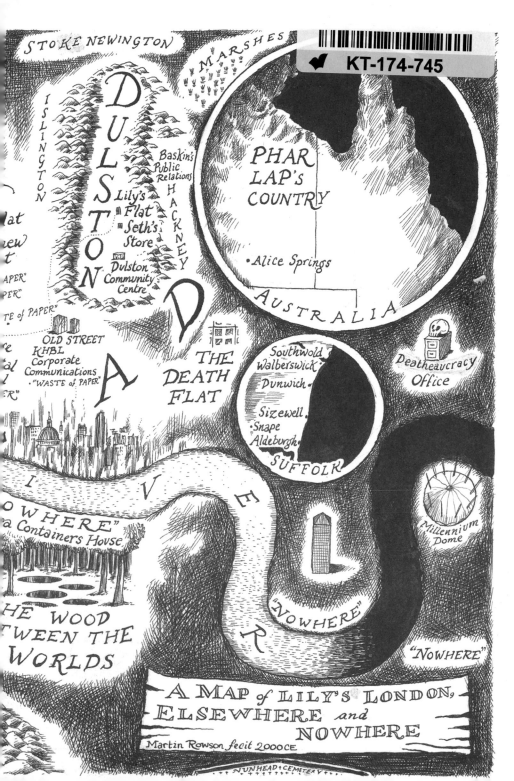

HOW THE DEAD LIVE

HOW THE DEAD LIVE

WILL SELF

BLOOMSBURY

First published in Great Britain 2000

Copyright © 2000 by Will Self

The moral right of the author has been asserted

Bloomsbury Publishing Plc,
38 Soho Square, London, W1V 5DF

A CIP catalogue record for this book is
available from the British Library

ISBN 0 7475 4895 1

10 9 8 7 6 5 4 3

Typeset by Hewer Text Ltd, Edinburgh
Printed in Great Britain by Clays Limited, St Ives plc

Endpapers © Martin Rowson

For Deborah

'As though in an initiatory mystery play, the actors for each day of the bardo come on to the mind stage of the deceased, who is their sole spectator; and their director is karma.'

W. Y. Evans-Wentz, Preface to
The Tibetan Book of the Dead

Epilogue

April 1999

We old women are easily erased from the picture of the last century. We're an entire demographic grouping of Trotskys. Like the once dapper Jew, we too stand with nonchalant unease at the base of that wooden pulpit, hastily erected on the platform of the Finland Station. Shorn of moustache and goatee our collective chin is rounded, awfully vulnerable, already anticipating the cold smack of the assassin's steel. Deprived of pince-nez our eyes are squinting into the limelight; what a mistake it was – we seem to be entreating future historians – to dress down for posterity. If only we'd kept our Trotsky costume on, not loaned our shoes to Lenin, then we wouldn't be facing this airbrushing out, this undeveloping, this eternal bloody deletion.

Where, oh where are the old women of the twentieth century? Where have we all gone? So few films, photographs and television pictures include us. Even when we were featured, the *real* intention was to emphasise the props: see how old that coat is/bulky that sack is/worn out those shoes are. And next to the great men of the age we were merely mothers, or women-old-enough-to-be-their-mothers, or women whose age made us childlessness personified, as time turned tail and our old vaginas, like ancient vacuum cleaners, sucked up the unformed, the unbecome, the unborn.

I'm not saying there haven't been exceptions, many many exceptions, crowds of exceptions like babushkas picking coal from the slag heap of the century. A legion of remarkable individuals humping hobo bundles down the road to where the *einsatzgruppen* were hard at it. Notable personalities grasping small, knobbly-haired heads between our withered dugs as the Interahamwe rampaged through the garden death-burbs of Kigali. Yes, we have been there. And I suppose, given our invisibility, our uselessness as anything but extras or crew – the gaffers, key grips and best boys of history – it's worth remarking that we were *in fact there already*. Yes, there before the director stopped shtupping his latest underage lover. There before the principals had any motivation, or the location had even been spotted. Like a herd of oblong-eyed goats, or a palisade of dead grass, or an enfilade of streetlamps, we were there. We old women – waiting for something to happen.

And if there are drifts of old women blowing across the fields of the living, why be surprised that the same is true of the afterlife? You look at the cityscape and see us tottering about in our insupportable hosiery. Look again and realise that while many of us are clinging on to the ledge of life, many more have let go already. As the living grow older, a sterile wad of humanity blocking up the generative drain, so we, the dead, accumulate like pennies on the ledges of a cascade game.

When the young die they're full of beans. Life hasn't exhausted them – why should death? Anyway, there are always vacancies in the provinces, or even abroad, for the morbidly mobile. Many young and middle-aged British dead work in the Gulf, the States, or even fucking Germany. But dead old women? Who wants us? In death as in life, we are the pavement-strollers, the window-shoppers, the bored, bunion-hobbled *boulevardières*. We're there waiting for something – anything – to happen. So we can be photographed, or filmed, or videoed, a backcloth of hysterectomies, in front of which events can be played out again, yet never exhausted. History is never in the round – it's always on a stage; and while the curtain may be death, why is it then that so many scrutinising eyes stud the proscenium, peering into the dimness of the stalls? Are they tragic or comedic masks – or not masks at all?

Earlier this evening – if this still is evening, we've waited so bloody long – I, Lily Bloom, picked my way down Old Compton Street. Yet another dead old woman patrolling the West End on a misconceived mission. My lithopedion scampered between my ankles, my Rude Boy was prancing in the road. Ahead of us the snake-hipped figure of Phar Lap Jones moved in and out of the gay throng. He may be old, but he's black, he's slim and – of course – he's a *karadji*, a *mekigar*, a wizard. Full of *buginja* power, possessed of *miwi* magic. With his finely corrugated matt skin and his thriving restaurant business, he might, it's often occurred to me, be the ultimate leather queen.

When I was alive I made it my business to zero in on my fellow biddies. Given a street scene like this – full of young people hurling themselves into the puppetry of lust, tying rubbery abandonment to their ankles and wrists before bungee jumping into orgasm – I'd've been taken by the tweed-wearers, the bearers of the capacious gusset and the porters of the nylon bag. The granny guild. I'd strike up conversations with these widows, spinsters and bints. I suppose I saw myself as a kind of reporter, researching a long article on the world, which turned out to be a profile of myself. I'd interview these old women, interrogate them as to who they were, what they were doing, where they were going, why they fucking bothered, and when they'd give it up. Later, I'd write their replies down in a notebook:

1. A Mrs Green, the widow of a minor civil servant. She lives in Hornsey in the house she owned with her husband, in

a basement flat knocked out by the son and daughter-in-law who cannot wait to inherit.

2. She's going to the Old Bailey to sit in the public gallery. It's good, cheap, wholesome fun.

3. Her basement is hot in summer, cool in the winter; it's good to get out.

4. It's not a question that can be answered at her age. She understands that life is not so much a journey from one horizon to the next as a survey of the world all around.

How wrong you were, Mrs Green. Indeed, I know you were wrong when I struck up that conversation with you, as you fumbled for the correct change by the ticket machine at Embankment, because this evening, as I paused by the sugary, munchy – and for me unreflecting – window of Patisserie Valerie, I saw you again. You were wearing the same worsted coat, now worsened by time, as you neatly stepped along the opposite sidewalk, hair coiled then crushed beneath a hat like a velour cowpat. Mrs Green, I never forget a face, even one as narrowly undistinguished as your own. Mrs Green, what were you doing in Soho? You have no need of butyl nitrate, or split-crotch panties, or charcuterie, or sushi. For shame.

Your husband died, aged sixty, in 1961. I first encountered you in 1974, when you were over seventy yourself. It's 1999! Ferchrissakes woman – you're ninety-fucking-five, yet don't look a day older than you did during the Winter of Discontent (which is not now). 'Has it not occurred to you, Mrs Green,' I might've let drop as I came alongside, 'that you must have died many years ago? That you are, indeed, dead – but won't lie down?'

'Ooh, I don't think so, dearie,' she might've replied. 'I mean to say, I still keep my flat up, pay the bills and such, do the shopping, go to bingo. I shouldn't be able to do all those things if I were dead, now would I?'

4

Oh but you can do them, Mrs Green. More than that, now that you're freed from the relentless popping of your cellular bubblewrap such tasks are a breeze, *n'est-ce pas?*

'But what about my Derek? He'd know I was dead – surely?'

'Oh, would he now – good at keeping in touch, is he?'

'We-ell, he's busy – '

'For life?'

'I'm sorry?'

'For life – he's been busy his entire fucking life, has he? Busy these past ten, fifteen, twenty, twenty-five years? Too busy to bother with an Abbey Crunch and a cup of milky tea – is that it then?'

'We-ell.'

'Well – nothing, *nada*, *rien du tout*. The well of life – pah! The well of death, woman – that's what you're down. Nope – you're dead. The reason your son doesn't keep in touch is that you're dead – and he's dead too! He died in the early eighties. First the cardiac arrhythmia, like a drum figure falling apart, then the big wrench to nowhere. Then Woking.'

'Woking?'

'Woking, Surrey, that's where he's spending his death. As to how come he doesn't keep in touch? Well, the dead find it just as hard as the living, you know – keeping in touch. It's an effort to call, to write, to pay a visit. Especially when your mother's dead but doesn't even realise it. Not that you don't have your uses, you know.'

'Uses?'

'You're an unquiet spirit – of sorts. Like all the unknowing dead, you're an exchange point between the living and the dead. This is true of many who die in their sleep, or inattentively, in stupors and fogs. If you don't know you're dead – and nor do the living – then it's easier for you to shout across the Styx than call along its banks. You could, for instance, take a message to my daughter Natasha.' This might have galvanised decrepit Mrs Green a bit; no one has asked her to do anything much but pass things – and only small things at that – for the last quarter-century.

'Your daughter, eh? What would you like me to say to her?'

'That it would be a remarkably good idea for her to insist on an abortion – even at this late stage. Saving that, she should wrench the fucking being out of her fucked-up womb and expose it, cast it on the fucking ground – that'd be just peachy.' Oh Christ – I've gone too far, she's backing off, turning, gathering her legs beneath her like stilts, piles under piles. She's moving away from me, fear and disgust curdling in her milky eyes. And that cowpat hat – my dear!

'You'd never have done it,' my lithopedion said, scampering between my own warped calves, as is its wont.

'I'm sorry?' I'd propped my brow against the plate glass of the patisserie, where cream cakes, croissants, Danishes and petits fours were massing with my strange thoughts.

'You'd never have done it – freaked out the old dead woman, Mrs Green.' My lithopedion was conceived and died in 1967, during the autumn of my love, which accounts for its hokey youthspeak.

'I forget that you know everything – have seen everything. I forget, I forget, I forget.'

'Not everything.' My lithopedion looked up at me with little, jet, periwinkle eyes. Mineral eyes. Its eyes have a black liveliness, so unlike its body, which is as grey as the York stone it stood upon. 'But everything that happened after my conception – including those five minutes of conversation with Mrs Green at Embankment in October 1974 – I remember.'

6

'You're' – and to the passers-by I suppose this looked perfectly natural, an elderly woman leaning against the shop-front and muttering at her swollen ankles – 'a most sagacious lithopedion.'

'I'm *your* lithopedion – *your* Lithy.' Sad that all my schooling paid off only in these, the last hours we spent together. But in the end Lithy did become the child I'd always wanted for myself, wise enough and sufficiently eloquent to re-parent me.

'Well, Lithy – and why wouldn't I?'

For the first time in the eleven years we'd haunted each other, it stopped dancing and spoke clearly. 'Because once you'd got going you'd've felt compelled to fill in all the detail. You'd've conjured up a charmless picture of her own demise for the poor, dead soul. A Zimmer-frame expiration, hmm? The retort-stand upon which time has experimented with human mortality, that's the sort of observation *you'd* make – but far cruder. She got up, and on her way across the parlour to get more tea, stubbing the Axminster with the rubber stoppers, died there, before she could make it to the linoleum.'

'It has a certain dignity – put like that.'

'Put like that, but you – you'd embellish the description. She died on the Zimmer, pitched forward, so that her body dangled over the crossbar. You've always said that all English women – '

'Of a certain age, a certain class – '

'Are pear-shaped, and in death Mrs Green inverts this state; when, quickening with putrefaction, pullulating with droso-phila grubs, head swollen with fluid, she becomes – for the first time in decades – the body of the pear, rather than its stalk.'

'Oh spare us this, Lithy, this pissy little guignol. Spare us, love – spare us. How about social services?'

'Social services – don't shake my tree, Mumsie, don't beat me Daddy-o ten to the bar – ' and Lithy broke off to do a little dance, which was far more in character.

Lithy is a minuscule cadaver of a child – about half the size of a kewpie doll – who was misconceived, then died mislodged in the folds of my perineum. There it petrified for twenty-one years until I died in 1988. Then, with the first faltering steps I took after my death, it fell from under my nightie, and clattered on to the linoleum of the third-floor landing at the Royal Ear Hospital. Phar Lap Jones – who was removing me from my deathbed at the time – stopped, stooped and picked it up. 'See you here, girl,' he said in that cheek-clicking, palate-snapping, percussive take on the English language which I've never ever been able to take seriously. 'This is a lithopedion, little dead fossil baby of yours, yeh-hey!?'

'How would I know,' I replied; at that time death had yet to mellow me.

' 'Cos I lu-urve yoo!' warbled Lithy, who'd had twenty-one years to come up with a better line but whose material had been garnered mostly during the first few months it spent in the pink pleats, when the pop rhythms still resonated in my tautish belly. 'I just like the things yoo-doo / Wo-on't yooo-doo-the-things-yoo-doo / Nya-nya-nya-nya-nya-nya-nyaaa! / Nya-nya-nya-nya-nya-nya-nyaaa!' And, surprisingly nimble on its misshapen pins (in truth, little more than the stubs that confirmed it as the true inspiration for the rash of 'Mother Goddess' statues found on Neolithic sites), the lithopedion began as it has gone on ever since, weaving between my ankles, shaking its little tush.

'Could be worse y'know, girl,' said Phar Lap Jones. 'Much worse than the little feller. You never have no abortions, no?'

'No.'

'Stillbirths?'

'No.'

'Miscarriages?'

'Not that I'm aware of.'

''Cos they snag round yer head some – to begin with, hey-yeh?'

'What d'jew mean?' His face was hidden by the brim of his ridiculous, white dude Stetson. In the small shadows a hand-rolled cigarette smouldered. At that time it was only the absence of pain that allowed me to concentrate, although ever since I've had plenty of time to run over all of this crap again and again in my head.

'Dead foetuses, newborn babies, whatever. With mothers who have kids, y'know, and they're young then – little, right. Well, when that woman dies they come and hang around. But see, hey, if they're real small they're still attached to the woman, danglin' off her, see – like this smoke. Older kids – they don't hang around as much, grown-up kids not at all.'

'Like life?'

'No, not like life . . .' He paused, allowing some nurses to pass by, even though this was irrelevant. 'In life, death drive you 'part, yeh-hey? Now it drag you all t'gether. I wonder which you'll like better. Anyway, you had a dead child, right?'

'You know this?' It was an old distress to me, a neat ring-pull on my canned emotions. A hungry pain, that loss – like the cancer.

'What good's a bloke like me for your death guide if I don't know this stuff? No way to get you off the go-round without it, yeh-hey?'

'There was a son. David. He died when he was nine.'

'And that was back from where you came, your country, hey-yeh?'

'Vermont. Not my country, it was where we lived at the time.'

'Well, whatever, hey. It'll take the little-boy stuff time t'get here see? But then he'll bother you proper. Nine years is a bad age for a boy to die. They don't take it well, yeh-hey.'

In 1988, on the dark landing, Phar Lap Jones spoke the truth while Lithy gambolled at my feet. Lithy never had any resentment or blamed me for its partial existence. Not so its brother Rude Boy – what else to call him? 'Dave' hardly seems suitable – who stowed away on a 747 and pitched up a few weeks later, while I was getting to know Dulston and attending the meetings. Rude Boy was there to remind me – for eleven long years – what it is to be a bad parent. Rude Boy is permanently arrested in the brattish mood of defiance that propelled him into the roadway, in front of the fifties fender which pulped his head then smeared it all over the asphalt. Now, in Old Compton Street, he's at it again.

In 1957, in Vermont, I'd caught him, playing out in the yard with two of his buddies. The three boys, naked save for their shorts, were smeared all over with black mud they'd manufactured using the hosepipe. 'What're you playing?' I called to David from the back porch. 'The nigger game!' he shouted back. I burst through the screen door and was on him in two strides, grasped his blond hair, smacked his head once, twice, three times. He'd only said it by mistake – this much I knew even then, even in the first fog of anger. I knew also that what terrified me about these casually ejaculated globs of race hatred was that they must be my own. My own dark truffles of prejudice, swollen beneath the forest's floor.

So, I smacked him and he ran and he got hit and he died. Now he likes to play in traffic whenever he can – and he's always blacked up for the nigger game. This evening, stood in the middle of Old Compton Street, still daubed with black New England mud, glistening on his straight, down-covered limbs, he shook his puny little fists at the illegal minicab drivers from Senegal, from Ghana, from Nigeria, and shouted at them, 'Niggers! Niggers! Niggers!' Not that they could hear him. They drove clear through him – like he was a will-o'-the-wisp bonnet mascot. Then he broke off and rounded on the cavalcade of clones. 'Pansies! Queers! Bum boys! Irons! Nonces!' he shrieked at them – and they too were oblivious. Hell, even if they could've seen him, what might they've thought? Nothing much. I've watched Rude Boy manifest himself tens of thousands of times in the decade we've been reunited – that's what the angry dead do; the rest of us are transparent with indifference, as invisible as the living. But much to his own disgust – and my weary amusement – hardly anyone in London seems capable of acknowledging the presence of a naked, mud-caked nine-year-old American boy screaming obscenities at them. In techie jargon – that argot of built-in obsolescence – they cannot compute.

It's like the pimply plump blonde I saw on the concourse at Charing Cross Station the other morning. She was wearing a sweatshirt emblazoned 'Hard Rock Cafe – Kosovo'. Har-de-har. When my two girls were little I took them to the first proper hamburger joint in London, the Great American Disaster on the Fulham Road. In time this transformed itself into the Hard Rock Cafe, and after still more vicious circularity, disasters were manufactured to decorate their sweatshirts. Cool, huh?

Oh, that Rude Boy! All he's learned in the eleven years he's spent in England is a plethora of pejoratives. No trips to the Wigmore Hall to hear Beethoven string quartets for him. No expeditions up Piccadilly to buy Burberry. No wry browsing along the Bayswater Road on a Sunday afternoon, laughing at the kitsch dangling from the park railings. No-no. What that foul-mouthed kid likes is to do what he did then, run up

11

behind me and plant one of his trowel feet – shaped like, as hard as – right in my fundament.

'Yah!' he screamed. 'Fuck you, you bitch! Fuck you!' The living may not feel or recognise or acknowledge the presence of the dead, but we can get to each other, as you know, when we're not expecting the intrusion. Rude Boy's foot usually passes right through me, but I was caught unawares – his sharp contempt lanced into my stupid, colourless indifference, and I turned to see his bony, mud-spattered little figure weaving away through the crowd. Having children may have been the whole point of life, but what it adds to death is dubious.

'Rude Boy, yeh-hey!' Phar Lap had backtracked to find out what was delaying me. 'He never stops ridin' you, hey-yeh?'

'No, I guess not.' We stopped. He rolled a cigarette, I got one out. We lit them.

'Mebbe it's time to tell 'im goodbye, move on, hey-yeh?' Phar Lap held his hand so it cupped my elbow and I turned to accompany him. Both of us pretended to touch.

'I daresay that's true – but can I?'

'Yeh-hey. It's not all gammin, y'know.'

'What? Reincarnation?'

'Yaka! Not a good word, that; iss like callin' sickies who fuck with kiddies "child-lovers", hey? No-no, y'see – you know this Lily stuff, we not gonna put it in a new body, yeh-hey? They don't make one body serve two souls, or one soul serve two bodies. Cleverer than that. You used t' think that you were your body – not so.'

'Not so.'

'No, what makes you Lily now? This lithopedion? This here cheeky one? Phar Lap has a way of gesturing all his own, elbows held tight by his serpentine sides, forearms angled out like the indicators on my father's *c.*1927 Hupmobile. When he

12

does this it's impossible not to pay attention – he commands attention.

We made it to the block after Patisserie Valerie, Rude Boy was in the roadway and Lithy lost in the velveteen folds of my sensible sack dress, when the entire frontage of the pub we were passing shivered, undulated and was then punched from within by an explosion. The matter percolated into the air like milk mushrooming into coffee. Coasters, bar mats, handles, straights, queers, the artworks formerly known as prints, stools, trousers, carousers, hearts, lungs, lights, blood, viscera, Britvic, gelignite, Babycham, carpet tiling, dry-roasted peanuts, penises – the entire gubbins of the bar gathered into a fisted force field and splurged into the street. I felt the afflatus of several souls stream through what might've been me, what might've been Phar Lap. Tatters of people. The blast curled around us, crinkling up the envelope of air as if it were paper.

Then everyone in Old Compton Street was lying down – as if a malevolent god had announced a nap-time for all the children. The only individual standing was Rude Boy. 'Faggots! Niggers!' he screamed. Lithy, stunned, clung to my ankle, and dangled there hitching a lift as we skirted through shattered glass – which as ever looked disassembled to me, a window jigsaw – and shards of wood; and the children, who now stirred, shuddering into shock; and the bystanders who unglued themselves from Pompeii poses; and the bits of the people. Goodnight mush.

Phar Lap clicked into my inner ear, 'Diddit with the punishment boomerang, hey. Walbiri one, hey-yeh. Very strong. Dragged it clear across the Balkans on my way back this time. Kickin' up bi-ig death dust for this year, hey-yeh!'

'Bullshit,' was my snappy rejoinder. We slowed to turn the corner into Wardour Street, swerving to avoid a dead old prostitute coming the other way. I recognised her; she has so many foetuses floating around her head – each tethered by its own serpentine umbilicus – that among the locally deceased she's known as Medusa. I went on disabusing Phar Lap: 'It's a fact written about in the press that this is the work of some far-right cell – an offshoot of the BNP, whatever.'

'Yuwai – it's speculated about. It's a fact that we're late – yeh-hey?'

Again he accelerated through the crowd ahead of me, a crowd which, as we strolled beyond its psychic shockwave, was exhibiting in reverse all the symptoms induced by the explosion. Sure, there were the emergency sirens' synthesised whoops – but aren't there always? And the pumped-up people seeking the violence anywhere but within themselves – but aren't there all the time? No, the bomb in Old Compton Street was a car crash and we hadn't stopped to gawk. Under the fake-porphyry columns of the NatWest bank, Rude Boy was waggling his little dick in the unaware face of a Dutch tourist who was having her cheese-head cheesily portrayed by an Ethiopian economic migrant. Lithy shinnied up, arm over arm, to grab the bottom bead of my amber necklace, and pulled itself into the shelter of my bosom.

How strange it is never really to be able to touch another. During the sixties I always wondered at those astronauts, not being able adequately to describe what it was like to be weightless. I figured that maybe they sent really stupid people into space, but over the last eleven years I've learned that some sensations are like that. When you're dead you can hold yourself against a thing, you can rub up and down, intent upon the precise degree of resistance the surface presents, but you won't *feel* it; it doesn't *touch* you. Still, we all do it – this pretence of touching one another. It seems to come naturally enough – wouldn't you agree? – when you're dead.

I've never altogether missed that aspect of life – the physical aspect, the insidey-outsidey part of it. I didn't even have a dead little twin to meet on the other side – like so many do. The idiot twin in my life was that big blonde slab-body I shlepped around with me, all heavy and stupid and inert and smiling thickly, for my entire fucking adult life. And then the cancer yet! I had a ridiculously late menopause for a woman so obviously past it. Fancy that – hardly had I given a final flush to the bloody cistern of menstruation when the alarm went off somewhere and the cells began to divide.

Some wiseacre told me – when I was actually fucking dying – that a foetus undergoes far more rapid cell division during ontogeny than any cancer. Great. He died three years after me – cancer too – and at that time I was still naïve enough to imagine that what the afterlife chiefly provided were unrivalled opportunities for unbeatable gloating, unbelievable schadenfreude. So English, that – a nation who've always been convulsed by the world's pratfall, when it was they who yanked away the chair. So, anyway, I went and had a look, maybe manifested myself a little – I don't remember – but I tried to make his death a misery, whispering, 'Dividing-dividing-dividing . . .' in his ear. Who knows. Who knows.

In Piccadilly there were unquiet spirits aplenty, the futile shades of dead junkies and drabs and auto-accident victims, who make it their business to whirl distractedly around Eros's standard. I'd like to see the seance that could get in touch with this roundabout of loons. I tell you I wouldn't even have noticed this crappy cavalcade had it not been for Rude Boy, who always insists on joining in, ripping the ectoplasm from their shoulders, flinging it into the air like he was a pizza chef. I shouted at him to come on, and Lithy piped up as well, 'Come on-comeon-Come on-comeon! D'you wanna be in my gang, my gang, my gang, d'you wanna be in my gang – oh yeah!' And this did bring Rude Boy over, but only to cuff

Lithy, who screeched and appealed to me, but I shoved it off and it kicked at Rude Boy and Rude Boy kicked out again. As ever it was difficult to tell what infuriated them more, their own hated consanguinity or their inability ever actually to land a blow, one on the other. So, they followed me on down through Piccadilly bickering and sniping and contradicting each other. Kids, huh.

Yeah, the unceasing awareness of underwear – I don't miss it. I remember being in Tuscany, in the mid-seventies, and all I could focus on in a beautiful Renaissance palazzo I visited, the only fucking thing in room after room of paintings and furniture and glass and Christ knows what, was a door-lock which resembled a bra-hook – flat eyes. The only thing I could hang on to all that hot, scented, beautifully touchy-feely afternoon. Must've been 'cause I had diarrhoea. It used to do that to me – crank up the unceasing underwear-awareness. Obviously.

Standing underneath Eros, I hoped the deatheaucracy had rented somewhere special for this meeting, because I wanted it to be a special meeting. I'd spent yonks dragging around their offices in Eltham, Ongar, Barking and Thurrock. You're familiar with the premises they favour, leased with the evidence of failed businesses still stacked about: Nobbo pegboards, Sasco year planners, redundant Roladexes, outmoded computing equipment. Yeah, this is the kind of swinging scene the deatheaucracy favours. Indeed, it's difficult – wouldn'tjew say – to see them in any other context, ratty little men in brown suits that they are. Just as it's impossible to imagine them not twiddling with their computer-games consoles, or fiddling with their Gameboys. Why can it be that the people who run death have such a reliable appetite for gadgets, fads, crazes – anything, in fact, that will allow them the opportunity to fidget for hour after hour, while the traffic clots in the arteries outside, and we shades gather among the shadows in the waiting room.

Still, as you know, not all the people who run death are male; there's the odd woman as well. And very odd they are too, these eternally plain Janes. They're the kind of spinsters who came of age immediately after both wars – women existing within the vacuum of a permanently absented purée of masculinity. Beneath umbrellas of cashmere and cotton they scampered away their lives, eluding the damp mizzle of testosterone. Now they're doing the same in death. Icky! Phar Lap says that most of these secretarial spinnies are unquiet spirits. But I protest that there's nothing quieter than these desiccated women, who tiptoe into meetings, only to deposit another buff folder into the tatty fingers of Mr Glanville, Mr Hartly, or Mr Canter – the mister who's given my application the most consideration over the years.

'You've set your heart on rebirth, then?' Mr Canter said at one of our last encounters, his fingers steepled over the graveyard of an open file.

'Yes, I think death has taught me all that it might.' I had my knees drawn together, my hands clasped in my lap. I clenched my fists and – hey presto! A half-century sloughed off and I was back in the unsuccessful interviews at Barnard and Wellesley, where they looked at my prominent nose from all kinds of angles.

'Oh really.' Canter was wearing his habitual, primitive, Norfolk-cut, Jaeger wool suit. I recognised it from the off as one of George Bernard Shaw's purpose-built garments, and pegged the deatheaucrat accordingly as a Shavian pacifist and freethinker of the Edwardian period. To begin with I was amused to see the people who run death sustaining their crankiness way past the grave – but perhaps it's only the English who do this?

I've always suspected that death American-style would've been both glitzier and more convivial. That Bobby Franks would've waited the twelve years for Loeb to turn up, so that the two of them could be pals, play pinochle and wait for Leopold to come from South America. That even a pair like that would eventually knuckle under to the defeat of the will.

It's a fact that you need a good background in bureaucracy to run death. I tested for a job with them a couple of years after I died, but, free of arthritis or not, I was told that my typing was too slow, my filing too haphazard. (Although there was general enthusiasm for me among the staff of the office where I was interviewed, when they heard about my background in pen design.)

Beyond this I don't believe there's any especial qualification, d'jew? After all, most of the deathly offices are hung with suits from all the decades of the last two hundred years or so. I've seen sharp 1950s sharkskin single-breasters, and tough 1930s twill sacks; 1890s nankeen frock coats and 1870s sawtooth cutaways. But mostly, the hideous brown-and-chalk-stripe double-breasteds of the 1940s predominate, I guess because this was when the bureaucratic type came to the fore – and we all went for a Burton. Left in charge by their more belligerent brothers, the paper-pilers and pen-pushers remained in the rear, both armies of non-combatants speaking ACRONYM, and perfecting the office management systems that would come to dominate the post-war world. Alan Turing was the originator of the spreadsheet, in case you didn't realise.

'Oh really.' Canter said it again and I savour it anew. There are some good things about death as well as many bad ones. The good things include the time to sit and stare. There's no hurry. In between the 'Oh' and the 'really' I had plenty of time to examine chipped chipboard partitions and dense slabs of

MDF. Time to see that in this office – above a dry-cleaner's premises on Willesden High Road – the Dexion cradle within which Canter's department carts around its *nyujo* occupies a dominant position. Canter and his staff have always loved telling me, 'Oh, you know, it's a very fine *nyujo*, a very perspicacious one – we do so like to keep it with us.'

D'jew know the *nyujo*? It's the petrified corpse of a long-gone scrivener, who saw fit to meditate himself into a crystalline state. The one belonging to this department achieved this by ceaselessly revolving on his Parker Knoll beneath an interminable succession of plastic demijohns of Buxton mineral water, upended by his disciples and set, one after the other, atop his Dexion cubicle. From time to time small basins of Tipp-Ex were thrown over his bowed head, staples fired at him from acolytes' guns, labels of all sorts affixed – Post-it notes ditto. Over the years this figurehead has swollen to alarming proportions – a dumpy Buddha, encrusted with stationery. Yet still he's humped from one defunct travel agency to the next busted electrical wholesaler's in his papier-mâché palanquin.

I expect you've discovered they're immensely proud of their statue of Anubis too? Pathetic isn't it, the way they drag it around whichever block it is that they're currently tenanting, as if it were a recalcitrant old pampered doggie. Still, I suppose it is.

The living, I guess, would expect the coincidence of different eras of suiting, and the presence of Cratchit clerks playing Nintendo, to give these offices an anachronistic air. We know it's not so. It's always the dumb mistake of the living to imagine themselves contemporary. 'Every period I've lived through has seemed like now to me,' my second husband was fond of saying – fondness was his forte. He was no more fond of me or his daughters or his mother than he was of his dog, or his golf bag, or his penis. Fondness was inscribed on his heart when I cut it out still beating. Only kidding.

Yaws kept prodigiously exact records of the Now during his entire lifetime, detailing every little particle of its extinction. When, after his own, I came to read them, they proved to my entire satisfaction that the over-examined life is hardly worth living; and that while ostensibly he had died of a routine cardiac infarction, he had in fact, like so many of his ilk – permanently adolescent, upper-middle-class, minor-public-school-educated Englishmen – strolled back to the Elysian pavilion, his entry in the scorebook marked 'Retired bored'.

'Oh really?' Had Canter said it yet again? He'd definitely caught me eyeing the fucking *nyujo*, because he continued, 'You hadn't perhaps considered becoming a *nyujo* yourself?'

'I'm sorry?' I replied – although I'd heard him only too clearly.

'Liberation through hearing on the after-death plane – you're familiar with it of course?'

'Of course.' They always talk like this, don't they, the brown suits, the deatheaucrats, effortlessly rendering the transcendent banal. 'But I'd rather set my heart on living again.'

'We've got all sorts of new animating principles available, you know – fresh harvests of anencephalic stillborn infants coming through all the time – ' He broke off to address a passing clerk: 'Mr Davis? You wouldn't be so kind as to bring over the Roladex with the anencephalic stillborn infants' animating principles on it, would you?'

'Truly, I have no desire to be *nyujo*, and I'd rather counted on being me on the next go-round, as it were.'

'You appreciate that you'll actually be more *you* if you accept a new animating principle, hmm? There'll be a more . . . how can I put it? . . . *porous* barrier between your assemblages of memories.'

'I know this, yes – but I won't be me. Me. Me.'

'Quite so.'

Yes, I kid you not – this is the kind of dreck he tried to palm me off with. Still, at least I wasn't among the living, stumbling about the joint imagining themselves painted up with the present, when it ain't necessarily so. Their minds are full of dead ideas, images and distorted facts. Their visual field is cluttered up with decaying buildings, rusting cars, potholed roads and an imperfectly realised sky, which darkens towards the horizon of history. They take in all ages in the one frame every time they snap the city with their Brownie brainboxes. Their very noses are clogged with dying hairs, moribund skin, stratified snot – they're smelling the past; and feeling it too – between their toes, their thighs, the pits of their arms: ssshk-shk! Peeling back the years. Whereas we, the dead, are the true inheritors of the Modern. The live lot assemble time into lazy decadences – ten-year periods of conspicuous attitudinising, which are only ever grasped in nostalgic retrospect. My second husband was a profoundly ancient man, a Neolithic stone-knapper. But we . . . we see it all; anachro-spectacles are the only ones we wear. So these interminable branch offices that I've revolved through, while Lithy sat in my lap and Rude Boy ranted in the vestibule, trying to piss on back numbers of the *Reader's Digest*, haven't been so strange, or so different.

Anyway, I'm getting off the point, which Canter never has. 'Thank you, Mr Davis,' he said, taking receipt of the relevant buff folder. 'You *see*, Ms Bloom – or rather your death guide . . . Mr . . . Jones, ye-es Jones, may have *told* you – we have our own calculus here, our own ways of proceeding?'

'I'm only too well aware.'

'This isn't' – then he really did take off his wire-rimmed spectacles, and run his hand through his sparse, sandy hair, giving me time to appreciate, once again, that instead of being determined by the magisterially pompous English gentile who I'd thought was going to decide it, my fate was in the waxy paws of a ratty little Jew – 'any longer a matter of how you conducted yourself on your last "go-round", as you put it.'

'Mr Canter, sir' – such honorifics came naturally when I was addressing someone who hadn't taken a shit since 1953 – 'I'm only too well aware of the implications of karma.'

'On the before-death plane perhaps – but after death? You died, in 1988, owing over two thousand pounds to the Inland Revenue. Monies which had, subsequently, to be disbursed by your estate – '

'Is this strictly relevant?'

'Oh yes, accounts are accounts – and we are – '

Accountants. Save for his peculiar colleagues, Mr Canter is well-nigh indistinguishable from Mr Weintraub, who, when I saw him for the last time – the cancer scooping out my left boob as if it were a fucking avocado – assured me he'd take care of the relevant returns . . . sitting in his aggressively Artexed office, off the North Circular by Brent Cross, playing with a Bic Cristal and annotating the accounts I myself had laboriously put together.

' – concerned here with totting up *all* the relevant columns. We'll be doing this for most of the next year, so don't be alarmed if your neighbours – you live in Dulburb?'

'Dulston,' I grunted.

'Dulston, quite so, a lovely area, very much village London. Anyway, if you should hear that certain enquiries are being made about you, rest assured that it's only us. And now,' he screwed his doughy butt into the swivel chair as if he were intent on sodomy, 'there's the matter of sex.'

'Sex?'

'Indeed, you will not, I hope, find yourself too discomfited by a resumption in sexual feelings, hmm? Merely psychic to begin with, but very real for all that.' He paused for effect and a zombie brought in tea and Nice biscuits.

Mr Canter and I sat either side of them for the remainder of the interview. After I'd left, another zombie returned to take them away. Funny how we dead never eat – yet still, some of us love to serve food.

Well, that was one of the last encounters with Canter, as I say. And earlier this evening, in Piccadilly now, I was beset by a liquefying inundation of orgasms – of dicks stirring me up. When I was abandoned in the wastes of late middle age, my flesh folding, then frowning into sour slackness, I wanted my sex cut out – and so it was; in death, at least. Who cut the cookie with the cookie cutter? But ever since Miles and Natasha got down to it in the gauche apartment on Regent's Park Road, I've been tormented by lust and jealousy. Who'd ever have thought they'd be welcome again in this old house, behind this envious green door? Ethereal fingers prinking my pussy. My first husband, jolly Dave Kaplan, he used to say that his beard was like 'wearing a pussy on my face – I've only got to stroke my chin and I feel real comfy'. It's Dave I thought of in Piccadilly. Or rather, it was the incongruous liver spot, adrift in his sparse hairline, that I pictured. It was always this scrap of yellow-brown I focused on as I willed myself towards another orgasm of crushing non-spontaneity.

Years after the marriage was over – the late sixties to be vaguely precise – when we'd occasionally meet in Manhattan for lunch – those good, wholesome divorcees' lunches, the only ones people who've been sexually involved can have and still enjoy their food – he divulged that while I was looking at his liver spot and imagining myself ecstatic, he was concentrating hard on the mole on my chin, while willing himself to detumesce. '*Touche pas!*' I laughed, and raised my glass of

Zinfandel. 'Yes,' he continued, 'I've spent possibly years of my life entirely absorbed in the pimples, blemishes and other imperfections of beautiful women.' And as if called to stimulate himself by this revelation, he meditatively stroked his pussy.

Spontaneous or not, I did use to orgasm with Kaplan. I did clutch his arched neck, groan, say things – I did that crap. I loved sex – or rather, like so many women of my era, I loved the idea of sex. Sex garbed in romantic weeds, sex with strong self-assured men rather than puling boychicks. Set against imaginings like these the real thing was never that great, natch; the dildo would have to be dressed. I knew even then, from talking to the boychicks themselves (and was there ever a century like the twentieth for chewing things over; 'Time as a Cud' – discuss), that their chief sexual hang-up was the reverse of mine – a hang-down, if you like. For all these guys sex was *too* sexy. That's why Dave confined himself to the mole.

We'd gone a couple more blocks and I couldn't see Phar Lap Jones ahead of me, when 'Oimissus!' – there he was, sitting, back against the wall, beside one of the alleyways that leads into the Albany. With the brim of his white Stetson pulled down low, he wasn't much more than black jeans, bullroarer and outsize punishment boomerangs. He looked just like any of the other alien sophomores who've enrolled for this year's London Summer School of the Didgeridoo. 'Oi!' He'd managed to mooch a meat pie from somewhere along the way. Strange, this being Kebabistan, rather than Fish-and-Chiplington. He chews up these hassocks of mince and onion after he's skin-popped them with brown sauce. It's a newly-coined Strine tradition of his. Meat-pie dreaming – I guess. But he never swallows it, none of us does, do we.

Anyway, as I say, there he was in the alleyway and I felt this aching desire to get in there with him, to cram myself inside that gully of old bricks. I was half-convinced that for the first time in eleven years I'd get some abrasion, some rasp – between Phar Lap and the wall, that is. I may even have begun insinuating myself, because he said, 'Juda! Lily, not in there, girl, that's bad, you can't go in there.'

'Where? The Albany?'

'No, that fuckin' buju, girl!' He made as if to pull me along with him and I followed in his wake, the two of us breasting the summertime crowds, who had now, like brown rats, sensed the explosion five blocks away by mood transmission. It made them all look as ugly as they are for a change. 'You feel that, didya?' he said.

'What's *that*?'

'No more of yer stupid colourlessness of indifference, hey-yeh?'

'No, I really wanted to get in that alleyway – '

'With me, yuwai, an' you been thinkin' 'bout rootin' long time now, yeh-hey?'

'Ye-es.'

'You've bin dead too long, girl, dead too long. Those dead souls on Old Compton Street, they passed clean through and you never broke step. I saw that.'

'So you – you do think rebirth would be a good idea . . . in my case?'

He stopped again, this time right next to a woman who was squinting into the air, arm outstretched, as if hailing a cab driven by Zeus across the fiery evening sky. Phar Lap was so close to her that he damped himself down a little – and so did I. We whittled our presences away. That's what we dead do, isn't it? Shave ourselves out of the designer-stubbled faces of the living. Rude Boy came and sat on the kerb by us. Lithy, amazingly, leant against Rude Boy's knee. 'Is it that you wanna get shot of these fellers, yeh-hey?'

'No! I mean – maybe. I don't know. But if I am reborn I've children to talk to among the living – even if I leave these two behind.'

'Yeh-hey! You don't wanna be alone ever, d'you Lily?'

'Do you?'

'I never am. Listen, don' go crawlin' into no cracks, not now. You hold back on those wantin' feelings you're gettin', yeh? You do bad shit now and you're done for girl, see? It'll come back at you like this here kayan – see?' He waved his big, black boomerang to bludgeon home his point. 'Now snap it up – Mr Canter is waitin' for you.'

He lifted his arm up in front of the vacant eyes of the living woman and grabbed the cab. That's how I ended up here with you. Stuck here in the waiting room, anticipating my final encounter with the deatheaucracy – for the time being.

Christmas 2001

Yeah, but there was more, hindsight multiplying me like opposing mirrors set either side of a restaurant booth. Because as we boarded the cab I remembered. This rush across this West End, ignoring the bombing in Old Compton Street, forcing Rude Boy to keep the pace: we were in a hurry – I was in a hurry. Now, that's one thing you never do when you're dead. There's no rush when you're dead. You may have scrambled up the dark stairs to confront it, nose to the musty carpet, anticipating its horror for every one of those fifteen steps, expecting it every inch of the half-landing. But there's no rushing once you've seen him, her and it. No rushing once you're there. Only pottering around. Pottering around for eternity.

Dying

'It's been quite a morning.'
The last words of Samuel Beckett's father

Chapter One

April 1988

They say you are what you eat and now that I'm dying I know this is the solid truth. Actually, it's not only a solid truth – it's a gelid one as well. It's also a sloppy, tacky, congealed reality. It's a pink blubbery blancmange of an evidence and a stringy gruel of proof. It's a gristly confirmation which swells like a filament of meat caught between teeth. Not, you understand, that I've had my own teeth for years now, it's just that recently I've found myself dreaming of teeth, of what it's like to have your own teeth. Dreaming of having teeth again. Anyway – you are what you eat: in my case, this hospital slurry, which seems to've been put together – insofar as it's cooked at all – for the express purpose of sliding through us near-cadavers as fast as possible.

'No need to give them anything but swill,' I can hear a pushy lack-of-nutritionist proclaim (funny how the profession attracts quite so many anorexics) at this meeting or that case conference; 'they're eating up half the budget of the NHS already – can that be right?' No, maybe not, but I've paid my fucking taxes, or at least I hope that ridiculous little man Weintraub has by now.

The other thing about this slick cuisine is, natch, that it doesn't repeat on you. Or rather, neither its odour nor its substance is likely to rise up in the faces of those poor overworked nurses. Good thing. We seldom get cheese – never smoked fish. Eggs are boiled to shit. Hard ovals of desiccated shit. No pickles. No rich sauces. No onions and emphatically no garlic. Not that I really liked such food when I was well, it's just that now, now that I'm dying, I realise that this capacity certain foodstuffs exhibit of reappearing in your mouth, spontaneously, hours after they've been consumed, is very much a sign of life. Life in its very repetitiousness. Life *going on*. I could murder for a shmaltz – now that I know I'm definitely going to die. After my teeth were taken out, in the mid-sixties – '63, '64, weird not to remember – I thought that I'd become immortal. I'd always assumed that I'd die with my teeth because they were so fucking painful. Anything that painful – I unreasoned – even if it didn't kill you itself, would surely be the end of you when it went. You'd die of bliss. But now, teeth or not, I'm dying.

I'm absolutely certain that I'm going to die because half and hour ago nice Mr Khan, the clinical psychologist attached to the ward, came and told me I was. Some wiseass once said that the miracle of life was that we all might die at any minute – but that we live as if we were immortal. I wish I could get this wiseass by his scrawny throat and throttle his life right out of him. Did he have any idea what it's like when you *know* the hour of your own death? And when it's announced to you thus: 'Erm – ah. I understand, Ms Bloom, that Dr Steel spoke to you this morning?'

'Yes, he did.' I put my crappy women's mag to one side, I show my dentures to the nervous Mr Khan. I'm being a good little cancer-ridden old lady. So easy to be like this when you don't have any legs. Legs make men think about pussy – even old pussy; and no one has legs in bed – not unless you're in there with them.

'Did he have a word about palliative care?'

'About giving me palliative care? Yes he did, thank you.' I'm still giving Mr Khan the glad eye but it's beginning to dim slightly, because let's face it, affirmative action or not, it's very difficult to see what the point of puffed-up Mr Khan really is. Sure, he's perfected that clever little Uriah Heep act which makes him appear ever so 'umble to his clients and employers, but my teeth aren't simply long – they're fucking eternal! And I know this covers up a typical subcontinental mummy's boy, a puling bully who lords it over the womenfolk when he gets home from a hard day talking crap to the dying.

'I'm sorry there isn't anything more that we can do for you . . . I can . . . do for you. Are you a religious person, Ms Bloom?'

'No, no *I'm* sorry.'

'You're sorry?' He's a fat thing, he hasn't got a hungry cancer chomping up his breasts, breasts which jiggle most unpleasantly inside his pressed, near see-through, synthetic shirt. Why do they always wear translucent shirts, these people who have everything to hide?

'Sorry that you're labouring under the delusion you've helped me at all. Done anything for me whatsoever.' And I pick up my abandoned *Woman's Realm*, get back to reading recipes I'll never make, ever, for sure now. Picking apart knitting patterns in my mind.

When I've absorbed another recipe for banana flapjacks – perhaps the two hundredth of my life so far – I look up to see that Mr Khan is still there. Having failed with what he imagines to be a sympathetic approach, and rising to my rebuff, he adopts a more scientific one: 'We – or rather I – wondered whether you might be able to help *us*, then?'

'With what?' I can't believe this shlemiel.

'We're doing a study – a survey of patients . . . of terminal patients'' – he's squeezed it out at last, that terminal 'terminal', popped it like a cyanide capsule into the mouth of the conversation – 'attitudes.'

'Attitudes to what?' Outside, on Grafton Way, I can hear the traffic whooping and growling. When I came into the hospital this time for the laughable operation (a lumpectomy – can you believe they really call it that? It's like dubbing a heart transplant a 'ticker swap'), it was such a relief to get out of the city, into a kind of refuge, but now I understand it's no refuge at all. There ought to be a sanctuary inside the hospital where patients can hide from Khan and his ilk.

'To, erm . . . to their quality of life.' He's got it out now and he's obscurely pleased; there's a thin smile seaming his stuffed, fat face.

'Let me get this straight, you're asking people who're dying what their quality of life is?'

'Ye-es, that's it. I have a survey sheet . . . a questionnaire, if you'd like to see it?'

'What do you expect to discover?' My tone begins sharp but steady, but as I enunciate the hated words the pitch rises, the words fray and shred. 'That the quality of a life gets better the nearer a cancer patient gets to death? Oh my fucking Christ I'm going to die. I can't stand it I'm gonna die. Not me! Oh God-ohgod-ohgog-jeezus-ogod-og – ' And here I go, choking into incoherent terror, the façade demolished by sledge-hammer sobs. I moan and I pule and I groan and saliva loops from my slack jaws. It's a most satisfying performance, I sense through the fog – for Mr Khan. After all, he's a trained grief counsellor – and here's *plenty* of grief. Sacks of it. But no – he can't cope, he's up and waddling off in the direction of the nurses' station while I tear up the *Woman's Realm*, lay waste to the paper Little England, and scream and cry.

I've always had a talent for hysteria, for plunging over the black edge of a mood, but this black edge is so much bigger. It's a Niagara, sucking into itself the whole water of my life. I feel like a stroke victim must – half of my world is gone. Half of that plastic water jug; half of that box of Kleenex; half of that fucking already half-eaten Battenberg cake which my junky daughter brought me yesterday afternoon; half of that crumpled tissue; that Staedtler HB pencil; that dust mote. For the first time in my life I can feel, utterly and incontrovertibly, what it's like not to be me. What it's like to be me feeling not me. It's so lonely. I'm so fucking lonely. Who would've thought that me, who's led a life that has known so much bloody loneliness, now has to face the solitude of death? I'm sobbed by racks. Oh my self – why hast thou abandoned me?

Sister Smith, one of those West Indian women of landmass bulk, who could be any age between thirty and sixty, rips me into my plastic cocoon with her arms arching like leaping seals, then sits down heavily near my mutilated breast. She's already got the unputdownable beaker, the easy-to-swallow capsule. 'Here,' she says – and I take the Valium. I've no problem with that; after all, I've taken a raft of the things thus far – why stop now? In the seventies, when I patrolled daily with depression's black guard dog, I used to pass by suburban newsagents, and seeing those sweetie-dispensers outside (you know the ones – ten pence for some gum and a plastic charm) I'd imagine them full of five-, ten-, even twenty-milligram Valiums. Go in, and the old stick behind the counter – hair greased straight back, cigarette fuming in his face – might say, 'Bad news today, Mrs Yaws, very bad news. Bomb in a pub in Guildford, many dead. Scenes of terrible carnage. Senseless slaughter. Unspeakably awful. Unimaginably evil. You'll be wanting a Valium with your *Guardian*?'

'There, love,' says Sister Smith, 'there you go.'

Gulp! I can feel her yellow-tinged, calloused palm through the brushed cotton of my nightie. A curious confusion of senses – and this alone serves to calm me, because it's only with blacks that I imagine I can feel their colour. What could whiteness feel like? A stupid colourlessness of indifference, I daresay. But the blacks – whom I touch always unwillingly – they *feel* black, or yellow, or brown, or in the case of the old man I tried to comfort after he'd been knocked down by a car outside John Lewis's on the Finchley Road – grey. He felt grey.

'I have to say, Mr Khan's not the best clinical psychologist we have here at the hospital, y'know.'

'I-I know. Believe me – I know. Ogodogodogod . . .' I would certainly like to hug Sister Smith. She's built to hug me, she's big enough to hug me. My mother was too petite to give me a proper hug once I was seven – not that she would've wanted to, for fear of rucking up her perfect bodice. And as for my father – I never called him Daddy; I never called him anything – he'd lift me up under my arms and swing me, but only as if intent on letting go.

'He really is well-meaning . . . but no one can find the right words exactly . . .'

No, or even fucking vaguely, or so it seems. Yes, I should like to be hugged by Sister Smith and feel her great reef of bosom support my shattered, decaying one . . . Full fathom five thy excised lump lies . . . I should like her yellow palms on my sallow shoulders. I should like to smell the coconut oil on her skin, the PH-balanced conditioner in her crinkly hair, but this would not be a good idea.

I'm sitting on the veranda of the old house in Huntingdon, Long Island, which we had, briefly, when I was a child. I'm sitting on the lap of a woman as solid as Sister Smith and as black and sweet-smelling. The sun is hot then cool on my neck as Betty plaits my long, blonde hair. Even then it was the best thing about me. Can she be doing anything as obvious as humming a hymn? Yes, she is. She's a religious woman – although when she did house-cleaning it would be the blues.

'Titanic Man' for the bathroom, 'St Louis' for the kitchen. She's doing my hair in a French plait, up and over and through. Hairy pastry. And while she plaits I'm kissing her. The softest and lightest of kisses on her neck and on her collarbone where it rises from her house dress. I'm being scrupulous with these kisses, they're really air kisses, perturbations of the atmosphere immediately above Betty, because I know – or I think I know – that this irritates her. But I want to kiss Betty because I love her. No, not love her – she's my world. Like all loving adult carers of small children, she has defined the world itself for me. My world is Betty – not the earth. Things can be assimilated in as much as they conform – or diverge – from this Bettyness.

Yes, I'm kissing Betty and I'm smelling Betty and I'm even subtly rubbing a bit of Betty's old house dress in between my thumb and finger – because she's my security blanket too – when I'm torn from her and deposited hard on the boards. 'You bad girl! You bad, bad girl! You *never ever* do this again. Never. Do you understand me? Do you!' One slap cross my tiny face, then back, then a third. My mother slapped me the way British actors playing Gestapo officers were later to slap their interrogation victims – but she wasn't pretending. Her diamond ring drew my blood and became this little girl's worst enemy. It was so out of proportion – the colossal violence from this petite, blonde woman – that Betty herself was stunned, left half-risen from the old rocker, her face a racist caricature of minstrel shock.

I never kissed Betty again. She stayed with us until I was fifteen – but I never touched her again. We would talk and I would confide and she would sympathise – but we both knew we could never touch each other ever again; that for me black flesh was an anathema. An evil substance. I cannot touch black people – unless I have to. How unfair that they may have to touch me. I do so hope I'm unconscious before it happens. And I find myself saying to Sister Smith, 'Will I know it when I die?

'Hush now,' Sister Smith puts a hand up and dabs at my dregs of hair – black women, blonde hair, my whole life has been wrapped in this skein – but draws back when she senses me stiffen. 'Y'know, you're not bein' good to yourself, girl – Lily. Dr Steel, he means well, but he's – how can I put it now – he takes a rather *technical* view of these things. He doesn't explain so well – did he say what you should be expecting?'

'He said that this time they couldn't get all the tumour, that it had hypo- hypo – '

'Hypostasised, yes, well, that jus' means it's spread, you see.'

'Anyway – that we could go on with chemo, with the ray gun, with a dancing shaman if I liked, but that he thought . . . he thought . . .'

'That there was no point now. That it would be better to accept it an' die with a little dignity – he said that?'

'Yes.'

'Well, he's nothin' if not dependable like that, but he's not a believer, y'know, he doesn't have no saviour so he can't comfort himself – poor man.'

Saviour. That's done it. Sister Smith is undoubtedly one of the rocks the Church is built upon. Although in her case it's probably a small revivalist chapel. I can see the tiny building in my mind's eye, actually shaking as Sister Smith and her sisters slam out the gospels. I notice now what I should've before – that wedged in the brown ravine of her cleavage is a gold cross. Her saviour must be tiny, it occurs to me – probably because my sardonic voice is the one that will be silenced last – if this is big enough to nail him up on. 'Thank you, Sister – but I'm not religious.' It's probably the most sisterly thing I've said in years – which is how long since I've had cause to thank my own.

'That's all right, Mrs Bloom, there's a special place with Our Lord for the Israelites, y'know – '

'I'm not Jewish, Sister.'

'I'm sorry – I'd thought . . . the name . . .' She wanted to say the nose – they all do.

'I was married to Mr Bloom, for a time.' The deception comes easily enough – since she made the initial mistake. 'No, I'm not religious – I don't believe in an afterlife, I don't believe in Big Cosy Daddy, waiting to swing me up into the sky. When I die – I'll rot. That's all, Sister – that's all.'

For a second I'm proud of this bravado, then she says, 'Y'know, Mrs Bloom, not all of the exoteric symbolism of Christianity should be taken literally. I can understand you'll not be wanting to see the minister, but Mr Khan – '

'Fuck Mr Khan.'

'Mrs Bloom – '

'Fuck him, fuck him, I don't wanna see him – don' wanna see anybody – 'And here I go again; the little stopper of pride has popped out of my gullet and a great foaming splurge of self-pity froths out in a spasmodic series of gulps, seagull cries, tears and then globs of white bile which have the ministering fundamentalist reaching for a cardboard kidney dish. Why shape them like kidneys – why not like a heart, or a lung, or a severed breast?

She leaves me after threatening me with the cold Steel, and I relapse into the *memento mori* nightmare which is dying. Half of everything gone – the flesh peeled back and the skull of things finally, irrevocably, exposed to view. I'm so shocked. You wouldn't credit it that I've been feeling the lump for two years now, that I'm so familiar with it I've even given it a baby name. Minxie, I call her – because she's going to annihilate me – the little minx. Yup, two years of the pet name, and then Steel's sharp pal cut Minxie out. But when the stitches were removed from under my breast and I had the courage to examine it, I found Minxie still there and bigger than ever. I think.

Before I knew I had cancer I was seriously frightened that I would die of it. Die like my own mean little mother, winnowed out by it until I was a wheezing grey cadaver, literally a mummy. Everyone I talked to, everything I read, everywhere I turned, I heard that smoking causes it – but I couldn't stop. I couldn't stop and I couldn't stop and I couldn't stop. I couldn't fucking stop. I couldn't stop when my lungs felt like they were full of napalm – that's what they felt like. They were napalming the Viet Cong – and I was napalming my lungs with Camels, with Winstons, with Marlboros, even with – when I was truly desperate – *British* cigarettes, with English *fags*. They were dropping Agent Orange on the forests – and I felt like I was coughing the shit up.

Dr Bridge, one of my second husband's perennial squeezes. A dry thing. It must've been dusty when they did it together – Yaws himself being such a dry stick. A dry shit. Any old shit on a kerbstone – that was David Yaws. Pass him by every city block. If only I had. Anyway this Bridge – *Virginia* Bridge, no less – she'd park up her ridiculously well-kept Morris Traveller, a silly little half-timbered car to go with her silly little half-timbered house, and come up to the bedroom where I lay drowning in my own phlegm. Then she'd sound me with her smooth, Atrixo-creamed hands, while speaking to me with her dry English accent, and say, 'Lily, really, I mean to say, you can't expect me to go on treating you for chronic bronchitis if you aren't prepared to give up smoking. I mean, it's not as if you don't know the facts . . .'

I couldn't listen to her. I was feverish, I was in pain – and she still wanted to chafe with my husband. Did she come to the house in order to speculate as well as employ her speculum? About what Yaws and I didn't do together? Imagining Yaws's and my daughters as possible versions of kids she might've had with him? I can believe that. She had a crippled husband. Paralysed from the waist down. Lucky for Virginia it wasn't from the waist up. Anyway, I lay there and watched as black-and-white documentary clips of the era showing baboons with masks lashed on to their muzzles, forcing them to smoke, spooled behind my eyes. Give it up. I couldn't – I'd rather die. Cigarettes were the best friends I'd ever had. More reliable than liquor, comforting – but not fattening. I'd sooner die.

Like the teeth, though – I had a fateful relationship with the unlucky Luckys. More than this, as I looked at Virginia's equine teeth (how could she keep such tent pegs clean?), it occurred to me that it didn't have to be my life on the line, someone else's might do as well. Like Virginia's. I closed my eyes tighter still – '. . . it's an addiction like any other, Lily, it will take a few days . . .' – and willed Virginia Bridge to die: O Great White Spirit, if I give up smoking will you take this woman in my stead? Yup, it did. She died only a couple of years later, and let me tell you I was sorely tempted to take it up again. Only kidding. By then I had the anxiety even worse. Every year throughout the sixties, more and more evidence kept coming out about smoking. I felt as if all my life I'd been driving towards an intersection, while Death was speeding down the main road, the two of us on a collision course. Really I felt no better when I'd given up. I had about a motorway's worth of tar to cough up, then I realised that I'd smoked so much that it was more than likely *too late already*. It was after-the-bloody-hemlock time. I began to refer to any discussion of cancer as being 'a self-fulfilling prophecy'.

A cigarette would be good now, though. Good here in an antiseptic ward. Blue smoke goes well with white linen. We may all live soapy, light-musical lives, but every woman has the right to die as Bette Davis.

A self-fulfilling prophecy. Nice, ringing phrase that – and I've always been something of a phrase-maker. I was a designer by training, not that I ever designed much of consequence except for the cap of a pen which has since been sucked by a billion mouths. It was a unique cap – they were generic mouths. That's the way I look at it. Still, designing is a self-fulfilling prophecy – if it's done right. But the thing about this particular self-fulfilling prophecy – death by cancer – was that the very articulation of the prophecy was bound to induce cancerous anxiety. Every time I said it, I knew it would come true. The self-fulfilling prophecy was itself a self-fulfilling prophecy. Even so, I was surprised to be diagnosed – funny, yeah? Real amusing.

I'd also said to the girls, who grew up with my dark moods, 'At least we can be miserable in good surroundings.' (Miserable because their father had left us; miserable because he hadn't paid the utility bills so we had no heat or light or telephone; miserable because I couldn't stop crying; miserable because I *couldn't find my keys*.) At least we can be miserable in good surroundings – ha! What a fool I was – I got it the wrong way round; I should've said *good* in *miserable* surroundings – that would've been the right way to carry on. Maybe if I'd concentrated on doing that I wouldn't find myself so fucking lacking in stoicism now, so scared of this pain, so sick of this nausea.

They give me drugs for the nausea – but they make me feel sick. Perhaps they'll give me still more. Yeah – they'll do that. They'll load me up with pills until I'll find myself cramming some into my mouth while I'm actually hurling others out.

Ha-ha. Here comes Dr Steel, tripping over the swirly lino, in between the mobile biers. He wears a white coat which although lovingly cleaned and pressed (by Mrs Steel?) has been imperfectly dry-folded, so that the thick cotton forms a series of rigid, square panels. It makes him look like he's wearing a peculiar tabard. St George, sneaking into the ward to do battle with the tumour dragon . . . 'Hello, Doctor.'

'Ms Bloom, your daughters are here to see you.'

'Oh goody.'

'*Both* of them.' I wonder which one it is he so disapproves of – either would be worthy of it. 'But before they come through I wanted to have a word with you about the future.'

'You mean the lack of one – for me.'

'Look, I know I didn't express myself terribly well this morning, I'm afraid that side of things isn't my forte . . .' No, I can guess that too. I think Steel is one of those doctors who doctors because he loves the *disease*, not the patient. Yeah, he loves the disease. He likes to look at microscope slides that show slivers cut from interesting cancers. He likes the surprisingly vivid colours and the complex whorls of tissue. Indeed, in his more reflective moments he's subject to philosophising on the nature of cancer. He expatiates on the fact that cancer was unknown in the ancient world, that it seems to have arisen at the same time as human reason itself emerged from the darkness. After a couple of glasses of a good single malt, he's probably been known to hazard that the peculiar morphology of certain cancers may be a function of their being, in reality, tiny cellular models of the Copernican universe itself! '. . . it's never easy to tell somebody that there's nothing much we can do.'

'I feel for you – truly I do.'

'Ms Bloom – this isn't helping. You can stay here at UCH if you wish – although I know you're as aware as I am that the bed is needed. Or I understand from Mr Khan that a bed could be made available for you at St Barnabas's – '

'The hospice?'

'Yes, the hospice.'

'In Muswell Hill?'

'I believe so.'

'I'm not dying in Muswell Hill – I wouldn't even go *shopping* in Muswell Hill. I want to go home.'

'Or, you can go home. Can your daughters arrange for nursing? You appreciate it will need to be round the clock?' Or, or , or – but you note: no either.

'One of them can.'

'That would be Charlotte, would it?'

'I can't see Natasha organising anything much – can you?'

'Erm, no, maybe not.' He's writing stuff down on a clipboard with a Bic Fine, gathering the panels of his virginal tabard about him. He's beautifully shaved, Dr Steel, marvellously groomed. When he gets cancer – and he must, eventually, it's a self-fulfilling prophecy – it will be a nice orderly one, a tiny tumour in his brain which will simply push down on a vital artery, like a light switch, and turn him off. Leaving his clothes all neatly pressed and his body unsullied.

Did he go? People are always doing that now – they don't say goodbye to me, they just leave. I guess they think all conversations with me are now intrinsically valedictory – no need to say goodbye to the old bat, she's already gone. And it's true – I do feel detached. I feel detached the way I did in the months of dropsical pregnancy that led up to David and Charlotte and Natasha. At the time I thought it peculiar – that I seemed to be absenting myself while these very important guests were arriving for life's party – but now I see it's all connected, there's a compensatory arrangement – arrivals and departures. Terminal life.

I suppose I must've slipped into unconsciousness for a couple of minutes, because when the girls arrive they wake me with their bickering.

'I don't mind giving you the money – I just don't want any crap about a loan.'

'But I'll pay it back.' This wheedling voice is naturally sonorous and beautiful.

'No you won't, you never do.' This reasonable, mature tone is strangulated by class.

'I will – I'm gettin' a job.' This mockney is so wrong.

'A job? You?' This hauteur is entirely believable.

'At the dogs – Hackney Dogs.' Hackney – how utterly unsuitable for this, this . . .

. . . vision of a thing. She's beautiful all right – my Natasha. She ought to be in elbow-length white gloves and writing on her dance card with a silver propelling pencil. Instead she's got the sleeves of a black cashmere cardigan pulled down to her wrists. I wish she'd shoot up in the soles of her feet. Her black hair looks as if its been cut with pinking shears. Her blue eyes have kohl round them, obscuring blacker circles. She's stoned – of course. Her pupils blighted points in each wilted iris. She's an inch or so taller than I used to be – five-eleven, I guess – but Natasha is coat-hanger thin. The last time I saw her naked I could count all of her ribs. They should've given *her* a fucking mastectomy – she'd never've noticed. Still, she's riding on her cheekbones, my youngest. Her cheekbones and her charm. How can anyone with that generous a mouth be so ungiving? It doesn't matter, though, because it isn't Natty's place in life to give – she's a taker. She'll take any man's heart, or wallet, and nowadays his credit cards and mobile phone too. Yup, I wonder if it's this ability she has – to solicit the answer 'Yes' before she's even posed the question – that has made her so incapable of resisting her own inner voices, her own charming demons. 'Have some heroin, Natty?' they sweet-talk her; and she replies, 'Sure, why not?' She says she's a painter – and it's true that she went to art school. Unfortunately, she's not well-to-do enough to be one of those girls-who-paint, so she has to be a woman who daubs on walls. She was doing a 'Muriel' – as she terms it – for some community centre, but judging from the bicker that's history.

'The dogs, how suitable,' says Charlotte. 'It'll be easy for you to get there, you know the way already.'

'Oh fuck off, you materialist bitch. If you don't want to lend me twenty quid – don't. Spend it on a pedicure, or a massage. Go and get your bourgeois bum sluiced out at the Sanctuary – see if I fucking care.'

'Twenty pounds is quite a lot of money.' How like Charlotte to say 'twenty pounds' like that. Deadpan. She knows the value of the words that are money. I peel up an eyelid to regard them both. Natty is standing by the sharply arched triptych of mouldering Gothic window. My bed's in a bay – I'm in abeyance. It suits her – the combination of grime and the ecclesiastical. It's easy to imagine her as the Madonna of grunge. Charlotte has taken Dr Steel's place on the chair by the bedside table. She's brought flowers and a bottle of barley water. I asked her for the barley water yesterday afternoon when this was what I desired more than anything else in the world; more than light, more than life, more than love. That was yesterday afternoon – now I'd sooner vomit again than drink the muck.

It's a bit like Charlotte, the barley water – both are things the anticipation of which far surpasses their actuality. No, worse than that – both are things you only want when they aren't there. Charlotte is one of those women – she is a woman, not a girl, although she's only thirty as against Natty's arrested twenty-seven – who make it their business

44

to maximise what nature has given them. She's a big, blonde, lumpy thing, like me. Sometimes she reminds me so much of the gaucheness of my own youth that I can hardly bear it. Yup, she looks like me: five-ten, carrying at least a hundred and fifty pounds; big, dirigible tits, still firm; high hips; thick hair. A no-messing, big, blonde woman. She'd be able to carry it off – just as I did – given the nose, but she doesn't have the nose, not the prominent keel that has guided me through life's seas. Oh no. Where it should've been sunk is her father's little blob, David Yaws's button nose. '*Retroussé*', his mother used to call it. 'Porcine is what you mean,' I'd reply.

So, she's got Yaws's nose and the rest of his face too. At times like these, as I bleary at her, it looks to me as if a snapshot of Yaws's face has been Scotch-taped on to hers. It might seem wrong of me to dislike my elder daughter on the grounds of her close resemblance to her father, but hell, it'll do. What other grounds should I dislike her on? That she's taken the place of the brother who died before she was born? Yeah – that'll do fine too. How about the fact that she's precise, neat and efficient – all those things I never managed. Mm – complementary, I'd say. Poor Charlotte, with her middle-aged, middle-class, quintessentially *English* face, all scrunched up with the effort of dealing simultaneously with her junky sister and her dying mother. Lucky she has Mr Elvers to rely on. Not that her husband is in evidence – he'll be in the day room using the payphone, or his mobile phone, or leaning out the window so he can shout instructions to passers-by in the street. He's nothing if not communicative, our Mr Elvers.

'She's awake, Natty, be quiet now.'

'I didn't say any – '

'Sssh!'

'Girls? Is that my girls?'

'We're here, Mum.' Charlotte leans forward and takes my hand, swollen with arthritis, in hers – which is merely swollen.

'Is that you, Charlie?' I'm cramming as much wavering sincerity into this as I can.

'Yes, Mum, it's me.'

'Then why've you got a snapshot of your fucking father taped on your face?'

Charlotte recoils, Natty laughs. 'All right there, Mumu? Still wisecracking, are we?' She leans down and plants a kiss on my mouth which is more like a blow.

'Mother!' Charlie exclaims – she's always chosen to regard my hatred of her paternity as a mischievous bit of play-acting. 'Dr Steel has had a talk with us both.' And now I know the game is up. While it was only the doctors, the nurses, the Mr Khans who knew, it couldn't be true. It was a messy but implausible fact – to be whisked away in a cardboard kidney dish. But now Charlie knows, efficient Charlie, well – my bones might as well already be being pulverised in that cremulator. I bet as Steel and she talked she was taking notes in her Filofax, under neatly underlined headings: Death certificate; Undertakers; Funeral. Dusted and done – that's Charlie.

'Natty-watty.'

'Mumu.'

'My baby.' I open my arms and somehow she manages to curl her near-six feet of limbs into my embrace. I can smell the henna in her hair and feel the coarseness of it against my sallow cheek, but she feels good, feels like my baby. When she's my baby – I'm hers. It's like that with the youngest child – for their whole life they make you feel like the youngest. I can never see any of David Yaws in her at all.

'D'you wanna go homey, Mumu?'

'It's shitty in here, Natty – the food's shit, the decor's shit; and my dear – the *people*.'

'You go home, Mumu. I'll come with and look after you, promise.'

'I thought you had a new job?' Charlotte says.

Natasha rears up. 'I do – but what's more important, eh? Making money or looking after your dying mother, hmm? No – don't answer that.'

'There are practicalities to consider' – Charlotte was born to say things like this. 'Mum will need proper nursing. I assumed you'd want to go back to the flat, Mum, so Richard's arranging for nursing cover and I've sent Molly round to clean it up – OK?'

'I guess so.' Guess so only because Molly – Charlie and Richard's Filipino factotum – has different ideas about cleaning to me.

'Now Mum – you can't be ill in a messy house.'

'I've been ill in it these last two years; what you mean is I can't *die* in a messy house. Go on, say it. Messy-messy-messy. Die-die-die.'

'Mu-um!' they chorus; and both are at one with this: the continual need to bring up Mummy, admonish Mummy. What will they do when I'm gone? There won't even be this to hold them together.

But it's good to keep up the contemptuous, dismissive, cynical pose – it keeps the fear at bay. I don't want to break down in front of them, not now. There'll be plenty of time for that later.

'Dr Bowen – the senior registrar – she's doing your discharge now.'

'It won't be the first time.'

'I'm sorry?'

'She's had to deal with a fair few of my discharges recently.'

'Oh Mother, really!' I'm really, really, really, actually sick and tired of hearing that 'really'. My life *really* might be worth fighting for if I could be certain that after they'd burnt out my remaining hair with their radiation and poisoned me with their drugs, no one would never ever say 'really' in that tone again, within my earshot. But Natty doesn't say 'really' – she wouldn't be so crass. She laughs instead. She's an earthy soul, my Natty. A farter and a laugher. Mind you, washed and groomed and suited and booted, Natasha looks as if she shits chocolate ice cream; whereas poor old Charlie only ever looks like she thinks she does. 'Richard will hang on and we'll drive you back in a bit – he's got the Merc.'

'Oh goody.'

'I'll come too, Mumu. I'll make you your favourite snack of the moment when we get there.'

'Double-chocolate-fudge goody in that case.' And while I sink back into the pillows (incidentally, the one good thing about modern British hospitals – good, big, clean, nicely plumped pillows; if it weren't for them this joint really would be the bed and breakfast of the soul), the two of them begin gathering up my pathetic little valise's worth of shampoo sachets and books and women's magazines and underwear. All my life my underwear has troubled me – soon, at last, I'll be free of it. The Playtex Shroud – separates you from life, lifts you up to heaven.

Of course in the sixties, when the girls were small, I still wore pantyhose and girdles, or stockings and girdles, or just fucking girdles. Anything to flatten that great Ceres of bellies, and strap myself into sylphhood. First came the girls – then the fucking girdles. If I wore stockings I'd snap them on to eyes that were actually *attached* to the girdle – what an embrasure of nylon and rubber and *steel*. In the sixties, spontaneous sex was unbelievably difficult to achieve. Any level of arousal whatsoever was bound to be damped down by the time he'd managed to insinuate a hand inside this lot – let alone a dick. It was like a three-minute air-raid warning:

'Aawooo! Aaaawoooo! Sex coming! Sex coming!' And *quick, quick boys – an ecstasy of fumbling*; but then, 'Aaaawoooo Mum-may!!' The not-all-clear sounded and it was too fucking late. Not that I enjoyed their father's love-making much – but it was the principle that counted. When I grew up, sex *really* mattered. We didn't have drugs, or many consumables – but we could hump. We'd come of age during the Second War, when it was *de rigueur* to rock 'n' roll with all and sundry. Then came the fifties and sixties, when every car that backfired sounded to me like a ten-megaton detonation. The Cold War didn't exactly give me the hots, but along with many many others I assumed that what I'd want to do while it all came crashing down was screw with Dr Strangelove.

That or kill the kid. Or both. Kill the kid while screwing Strangelove – that was the early sixties for me. But *really* it was kill the kid. 'When they drop the bomb we'll have to kill the kid,' I'd say to David Yaws. 'You realise that, don't you' – I'd say it over dinner; in those days everything was over dinner – 'because even if we survive the bombs they drop on London, we'll wish we hadn't. It'll be the kindest thing to do.'

'Really, Lily,' he'd reply, shovelling his food up in the English fashion, the fork a little bulldozer, the knife a petite barrier, 'the Soviets may have walked out of this round of negotiations, but they'll be back. They know a nuclear war would be madness – just as Eisenhower does.' Christ! What a sententious prick the man was. He always spoke as if he himself had recently been consulted on the matter in hand: 'Is that Mr David Yaws, the ecclesiastical historian?' 'Speaking.' 'I have the Chairman of the Politburo on the telephone for you . . .' While I could hardly bear to look at a newspaper, Yaws devoured crisis after crisis, confident that none of it would touch him, that he'd sail on by as he always had.

Yaws had been in the Royal Navy during the war. 'I was on

the North Atlantic convoys' was the way he used to put it, in lounge bars, golf-club bars, train buffets – wherever he could adopt the correct hands-in-flannel-trouser-pockets pose. But the truth was he'd been at the pushing-off point for the Atlantic convoys. He was the guy who checked they had enough bullets and biscuits or whatever it was they took with them. He was the fucking quartermaster. And he wasn't out there in the ocean getting his balls frozen, oh no, not Yaws. No, he was tucked up on shore in the Orkney Islands, billeted in a cosy farmhouse with a lonely farmer's wife. I daresay there are a few middle-aged Orcadians walking around now with Yaws masks on. Amazing that such a slow-witted man should have had such a slick dick.

It's the baby talk that made me remember all this, the baby talk I talk with Natty. I always talked too much baby talk with her, which must be why she's turned out such a baby. I talked it with Charlotte as well, but I think that was to try and make her seem more like a baby and a little less like a scaled-down version of Yaws. One night in May of 1960, Yaws and I went to have dinner with his sister and brother-in-law. Bunny, that was his sister's name. The whole family had corny nicknames, the world was their nursery. Anyway, Bunny had gone to the trouble of getting us quail. The little birds lay on our plates with their feet clawing at the rim and their heads bisected and laid alongside. This was so we could lick the brains out of them like the sweetmeats they were. I quailed over the quail. The idea of crunching into the eggshell heads revolted me, all the more so because the assembled company were doing just that, and noisily. I felt like I was in a Kafka story. When I tasted the flesh it seemed fishy to me, and when they weren't noticing I tucked my brace up under a big, limp lettuce leaf.

'Lily thinks we'll have to kill Charlotte if they drop the bomb,' Yaws said, and Bunny and Mr Bunny cackled obligingly. To me it sounded like 'Lily tinks we'm gonna kill Charlie-warlie when bomb-ums goes off.' Both baby and, curiously, black talk. When we got home that evening and Yaws turned on the television, the news was being broadcast in baby talk: 'De Soviets dem do' wanna negoshyate. Dem angwy. Dem no like West. Dem baddies.' I told Yaws the newsreader – a drunk whose shtick was being so – was talking baby talk, but he paid it no mind. The next day, after *Mrs Dale's Diary*, I heard a radio announcement in baby talk, and when Yaws got back from the university he found me telling Charlotte, who was two, that she would have to die – in baby talk, naturally. Virginia Bridge was round with her black Gladstone before you could say 'barbiturate'. Or even 'bar-bar-boo-boo-bituate'.

It was barbs in those days. Virginia called it the 'yellow medicine', but I knew damn well what it was. She kept me lounging on a yellow chemical bed for the next six months, and then I discovered I was pregnant with Natasha. I wonder if it helped usher her into the arms of Morpheus, that amniotic bath of yellow medicine? It helped usher me into even greater anxiety. After David was born, in 1948, I was claustrophobic; after Charlotte was born ten years later I was agoraphobic. But after Natasha was born in 1961 I couldn't stay in *or* go outside. I would stand in the back doorway, the baby in my arms, wavering between the awful non-alternatives. I suppose that's one good thing to be said about dying: it gathers together all those irrational fears and effortlessly trumps them with the Big One. All bets are off. *Rien ne va plus.*

'I like the way they allow these cats to come on to the ward,' I say to Natty, who's packed the valise and is now helping me out of my nightie, into my clothes.

'What?' I daresay she's thinking about other, more lively concerns – like where her next fix is coming from, now she hasn't managed to hit on her sister for a loan.

'The kitties – on the ward. They don't seem to mind about them. There's a tabby who sits over there on that old lady's bed all day; and there's a tortoiseshell who comes in this window from time to time and curls up right on my tummy. It's so comforting – I wonder if it's a new therapy they've devised?' But this doesn't draw her out either; she only gives me a funny look. The funny look. The look you give dying people who're seeing things.

Now, here come Richard Elvers and his missus. See how fine they look together – all the deportment and elegance that money can buy. You'd have to say Charlie's chosen wisely, because they complement each other well. Both fleshy, both anally retentive, both driven. Elvers is a big, sandy-haired man with a safely red complexion (he doesn't drink). He favours dark, double-breasted suits which rationalise his fat. So does she. 'Hello, Lily' – he leans and pecks at me, as if I'm carrion already – 'I've just spoken to Molly and she's given the family seat a good seeing to.'

'Oh, that's good.' Now the Filipino's got her act together – I shall return!

'The car's right outside on a double yellow – so we'd better get going.'

'Upsy-daisy,' says Natasha, and she and Richard lever me to my feet. I bestow a few valedictory smiles on the super-numeraries in the other beds – no need to say *au revoir*. Sister Smith is at the nursing station together with the two nurses who're coming on for the night shift. 'Good to see you up, Mrs Bloom, and on the arm of such a handsome gentleman.' She has, presumably, assumed that Elvers is one of mine. For shame – really the woman is a fool. Still, I smile as best I can, give her a flash of the plastic. After all, this will probably be the penultimate time I leave the hospital.

Chapter Two

I'm glad he's got a ticket – although sad it's only an interim, sixteen-pound, fine. He deserves an unfixed penalty, our Richard; a free-floating axe should swing permanently above his head, ready to cleave him if he *ever* does *anything* wrong. And wherein lies his fault, this upright entrepreneur who's had the good grace to marry, look after and even *be faithful to* a daughter I myself could frankly do without? He's successful – we don't like that. After all, anyone can be a success, but it takes real guts to be a failure. Richard is gutless – which perhaps explains his boyish buoyancy. There's nothing in that puerile belly of his save for the gas of marketing, without which – as any fule kno – there can be no oxygen of publicity.

So, we settle ourselves and our tumours in the blue confines of the Mercedes and set off. Richard is fuming a little – but only internally. The car is like Richard himself: stylishly unstylish, corpulent, solid, efficient. And navy – part of the senior German service. Mercedes pride themselves so much on the longevity of their vehicles it surprises me they bother to bring out new models at all. One would rather think that now, as we power down the home straight – I say 'we' advisedly – towards the millennium's end, they'd reintroduce the older models again. 'Ladies and Gentleman, *meine Damen und Herren*, Mercedes-Benz of Düsseldorf, for a few seasons automobile-manufacturers by appointment to the Thousand-Year Reich, are proud to present the all old, all new, Horseless Carriage! Assembled lovingly by three ancient artisans, veterans of the Battle of Sedan, the Horseless Carriage features an entirely wooden body and a solid metal dashboard! Vases and reticules are optional, but every single Horseless Carriage comes with antimacassars as standard – '

'Look, Mumu,' Natty breaks in – she's in the back with me, the grown-ups are in front – 'there's *Jew*mar.' And indeed there, on the corner of Prince of Wales Road, is Jewmar – or what used to be Jewmar when the girls were kids. All that remains now is the black outline of lettering stencilled on the brickwork. Jewmar – or Lewmar, to give it its correct name – was a dry-goods store owned by Lewis and Mary Rubens, the couple who lived next door to us in Hendon in the sixties and seventies. Lewis and Mary – hence Lewmar; hence, to our anti-Semitic wits, Jewmar.

I couldn't believe the Rubenses when Yaws and I, together with Charlotte, aged one, moved to Hendon. Here, strained through net curtains, rustling about in a nylon, gingham-patterned house dress, and dumped down on a velour-covered three-piece suite, was all the sour, affected, sub-gentility of my own lower-middle-class, Jewish upbringing. The Rubenses' place smelt of gefilte fish and matzo balls – despite the fact that Mary Rubens cleaned relentlessly; she was a laving engine. And once every surface was spotless she'd re-cover it with glass, or plastic, or vinyl. There were glass covers on all the tables, stippled strips of transparent vinyl on the edge of every carpet, plastic covers on the seats. The whole joint was encapsulated – but it only served to keep the odours in. Meanwhile, over the hedge, next door, I'd be popping Librium and ironing creases into Yaws's shirts. After all, I'd married into true shabby gentility, and there were standards I *had* to fail to maintain.

Jewmar, its austere naves lined with boxes of Brillo pads and its rococo chapels writhing with mop-heads, has long gone, to be replaced by a branch of Waste of Paper, part of a nationwide chain that sells prints, posters, postcards and decorative stationery. These stores started up in the seventies, flogging post-hippy tat – flowery bookmarks, bookish flower presses, you know the cack. To kids mostly, I suppose. I remember the original outlet, which was in the basement of Kensington Market; and I recall too the tubby, pimpled, bum-fluffy proprietor, one R. Elvers. Yup, Elvers is the man behind Waste of Paper, which is why Natty says '*Jew*mar' in this heavily ironic way, with the accent on 'Jew'. Not that Elvers is Jewish, you understand, it's only that like so many liberal Englishmen he finds our Jewish anti-Semitism hard to take. Ach me! So many people left to disparage – so little time.

Yeah – but y'know what? Jimmy cracked corn and I *really* don't care. I'm annoyed that Richard has over two hundred Waste of Paper outlets. I'm aghast at the way he buys taste wholesale not just for his stores but for himself and his wife as well. Did he have any taste grubstake to begin with, I wonder, or has he never staked any claim at all? 'Nearly home, Mother,' says Charlotte – as if it were true. But now that we're pulling up Kentish Town Road, and turning into Islip Street so as to negotiate the one way-system, I'm not so sure that this is my home at all any more.

When I think of the colossal effort I made to integrate with this neighbourhood when I moved here ten years ago, it makes me realise how pathetically small all my life's endeavours have been. My efforts as a homemaker were like playing with kids' constructor toys, Lincoln's Cabins Stateside, and Betta Bildas when I crossed the pond. They were childish, out of scale, and inevitably, once I'd completed them, I'd smash them up in a giant fit of pique.

I have to say this much for David Yaws – in his demise he exhibited a genius for timing which was entirely absent in his life. Having been late for everything, he finally left me in the winter of 1970, not to shack up with Virginia Bridge, or

Serena Hastings, or any of the other uptight genteel fucks he'd strung along since – in some cases – *before the war*. Nor did he get it together with Maria dos Santos, his fellow ecclesiastical historian and stereotypically hot Iberian lover. Maria was the one he actually *chased* all the way to Seville, where he *howled* outside her door like the dumb dog he was, until she had to *climb* off of her back terrace and go to her mother's house, in order to telephone *me*, and ask *me* to leave a message at his fucking hotel to tell him to *come home*. No, not Maria – who I always rather liked anyway. No, he went off to *Crouch End* of all places, where he had effected a liaison with a little old lady called Wix, Wendy Wix. Who was so little and old and wrinkly and fucking genteel that according to the girls she was like a cross between a gnome and their *grandmother*.

I suppose Yaws was missing Mumsie, his mother, who he'd managed to neglect into the grave the year before. Either that or he really was a gerontophile. A sinister thought, but then as the decades passed and the prissily precise accents of his comfortably padded, inter-war youth were drowned out by the current babel, he must have developed a genuine yearning for a brief encounter with the past. That was all he got, for having failed as a gentleman, Yaws copped out of being a man as well. By dying. They said it was a heart attack, but this sounds far too speedy for Yaws who wandered through his entire life in slow motion. No, I'm more inclined to think that his mortal coil simply uncoiled. His tick-tock clock ran down and no one troubled to rewind it. His heart pittered, pattered, skipped a beat, thought, 'Screw this,' and halted. He was fifty-six, another droning male who failed to make it out of the killing jar.

How strange that Jews should've silted up the backwaters of suburban London. How peculiar for the diaspora to end behind net curtains. Net fucking curtains. Rather than going to Hollywood or the gas chambers I joined this gauzy crew. Richard turns the car carefully into Bartholomew Road and we purr down it, the Nazi suspension eliminating the potholes. Not that Kentish Town is anywhere near as dismal as Hendon; it's wedged into the core of the city far more tightly, a sliver of a district. I moved here in 1979 when Natasha went to art school, and once again, as I'd done so many times before, I organised my own induction: getting a library ticket; finding out where the good deli was; pacing out walks; window-shopping; acquiring neighbours. Christ – I'm glad that's all over with now, I don't think I could stand to do it again. I'd sooner move back to Madison, Wisconsin. Where Dave Kaplan and I spent the Eisenhower years – or at any rate some of them. Madison – now there was a town for claustro-agro. A radial of avenues, swept by the chilly winds off the lakes, and all of them aiming towards the fake Capitol, the vanishing point of democracy.

'We're here, Mumu, let me help you out.' Why's she being so solicitous? Out the door in a flash, round to my side, and a rail of an arm to lean on. Oh! Pain and nausea. Which came first? Certainly the pain makes me feel sick, but could it be that it's feeling nauseous that gives me such pain? We totter to the kerb. I'd forgotten it was spring, although in London this often only means a jaundiced outbreak of forsythia. The street looks different the way things do when you've been away; and when you've been in hospital the familiar usually looks tremendous, the vitality of the fresh outside a glorious part of recovery. With all three kids – even after the painful, embarrassing delivery of Natasha – I felt immeasurably better when I got out of the hospital. I'd like to say that it was the transcendent feeling of New Motherhood, of Cosmic Beginning – but it wasn't. It was me being well again, de-lumped, un-bumped, unpicked and free.

It's not like that now – I'm only coming home to die, so the street looks like crap to me, blobbed with dog shit; spattered with chewed-up gum; cluttered up with cars on either side. The bricks of the three-storey terraced houses are bilious in the sharp sunlight – what's London made of? Why, London bricks, of course. I feel horribly exposed in my crappy old overcoat and my Cornish-pasty shoes, with my scalp showing through my sparse hair. Each step brings a dollop of bile into my mouth, so by the time we've reached the front door, entered it, broached the flat's front door, shuffled across the vestibule, staggered through the front room, and made it into the bathroom, I'm ready to vomit. Which I do. Natty holds on to me all the while, not exactly whispering, but at any rate muttering reassurances. 'That's all right, Mumu, on you come now, don't worry, that's OK, on you come, there you go, do you want a flannel?'

A washcloth? Eurgh. It smells when I clean my face with it – everything smells too much. I long for the days when Churchill was in power and all I could smell was the smoke from my Winston. You couldn't get them in England then, I had to have friends bring them over from the States. We stutter back into the main room of the flat, then through the double doors to my bedroom, where I sink down and Natty kneels to remove my pasties. My little flat – why can't *I* keep it clean? Without Filipino assistance all the surfaces are covered in crumbs, the carpets wefted with cat hair, the lampshades furred with dust. But why should I bloody care? For once in my life, entropy is in fashion. The Second Law of Thermodynamics is *the look* for 1988. Says top designer Stephan Shylock, 'No need to worry about taking the trash out, dusting, ironing, or cleaning the drapes. Let that dirt build up mightily and allow your living area to reflect your own inevitable dissolution . . .' Pity Molly had to spoil the spoilage.

Where *are* my kitties? There were plenty at the hospital – or were those mine? Or has the Filipino sucked them up along with their hair? Do I even care? My girls will be adequate pet-substitutes – for now.

'Mumu, d'you want to climb into bed?' Why is she bothering me? It's comfy here, slumped down on the bedside – why would I want to lower myself into that chilly linen tomb? Old Lazarus has just managed to clamber out of the last one. But – hey! It's not up to me; she's got me back on my feet and we stagger together like two marathon dancers nearing the end. Off with the coat – down with the dress. I only dress down nowadays y'know – I only wear dresses that can be taken down. My days of upwardly-mobile undressing are over now. I was never exactly free with my body, but before my second was born I had no qualms about crossing my arms and pulling my dress over my head. Then advancing, open to whichever man, open to the world.

'That's better.' Better for who, exactly? Better for you, you round-heeled little tart? Better for you to have me supine so you can rummage through the flat and see if you can turn up any loose cash, dollars maybe left over from my last trip to New York. Whatever. Natasha would purloin a wad of zlotys if she thought her drug dealer would accept them. I used to be a big blonde with big tits and a big nose. Now I'm a big grey blob, with one and a half tits and a sharp beak. I'm a game bird – I hope. No, on reflection I *fear*, I *quail*.

'Errrrrr!' The flat has an intercom buzzer that sounds like hesitation.

'That will be the Macmillan nurse,' says Elvers – because he's paying for it.

'I'll let her in,' says Charlotte – because she is, too. Natty stays pennilessly put. Then a tangle of voices which I can't be assed to unravel. They are, presumably, showing her the flat and going over the drugs with her –

The drugs! That's why Natty was so keen to come back with us – she has her eye on the Oramorph (one milligram of morphine sulphate per cc of liquid), and the diamorphine (handy hexagonal pills, twenty-milligram blues and ten-milligram browns, to be taken sub-lingually), and the Valium – of course. I've already heard her thinking aloud about 'when they'll give her Brompton's cocktail'. While Sister Smith knew better than to hand her the hospital-issue paper bag full of the stuff, she did give it to Charlotte. Natasha has swooped in its wake like a seagull. Jesus – how grotesque. You're dying and your junky daughter comes over to rip off your pain relief – 'Natty!'

'Yes, Mumu?' Her lovely wasted head pokes through the double doors to the living room.

'What's the nurse like?'

She enters and pulls the doors to before replying. 'She's wearing a ghastly yellow cardy which makes her skin look sallow and ugly.'

'Indeed – and d'jew think that reflects on her healing arts?'

'Dunno – you asked what she was like. Charlotte's showing her the kitchen and Richard's making up the sofa bed for her.'

'What time is it?'

'It's nearly five, Mumu.'

'You must be feeling sick, precious – tell Charlotte to bring my drugs in.' That gets her trotting off coltishly – my little junky pony.

'Aren't you feeling well, Mum? Are you in pain?'

Oh yes – it pains me to see your round face. It pains me to see that I've squeezed out a further dollop of Yaws's white, adipose body. Never allow yourself to be swayed by a man with a surname that can be read backwards. 'I want my pills.'

'Dr Bowen thought you wouldn't need any more until this evening.'

'Well . . .' It's becoming a real effort to say things; I have to punch a hole in the wobbling membrane of nausea that envelops me, simply in order to ejaculate them. 'I don't believe Dr Bowen is *that* sympathetic. I mean – it isn't *her fucking pain*!'

'I'll get them.'

More muttering behind the doors, then they swing open again. Why am I insistently reminded of cowboys being thrown out of saloons in old westerns? It's the movies, kid – enjoy. Natty was right about the cardigan. 'Ms Bloom?' She's revolting – arguably more cadaverous than me; a ministering angel – of death. 'I'm Deirdre Murphy.' I'm an authority on arrogant contempt – perhaps the world's foremost. 'I'll be looking after you for the night.' She has a rapid yet limpid voice – no Irish accent.

'You're a bit early, aren't you?'

'Normally the night nurse will come on at eight in the evening and stay 'til eight the following morning, but the agency thought it would be a good idea if I came earlier this evening so that you wouldn't have to deal with two new carers in the one day.'

'How considerate of them.' To consider their own profits.

'Yes, well, we are here to help.' Indeed you are, you're helping me to let go of life already – with cardigans like that loose on the surface of the world, it's no longer a safe place for anyone with any sartorial taste. 'Your daughter said you wanted some pain relief?' She's got the bag.

'Yes, where they took the stitches out – it's very raw.'

She disappears into the bathroom and I can hear her stacking the packets and pots of pills. She reappears with the Oramorph.

I wave her away. 'No, no, I need a pill – that stuff doesn't work.'

'You've already had twenty milligrams of diamorphine today, Ms Bloom – any more will make you awfully constipated.'

'*Awfully?*'

'I'm sorry?'

'There's nothing awful about my constipation, madam. I cherish it. I hated having to crap – and now it's over.'

'I – I was going to ask you if you'll be needing a portable commode?'

Only to stuff your head down. 'No, no – that won't be necessary, just gimme the pill.' And she does, worn down by my irony. I put it in my mouth and when she turns away palm it. If life has been a prison – what better time to break the rules than when you're dying? I wish I'd had more sex – and more unsuitable sex. Now one of my descendants will have to have it on my behalf – a groaning legacy. 'And Deirdre.'

'Yes, Ms Bloom?'

'Call me Lily, please, and would you send Natasha through now?'All this coming and going – so little discussion of the Great Masters.

'Yes, Mumu?'

'There you go, honey.' I display the brown pill in my palm.

'What?'

'Here's some heroin for you, darling, better you should take a pill than make your arms more of a pin cushion than they are already. What's this . . .' I squint at the pill, which is slick with saliva, '. . . ten milligrams, is that enough to hold you?'

'Not quite – but why're you doing this, Mumu?'

'Not quite, huh? Go in the bathroom and get me the pot.' She complies and I shake her out two more. 'Enough now?'

'Yuh.' She dry-swallows them. 'But why, Mumu?'

'Listen, I've been to those crappy meetings 'cause of your drug problem, I've sobbed in doctors' waiting rooms and casualty wards, and you're still taking this shit – though Christ knows what it does for you, it does nothing for me. So, if you want to hang out here with me I don't want you always on the lookout for cash to steal, or drugs, and I don't want that junky pal of yours coming round here either – what's he called?'

'Russell.'

'Yeah, *Russell*. Him I could really do without seeing. So, if it's all the same to you I'd as soon I was your pusher for the time being – suit you, madam?'

Oh, it suits her all right. I can see that. I thought heroin made people who took it comatose zombies. In my own case it would be all but impossible to tell the difference, but Natasha is peculiarly charged by the drug – and even by the mere anticipation of its effects. She shifts from being vulnerable and skittish and withdrawn to being strong and steady and extrovert. She's told me before that it makes her feel 'complete' and 'confident', and I can see what she means. When she's off heroin she's a fucking nightmare – when she's on it she's a peach. It's not what a mother should feel about her daughter, but I do, I do, I do. She's positively cantering around the room now, hanging my clothes in the closet, ordering my bedside table – books neatly stacked, little radio to the fore. 'Do you want me to crash here, then? Stay in the flat?' She stays at Russell's flat, I know. It's right around the corner from here, over a bookie's on the main road. Natasha stays there so she can have her fix in the morning – her 'get-up', she calls it.

'No, that won't be necessary – there isn't any room anyway. Besides, I thought you were staying with Miles at the moment?' Miles is the boyfriend – there would have to be a boyfriend. Natasha couldn't live without a boyfriend.

'Oh yeah – but . . . well y'know.'

'What, what do I know?'

'He's so *dull*.' Oh yes, my daughter the thrill-seeker. Perhaps if I hadn't brought her up to thrive on high drama she wouldn't approach her life in this stagy fashion. My mistake. I would say *mea culpa*, but in the commercial premises I currently lease there's a discreet sign by the cash register that reads: NO LIABILITY IS ACCEPTED FOR ANYTHING WHATSOEVER. FOREVER.

'Well, are you staying with him?'

She is. This is confirmed by another burp of hesitation from the intercom – Miles has arrived. Miles by name, miles by nature – for he walks, rides and drives many many of them in pursuit of the lovely Natasha. I feel like drawing nice Miles to one side and warning him that this will always be his fate. That he will spend a lifetime trailing after this no-cash cow, as it grazes on other men and more drugs; and that if he's fool enough to impregnate her it will be worse still. He'll find himself shouting through letterboxes to check that his kid is still alive, that its mother hasn't dropped dead from an overdose, leaving it to bang around by itself, in a squat full of rusty nails angled so as to inject tetanus. Poor Miles.

In he comes, looking dutiful – as if he were my son. He opens the double doors like a flunkey or an ambassador, parting them in front of his face, then deftly marrying them again behind his ass. 'Mumu?' He partakes of the family lingua franca, the gooey argot. 'How're you feeling?'

'All the better for being home, Miles.' I manage to look at him with feigned betterness concealing my real bitterness. He's a severely attractive young man, straight black hair, burnished features – he's far more handsome than anyone I've ever been with. Not that I could've summoned up a smidgen of lust for him, even before Minxie came along. No, my lust grew old along with me. In my thirties I only found thirty-year-old men attractive; in my forties, forty-year-olds; and in my fifties, men who were, quite frankly, moribund. Now my lust has died alongside them – and so I'm dying. How I used to hate putting on the convict's costume of feminine allure, so that all the arrows pointed towards my sex – yet how I miss it now. It transpires that my life may well have been for lust.

'I was going to take Natasha to a film – if that's all right with you?'

'Perfectly fine, although I shan't be accompanying you.'

'Would you like me to bring the telly in here?'

'No, don't worry, I've got my little radio. I like the BBC voices. I like the news bulletins. I bet they'll have them even in the grave.' His shapely mouth becomes amorphous with concern, but he doesn't blink. Bit of a catastrophile, our Miles – comes of being raised by a drunk old hippy. He's told me that he spent much of his childhood prising her insensate fingers from bottles of Merrydown cider, and checking to see Isis (that's her name – I kid you not) hadn't wet herself. Yup, he's right at home with the incapacitated, is Miles, which is presumably why he finds Natty so bloody irresistible.

'If there's anything I can do, Mumu – anything at all.'

What service does he imagine he can perform for me? Does he really *want* to give me an enema, a blanket bath, an injection? Or is his heart set on something even more sinisterly invasive? Is he looking at me in the way Dr Steel does, seeing the patient as merely the container of the disease? Steel, a pathologist *manqué* if ever there was one, clearly cannot wait to unzip me and have a look at my malignant goodies. Good luck to him – I'll be elsewhere. 'No, Miles – you head off. And Miles.'

'Yes, Mumu.'

'Natty's had thirty milligrams of my diamorphine, so don't let her anywhere near that creep Russell, OK?'

'OK Mumu.' He withdraws, his idol face determinedly void of consternation at this bizarre role I've adopted.

Yes, Miles. Trying to look sharp and hip and funky in his all-black denim costume, his three earrings, his teased hair. Miles, who like so many of the kids of bohemians is in fact desperate to conform. Miles, who would've made the perfect partner for Charlotte. Charlotte, who now bustles in efficiently with what appears to be – actually *is* – a checklist. 'Mum, I've filled in Deirdre on the kitchen, the heating and the cats. Richard has arranged for Molly to come by for an hour each morning and give the place a once-over. Natty says she'll check on you later, and I'll be back late tomorrow morning – I have an early meeting.'

'OK.'

This downbeat reply doesn't please her, and her fat lips give a Yaws moue, as if disappointed in the world that has been organised. 'Are you OK, Mum?'

'Charlotte,' I lever myself up on the pillows so that I may get more uncomfortable, 'I'm not going to go gently.'

'I hadn't thought so.'

'I'm scared.'

'So am I.' She comes over and kisses me on the forehead. I cry a little and when she's comforted me a little I forget that she's there and even who she is. When I remember – she's gone; and so, apparently, are the black-denim twins.

With the girls and their swains departed, I'm free to meditate on the way time will drag to the fore their presently obscure resemblances. With Charlotte, as I say, so far there's nothing but Yaws, and with Natasha there's still nothing of him. But I know this isn't true, know it from my own experience. As I've grown older, increasingly the disliked and heavy face of my Aunt Rhea has stared back at me from the glass. This face has been hidden from me for all these years and comes upon me now in mockery – or so it seems. I wonder who'll rise up to mock my two? Neither will know until they reach the age I was when I raised them. Then the memories of their own bodies will inform them who they genuinely are. What if they turned out to be Aunt Rheas as well? That would be worth waiting for – the three fat Rheas sitting stitching malicious tapestries together. I think not.

I guess I kept the delusion of being my own woman too long, blowing hot and cold so that eventually I was annealed by my neuroses. If I was my own woman, why was it that these impersonal anxieties and mass phobias could jerk me around so, like a dope on a rope? Let alone lust. Or even: *let alone lust!* Lust was a positive high-tension cable, plugged into my core, activating a near-epileptic seizure of conviction that this was the one thing I *had* to do in life.

Deirdre comes tiptoeing through to check on me. 'Would you like a snack, Ms – Lily?' Sounds like 'Mizz Lily' and for a moment I'm back in the thirties being waited on by a negro – which is what they were then. What's she gonna offer me, corn pone? Jell-O?

'Thank you, Deirdre, I'm not hungry.'

And she withdraws through the double, ceiling-high doors, which are really the only original feature left in this heavily converted apartment. And isn't the same true of me? All that was once me has been dispersed through the flux of a thousand thousand experiences. The 'I' has been partitioned off, remodelled, resurfaced and re-insulated, so that it cannot even remember what the original dados or mouldings were like. They say ninety per cent of house dust is dead human skin – and that's me. Dust on a windowsill, in a converted apartment, in a foreign city.

I suppose I should've written a memoir before it was too late, but unlike fucking Lady Asquith I never kept a diary. The towns and cities and areas I've lived in, on two continents, over sixty-five years, merge into a composite Unpleasantville.

The people I've known are resolved into types, appearing to me now as a play set of plastic figurines: 'Typical People of the Eastern Seaboard of the USA and London England from the Twentieth Century – .030 Scale'. Only lust can grab me in its bra-cinching hook eyes, drag me down through the undertow of nausea, into a past which could be mine.

1955. Dizzy Gillespie and Miles Davis are duelling through the door. It's a jizzed jazz scherzo, so jizzy that globs of jizzum must be shooting out of their horns. I'm leaning against a General Electric fridge of such purring, juddering, aerody-namic aspect that were I to unsuck the rubber-flanged door and climb inside, settle myself comfortably in amongst the bowls of chopped liver, the packets of frankfurters, the crinkly heads of lettuce, it might well lift off for the Forbidden Planet. Yup, Dizzy and Miles are going at it next door, and I'm leaning in here talking with a man who isn't my husband. He's a tall, stooped man – quite unlike Dave Kaplan – and he's wearing a suit, which Kaplan would never do. We're talking around Norman Podhertz and the *New Republic*, or the poetry of William Carlos Williams, or the pickling of Ein-stein's brain, but we're talking *about* lust. Sex. Screwing. He's saying, 'I want to screw you, but I don't want to break up my marriage.' And I'm saying, 'Let's just make love – and damn the consequences.' I communicate this by staring straight into his remarkably deep, black eyes. He expresses his demurral by peering at a point just above my left shoulder, a vantage allowing him to see his wife's arms, which are waving about animatedly in the next room. It's 1955 – and I'm armed with my own teeth.

It's a party. A party in his house. Kaplan and I barely have an icebox – let alone this Mercury rocket of chilliness. And Kaplan doesn't really like bebop; sometimes I think he'd prefer to listen to klezmer. The party is full of arms – fifties parties always are. It's the smoking, the puffing, the gasping. If you're gonna hold on to one of these burning babies you have to port as well as aim it. So the arms are all out at angles like the limbs of trees. Winstons and Pall Malls and Camels and Luckys and Newports, all fuming away wherever these particular people congregate. But the house isn't too smoky, because the windows are wide open to admit the thrumming heat of a New England evening in late June.

The man – whose name is Bob Beltane – isn't smoking, which gives him a certain mystery. To add to his allure, Bob is a poet – and I think this fabulously cool. His verse isn't that bad – perhaps a tad mannered, but he dares to recite it to me which I find irresistible. He also declaims other poets, and now I can tune in he's saying, '. . . September, when we loved as in a burning house . . .'

'Is it going to take that long?'

'What?'

'For us to love? D'jew think I should set the house on fire now? We could let the calendar look after itself, huh?' To show I'm not kidding I flip my Zippo and apply an inch of ivory flame to the corner of one of Jean Beltane's cookbooks, which are piled up on the ceramic-tiled breakfast counter. To do this I have to lean forward across Bob, so that my stomach momentarily nuzzles at his crotch. He recoils as if I've zapped him with a ray gun – and I recoil as well, shocked at how little of my belly there is. It's as flat as a pancake and encased in slacks – black *slacks*! I've got some kind of a gingham shirt on, the tails of which are tied in a knot under my boobs. I'm thirty-three years old and I have my own teeth – even if they're rotting in my head – and I know I'm going to live for ever in . . .

. . . Hendon. Crooked Usage – that's the name of the road. A little elbow of three-up, three-down semis, angling away from and then back towards the Hendon Way. You can never get away from the Hendon Way. I'm having a recurring dream which is always set in the house Yaws and Charlotte and Natasha and I lived in. I may have swapped continents and changed men, but I still got a hateful house – another joint I could never be bothered to decorate, or maintain, or cherish. Which is perhaps why these characters have pitched up – a dusty mob of them. Not what you associate with London. London – even the 'burbs – is a grimy enough city, but this crew are thick with real dust, whitish desert dust. They're erecting a tent, or constructing a lean-to, maybe even a humpy. Whatever it is, it's clear they're intent on staying. One of them comes to the back door; I can see him from where I'm standing at the kitchen sink. I've got such dreamy views – from all windows of the house at once. He's wearing a white Stetson, of all things, and asks for water: 'Git inny water, missus?' he says. 'Git inny water, missus?' I feel that I have utterly *incomplete information* about all of this, a not unusual intimation whether I'm asleep or awake.

Chapter Three

'**G**ood morning, Lily.'
Morning – what the fuck's she talking about, this bog-trotting drab? This isn't morning, it's grey and insipid outside – what the city that always sleeps palms off on its somnolent inhabitants as dawn. 'What time is it, please?' The 'please' is a compensation for my inner baddy thoughts. It always is – isn't it. No politeness is ever justified. Even in *Pride and Prejudice* the Bennet sisters were fucking people over, and screwing them up, and shitting on them – when off the page.

'It's nearly six-thirty, you've been asleep for almost thirteen hours.' That'll be the diamorphine and the Valium, drugs so powerful they're like the boots of heavy men stamping down on my neck.

Jesus – the pain in my *neck*. 'Oh God!'

'Is it a pain?'

'My neck – my neck, it feels like it's broken.'

'It's the angle you've been lying at. I tried to move you late last night, but I'm afraid I wasn't able.' She's up close now, my Deirdre, still in the ghastly yellow cardy. Amazing – I've never seen a ball of pus-coloured wool. 'You were sweating a lot in the night as well.'

'Was I.' *So* unladylike, that, I must have a word with my sebaceous glands, whip them into shape.

'It might be a good idea to clean you up a bit, get you into a fresh nightdress for the day.' She's playing it quietly, clever Deirdre. She realises that although toothless, I can still bite. Now she's close up I can smell soap on her. She must've brought her own, because I don't recognise it. The odour is surprisingly pleasant, forcing on me the awareness of my own well-matured stench of sweat and disease. I feel like puking.

And do – 'Heroosh!' – an abrupt, third-personal, highly feminine piece of puking. Or so *I* like to think.

Deirdre and I now have to go through a whole rigmarole. She rocks me up and rolls me out of the bed – I'm so fucking weak, the latitudes of impotence extending from under my mutilated breast and circling the toxic planet that is my body. I'm far, far weaker than I was yesterday, my strength is gurgling out of me, all that anger – surely it can keep me alive? I keep flopping over the arms of the chair as Deirdre mops at me with flannels and bowls, flopping over like an unstandupable toy: 'Whistler's Incredible Dead Mother – Push Her Over and She Stays There – For Ever'. Not funny ha-ha really, more funny peculiar.

Deirdre bundles up the soiled nightie and the soiled bottom sheet. Someone's put a plastic sheet on the mattress underneath it. How sensible. It must be the same procedure for home deaths as it is for births. The chair she's put me in is a little Regency fake which I recently had covered. Looked at this way, my decline has been sickeningly abrupt – there are library books unreturned, a tax return inadequately filed, letters unwritten, even appointments I've yet to cancel. Who knows, I might make a sudden recovery, Minxie might gather herself together and quit her temporary home, leaving me free to attend a flower show on Saturday with Susie Plender. O frabjous day! Callooh! Callay!

'I'm sorry, Lily?'

'Nothing, Deirdre, nothing at all.'

I don't mind Deirdre; more than that – I'm grateful to her. Dying should be done with strangers – it's not so bad for them, mopping up the sweat and puke. After all, it's not as if the cancerous burglar has broken into their corporeal house, laid a tumour turd on their cellular carpet. So, I guess it's a hell of a lot easier for them to clean it up. It must be the same with undertakers. They must be the jolliest guys around, going into work every day and knowing they'll face tragedies not their own, *such* a relief. And English undertakers must be the jolliest of all, given their unrivalled propensity for schadenfreude: Ho-ho-ho! You're lying down on the ground covered in blood, *what* a silly pratfall. They don't need to be venal and money-grubbing the way Americans are, because they actually *enjoy* the work – they'd *pay* to do it. And anyway Deirdre holds me well, touches me firmly. She's a nurse – I'm a child. This will be the only way the English handle me now, until they chuck my corpse in a cheap pine coffin with no bogus ceremony at all and I disappear up the pillar of chimney that supports the grey sky over Hoop Lane. I do *so* like Golders Green Crematorium – did you know that children under five are burnt for free? So very humane.

She dries me off, dresses me up, tucks me back in, smooths the duvet, smooths my hair. I wonder if all nurses played with dolls a lot when they were little girls?

'Do you think you could manage a snack now?'

To my near infinite amazement I discover that I might be able to choke something down. 'In the cupboard over the stove you'll find some Ryvita – would you spread a couple with a little of the cream cheese in the fridge? And perhaps some fruit if there's any?' She shuffles off over the carpet I've never liked, into the kitchenette which has always been too small. I suppose I could've stayed at the house on Crooked Usage – the kitchen there was fine. But what would I've done in it? Cook gigantic meals I was incapable of eating without ballooning still more than I had? The entire fucking house was defaced with the evidence of my bouts with the bulge. On every wall there were pencilled lists of my daily weigh-ins:

'April 5th – 186 lb. April 6th – 184 lb. April 7th – 183 lb. April 10th – 189 lb. SHIT! SHIT! SHIT!' I must've gone away for the weekend – to a fucking bakery.

The seventies were my fattest decade. Overall I think the seventies were distinctly bulbous. People looked chunky, type-faces were rounded, writing implements penile. I liked to think I was maintaining an aesthetic unity, as my weight shot up to two hundred pounds and I became a Mrs Pepperpot of a woman. Sheer bravado – I hated it. I hated my fat. I'd sit sobbing on the side of my bed – things never change – and grab folds of myself up in order to present them individually with my derision. The effortlessly skinny girls would gather whispering on the landing – was it safe to approach the obese old dragon? Emphatically not. I loathed and resented the sylphs I shared the house with. I hated their nascent curves and their burgeoning sexuality – and probably showed it too much. Said too much about quite how shitty it can be to lie with a man. Said it to Natty – in baby talk, naturally. *Pas devant les enga-fengas.*

Up and down went the scales, the dial flickering over weeks and months. I reckon that between '73 and '79 I must have lost and regained, lost and regained getting on for seven hundred pounds – three whole obese mes. Me-me-me. Then I stabilised as a fat old pear-shaped woman. Not obese, simply fat and old. It seemed that I'd acquired the naturally pear-shaped body of the middle-class, late-middle-aged English-woman. My adoptive country's lard had taken me for its own. How nice. No wonder Hedley didn't fancy me. Natasha caught me sobbing on a transatlantic call: 'I was like a seal,' I moaned, 'like a seal.' I was referring to my agility in bed, but he took it to be a reference to my size and replied, 'It's not that, Lily – it's not that you're fat, believe me – ' I hung up and saw black bangs dangling over the banisters. 'Whyd'jew say that, Mumu? Whyd'jew say you were a seal?'

Here comes Deirdre with the inapposite slimmer's snack. I don't need fucking Ryvita – I need food substantial enough to give me back my life, my vigour, my health. I need to eat an entirely new Lily Bloom, so that she can be me. Deirdre's put it all together quite well, and she's found the grapes in the front room too, but I should've told her where the trays were, tucked beside the cooker, because the crackers are sliding around on that blue plate like pucks on an ice rink. Even when the plate's propped on my withered boobs I can't seem to keep the things still enough to grasp them. Deirdre's set herself down in the blue chair and is ostentatiously pretending to read her notes from the nighttime. Oh Christ! If only now were the bite time, but I know it isn't, even before the carious corner of one of the crackers stabs into my gum, underneath my bottom plate, and inflicts a wound nasty enough to bleed. Blood on the snacks.

Hedley. *He*'s still alive somewhere. He sent me a chess set only last year, even though he knows I don't play. But then he does have a chess shop in the Village – and his house was always cheap. Dead cheap. He doesn't own a car to this day – doesn't need one. He walks from the brownstone his gonif papa left him in the fifties, trolling down Broadway in a seersucker suit and a straw panama, all the way to the Village – where he sells his chess sets and his checker boards. Not exactly demanding work. It leaves him plenty of time to concentrate on the only problems he'll admit into his life – chess ones. Hedley, the last man who ever touched me intimately – saving Dr Steel, but then *he*'s barely human. More of an animated scalpel.

Hedley. Together we would lie in the flat in Brooklyn I borrowed from Esther – 'Darling it's rent-controlled – so I can't be assed to rent it!' – naked on the bed, like two parentheses indicating the presence of passionate language, of sex. Of course, he'd never leave his wife. His invalided wife. I mean to say, he'd leave her – in order to come to me; but he'd always go back again. Back to put her on the machine (she is – was? – a diabetic), or take her off the machine, or give her a shot. I asked him once if, given that he had a mountain of cash in the bank, he couldn't arrange for her to have a kidney transplant. He looked the most flustered I'd ever seen him, more abandoned by his reason than when he orgasmed. He said something about tissue types, rejection, unavailability, unsuitability – but I didn't believe him. Like I say, the house was cheap; and more than that I think he actually *wanted* her to be housebound, wanted her there whenever he eventually came home. What a psycho. Good riddance.

Eight o'clock, and outside small birds are going 'cheep'. I can hear cars grinding into motion and the relentless stutter of lorries on Kentish Town Road. Hard to believe, as I lie here listening to the *Today* programme, that six weeks ago I would've been leaving with them. The Italians call this kind of cancer 'the whirlwind', because it blows down on the person and winnows them right out, like a husk. It's blown away all my precious routines, my rounds of errands, my staggered sociability, my little trips – all gone. And with them the people.

No need to see Susie Plender any more – although she's called, naturally. No need to see Emma Gould either and hear about her latest man-trapping escapades. She's not a fifty-year-old woman – she's a tethered goat. No need to see Jack Harmsworth, my alcoholic bibliophile friend – although him I could bear the most. Like Natty, I guess – addictive person-alities are peculiarly restful to the dying, because like us they operate within tiny windows of temporal opportunity. And no need to call Mr Weintraub. No, actually I *must* call Wein-traub, or get Charlotte to. I must sort out this tax business before – before – well, let's just say it has to be dealt with. No need to see Tim, my boss, although the sweetie did come and visit me in the hospital last week. He was terribly uneasy and his wife, Lola, a squint-eyed Spaniard, kept looking around the ward as if she could see something we couldn't. Something terrifying.

Nope, no need for any of them. Hedley's history. Yaws is dead. Kaplan – well, Kaplan, there lies a tale. Anyway, I don't expect to be hearing from him, oh no. It'll be Natty and Charlotte and Steel and Deirdre from now on in. Not that Deirdre's here for the duration; I can hear her next door passing the careful baton as I muse.

'Here's my time sheet, Mrs Elvers. Your mother had a very quiet night.'

'Did she?' You note there's no move to informality from my stuck-up daughter.

'Well, I say quiet, but in truth I have to say she's . . . she's . . .'

'Fading fast?'

'I – I wouldn't want . . . it's . . .'

'Please, Mrs Murphy, please – don't be afraid to express an opinion.'

'She does appear to be in a rapid decline. It happens quite often – when a . . . terminal patient comes home.'

'I see. Is your colleague here yet?'

'No – '

'Errrr!' Yes she is, and hesitating for admittance – but no:

'Hiya.' It's Natasha, come for her get-up, I daresay – well, I did tell her to – and:

'Errr.' A bit less insistent, that – it'll be the Murphy-substitute, another certain woman of a certain age in the slick, professional housecoat of death. Their Father's house has many mansions, and they're intent on dusting the vestibules.

From the main room of the flat come scraps of conversations, leftovers of sentences which float through. Then there's yet another burp from the intercom, and Molly, the Elverses' maid, arrives to clean. Jesus! It must be like the stateroom scene from the Marx Brothers' *A Night at the Opera* in there. I wonder if I'd find them funny any more. I wonder if there's a last particle of amusement left inside this rotting body. Perhaps if I vibrated at the right frequency the worms would quit me, like a stream of rats running out of Hamelin. In truth, I never thought them *that* funny. I always equated Groucho Marx with Hitler – saw him as Hitler, with his bogus, greasepaint moustache and his rapid-fire delivery of deranging demagoguery. Like Hitler and like my father, with his big hands, his scarred face, his Indian-head money clip, his wiseacre's patter. 'A child of five would understand this. Send somebody to fetch a child of five.' So that he can perform unnatural experiments on it, flay its skin off for a nightlight's shade. Yeah, nothing cosy about Groucho, giving the lie to Hitler's own Semitism – surely *only* a Jew could hate Jews with such intensity, wish to rip out the kike sleeved within the Jew? I married Dave Kaplan, I understood later, because of his own – soon to be manifested – Jewish anti-Semitism. 'Y'know Kaplan isn't my real name,' he used to say to people, 'I changed it in order to appear Jewish – my real name's Carter.' And this from a man with such a melting-pot of features – it was irresistible.

Dear Dave – he styled himself 'the Fatalistic Funnyman', or even 'the Ya-Ya Yid'. I suppose his defiance was beefed up all the more by my appearance – at that time willowy and very blonde. It was quite a thing in the forties, in the States, this marriage between a Jew and an apparent Gentile. When people caught on that I *was* Jewish as well it was already too late, we'd moved on, doubtless leaving an unpleasant taint behind us. Moved on. The late forties and early fifties were a succession of hole-in-the-wall appointments for Kaplan, whose communist sympathies made it impossible for him to teach politics with any candour. So he drifted into admin, which is how we ended up in Vermont, in 1955, in time for Dave Junior to rendezvous with that fender.

It destroyed the driver's life – hitting my child. Destroyed it. He went crazy – or rather, he had a breakdown, and in those days, in that place, if it was severe enough they'd put you in an insulin coma and hook your temples up to the mains. I felt sorry for him even when I was caught in that vile ballet of shock – the five steps to where Dave and his pals were playing. Sorry because I was always guilty, ever in the wrong myself. I was on him in two strides, grasped his blond hair, smacked his head once, twice, three times. Then he was out in front of me, his narrow little ass covered in mud, out of the back yard, across the front yard, and then WHACK! A twisted scrap of flesh on the asphalt. The impact was so strong it split the child's head in two. In two. His face was hanging off like a crumpled bit of cloth – and there was blood and grey stuff. Kaplan and I lasted a year after that. I don't think he ever styled himself 'the Fatalistic Funnyman' ever again. Not after I'd taken all of my guilt out on him and remoulded whatever love we'd ever had for each other; fired it in a kiln of white-hot anger and smashed the fucking ugly memento.

'Mumu?' Here she is, looking scrubbed in jeans, sneakers, sweatshirt, black hair back in a ponytail. Looking very *American* today.

'Natty.' I'm alarmed by my croak, it sounds like 'N'nerr'.

'Mumu!' She swoops down on me, crying. I suppose the junk is out of her system and a little of the real world is seeping in. She plants kisses on my moulting skull. 'Mumu, Esther's arrived.'

Esther, eh, now there's a turn-up. 'Where is she?'

'At the Ritz, I think.' Natch, although it could be the Royal Garden, or the Savoy, or Brown's. 'She called – she wants to come straight over.'

'I don'wanner here.'

'What?'

'I donwannesther here.' Only my older sister's arrival could galvanise me in this fashion.

'What do you mean?' Her scrubbed appearance is being sullied by the seepage of sweat along her hairline.

'We'll meet her elsewhere – anywhere else we can.' This morning I not only have to punch a hole through the nausea, I have to punch through indifference as well. It's clear to me – transmitted on a special frequency employed by the British Broadcorpsing Corpsoration – that I no longer matter. Sure, I'm the pretext for an intense endgame, a dramatic enough finale, but then? I'll be forgotten in months – years at the outside. Of that much I'm certain. Oh, I don't doubt that the girls will remember me after a fashion, but there'll be no gathering of people where my name will animate the conversation, no spirited chat that in turn will reanimate me. No, I *know* not. The Lily Bloom who commanded attention has quit already – except for this one final fling, this defiance of Esther. 'I don't want her coming here – she's such a fucking snob.'

'Oh Mumu – does it matter now?'

'Now more than ever.'

'Ms Bloom?' It's the new muck-shoveller and she's black – natch.

'Hi.'

'I'm Doreen Matthews, I'll be handling the day shift, I wanted to introduce myself.'

'Pleased to meet you.' She's dazzling, this one, a coffee Nefertiti with sugar-almond eyes. I could look at her all day; women simply *are* more beautiful than men – just as Jews are smarter than the goyim.

'How're you feeling, Ms Bloom?'

Punctilious, this one – I can tell, I've had my tilly punked more than most. 'Lily, please. I feel better, since you ask.'

'Then will you be needing these?' She's got the entire assortment with her – pain relief, anxiety relief, nausea suppressant. They should come in a dear little choccy box, with a book of words attached. Natty is looking avid, as if she might swoop down on Doreen's palm and snaffle the drugs up like the raptor she is.

'Yes, yes, I think it would be a good idea . . . you never know.'

So, pills mouthed then palmed, water dribbled, nurse exited and drugs passed on to lurking junky daughter. Charlotte understands immediately about Esther and goes to phone her – we'll meet at Kenwood, in the Old Coach House. There's considerable consternation about dragging my bag of bones out to the Heath, but then – as I observe to all and sundry – it's not going to kill me. The cancer's going to kill me – but not before I'm a lot thinner, I hope.

'Are you absolutely sure about this, Mother?' Charlie is in another suit today, fresh from meeting with Wiggins Teape or Reed International. An A-line skirt is not her, her ass is too big, legs too chubby. But it's cut exceedingly well; once you're up above a 14 the best you can hope for is a clever cut – colour must be inconspicuous.

'You know what she's like, Charlie, I'm amazed she's here at all.'

'She's genuinely upset, very tearful on the phone.'

'Great.' She's going to live for ever, Esther, she's never had a day's illness in her life. She's seventy years old, she smokes like a house on fire and she drinks as if she were trying to extinguish it. She spends more money than the Colombian government and earns more than the Medellin cartel. She's a fucking nightmare – my sister.

Leaving the apartment proves difficult, a protracted, staggered departure, which sees me arrayed successively in day clothes, an overcoat, a rug, while supported by daughters and paid servitors. I feel Lear-like – and wouldn't be that astonished if Natty were to begin addressing me as 'Nuncle'. Charlie's got the Mercedes today, Elvers must've walked in to the head offices of Waste of Paper. He's the kind of man who likes to say, 'Yes, I walk *everyhere*,' as if he'd recently spent a summer crossing the Antarctic with Rheinhold Messner, not twenty minutes strolling through Regent's Park from his Nash terrace apartment to his Terry Farrell office. What a creep.

We purr up Kentish Town Road and on up Highgate Road to Gospel Oak. There's apple blossom and cherry blossom and light industrial units and gentrified nineteenth-century terraces and lots of cars. There's London. I read in a magazine – not *Woman's Realm* – that the human brain recognises composites rather than elements; which is why – I guess – I know this is London and not New York, or Chicago or Rome, because it doesn't matter to me any more. I've shut down all the outlets and there are tacky signs up on the insides of my eyes: 'CLOSING-DOWN SALE – ALL MEMORIES MUST GO!'

Memories of my dad and his card files of smutty gags; his Indian-head, mother-of-pearl money clip; his lack of funds for it to clip. In the Depression he took jobs doing *anything*. Esther told me once that he was a pimp for a while, and I can believe it. Although he wasn't an overtly sexual man, there was a greasy feel to him, a greasy *Jewish* feel. I would imagine that he had a large pimp's penis. But the job I remember best was the one he took closing down department stores. He was good at this – firing the staff, arranging for the stock to be discounted, selling the premises. He functioned better during the Depression than he did either before or after. Very much a twentieth-century man – my father. A boom-and-bust jockey. An economic cyclist.

We tip up on to the steep slope of Highgate West Hill and drive between wealthy villas. Then along the Grove at the top, past Yehudi Menuhin's imposing house. I hate Menuhin. I sent Natty to audition at his school when she was eight. She was a not untalented little pianist – but I knew not good enough. But that isn't why I hate him – I hate him because he never crossed a road alone until he was twenty-five, or so they say. Just fancy! The ultimate effete, artistic Jew – and this is meant to be impressive? This racial cosseting. Yuk. He'll live for ever – of that I've no doubt. Live for ever in a gilded cage of sound, a cat's cradle of golden harp strings. Double mint choc chip yuk. Thirty-two flavours of Baskin-Robbins's best nausea.

I know it's got to my liver, this cancer. I can feel it as we tilt down and turn into Hampstead Lane. I can feel the fucking thing swollen inside, each lurch of the car pressing on it so that, like a filthy sponge, it oozes poisons. The body's oil refinery is itself polluted. The crazed enzymes have taken over the asylum – oh, for a sane axeman. Two fucking lumpectomies that fraudulent pal of Steel's did on me. He scooped out my boobs like a counterman in Baskin-Robbins . . . Maybe I *want* ice cream, that's why I keep thinking of it. 'Natty.'

'Mumu?' She's in the back with me again. She has darker skin than me – but finer-grained, to go with her long narrow nose, delicately flared cheekbones, violet eyes. Little bitch.

When she was a child she went red in the sun, but if she'd let it get to her now she'd turn a pleasing olive. But she'd rather be sallow, clearly. Under her preppy clothing are track marks, sores, infections, all abraded by her serrated nails. I wonder how Miles can stand to touch her.

'I wonder how Miles can stand to touch you.'

'What?!'

'I want an ice cream; no – an ice lolly.'

'OK – they'll have them at Kenwood.' She heard me, but hey – let's not make waves.

If I were dying when I should've, say in the late sixties, when I thought my head would explode with howling misery, when every time their father opened his fat mouth I thought I'd have to kill him, then – then I would've written the girls affectionate letters, telling them of my sadness, and how much I loved them, and how sorry I was to be leaving them. Too late. They're here, they're grown-up, they're crap; and so we'll bicker towards oblivion.

I must've dozed a little, or zoned out, because when when I'm conscious of myself again I find we're hobbling down the hill towards Kenwood House, a fuzzy blob of off-white Palladian which wobbles amazingly for something so heavy. The girls have me under either arm and I'm saying to them, 'You must remember how much easier dying is for a pessimist like me than it would be for someone who'd expected anything from life, who'd counted on anything.'

'Yes Mum.'

'I mean to say – I've always been hunkered down on the starting line, waiting for the pistol shot so I could race to the next bad thing.'

'You wanted it badderly,' says infantile Natty, in baby talk.

'Oh, I did, I did.' I clutch her hand tighter under my armpit, and I guess she thinks this affectionate, but it isn't.

Kenwood. I've always known I was going to end up here. When I first came to London it was my favourite park. I'd come here alone and sit and read a book, or strike up conversations with old women, or down-and-outs. In the States I was never gregarious in this fashion, never. It was all that English dissimulation that forced my cards, made me play my crappy little hand: 'Oh, how interesting – *do* tell me more.' And they would, by Christ they would. That precious fucking reserve, it transpired, was only the thinnest of hoary mantles, beneath which was a positive torrent of chilly drivel. No, there's nobody like the English for inconsequential chat and I hope they all fucking choke to death on it. 'How's the wea-*theurgh*!'

In the sixties this place was primmer, more proper. The prams looked positively nineteenth-century – great black things, pushed about by pudding-faced nannies and mums, all belted up in coats and hats and even *gloves*. Now it's spring, and track-suited, androgynous parent-substitutes are shoving McLaren buggies loaded up with hothouse weeds. There are faggots flexing their muscles on the shaven grass. Yaws would come here every weekend before Sunday lunch and force the girls to accompany him. Yaws had played lacrosse when he was at the varsity. *I kid you not*. And he thought it would be nice for the girls to learn to play it with him. Nice for whom? Not me. I'd stay back in Hendon, overcooking Sunday lunch in the prescribed way. Granted – I'd take the task on, but what were we going to do otherwise? Yaws himself, notoriously, could survive for days on a heel of bread smeared with Frank Cooper's Oxford marmalade. Cunt. To think I washed his underwear. Double cunt. Double choc chip cunt.

The only thing that remains unchanged in this ersatz landscape are the little brown men. They're *exactly* the same, in their trilbies and brogues, spiking litter, checking notices to see that they're officious, driving dinky vans full of dead leaves. The suits themselves may be nylon now – they certainly look cheap – but the men are as fawn as ever. Fawn-coloured – and they look like fauns too. Camden Council must have an Affirmative Faun Action Programme. I've never seen a truly brown little brown man, though, never. The brown men are important – they minister to the memorial benches. I always fancied a memorial bench: 'In Loving Memory of Lily Bloom 1922-1988, Who Loved to Take Our Products on This Bench. Hoffmann La Roche'. But when I looked into it two years ago (I did this when I discovered the lump, did it even before I called Sydenberg, the GP), I discovered that the Heath was bench-saturated, that if you wanted to evoke even the tiniest bit of recall here in the future, you'd have to have your name put on a marker along with a lot of others. Doubtless, as with the benches, relatives scatter ashes around these markers. A delicious irony – those of us Jews who escaped the Holocaust, none the less interred in mass graves with our kikey kind. How unkind.

Inside the tea place it's dark, despite the whitewash on the walls. This is the old stable block of the house, and even now – or maybe *especially* now – with its stalls full of horse-faced Englishwomen slurping down Earl Grey, it feels like one. The only non-horsey face in the place is a version of my father's. A smaller, painted version of his face – like Dad's funerary mask. A Jewish face. A New York Jewish face. An Upper East Side New York Jewish face. A UESNYJF. Esther, my sister.

'Lily!' She's on her sharp heels pointing her beak at me, and her claws are out.

'Esther.' My piece of dead veal collides with her facial. Esther doesn't have a face any more – only a facial. Not that she's had nips and tucks – she knows better than to do that, because she's going to live for ever. If she has a facelift now, in thirty or forty years' time she'll be looking like Methuselah.

'How *are* you?' Incredible, only the tactless can live for ever – that much is obvious. 'Let me *look* at you.' Why would you wanna do that, dumb ass? Well, let her – looking is all you'll get.

I slump there in my cancer cloak while the world goes on dancing about me. They give me a little pot of Cornish ice cream, which sits in front of me on the table uneaten. I mean to say – it's hardly likely to repeat on me, now is it? And anyway – I *asked* for a lolly. I regard Esther critically; it's interesting looking at a version of yourself that has achieved immortality, courtesy of Saks Fifth Avenue, Tiffany, Bergdorf Goodman and all the other temples of dressage – which is what these English horses could do with, even my little ponies. Americans always look so clean and scrubbed and presentable – is it any wonder I ended up a slut living in this dungheap? Is it any surprise I lost my teeth grazing on this rotten dump?

Esther has brought presents for the girls. Yup, Tiffany – thought so. A brooch for Charlie, which she'll treasure along with the rest of her hoard, and a little gold watch for Natty, which she'll pawn the first time she claps eyes on some dangling balls that aren't attached to a man. They chat away as if I wasn't here. Esther tells them about her hotel, her art gallery, her other shops, her properties, this business, that business. Natty's lovely head is heavy with heroin now – that much is obvious – but Charlie keeps on nodding and interjecting and chatting with her mummified aunt. Her made-up aunt.

I had hoped that seeing Esther would provoke some flood of recall. I wanted – God knows why – to immerse myself in childhood again. I wanted to summon up sarsparilla and kewpie dolls, baseball cards, jitterbugging, kreplach, jitneys, the surrey with the fucking fringe on top. I wanted us to mull over the proportions of all the houses and apartments we grew up in and the foibles of all the friends we'd had. I wanted to reach back to a time when Esther and I loved each other more than anything else in the world, when the only thing in the world we feared were our poor, sad, frightened parents. I wanted to turn the leaves of the high-school yearbook with Esther (Class of '35 – 'A flair for business is an ornament for the whole world') back to a happier time. But now I set eyes on her, all I can think of is 'The Relic' by Donne, and how, despite the fact that her expensive watch is shackled on to her skeletal wrist, she's going to live – while I'm definitely going to die.

One thing to be grateful for is that there's no waitress service here. Esther always abuses servants with her familiarity – 'Hi! What's *your* name, then? Mark, eh? I bet you've made one here . . .' – effortlessly engendering their contempt. And mine. Although it's not hard to feel contempt for surly English service. England – where the waiters respond to any orders that transgress the menu as if it were carved in stone and they were terrifying and incomprehensible heresies. 'Hold the mayonnaise?! You mean to say the world is round?! God is dead?! Good and evil are conterminous?!' There's one thing I can do for Esther, though, one bequest her lumpy, liverish, cancerous, moribund sister can give her, and that's to not talk about anything of consequence whatsoever. Don't talk about dying. Don't rupture her great reservoir of denial and watch her sang-froid escape into the hell of the present. Heat up, bubble, boil, evaporate – leaving this little old Jewish lady just as terrified as this big dying one. Oh no, save her. Together with her savings.

I can't be damned to listen to people's chatter any more.

Everything they say bears upon a future that doesn't include me. I don't even notice if it's Esther who leaves, or us. The fact that I'll never see her again is obscurely satisfying – and I prevented her from visiting my shitty little apartment, propping her narrow JAP ass on my dusty cushions. She's the sort of woman who wants the earth girdled with a sanitary strip – for the duration of her stay, which, as I believe I've mentioned, will be for ever.

We're in the car again and heading down the hill from Highgate. Charlie is a very good driver, much less impetuous than I used to be, far steadier. She knows how to pilot this big Kraut box, this steel egg-carton containing a diseased yolk. Pain has been cracking on the edge of me for hours now. I'm drenched with sticky pain, and Natty's lying – cool and dry – on an ottoman of *my* heroin.

Miles is waiting outside when we get back, resting his beauty on a wall. I wonder how many he's travelled to get here this time? He's a law student, he studies hard – what's he doing with this skittish trash? They unload me and hustle me inside, to where Molly and Doreen have made enormous inroads on the entropy. Seat covers have been cleaned! Shelves dusted! This is real housework going on. I like to think I could've been a good housewife – I should've adored to keep house for a man I admired. I'd've ironed Trotsky's shirts like a dervish, then made love to him like a seal. But the men I was with were always feeble suppliants, wanting sex the way little boys want sweets. Pathetic. No wonder I'd discover myself day after day cursing and moaning and even screaming as I wiped up their shit, cooked for them, ordered their little play-dens. I'm glad that's over. I'm glad house-cleaning is over. Goodbye Jif, fare thee well Flash, *au revoir* Harpic – I'm sure we'll meet again some su-unny da-ay.

They've cleaned the flat up because they're going to sell it.

Charlotte's going to sell it. I wish my will wasn't in order, I'd've liked to gift little Miss Yaws at least a duplex of litigation, if not Bleak House itself.

Competent black hands are all over me now – and d'jew know what? I don't care. I can feel each black handprint as she pushes and plumps me like a pillow, but there's no Pavlovian revulsion, no sick decoction of petty-minded bigotry. I used to torment Yaws: 'You're the fucking black man's burden!' I'd scream at him. 'Look in the fucking dictionary, you creep! Read it – "a contagious disease of Negroes characterised by raspberry-like tubercules on the skin" – that's you, pardner, that's you!' Usually, at around this stage I'd begin hitting him, and wouldn't stop until one of the kids intervened. Do I feel guilty? Not any more, not now. Junky will have to wait – I've had the diamorphine for my lonesome, and the Valium, and whatever other shit it was that Doreen gave me. Junky will have to wait now.

Doreen's got me down and my little radio's on, warbling. It's the evening repeat of *The Archers*. People hate the way the media repeat things – but not I. I love it. I wouldn't care if they echoed this episode again and again and again, as long as I was there to hear it, as long as I was still alive. From a region deep in the darkest, most diseased portion of me an old blues man is warbling. What is this, some song I heard when trailing my rag dolly behind me, clumping through the dirt on the other side of the streetcar line? Who knows, but it's old, as old as me: 'I wish I was a mole in the ground / Like a mole in the ground I would root that mountain down / And I wish I was a mole in the ground.'

Not long now. Next door there are voices raised above the pseudo farm life: 'Do you think we should call her GP?' I daresay Charlie already has her mobile phone out; she wields it as if it was the future itself.

'I think it might be an idea. I don't honestly think she's going to be able to stay here much longer.' But I want to stay here – I want to stay with you, Doreen. 'But – ' And here her voice dips beneath my hearing range, allowing me to tune in to the other voices in the next room, Natasha and Miles bickering about where they're going to eat. Who would've thought everything was going to happen so suddenly?

Chapter Four

Sydenberg is on his way – goody gumdrops. Sydenberg, the last tailgating medic in a queue which stretches back to the late forties. You cannot fault me when it comes to providing employment for these interns, I've always been a zealous customer of the house call. For what is hypochondria, if not the midwife of all the other, littler phobias? When the girls were kids I'd get Virginia Bridge out at the drop of a hat. My motives were mixed, I guess, because as much as I wanted her insipid reassurance, I also liked to observe Yaws with his auxiliary squeeze. It amused me when, like a kid himself, he was confronted with an ice lolly in either hand, not knowing which one to lick.

I also liked the doctors' being at my beck and call – or so I thought. I realise now that all I ever represented to them was diseased throughput; another sick shell of a human requiring a missing component to be bolted on. Modern Times – no wonder these assembly-line workers find themselves unable to cease making diagnoses when their day's work is done. Sydenberg is by no means among the worst; certainly better than that snotty twerp Lichtenberg who 'psychoanalysed' me in the early fifties. I remember that all too well. He was a friend of Kaplan's – and there was a sinister congruence in the attitude they'd take towards my *crise de nerfs* in any given week. I said at the time, 'You two are in cahoots!' but they denied it.

Lichtenberg was an orthodox Freudian who related every single aspect of my psyche to my early childhood. Well, while my childhood may have been extra shitty, I should've been concerning myself with Dave Junior's – which was actually under way. But no, Kaplan was in favour of the analysis, the Eight Couples Who Mattered (our incestuously entwined coterie of friends) were in favour of it, and the fact that it kept me mired in the past hardly seemed relevant – at the time. Lichtenberg actually gave me *licence*, encouraged me to have affairs. He felt it would help me to undermine my negative relationship with my father. Bullshit. The truth was that all this Freudian sex talk was the preview, a blabbermouthed precursor of all the feckless promiscuity that was to follow in the sixties. Although not for me – by then I'd relapsed to the talking bit. Mostly. I wonder what Lichtenberg would say regarding the current impasse? Probably quote Freud: 'The aim of all life is death.' I wish I'd killed the creep when I had the chance.

From city to city, from burg to burg. Sailing through the bergs and into the arctic night. Sydenberg is one of those English Jews who are more English than the English. Actually, nowadays, almost anyone is more English than the English. Since the late seventies the English have abandoned their reserve, their coolness, their rustic urbanity. They've always complained about their 'Americanisation', meaning chain stores, supermarkets, advertising – but what they've failed to account for all along is the creeping cosmopolitanism that's transforming their culture – if not their precious fucking society. I noticed in the seventies – that bulbous decade – that the English were beginning to get wiseacre Jewish-American humour, to find it genuinely funny – and that was the beginning of the end. The indigenous Jews were too dull and conformist a group to crack real jokes. They were the ones left behind in Liverpool while the rest of us headed on to the New World. As soon as they made some money they retreated, Rubens-like, to the 'burbs, to live out their days in colourless indifference. Jewish Anglicans. The English had to turn to American Jewry for entertainment, and so began the proper Jewing of London. Now every little Cockney punk you meet cracks wise, kvetches, shmoozes and cheats. Great.

Anyway, Sydenberg – here he is: tall, stooping, grey, bespectacled. His suit – unlike my body – is double-breasted. He carries an ugly, modern, vinyl attaché case, which he places by the side of the bed before methodically retracting himself down to my level. Bedside manner – what an expression. All the doctors who've ever come to my bedside have looked, suitably enough, utterly uncomfortable. I mean, what could it be like for them to be completely at ease – to put you completely at ease? They'd have to put their cases down, then pull their pants off and get into bed with you. Now *that* would be a bedside manner.

'So, you came home, Lily?'

'As you can see, Dr Sydenberg, as you can see.'

'How's the pain?'

'It hurts.'

'And the nausea?'

'Sickening.'

'I see.'

He does see, he sees through thick bifocals which prise his oyster eyes open with enlargement. I wish he had a better bedside manner, though. I wish he'd get into bed with me – I want someone, anyone, to hold on to. I'll try another tack. 'I'm frightened.'

'Of dying?' Good man. Direct – I like that.

'Of dying, of what they'll do to me after I die.'

'You told me that this didn't concern you, that you'd told Natasha and Charlotte to have your body cremated and drop your ashes in a skip, or a bin, or anywhere.'

'I'm worried they won't – Charlotte's too sentimental, and Natty's too stoned.'

'Well, given your convinced materialism this would hardly matter – would it?'

'I don't want to be embalmed.'

'That's an American thing – we don't do that here. Remember, the vast majority of English people are cremated; I think it's something like seventy per cent.'

'I know – it's a great country to burn a corpse in. They won't even have to take my pacemaker out – 'cause I don't have one. D'jew think you can still feel it when they burn you?'

'Lily.'

'I'm serious. What if I'm wrong? What if you can feel everything, what if you can feel it when they crush your bones in the cremulator?'

'Cremulator?'

'It's like a spin drier full of steel balls – they use it for bone-crushing, for making human bonemeal, so that the relatives aren't freaked out by spare ribs or odd vertebrae when they collect the urn and sift through the leftovers.'

'No, no, come now, this isn't right – I think you must be suffering from taphephobia.'

'What the hell's that?'

'An irrational fear of being buried alive.'

'Unlike people who live on the San Andreas fault.'

'Quite so.'

Wow, taphephobia. And I'd thought death was the great phobia-eradicator; now I discover that I'm to be irrationally fearful – even as I die. 'How about decamping to Palermo?'

'What?'

I can see that this conversation is beginning to discomfit him. Good – I can't keep it up much longer. 'Palermo – or Paris, anywhere where they have catacombs, where I can be strung up on a wire wearing my best M&S dress, my sensible flat shoes, my raincoat.'

'That's not altogether practical, is it?'

No, it isn't, and I don't want to hang around – I don't want to be a *drag*. Nor do I want to be planted out in Wanstead at the municipal necropolis. I've had enough difficulties with paying for living space as it is; the idea of mortgaging a grave plot is unspeakable. I've read too much about it, I *know* what goes on. I even know that there are giant American corporations in the process of taking over the British cemetery industry. These saps – they think they're going to heaven; but even if they are – which I very much doubt – their earthly remains are being transformed into a very worldly profit for fat, unscrupulous investors. Fools.

I'd like to convey some of this intelligence to Sydenberg, who's been proving such a good listener, but by the time I realise my eyes have been shut for a while, and then manage to open them, he's gone next door for a case conference.

— I'm afraid there's very little to be done.

— We understand. Do you think there's any point in calling round the hospices?

— Not really, we can manage the pain just as effectively here. You've arranged for twenty-four-hour cover?

— Yes, so it'll be here then?

— As long as there isn't any major change, as long as it's possible to give her her medication.

— And you think it will?

— It's impossible to say; if there's any radical acceleration, rather than . . . a slow fade, well, I'm afraid you'll have to call UCH.

— She doesn't want to die in the hospital.

— Frankly, Charlotte, it's that she doesn't want to die; your mother's a relatively young woman to be dying. I think all this talk about remains and burials is a diversionary tactic. Has she discussed the future with you at all?

— A little. She slides in and out; sometimes she appears reconciled, but mostly she's very very angry.

— Well, this is to be expected.

— I'd hoped she might be a bit more philosophic.

Philosophic – ha! That's one of Yaws's catch-words – 'philosophic'. He was very phucking philosophic. Philosophic about everything but philosophy – that he couldn't manage. Yaws was an ecclesiastical historian. He wrote his thesis on Trollope and the nineteenth-century clergy as depicted in his novels. I'm not saying it was a second-rate subject, but it was notable how many second-rate minds were engaged by it. I used to have to make tea for them, entertain greying perpetual students on perpetual, grey English afternoons: 'Tell me, Mrs Yaws, which would be your favourite Barchester novel?' Any that was in a small enough format for me to *shove it right up your ass you dumb motherfucker*. I wish I'd been less polite to these people, who didn't matter at all, and more polite to the ones who did.

So, I'm to die here, am I? Here in my dingy little flat. I'd better do an inventory of my dying space, my ideal tomb, my gentrified sarcophagus. This latter meaning – as I know only too well – 'flesh-eater'. Hear that, Minxie? You're not the only flesh-eater around here. And the cancer, like the faithful dog it is, gives me a maul with its deathly awl. I'd almost forgotten what a wild, exquisite pain there is to being hungry – until *you* reminded me. So, tatty furniture, mismatched pots, boxes of postcards – why the fuck did I buy them? Memo for Another Lifetime: never buy more postcards than you're going to send, no matter how attractive the pictures are. Bibelots; books; racks of shabby tent clothes; cupboard bottoms carpeted with pasty shoes; baskets and shoeboxes crammed with damned knitting and odd bits of sewing that've gone to hell; drawers full of sad underwear and sadder letters. Letters – why keep letters? Do I want to read letters now? Do I fuck. In the kitchenette cupboards there are jars of congealed preserves; in the bathroom cabinets there are half-used cans of talcum powder and suspect unguents – bring them to me! Bring me my chattels! I want to die with a pot of blackcurrant conserve in one hand and a straw place mat in the other. I want to expire with all the records of my tortured heart, the minutes of my faithless meetings and the proceedings of my dishonourable societies to hand. Don't I just. Aren't I *keen*.

As is Dierdre, who's arrived and processes across the bedroom to where I lie, news of Ivan Boesky burbling in my ear. 'How are you feeling, Lily?' she enquires.

'Downsized,' I reply. 'They're selling off bits of me, leaving only the profitable core.' I want to say more, but I can't, because there's a new sensation to contend with, making me more fearful than the terror, sicker than the nausea. It's the mother of all sensations for this mother – who's always had to run and hide when things got too much to bear. I'm paralysed. I can't move, I can't blink my eyes. There's a fat bastard sitting on my chest crushing the life out of me and it isn't me any more. Deirdre gets a fork of hand behind my neck and lifts me up far enough to drop the pills into my mouth, then tips my head back so that water can be poured to sluice them down my throat. Pain relief has now become an engineering work rather than a medical operation.

'There you are,' she's got me back down on my pallet, 'I'll mop your face and neck with a flannel – you'll feel more comfortable.'

When I was a functioning mother I had this routine down pat, the index finger tightly cowled with hanky; the child's mouth imprisoned on my hard hand, the tiny gummy lips attacked with the adamant prong. If I'd only known this technique was going to be applied to me again, I'd never have been so brutal.

— I just thought I'd drop by, see how she is.

— She's as well as can be expected, Natasha. She's sleeping now.

— It's – it's Deirdre, isn't it?

— That's right.

— D'jew think it's gonna be soon?

— That's not the sort of thing I'd like to say.

— But what d'jew think?

— [*Sigh*] I've seen people in your mother's condition linger for weeks and months or go in seconds and hours. Death, Natasha, doesn't abide by our schedules.

— I'm going to the loo.

Natasha's normally husky voice has gone up half an octave and the vibrato is quite intense. I can smell the fearful sick sweat come off of her as she canters through my bedroom – why doesn't somebody give the junky pony a rub-down? I can hear the Vent-Axia stirring up the lint in there and the taps running and the loo flushing and she seems to be out in seconds and rummaging in the bedside-table drawers.

— Are you looking for something?

— Just a letter – a bill; I left here.

— There's some papers on the table by the front window.

— Oh, oh – are there?

Busted. Deirdre's quite a smooth operator – despite the cardy. She's got little Natty's number. I daresay Deirdre hasn't a great deal of time for spoilt middle-class brats like mine. She's certainly not about to let Natasha walk off with my medication. Damn – I should've given her a supply while I still could. Now it'll be Chez Russell – I wonder how many miles she's managed to put between herself and Miles? I don't even hear her go – my own daughter; but then I didn't feel myself deanimate – and this is my own body.

I remember this lack of sensation; it's happened enough times to me in this bedroom, usually in a ginny mist, a forest of juniper. Lying here, desperate to get to sleep, the World Service revolving in my ear. *So* desperate to sleep, thoughts buzzing in my skull, pinging off the inside of my eyelids. Eyelids which at first cannot be opened and then can't be shut; which are rolled up like recalcitrant blinds. Then it occurs to me – my body has fallen asleep while my mind is still awake, hence the paralysis. It's a reversible jacket of a mind, mine is; ever ready to play an ironic trick and confound me. It's petrifying – this paralysis. Ha-ha. I thought you became petrified *because* you were terrified – but now I realise that the reverse can also be the case.

Why aren't I more frightened than I am, lying here, while the plummy radio accents describe rotten events? Unable to move, to escape. Claustrophobia and agoraphobia – all these years I'd thought they were to do with external spaces, but now I understand that both fears are – in Lichtenberg's dumb jargon – 'projections'. That it's the body itself that is either too vast for the tiny mind that wanders over it, or too small to contain the myriad perceptions that pile up in its memory like dishes in a sink. Christ – I'm waxing philosophic and I'm waning into a reverie of Penn Station . . .

. . . which I trot through on clicking heels, from the tracks up the iron stairs, clack-clack-clack, and into the General Waiting Room, click-click-click. I move from one huge vaulted space to another, the distinction between them being that the body of the station is an exposed skeleton of cast-iron ribs, vaunting pelvises and soaring, arched spines, whereas the waiting room is fleshy with coffered plasterwork. You might think that Penn Station – or indeed any station – would be the last place I'd want to hang out, given that it has so much of the outside inside of it. Not so. I prefer to think of it as being solely an internal construction, a huge den tucked securely in a corner of the city. It helps with the claustro, eases the agro, that there's a stench of train exhaust and the breakfast breaths of ten thousand thousand. It helps the station towards classical immortality that the façade was modelled on the Caracalla Baths. Not that this morning I pause under its heavy pediment – I've more important things on my mind.

Today is the launch of the new Rose's Rocket – and I'm on the sharp end of a revolution in writing materials. Yup, it may be the closing stages for the war in the Pacific (VJ Day is only weeks away), but the only projectiles bothering me are Rockets with a cap 'R' – and the only flaks present will be wearing snap-brim hats. It's the press day for the Rose's Rocket, the first continuous-inkflow pen to hit the US market ever. Oh sure – the idea's been around for ages, patented as far back as 1888, but hell, what's inventing something when you can copy it? The Japs created an entire manufacturing economy off the back of copying things after the war, but they copied the copying from the likes of Rose. Bob was well ahead of the game.

In Buenos Aires, to be precise, buying supplies of raw wool for his business. Rose was a Chicago businessman who'd made a wartime fortune out of stuffing things with wool: flying jackets, helmets, sleeping bags – you open it, he'd stuff it. In the Windy City they called him King Stuff. Anyway, Rose saw some of the original Biro pens on sale in a department store and, cottoning on instantly to their potential, bought them and brought them home intent on copying. Poor old Laszlo Biró; he sold his North American rights to Eversharp, but never bothered with a patent – the way was clear for both of them to be stuffed by the King.

Rose was an old college buddy of Kaplan's. Kaplan was away at the war. That's what we used to say: 'He's away at the war.' It made flame-throwing Japs sound like a ball game – and I liked it that way. I was a selfish, headstrong, oversexed girl of twenty-one when Kaplan was drafted; we'd been married a year. He was, as yet, without his pussy. A square-jawed, wiry man of medium height with brown, wavy hair, who could always raise a laugh with his 'I changed my name to Kaplan' routine, because he was so all-American as to have an indeterminate feel about him. He appeared no more Jewish than he did German, or Italian, or Irish, or anything else. Jolly Dave Kaplan, the genetic blender.

We had a cold-water apartment in the run-down wreck that was the Rhinelander Gardens on West 11th Street. Not that there were that many hot-water apartments in Manhattan in those days – the war was on and so was the housing shortage. I had a job selling war bonds for a while, but then so did everyone else. I was crap at selling war bonds – Kaplan had infected me with his café communism, and his Jewish anti-Semitism. Canter – that was the guy who ran the war-bonds outfit. Ratty little man – a British emigrant. I couldn't stand him. 'Your heart isn't in this,' he'd say pompously, sanctimoniously – as if I were personally responsible for Pearl-fucking-Harbor, and fucking over Mrs Miniver.

I did other war work for a while, putting radios into Flying Fortresses, which was kind of fun. I thought I looked good in an overall when I cinched it tight, but I had to go way out into the Jersey boondocks to get to the factory, and, well . . . I had a real yen for Manhattan at the time. Didn't make any difference whether I was a V-8 or a V-girl – I still had to be sucking on that big lozenge of masonry.

So, anyway, I'm coming out of Penn Station, because I like to detour there on my way to Rose's offices, which are in the mid-40s (I can't remember where exactly – could you?), and I'm cock-a-hoop because we're launching the first continuous-inkflow pen in the entire US of A. We've beaten Eversharp's Capillary Action to the stores by five clear weeks, and the Rocket's smooth, futuristic design sold it in as much as its revolutionary ink-delivery system. And who's responsible for this design? Why, me of course. Little ol' missy. I'd taken design classes as part of the art syllabus at Columbia, although I'd never intended becoming a professional. I didn't want to do anything much at all when I was young. I saw myself as a Zelda Fitzgerald type, married to a successful writer or artist, running a salon, drinking too many highballs, crashing my Hispano-Suiza into the Mediterranean – whatever. I was a fantasist; the only part of it I could realistically manage was the drinking. The only things I had going for me were a big, blowsy body, a dirty imagination and a talent for back talk.

Rose sent me a wire because we didn't have a phone. Like I say, I can't recall exactly where his offices were, but from his window you could see the Times Tower. As for what the suite looked like – well, it was full of stuff, natch. Rose was – to my considerable chagrin – a big guy, a blond as myself. 'I changed my name to Rose so people would think I was Jewish,' he told me; 'it's the only way to get on in business.' We laughed about this; then he showed me the designs he had for the pen, and asked if I thought I could help. He didn't want to use any established product designers, this had to be done in total secrecy, I was his pinch hitter. 'Like the atom bomb,' he said, 'this pen is going to revolutionise the world – you'll see.'

Trouble was that as yet the Rocket was a stumpy, bulbous thing. The body of the pen and the mechanism had to be made as one unit. To keep costs down, Rose was planning on using the injection mould for a fountain pen. The original Rocket would've begun looking contemporary around 1971. I had a brainwave: 'You say, Mr Rose – '

'Call me Bob.'

'Bob, then. You say, Bob, that the principle by which the ink is placed on the paper is a freely rotating steel ball in the very tip of the pen?'

'That's it.'

'And you want the pen – the Rocket – to look like its namesake, to be aerodynamic, futuristic, huh?'

'That's the idea.'

'You recall the World's Fair in '39?'

'Who could forget it.'

'Well, it seems to me that your tiny ball is like a small-scale version of the giant Perisphere they built for the Fair; and that it should be housed inside the Trylon.'

'Trylon?'

'You remember – that huge, tapering pillar; it was seven hundred feet high.'

Bob Rose stuck his hands in his waistcoat pockets and wiggled his fingers as if he were a marsupial. Gesture I usually remember – appearance I mostly forget. His eyes rounded with credulity. 'That, Mrs Kaplan, is one helluva good idea.'

He paid me fifty bucks a week and I worked at my apartment. The Rocket had a detachable cap which closely resembled the nacelle of a fighter plane. I dropped the decorative aerofoil projections Rose had put on the base of the pen – they rubbed your hand when you wrote. I made the pen slimmer and steelier. It was an instant hit. At the press launch on that May day in '45 I sold units off of a tray, like a cigarette girl. We shifted nearly five hundred to the press and the flaks alone. The following week the Rocket blasted off at Gimbels and shifted ten thousand units in the first day. It was a dizzy time – and I made a point of going to Penn Station every day, whether I had to go uptown to the office or not. It was only there, inside the outside, that I could put my fierce pride in any kind of perspective – and my new anxiety. For at the same time as I was designing Rose's wholesale Rocket for him, he was putting his retail one inside of me. His cock, I mean – retractable ballpoints were ten years away yet.

He was quite a cocksman, old Bob Rose. We'd do it in his office, at my apartment, in hotels and flophouses, at parties – wherever we could. He had deft fingers, Bob, he could get into my panties in seconds and out of them in minutes. It sounds kind of yucky – but believe me, it wasn't. Bob was no hypocrite – he never talked crap about being 'unhappy with my wife'. Not that I'd've taken it; I was young, I was proud, I was confident. I thought I'd soon be given a proper job with the company, that I was in the up elevator. I was already working on designs for a whole squadron of Rose's Rockets when the troubles started. The Rocket was leaking, skipping and just plain wouldn't *write*. The original manufacturing run of pens were still the ones on sale in Gimbels, so steep had the sales parabola been. It was the design that was at fault. Bob reamed me out: it was my sloppiness, my inexperience, my *amateurishness* that had led to this, this *débâcle*.

He was actually inside me when he said this, the two of us screwing away on his desk, buck-naked from the waist down, me on top. People used to do this – talk when they screwed. Screwing itself was so novel – or seemed so novel, so twentieth-century – that an etiquette for it had yet to develop. We would talk while we screwed, listen to music, smoke – which I always considered to be the best way of deflating a man's ego – even drink a cocktail. Mind you, I wasn't about to take this crap from Rose; I stood up over him and let the load he'd dumped in me trickle back down on top of him. 'Your pen leaks, Bob,' I said, 'and so do I.' He had, of course, promised he wouldn't come. 'And you wanna know why?' By this time I was down off of the big desk, putting on my panties and untangling my stockings and suspenders.

'Why?' He was up on one elbow, looking flatly surreal, with his bare ass on the blotter and his naked foot resting against the intercom.

'Because neither you, nor your fucking pen, has big enough balls.'

Good parting shot, huh? It was the best I ever came up with. And I was right – it *was* the balls. Ten years later they had tungsten-carbide balls with abrasive surfaces which held the ink perfectly, but the Rocket's balls were only steel; too smooth – and too small. Rose's business folded and the Eversharp Capillary Action pen never made it either. A decade later Parker brought out their Jotter ballpoint, and that little fucker sold 3½ million units in a year, priced at a mere three bucks. The Rocket was history – except for one minor point. When Bic bought out Waterman in the early sixties and began to dominate the ballpoint market with their still cheaper and still more efficient pens, I saw that they'd mooched one part of their design from me – the cap. Yup, even today the cap of a common-or-garden Bic Cristal (daily worldwide sales of 14 million units) is a direct steal from my original Rose's Rocket.

Am I proud of this? You bet your ass. Very proud. Even now, a billion mouths must be blowing on something *I* shaped, a piece of plastic *I* gave form to, as surely as if my will had been the forces at work in the injection-moulding machine. Proud? Yeah – sure am. Very. It's a beautiful irony that it should've been a woman who was responsible for crafting this tricky little prick, this rinky-dink dong, this tiddly wiener, which has annotated so much of the post-war world. I must be one of the most marginalised people this century – if you get my drift.

Did I go on after this débâcle? No. I never designed any-thing ever again for commercial sale. In the seventies I wrote to Berol. I suggested that they were making a profound mistake with the cap of their new Rollerball pen, which looked to me like an old Nazi pillbox. But they weren't interested – although I got a polite enough reply from the R&D manager. In fairness to Berol, their Rollerball has been a great success. I saw Deirdre filling in her time sheet with one not ten minutes ago. No one appears to notice the little pillboxes they're capped with – or perhaps they do? Maybe that's exactly why they're so popular?

Kaplan came back from the war and said to me, 'Why the fuck did I bother to defend my country?' when he found out I'd been screwing around. I said, 'Why don't you get down off of your character heights?' And he did.

But the real pride I felt over the whole Rocket incident was that it gave me a grasp on progress, which not many people seemed to have at that time. The whole USA was on a binge of modernity after the war. The big-assed auto models of the thirties and forties gave way to the skinny-butt rapiers of the fifties – vehicular rockets if you will. Everything had fins – not only the cars. You could get spectacle frames with fins, radios with fins, shoes with fins, fridges with fins. By 1957 I wouldn't have been that surprised if Dave Kaplan had pulled down his shorts to reveal that his cock had fins. Fins were the future and we were speeding towards it. I guess the point here is that the ballpoint pen could hardly have been said to be before its time – not in a world that, within weeks, witnessed the press launch for the atomic bomb, complete with its own dear little stubby fins. More than that, when I look back now, the idea that the world didn't even have the *fountain pen* until the turn of the twentieth century seems preposterous, like some alternative sci-fi reality in which the Nazis won the war. Fuck it, until then they were dipping nibs, which to all intents and purposes were unchanged since Egyptian scribes squatted in front of papyri five thousand years ago, with fucking *reeds* in their hands. Progress – shmogress.

Pride is a cosy feeling wrapped round the individual and pumped full of wool. King Stuff. Is it pride or junk that's making me cosy in my paralysis? It's hard to say. Is this a real memory – or a false one? A 'screen' memory, as the Freudian motherfuckers would have it. Who knows. We allowed our lovemaking to become neurosis-manufacturing when we let those Jew-boy jokers loose on us; and we also allowed all our memories to become false floors, but thinly covering a yawning oubliette full of untold ghastliness. Memories like the corners of our minds – ever ready to snag a piece of clothing and tear the shirts off our psyches. I could do without them. Will do without them.

Radio 4 has become the World Service as I skip over the surface of consciousness then dip beneath it. I've slept like this for the last ten years – with the radio pancaked beneath my ear. The wholesome, middle-class, middle-aged, well-spoken announcers substitute for all the wholesome, middle-class, middle-aged, well-spoken lovers I've never had. They murmur consolingly to me of war and famine and insurrection. Then they murmur consolingly to me of horsey victories, tennis tourneys and cricket scores. They are the world's groundsmen, gently dragging an enormous groundsheet of dull comprehension over the darkening playing field.

Chapter Five

The semi on Crooked Usage was absolutely that – half a house, with its own disordered demi-monde. Half cluttered with the Yaws family pieces, which had been kicked down the generations – heavy sideboards, heavier bookcases, solid and ugly chairs. And the other half decked out with the half of nothing much salvaged from my first marriage, crated and freighted to this damp isle. There was nothing beautiful in the house, or loved, or remotely modern – save for little Natty.

A red-brick garage was tucked up beside it in its privet bed. The house was never clean or tidy, but even if I managed – along with Mrs Jenks, my dirt-rearranger – to get it into some semblance of order, there was always the garage to serve as a museum of chaos. That garage – no object that entered it ever re-emerged. It was a memorial to going nowhere. The family car camped out in the driveway. That the garage was built to match the house – red brick, slate mansard, metal mullions – belittled the latter rather than exalting the former. As for the interior, a cenotaph of steamer trunks was piled up in the middle of the floor, and a tea-chest columbarium ranged along the back wall. In the far corners, old bags of Yaws's golf clubs lowered in the gloom, like outsize dental instruments, once used for messy operations on mossy mouths. Crooked usage indeed. A family grouping of decaying bicycles – mummy, daddy, baby-with-stabilisers – leant against one another, festooned in cobwebs, roughened with rust. Those were the main props in this Garage of Usher, but there were also sodden newspapers aplenty, books ditto, bulging cardboard boxes prolapsed with mildewed old clothing, toys; all kinds of trash no one had troubled to sort through, bothered to discard. Over all of this there hung the distinctive – almost sacred – odour of Three-in-One oil.

The girls played in there when they were small. Or rather, Charlotte – true to character – attempted to impose the order that so eluded her mother. It was Bob-a-Job week times fifty-two for that little miss – while her sister smashed old panes of glass or imprisoned pigeons the cats had maimed. The garage was beyond Yaws's ken. As I've said, he sauntered through his life as if it were an unusually large cathedral close, and although he could drive, his expression as he pushed down the accelerator, and the Bedford – or the Austin, or whichever crap car it was we currently suffered – lurched backwards out of the drive, was one of clerical distaste. He was the only man I've ever known who drove a car as if it were an unseemly act; as if he were committing adultery by betraying his own, huge feet.

Mindjew, this wasn't an act of betrayal that would've truly bothered him. ('Bothered' – another great Yaws word, used as noun, as verb and even – Oh! corny hallelujah! – as an exclamation.) Yaws was tight-fisted with his things, his pid-dling private income and his pathetic mementos of the Yaws family. When tipping girls (whether servants or his own children – both were liabilities to this neo-Victorian), he'd often be unable to let go of his end of a ten-shilling note. If they snatched, father, daughter and bill were divided.

Tight with things but free with his body. He stalked the unlovely environs of Crooked Usage in his yellow flannel underwear, one thick sock in his hand, plainting, 'Bother! Lily, have you seen my other sock?' Which I'd hear, natch, as 'have you seen my other cock?'. 'Think back to which frumpy cunt you last saw it in!' I'd snap – and he'd look bemused, or else rise to ire: 'Now look here, Lily!' Jesus, he was an asshole.

Christ, he had a skinny Shylock for a heart, enfolded in his fat form. He was that emotionally tight-fisted a man – with his smile which was like a 'Keep Out' sign.

If the late sixties proved anything to me it was that not all phobias are irrational. There was I – who'd spent the first half of the decade prostrate beneath the bed covers, as if they'd shelter me and my babies from the fallout – striding out into chilly arena of Grosvenor Square in order to hurl my hoarse barbs at the American Embassy. *So* dumb to be protesting – when I was always happier to be alone in bed, reading recipes and cracking up with Jacob's Cream Crackers. But I knew I wasn't a little girl running down a mud road with a napalm cloak flaring from my shoulders; and I knew I wasn't a Viet Cong suspect, dying in a short-sleeved, tartan-patterned shirt, from one of General Loan's bullets. Strangely, the very intimacy of these extinctions – now brought to us near instantaneously – made them quite inapplicable to my sad sack. I was safe while all the baddies were off on a peasant shoot in Indo-China. Safe enough for idealism to blossom anew in the neglected, North London borders of my mind. Safe enough to lust after Gus.

Gus, who strode athletically off the plane, and came to us from London Airport wearing the American student uniform of the time – blue jeans, college sweatshirt, sneakers and duffel coat. Within ten years this gear had been fully adopted as an off-the-peg, pre-unwashed, counter-cultural, dressing-up costume, but then it was preppily pressed. Decadences are just that. I remember the crowds at Grosvenor Square only too well, the young men with parted hair and heavy-framed spectacles, the young women in thrifty knitwear, some even sporting *twinsets*. My girls now ask me what the sixties were like – and the answer's simple enough: the fifties. Yup, just like the fifties; the great mass of youth merely aped the styles and modes of their elders who'd advanced half a generation further into the future fray. Naturally, the fifties themselves were not unlike the late forties, which in turn were umbilically linked to before the war. And to me England was a retard society anyway, empty of fridges, devoid of drive-ins. If I squinted at the Aldermaston crowds of plump-faced CND demonstrators only a little, they became hollow-cheeked Jarrow marchers.

Anyway, Gus was the son of one the Eight Couples Who once Mattered, and – far more pertinently – one of Dave Junior's friends, the mud-streaked skinny-dippers who'd been playing the nigger game on the day my love died. Gus, who'd mysteriously fallen through all the bafflers of influence and gratings of exemption designed to prevent good middle-class boys from going down the Vietnam pan. Gus, who'd actually been *drafted*; and who then took to his heels, hiking his way out along the Long Trail into Canada, where he waited for a money order to arrive from his parents before jetting on to Europe.

There was no room in the house – so Gus moved into the garage. He bivouacked in among the discarded luggage of the previous two decades. In order to dodge the VC he had to hunker down in the dark jungle of my peripatetic life. I'd never been anywhere for long – he was not to be long in the leavings of it. Nights we'd watch the nine o'clock news together, our asses rammed to the back of the vomit-coloured, oatmeal-textured divan. Yaws took a similar line on Vietnam to the one he'd taken on the Cuban missile crisis: this too would pass, leaving the Warden intact, a crumpet *en route* to his lips. Yaws didn't suspect anything sexual between me and the kid. It wasn't so much that he'd rationally dismissed the idea, rather, it couldn't even register on his smutty radar. Gross. I can't have slept with Gus more than four times – five at most. All that stuff about teaching young men the ways of love is so much horse shit. All you have to do is feed 'em into the groove and they'll do the hammering. Every time we did it I was amazed that he wasn't discommoded by my sour smells and puckering cellulite. But I guess there was plenty of vagina, heaps of bosom.

It was last time in my life that sex held any quality of conviction for me. In the cooling pretzel of tatty linen, still aromatic with Yaws, we'd thrash about. He did it hobbled by his jeans. I did it hobbled by Librium. It was a big period of mental freedom for me. I hauled myself up in the morning and cooked the kiddy-winkies breakfast in my nightie. Then I drove them to school in my nightie. Then I came back to Crooked Usage, took my nightie off, and climbed back into bed. I felt like I was on the night shift. Haig was the blended Scotch people drank in those days. It was advertised with the catch-line 'Don't be vague', when that's exactly what it did to you. To me.

On that particular cold March afternoon, shlepping from Marble Arch with all the other bleeding hearts and closed minds, I was tired. I was always fucking tired. Natasha'd kicked seven kinds of hell out of the insides of me; I still smoked forty a day; I was often vague – and there was the Librium. It didn't lay you out like sodium amytal, but it still made me pretty laid back. Laid back on a cushion of Librium, my young lover by my side, I railed by the railings at the boob-helmeted policemen. Over the grey haunch of the American Embassy the tessellated greenery of Hyde Park tossed with wind and drizzle. The coppers linked arms and forced the beatniks and beatific old Quaker women back from the entrance. Lots of the duffel-coat-wearers – and Gus, to my shame – began to chant, 'Ho! Ho! Ho-Chi-Minh!' Absurd – what did they think an ageing, intellectual, highly ascetic,

Vietnamese Communist Party cadre would have to do with these truants from the bourgeoisie?

That's all gone now, social revolution as an aspect of the gap year. It's all there was to left-wing radicalism in the West after the war anyway; doctoring the social fringes was as much a fashion statement as cutting your hair, or growing it, or shaving it off. I fell for these cheap nostrums as did many others. Protest marches were my weight-watching; and I used to see plenty of other women, nearing middle age, verging on being pear-shaped, who smiled ruefully at me as they toted their placards.

But I was tired – fucking exhausted. As the police moved in, blows were exchanged and they lost control – marvellous expression. They lost control, fists tried to fly but crashed into skulls and cheekbones. Fleet feet fled through flesh. I snuck away – leaving my young lover to the shlemozzle. But not before seeing more striking slow motions – heads going like the clappers, the impacts were so percussive. I saw one beefeater thug smack a Buddy Holly lookalike the way British actors playing Gestapo officers smacked their interrogation victims. Back and forth and back again. I never ever wanted to be that close to violence again. I'd never intended it, my life wasn't meant to be like that. I'd understood that I was to be excluded from this section of the twentieth century, that I hadn't been selected. I saw it as my role to skulk in history's wings, observing the actors once they'd been bandaged, or otherwise made beautiful.

Even the noise of a riot soon fades if you tuck your head down and ignore it. While bottles, bricks and splintered placards punctured the drizzly sky, I made my way to Berkeley Square and sat down on a bench. Here, then, there were elms not yet diseased – I think. I sat and lost myself in the damp leaves pressed into the pavement, the old people fizzling out. Come in cigarette number 34, your time is up. I'd never felt, it occurred to me, more depleted. Or, to be correct, more indolent. The very effort needed to register my own fatigue was . . . too much. Seeing made me yawn. I was only forty-six, but I couldn't conceive of how I'd make it through the remaining years – they'd have to spool them in front of my eyes. Pathé life reels.

Eyes which are now jammed open in the enclosing darkness. I wake from reveries of the late sixties to this nighttime paralysis. Waking takes long enough for me to realise that these memories – undoctored and unedited – are a crude gloss on the badly painted present. More precisely – that the tank of tiredness is itself now empty; and I feel fatigued by this fact alone. I'd thought that at least I could always depend on this numbing languor, this painful drowsiness. That it would be the layette of my lifetime; and that sleep – for so long dispensed in famine rations – would now, at long last, be in plentiful supply.

Not so. The devil is looking at me with malevolent red eyes shaped like twos. They blink with electronic implacability. Coiled around the bedroom the plumbing gurgles like a gassy gut. The pain comes galloping towards me, ravening white horses which chomp though everything in their path. Hurricane pain. Pain that leaves me clinging to the driftwood of my own consciousness; battered into not being me. Maybe now I die? I allow myself to be lifted up by this anguish like an oscillating mote. Higher and higher I rise in the fusty darkness, while below me the duvet's pattern dissolves into the grid of Manhattan, as a clarinet intimately moans: 'Ooooowaaaa-wa-waa-wa-waa-waaa-wa-wa-wa-wa-wa-waaaa . . .' then a string section cranks up the pace: 'Diddleumdumdumdiddle-umdumdumdiddleumdumdum!' until the clarinet gets eloquent on behalf of its own misery: 'Wawawawaaaawawa-wawaaawawawawawawawaaaaaaaaaaaa . . .' and not to be

outdone, the strings crank it up some more: 'Diddleumdumdumdiddleumdumdumdiddleumdumdum!'

'Wawawa-waaaa!' Christ alive – it's fucking *Rhapsody in
Blue*. Christ penetrated by the Lord. Christ jacking off the
Holy Ghost – how I hate this tune. Three in one. It's a tune –
not a rhapsody. A tin-pan-crash-bang bit of Yid slickery,
played out in the trash-choked alleys around Times Square
and Broadway.

The city of my majority swims towards me out of the dusty
deathly darkness of this suburban room an ocean away. At first
I'm relieved to have this effortless ascendancy; rising in a
smooth parabola from the coxcomb of Liberty into the clouds
over the toe of Manhattan, so that the leggy length of the island
rears below me, each neon street switched on by my own
awareness. 'Diddleumdumdumdiddleumdumdumdiddleumdumdum!' A set of a certain unreal age, with no distinction
between the fabricated and the constructed, between interior
and exterior. A musical New York peopled by eternally young
songsters clad in sky-blue Runyon shmutter. See them dance
down the block, swing around the corner, leap into the sub-
way, while Top Cat trades gags with Officer Dibble and the
Jetsons head home in their flivvers to White Plains.

As if the streets were sore throats gargling the violence of
their own dissolution, it's a *memento mori* city in which a
flayed cop rides a flayed horse, half of their skulls and half of
their skeletons exposed. And these picked-clean knights are
predisposed to shepherd a funeral which emerges from Har-
lem to march across 121st Street and downtown. A black
funeral – what repulsive fun. How much black silk and black
crêpe, how much bombazine has been draped over these black
bodies? The tubas and cornets are pooting out the hated
moans of Jew urbanity. This black has decided to belong
to the Jewish Death Club – which is happy to accept him as a

member. This Jew has declined to attend meetings of the Black Club – but she's being forced into the procession for all that. Please don't let Death touch me with its black hands; please don't let Hitler kiss me with his greasepaint moustache.

'Ooooowaaaa-wa-waa-wa-waa-waaa-wa-wa-wa-wa-wa-waaaa . . .' I managed to squeeze that one out, project it above the murmurous, murderous news of Kurt Waldheim's rehabilitation.

— Ms Bloom?

I try to reply, to ask her to move me, feed me, drug me, comfort me, but all that emerges is more blueish rhapsodising. 'Wawawawaaaawawawawaaawawawawawawawawaaaaaaaa-aaa . . .'

— Ms Bloom, are you all right? Is there something I can get for you?

And now the beat is doubled up: 'Diddleumdumdumdiddleumdumdumdiddleumdumdum!' Deirdre has opened the double doors to the living room, letting in a big wedge of yellow light. She returns to my bedside.

— Ms Bloom, can you hear what I'm saying to you?

'Diddleumdumdumdiddleumdumdumdiddleumdumdum!' Oh yes, and I can also see the greasy blackheads like Braille on your yellow vellum.

— Ms Bloom, could you blink, or close your eyes if you can understand what I'm saying?

No. No – that's beyond me. It's happened. I've been buried alive in the flesh-eating box of my own body. My eyelids, intermittently and unpredictably, sweep wet streaks across my view – like demented windshield-wipers. Time doubles up in their wake. 'Diddleumdumdumdiddleumdumdumdiddleumdumdum!' And my voice is compelled. 'Wawawawaaaa-wawawawaaawawawawawawawawaaaaaaaaaaa . . .' This definitely gets things going. Deirdre recoils as if I've spat in her face. I *have* spat in her face – she's wiping the spittle from her drippy nose. I can hear my clarion cry echo around the room, my hearing must have a delay now, a sound-lock. But in place of Gershwin's bombastic klezmer, it's become a hideous life-rattle, a gurgling, gasping, aspirated screech: 'Hhhraarrghhh-resheo' Hyayyayrhg-h'- h'h'hergh'!' This is a terrorist alert in the language centre itself; vowels and consonants evacuating at top speed from the Tower of Song. Christ! You would've thought such a bestial noise would get windows banging open all over Kentish Town.

— What's the matter?!

Sweat damp in her knickers and wearing a Che Guevara T-shirt, Natty appears in the yellow wedge.

— Your mother is declining very rapidly, Ms Bloom –

— Mum! Mumu! Can you hear me?

— I'm afraid she's no longer lucid –

'Wawawawaaaawawawawaaaawawawawawawawaaaaaa-aaaaa . . .

— What's that dreadful noise she's making?

From the terror in my youngest's porcelain eyes I can assess the mess I must be. If I try hard I can re-establish contact with this steadily departing vessel of cellular mush. I can feel its dismasted no-progress – limbs flapping like collapsed sails, as it no-heads round into the afflatus of extinction.

— I'm afraid the cancer must have entered her brain –

— Her brain?

'Wawawawaaaawawawawaaaawawawawawawawaaaaaa-aaaaa . . .'

— That's awful, she . . . she doesn't sound –

Human. I don't sound human. I sound like a fucking animal. A gurgling cow. My brain's been vaccinated – with cancer.

— Please – Natasha. It isn't her, these noises are involuntary. It's breakthrough pain.

Oh, it's a breakthrough allrighty. Brand-new pain for a brand-new era – coming soon to a nerve ending near you.

— What can we do?

— I'll have to phone the hospital, see if they'll admit her.

— Admit her, why?

— I haven't been able to give her medication for eight hours now – it's likely she's in a lot of pain. I can't tell. She'll have to –

Make sure you know quite how far things have got by my skilled employment of the voluntary involuntary action; in this instance an arm swung wide in the shadows, swiped in a spastic butterfly stroke, then whipped back again. Whack-whack-smack! I catch Deirdre in the lower belly, Natty on the thigh, paperbacks and the little radio fly from the bedside table.

— go on a drip.

Drip-drip. In fairness to Natty she's exactly the same as everyone else. It's only that unlike the others she can't prevent the naked self-interest from showing. Especially not now, not near naked, in frayed M&S bikini briefs, sweat on her thighs, sweat on her neck and sporting a sweaty tiara. It's a sweat T-shirt competition – the sweat plastering Che Guevara's noble brow between Natty's once proud tits. So, she stayed here last night. Evidently Russell wasn't available; absent, I daresay, at some junkies' soirée – pass the Vicar, tea-head. Miles would've been small comfort – and miles away if he's any sense. So, best for her to hang out here in the hope of a few crumbs of pleasurable relief. You would've imagined that this – the live burial, the uncoupling of mind from body – would plunge me into final despair. Not so. Can you hear me? Not so. All those injunctions to *let go*; to accept and *let go*; to walk into the garden and see spring invest the saplings and *let-fucking-go* – when there was no need. I can kick and punch and scream as much as I like, I can hold on for dear life if I want, because it makes no odds. Dear Life is rearing up above me, rearing over me as my fingers scrabble on mortality's cliff edge; and Dear Life's boot is coming down on the back of my hand. Hard.

Life has left me in a plastic-curtained cubicle. Life has left me in the family way. I'm fully gravid with Death; Death is engaged now – his bony head nuzzling my cervix. Perhaps that's why I'm so detached, and able to witness impassively my spasmodic movements, my stuck-pig cries. My sick and sickened daughter.

Deirdre hits the overhead light and banishes one kind of darkness. Natasha sinks down on the chair and stares at the animal who used to be her mother. I can't focus on her – I can't focus on anything. I have no more control over my eyes than I do over the rest of my body. Perhaps that's why I'm achieving such glorious indifference? After all, it's foolish to take any responsibility for involuntary actions, to weep for sneezes, cry for hiccups, mourn for yawns.

— I think the best course would be admission. Is it possible to send an ambulance? 256 Bartholomew Road, ground-floor flat. The name on the bell is Bloom.

Efficient Deirdre comes back to deal with dreck girl:

— Now, Ms Bloom – Natasha – I know you're not feeling well yourself –

— Can you help?

What a chancer. Deirdre glares at her with a what-kind-of-an-inhumanly-selfish-bitch-are-you expression. Natasha isn't chastened.

— Look. I know what you're thinking, but Mum –

— Was giving you some of her diamorphine? I'm well aware of that, Natasha, but as a registered nurse I'd be risking my career as well as breaking the law. Now, if you can forget your own sickness for a moment and remember your mother, perhaps it would be a good idea if you called Mrs Elvers? *And put some clothes on!*

This last is mine; sensible Deirdre wouldn't say such a thing

– even to the junky daughter of a moribund patient. She must also sense that Natty is well capable of striking out. Like me, she has a hair-trigger temper; an element within her which incandesces. Not that you'd know it to look at her now, gathering herself up, limping off to the spare bedroom, her wasted buttocks looking, from the rear, like the kneecaps of a starving child. And that sweat.

Mrs Elvers – now she's doing the mothering I think it behoves me to address her formally – arrives in good time. Why wouldn't she? She'll've been dozing lightly in their big, white bed. Their bed so big she need hardly sleep with Mr Elvers, merely in his general vicinity. There's a lot of padding in the Elverses' world. They sleep swaddled in linen and duck down, while propped against goose down. Charlotte's skeleton is sheathed within her own foam rubberiness; and when she arises – moving with the spirited jiggle of the plump-yet-fit – it's to encase it in more softness, before carting it downstairs and buckling it into the foam rubberiness of the Mercedes.

It takes Charlotte five minutes from Regent's Park to Kentish Town. She brings the dawn with, and comes in through the double doors to my bedroom with a grey corona behind her. Funny how the light is frightening to me – the dark was better. Her rumpled sister meets her by my bed and they embrace, anxiety cancelling out enmity.

— Oh, Charlie, it's terrible.

Natty gasps in her older sister's hair, then they awkwardly decouple. Charlie leans down to look at me, and I have the bizarre sensation that I'm an aquarium; that my convex elder is peering in through my toughened glass eyes, to admire my lazy eels of thought.

— Her eyes are open, but she doesn't seem conscious. Mum? Mu-um?

I'm in here, dear, dressed in a fleshy winding sheet – but still alive. I'm in here, dear, still conscious but suffering no fear. I have no volition any more, you see, there's nothing I want, nothing I desire. The world is cold, grey Ryvita – and I'm, as ever, on a diet.

Deirdre comes through and pronounces with equestrian authority:

— The ambulance has arrived, Mrs Elvers.

Then all hell breaks loose. Two big men and one man-sized woman are in the room. They're all wearing green nylon coveralls and stomping on the carpets so hard I can see plumes of dust explode from beneath rubber soles. They talk in very loud, workaday voices.

— In here, is she love?

— This is Ms Bloom, yes.

— Double doors no problem –

He looks at me as he says this. Looks at me where I lie twitching and spluttering. Looks at me with no more empathy than he would regard an awkward piece of furniture.

— but the vestibule is tricky, both doors open into it. We can't get the stretcher through there. Have to be the chair. Ron! Ron! Get the chair out of the van, woodjew?

No attempt at volume control at all. He might be in a warehouse. My daughters are frozen in mid-flinch. They clearly expect their dying mother to be handled like a piece of gold leaf, blown upon and gently applied to the hospital. The other two manual workers are shifting the furniture about, shoving the sofabed, the Danish modern armchair and the recliner into a cramped ménage. Deirdre is off to one side, feeding her pasta knitting into her working-woman's holdall. Both our shifts are over. If my body has a mind of its own, then whose mind is this one? For I'm convulsing again and the blue rhapsody of dissolution streams from my mouth. 'Wawawa-waaaawawawawaaawawawawawawawawaaaaaaaaaaaa . . .'

They all turn to goggle at the lowing, thrashing bovine in their midst. Then they all redouble their efforts: must remove this farmyard detritus from this domestic context. Get it in the van. Drive it to the abattoir. But Natty is transfixed by her own particular agony. Christ she looks ill in this cold dawn light. I can see the gross pores pitting the edge of her fine jaw. I can apprehend the agony of her jarred pelvis. I feel no compassion.

The chair is in the front room. It's highly utilitarian – a kitchen stacking chair with extra foam-rubber padding and many straps. The two ages of woman: in the morning you toss your food about in a high chair; in the evening you're trussed up and carted off in a low chair. Ron and his mate bring the thing in. They smell of diesel exhaust, bacon sandwiches, sugared tea, smokes. They clomp and stomp, their hands are square. The woman – who's a bumpier version of her colleagues – has finished clearing the path to the door; so, without any ado, they yank off the duvet, yank me upright, get a wispy shawl around me, lift me off the bed, slam me in the chair, strap me in, lift me fore and aft, lug me out.

In quick succession, as we go, I see the following: the Yaws family silver in its box – atop a mouldering Yaws family Bible – alongside a dust brush for LPs – alongside some carpet – alongside some skirting board – underneath a wall – on which hangs a dark oily daub I bought in a flea market – up above a plug socket – over which dangles a crystal, which flashes facets of this space where I have lived into my dulling eyes. This is how you leave your home to die – with a bang and a 'Wawawawaaaawawawawaaawawawawawawawawaaaaaaaa-aaa . . .'

In the ambulance things are getting uglier. There's an opaque, green-tinted gloom-roof in this vehicle which would turn blood to sap. The green light makes everyone appear deathly. How comforting. Charlie looks so like Yaws, it might actually *be* Yaws – or his corpse, dug up and propped in this vehicle – lurching through London. Her and her sister's faces are paralysed with nauseous shock. They can't put their eyes on me. I must be quite a sight. I can read the disgust, though, when they glance at me, then peer to see if it's really true: that the lights are all on, and the Old Dear is finally absent.

But I'm not. I'm hiding under the bed in the spare room of my mind, waiting for the men in the death's-head uniforms. So foolish to have bothered to avoid the Holocaust, when it was waiting for me all the time –

— Can't he drive a little more gently?

— We've got to get there, haven't we?

— Why – are you gonna save her life?

Good. Nice sarcasm, Natty. Nice crappiness. Puts these hirelings in their place – 'Awoo'wooo'wooo'wooooo-a'wooo' – until they put on their siren.

— Is this strictly necessary?

Asks Charlie, giving her version of the family contempt. But the Ronette, who's right alongside where I'm pinioned in my low chair, feels no need to reply. She's fortified by her mission of senselessness and her professional discourtesy. Although fundamentally unchristian, she ecstatically sways as the ambulance takes the chicane over the humpback bridge at the top of St Pancras Way and barrels down towards Somers Town. The girls fatalistically lurch, like davening frummehs accompanying the remains of some great sage of the kabbala. Their faces suggest to me that they really believe things cannot get worse. And this would touch me deeply – were I not already beyond reach.

We arrive at the loading bay on Grafton Way primed for more industrial medicine. This new wing of University College

Hospital – completed on the cusp of the bulbous decade – has a defiantly factory air about it. Whumph! go the front tyres on to the ramp. Crash! go the doors. Smash! goes the chair as they dump me down to the ground. Then dreedle-squeak-dreedle-squeak-dreedle-squeak – they wheel me into the low-ceilinged, yet cavernous, Casualty waiting area. It can't be later than eight a.m. and the atmosphere reeks with last night's violence. The air rings with a silent tintinnabulation of many heads clapping. It stinks of smoked cigarettes, their rotten corpses, their dead essences. Who cares about the fucking humans dying of cancer – what about the poor cigarettes being wilfully exterminated by humans? Cruelly sucked up, then ruthlessly stubbed out.

Whumph! Banged into a wall like a bowling ball coming to rest – but there's none. Only the two Ronnies lifting my thrashing, groaning carcass on to a trolley, then making off again. Hairy jerks. I'm conscious of the susurrations of a conversation which is being rushed alongside me:

— This is very sudden.
— Have you got a bed for her?
— We'll see, we'll see . . . I've spoken to Admissions already.
— But have you got a bed for her?
— We'll find one.
— Where? Here?

No, not here, please. Not. It's a long, lowering, warped spine of a tunnel, which plunges beneath Grafton Way, then runs, north-south, parallel to Gower Street, connecting all the various organs of the hospital. It's simultaneously chilly and food-odorous down here. Quite an achievement. The tunnel is green-tiled, stone-floored, strangely reminiscent of the foot tunnel beneath the Thames at Greenwich. Must be the same vintage. And like the Greenwich foot tunnel, this one feels pressurised, weighed down by the many millions of tons of water overhead. No, not water, the effluvia of disease itself. A rambunctious river of pus and gleet and ichor; a cascade of mucus and bile and gall. An impressively engineered Victorian snotqueduct. The medics here are only lock-keepers; they can check this mighty Orinoco momentarily – but never dam it.

Dreedle-thwock-dreedle-thwock-dreedle-thwock. The trolley wheels leap and skitter over the joins in the floor. Sensible daughter is keeping pace well in her fashionable sports footwear; with each stride she glances at my face, as if hoping to find new life. Sick, junky daughter is doing less well. She shuffles and snuffles in our wake, all wiped-upon cuffs and bleary features. To be fair to darling Natasha it's been quite a morning for her – she's had to face it straight, for one thing. Now she's sick with heroin withdrawal, and although I've never experienced it myself I know with certainty that it's a lonely, silent hell of vulnerability. Poor Natty – it's all about boo-hoo you, *n'est-ce pas?*

We've stopped half-way along the tunnel at its lowest point. The trolley splashes into a brackish puddle of tears. There's a consultation between the Ronnies, then Dr Steel emerges from a small, glassed-in office at the side of the tunnel. He's so well pressed – it looks to me as if he's climbed out of a trouser press where he's spent the short night. His face is ironed into professional impassivity.

— Hello, Mrs Elvers.

— Dr Steel.

— Natasha.

— 'Lo.

He's got the titles correct here. He's right to address Charlotte sensibly and Natasha indifferently. If any doctor addresses Natty with a modicum of interest, she'll hit on them for an RX. I'm looking at the globs of Blu-Tack that have been used to gum rosters and schedules to the windows of the office. When the girls were kids they played with Silly Putty – is it that recreational stuff that has evolved into this working material? I've stopped groaning and thrashing. The warm breezes smelling of cabbage and boiled fish play upon my slack face. On some seats at the far side of the tunnel a small Asian family – tiny bejewelled lady, tiny suited man, tinier boy in well-ironed shorts – sit in a respectable line, as if decorum were part of their cure. The little boy has a toy metal car, a toy plastic cow and a toy plastic harmonica. As I watch he carefully balances these three objects atop his flattened thighs. He tries car on top of cow on top of harmonica, then harmonica on top of cow on top of car, as if he were investigating the possibility of new Hindu cosmologies.

— Hmm.

Steel is reading notes handed to him by Charlotte. Must be Deirdre's report of the night's jam session.

— I'm afraid this is it.

— It?

— The cancer appears to have metastasised into the meningeal fluid.

— Meningeal?

— Her brain – your mother's brain. The fluid is in a column inside the spine; once cancer is present in this fluid, it will rapidly move throughout the brain.

— It's – it's like she isn't there any more. Like she isn't sentient.

— Well, who knows . . . but our priority is to keep your mother as comfortable as possible.

— Until she dies.

— Yes, until she dies.

I like this finality, this spade-calling. I like it well. Of course, like so many others, I had hopes of attaining the gift of perpetual old age; still, finality I like as well. But Natty doesn't – she'd like some histrionics. She feels everyone present would benefit from an improvisation of her love.

— You're fucking giving up!

— Natty!

— Shut up, Charlie. You – you're fucking giving up.

— What're you talking about?

— You aren't even trying to help my mother – to *cure* my mother. You've given up. I thought you lot signed some fucking *oath*, that meant you had to try. What about a fucking transplant? They do them now – liver transplants. I read about it in the paper, why don't you do one – or aren't you a good enough doctor? Good enough with your fucking *hands*.

Disregarding the fact that Steel, of course, is not a surgeon, I still think this last shot of Natty's is a good one. I mean to say, there's the competence of the doctor and the sexual *amour propre* of the man, both nicely insinuated. If I were Steel I'd be chastened – but then I'm not, and he isn't.

— Listen, Natasha, your mother isn't the only person who's dying. Not in the world, not in this hospital – not even in this corridor. Yes, they can do liver transplants. They do them in California. If you can lay *your* hands on the thirty thousand pounds necessary to pay, and can organise air-ambulance transportation for your mother from here to Los Angeles, then you might – just might – have a chance of saving her life. But not her brain.

— Jesus! Wha'kinduvafuckin'monster'reyou? Oh – h'h'-h-oh! Those ambulance fuckers smashed her all about, an' now you're gonna put her on a fucking drip in this fucking *tunnel* and leave her to die. National-fucking-death-service – that's what you are.

— The ambulance crew did their level best to get your mother here as quickly and as smoothly as possible. We will do our best to care for her now she's here. If, Natasha, you cannot control yourself, I will have to ask you to leave. If you then won't leave, I'll have you removed. Now, Mrs Elvers, we have a bed for your mother in the Royal Ear Hospital. It's not available yet, but she shouldn't have to wait here for too long.

Steely Steel. Now that's telling Natty. I don't imagine many men still capable of maintaining an erection would've dared to tick her off that severely, but then Natty's junky allure is totally lost on him. He looks upon her – quite rightly – as another of the diseased. And she self-pityingly leaks, dabs black cuff to bruised eye, shuffles off to one side, into the shadows of a temporary oblivion.

Chapter Six

We're rolling again. Dreedle-thwock-dreedle-thwock-dreedle-thwock-crash! That was a corner. The Rons have long gone, and in their place there's an authentic porter; a neanderthal shvartzer, whose brows beetle all over the place as we squeak forward. Charlotte marches in step with him, looking down at me now as if I were a vast dog turd which *has* to be removed. The Royal Ear . . . mmm. How suitable, when it's my hearing that looks like being the last thing to go. My ears . . . mmm. So curiously hand-moulded – like all the rest of the human clay. My ears – the last part of me that will feel the claw of cancer.

The trolley has assistance – or are they assistants? Anyway, along either side, like oars thrust through the gunwales of a galley, are many many legs. Fat legs, thin legs, hairy legs, smooth legs, waxen legs, dusky legs. They have nothing in common with one another save for being dead. Dead legs. Dead legs streaked with the miasma of gangrene, or swollen with purulence, or shattered by impact. They're severed and stuck along the trolley's sides, so they may bend and push, walking with me to eternity.

They are – I realise this joyfully – the leftover limbs of amputees. This hospital is famous for its amputations – the first ones ever conducted using ether. I read it in a helpful historical handbook before I was past caring. These must be the ghostly legs themselves; left to hop for ever along the strip-lit cloisters of this mundane monastery.

The Royal Ear Hospital – it has a ring to it. I can imagine one periwigged courtier saying to another, 'I have the Royal

Ear.' And the other replying, 'But I understand it's in the hospital.' Where do they keep the Royal Ear, I wonder? I think of it as very large – as big as a dinner tray – and very red, angrily red. They probably keep it in an incubator in the sub-basement of the hospital, where it's tended by a succession of pasty-faced flunkeys, who rub saline solutions containing royal jelly into its swollen lobes. *De temps en temps* a minister will arrive from the Palace to impart matters of state to the Ear. He'll sit on a folding chair and mutter into the fleshy toilet bowl. Naturally, the Ear will be unable to respond, so in due course the Minister will repair to the Royal Mouth Hospital, where he'll learn the royal edict.

They're removing the imperial dentures from my royal mouth. O well-formed acrylic, fare ye well! You never required additional grip or adhesive. I bathed you in Steradent so you never rotted or stank. I handled you with the utmost gentility so you never chipped or broke. You cleaved unto me and I cleaved unto you – we were as one, snugly snogging each other for a quarter of a century. You two plates and I – we were the true and loving trinity.

— Blood pressure forty over seventy.
— Have you brought a bag for her?
— Sister, could you find me a seven-gauge one of these?
— Would you take five cc and take it to Bloods?
— I'll need saline, sucrose and diamorphine.
Ssshk-ssshk-ssshk-shk.

They've shucked the nylon curtains and screened me from the incurious eyes of my fellow mothers. We all know what's in store for us, so why bother to act in this coy fashion? Still, what can you expect from a medical staff who have the bodies of humans and the heads of pussy cats? It's true that their paws are surprisingly deft when it comes to putting in catheters, arranging feed lines and filling in charts. But I can't help suspecting that their chimerical nature has contributed to their failure to treat me properly. To save at least one of my nine lives.

Perhaps I should've examined my own breasts a little more thoroughly. Possibly I should've attended screenings more regularly. But you know what? I couldn't fucking find one of my teats amid all that tawny chest fur – let alone six. By the time they gave me a CAT scan it was already too late. The radiation only singed my fur and burned me. Oh! How vile it is – the feel of exposed feline skin. It made me puke. I lost the wild exquisite pain of being hungry. Not even Whiskas appealed to me. They gave me tamoxifen. Then more tamoxifen. Then more. My fur fell out in clumps – I went right off . . . everything. Now they've got me here, in the cattery, morbidly pregnant. Full of the kitties of death. And here's kind Dr Bowen annotating a clipboard with a Bic Cristal as she stands at the foot of my basket.

There are moggies in here with deadlier enteritises than mine. Moggies who've been out on the tiles. Moggies who now lie emaciated, blind, forsaken. Mewling pitifully. Herpes was a trailer for Aids – that much we now understand. 'Coming Soon to a Body Athwart Yours!' was how the titles read, spelt out in precise, warty eruptions. Of course, you had to get right down on the relevant genitals to see it – not something I was in a position to do. The appetite for oral sex is, in my experience, entirely vitiated by an inability to touch your own toes. Even when seated. Oral sex – yummy. That's what it made me to Yaws – yummy. Couldn't keep his eyes off my mouth. He'd never been blown before me, they didn't do that kind of thing in Barchester. If you were lucky the Dean of Chapter's wife would let you touch her stays, or jack off into her under-petticoat. Wow! Those were the days.

I only mention it because I've still the hunger for sex – still, with Death licking me out, nuzzling me with its bony head. And while I concede that it's peculiar, I have an awful kind of jealousy towards the Aids patients in here. They had more sex and more unsuitable sex. I had more cigarettes and more liquor.

It was Natasha who clued me in to all this – told me who had what. Natasha, whose attendances at my radiotherapy sessions were an amusing sideshow. In among the prematurely bald boys and scoop-breasted women, Natty was at once exotic and right at home. She knew the medical ghetto well enough – she'd trailed her own trailer to James Pringle House for treatment; and in the casualty wards and drug-dependency units she'd watched the skinny junkies getting far far skinnier. Can her pallor be the result of radiation? thought all who saw her slumped against me, the two of us purring feline kitty talk to each other.

'Will it be the dykey one today, Mumu?'

'I shouldn't be at all surprised. Mindjew, I always feel better when it's the lesbian radiographer, Natty.'

'Why's that, Mumu?'

'Well, it strikes me that she may be that much better at handling boobs – given that she enjoys it.'

'S'pose so.'

She'd come with me, in amid the clanking equipment, which was meant to smoke out the smoking-related disease. It banged and whined – we both cowered. At the time there was no sensation, although I always thought I could smell the cells singe. I daresay anything nuclear looks the same – power stations, weapons systems, whatever. All these inhuman forces, these isotopes of Vishnu, being flung out by lesbians in tightly buttoned nylon coats, snapping heavy switches at Bakelite consoles. Singeing us to no avail.

Then we'd head back out into Grafton Way, turn the corner

into Tottenham Court Road. It was OK to feel like death with my youngest, who, after all, had been suiciding for ten years already. We'd drag our heels around Heal's, then go for coffee, then back to the flat. She'd slide off to score. I wouldn't remark on it. It was a deal between us: don't mention death – I won't mention smack. Even-steven. I grew hollow-cheeked, my eyes bruised, my hair thinned, my breast burned. Natasha paced me in my race to the grave.

It wasn't always thus – so I was genuinely glad of her company. She may've been untrustworthy, unreliable, selfish, sluttish and even – and to say this of one's own, one must *really* have chewed the cud of irony until it's bitter as wormwood – pretentious. But then that was far better than boring, which is what all the other women in my life – all the other 'friends' – had been for years. All the Susies and Emmas rationalising their loneliness, their very raw lack of the manly tumour that surgical lawyers had so efficiently excised, by an appeal to sociology, or demography, or even – laughably – fucking biology! Nope, better my junky own.

They meant nothing to me – she did. Mrs Elvers has gone now – but Natty remains. And they've taken my false teeth out of my fake face – I must look like death warmed over. A nurse enters the shucked-in space pushing a bag on a stand. She uncorks the catheter stopper on the back of my hand and plugs me into the drip. I feel more affinity to it than to her. She's tiny – all her work is up above her. So she ups and stretches, and the wide elastic belt cinches her tiny waist tighter. Her pinafore is fine-striped, she's blonde, her calves heart-shaped, her elbows dimpled. Natty – that crow – stares at her with avidity, as if she would eat the girly nursling. Oh yes, they say you are what you eat, my daughter – but then you hardly eat at all.

Shucked in here, in this nylon shoebox, and shucked in here

behind grating lids. Shucked-in eye, walled-up eye. I am obscured by my own tatty beliefs – entertaining any company with very much banked fires. Eyes that rock to rest at the bottom of either socket, or lunge at a glance. Outside in the mid-morning Mrs Elvers will be calling her husband Richard on a mobile telephone which looks like a black plastic tibia. Inside thirty-odd of his outlets, thirty bored sales assistants are wrapping up some wrapping paper, then ringing up the sale. It's not too early to leave after all.

But I can still summon up the past – even now. Even now as the cancer, this inky antagonist, corners my very sentience and readies its suckered tentacles. Let's face it, anything that has suckers sucks. Yeah, I can summon up the past. Howdy-doody past! Yo Main Street USA! I gwyne to talk with yo' – hairball. I gwyne to drop yo' on de floor an' see how yo' roll. Nope. The past is too dense, too digested to act as an organ of prophecy. If I attempt to feel it, its falseness is overwhelming. It's not of me – I was of it. I glibly made a profound mistake. I thought I was getting wisdom – it was getting me. They were staying away in droves, and I'll be droving away in stays, cinched by the knowledge that the cap of a Biro is all I leave behind me. A flimsy plastic nose cone crewed by twenty thousand metres of potential expression; a long line of sense, as yet unformed, unbecome. The registrar will probably pull one off to warrant I'm dead.

'Y'not in godzone yet, girl – yeh-hey?' It's a middle-aged black man wearing a white Stetson. He parts the curtains, thrusts his head inside – the hat so crammed down on his dusty tumbleweed of hair that it flares in his mirrored shades – and says, 'Y'not in godzone yet, girl – yeh-hey?' Then goes. Why doesn't my daughter register the thrust of this masculine head? Oh, I see, although it's not cute the way she chews her cuticles. Did the black man wave a boomerang at me? Could he be an Aboriginal? He's back. 'Not long now, Lily, see, I'm tellin' you. Yer djang unravellin' now, see? Gonna curl up new time. Curl roun' *her*.' It is a boomerang and he points it at the nail-biter. 'Mek a new rainbow . . .' His accent is a peculiar mishmash of cheek-clicks, tongue-slaps on palate and wide open Australian vowels. What the fuck is he on about? Who the fuck let him on to the ward? Wait 'til the Royal Ear hears about *this*! Christ! No fucking security in these places; any psycho who pleases could run in and molest me. Steal me, even. Snatch Mummy from her baby. Ha-ha. Aha-ha-ha-

'Hhhraarrghhhresheo' Hyayyayrhg-h'- h'h'hergh'!'

— Sister! Sister!

Natty's up off her chair and out of the booth. She'll scream for any sister but her own – like me. And one's to hand, lurking, an older, flushed brunette. Well groomed. How the fuck can she be bothered?

— Right. What's the problem here?

'Hhhraarrghhhresheo' Hyayyayrhg-h'- h'h'hergh'!'

She leans down and shines a flashlight in through my eyes, not to see if I'm inside, but merely to check the reflex action of my pupils. It's uncannily like being a boiler and having someone lean over to check your pilot light. She straightens, stretches, adjusts the translucent spigots on the dangling bags. I become equally transparent, like a child's educational model of the human body. Like a Biro. I can see my capillary action, the veins and arteries slurping down the sedatives, siphoning up the opiates. There's no pain any more. No discomfort. I thought you might like to know that. I thought . . . you . . . would . . . keep . . . shtoom. Mum is the word.

No pain, because no me. No me? No – you. The pain was about being other – I guess. The pain was about being me. The pain was about being me remembering so much trivia and you – petty *pain* – being a big part of it. Petty pain, my heavy-petting date at the fucking prom. Pain took time – time was painful. Could it be that . . . time . . . and pain . . . were one . . . and the same? Pain was a pebble tossed into the widening and senseless torrent of trivial innovation, which I can feel myself breathlessly breasting – or is it breastlessly breathing? – smacked in an eye by a digital watch, hit in the shoulder by a juicer. I'll stop struggling soon and float downstream. Remember those seventies gadgets that were meant to hoard all the labour of chopping onions? Save it to spend on a leisurely, unweepy old age. A zigzag blade stuck inside a plastic cylinder, then thrust up and down with a spring-loaded plunger. The results were never as good as you hoped for. It was also a fucking pest to clean.

I've been chopped up by a zigzag blade, and oblique chunks of messy old me lie about the Royal Ear. My body reclines here on a subsidised bed, yet whatever impoverished sensations pertain to it reside over there, outside the curtains. As for feelings – who needs them when there's no one left to feel? They were useless anyway, emotions – only the dead skin of our insensitivity; which we rubbed away, each from the other, until it was all dusty down below. Who has the right attachment to vacuum up these grated calluses? Who wants it? Consciousness of what? Going where? With whom? And why, why, why, Mummy? After all these years of being assured of my own loneliness, at last I know what's it's like to be by myself.

I was by myself fifteen years ago, in the flatlands of East Anglia.

No, I *am* by myself, in Aldeburgh, where the sky is exactly the same washed-out grey as the candlewick spread, on the lumpy bed, at the Ship Inn in Dunwich, where I spent last night. More of a pub than a B & B; the landlord looked very much the part – mustachios, waistcoat, key fob – rushing between the stone-flagged bar and the kitchens to the rear. He was seemingly doing everything on the premises at once: tending the bar, cooking the food, serving it, showing fat guests – actually there was only me – to our lumpy beds.

This won't do. This is a recollection within a memory – and this won't do. The sky over Aldeburgh is the same washed-out grey as the shuck-shuck plastic curtains, and like them it's being shucked off to reveal Steel and Bowen and the sister and the edible girly. The giant medics are set against an inconceivably lofty, cavernous universe of a hospital ward. A rough terrain of fire-resistant tiles floats in the middle distance like flat earths. The staff foregather and bear down on me. Hard. Better get away from here – get back.

She began to take exercise far too late, embarking on tiny cycling tours to music festivals, or flower shows, or doing the rounds of churches – there were so many spires in her uninspiring adopted home. Three kids, one episiotomy, two continents, many phobias, lots of depressions. Old fat lady's underwear. It was all a curse upon cycling, which she'd taken up for what reason? Believe it or not, even in the bulbous seventies there were still bulbous, middle-aged women such as she, who thought that the *principle* of cycling meant something. They cycled and they ate in health-food restaurants like Cranks or Ceres, their cussedness aimed at appeasing the Earth Goddess herself. They almost fucking *overdosed* on grated carrot; while sipping fucking *prune* juice. They *invented* being environmentally-conscious, with their vegetable-buying co-operatives which gave them an excuse to put gumboots on in town.

Poor Lily. Poor, infinitely pathetic, fat, old, blowsy Lily; a *jolie laide*, who should've been laid out years before. It was sad to witness her, in her final fifteen years, assiduously picking up litter – tin cans, wrapping paper, cigarette packets, whatever – and secreting it about her person. Tucking it inside her coat pockets, or even her handbag, then carrying it back with her, one corny footstep after another, until she reached whichever place it was she was currently calling home and lodged it with more of its own kind. No wonder she always called her kids' attention to bag ladies – she was one, albeit of a bourgeois stripe. But unlike her, at least the litter got to be with its own, then more of its own, then more. Each stage of the litter's journey involved rooming with more rubbish; until the final journey, down the Thames, in the big steel barge, to Trashy Yar.

In Aldeburgh, having propped up her Raleigh Tourer, Lily stands by the Moot Hall observing an eyebrowless man who's pottering in his front garden, fussing at some ferns with secateurs. Peculiar, she thinks, how the absence of the one usually unnoticed feature renders this man so sinister, so maimed, so odd. Funny also – and here she shifts from one corny foot to the other, feeling newly-acquired blisters, pedal-pushed into painfulness – that I bother to observe this. I should never have spent all of this time observing people – they mean nothing to me. How many more of these stakeouts have I left to endure? Five a day? Ten when taking little cycling trips? How many more years before I fulfil my own prophecy and the crabs crawl out of the dark sea and begin to clip away at my ferny flesh with their secateur claws? Ten, maybe – in which case I'll die in 1984. Or perhaps fifteen? Who knows. No woman may know the hour of her death, nor stare at the sun. Not in Aldeburgh. Not during this June, which is unseasonably grey and blowy. There may be rain this afternoon. She's glad she brought woollen underwear. Big woolly pants.

Lily goes round the corner to the little box office for the

Festival, which is opposite an equally dinky cinema. On the way she deposits a bit of trash in a bin – a sweet-wrapper she's been carrying for at least two days. Paper ballast – no wonder she's so unstable. She likes Aldeburgh and its environs, does Lily. It's the England she came here for, a country of gabled houses, genteel old ladies, secateurs, gently undulating countryside, a good social-security and health service. It's Holland – the England she came here for. Lily buys herself a ticket for the concert that afternoon. Peter Pears singing Schumann's *Liederkreis*, accompanied by Murray Perahia on the piano. She's inordinately pleased to have secured a ticket; this has to be one of the most popular events of this year's Festival. 'I'll buy a packed lunch,' she thinks, 'then cycle up towards Snape along the lanes. Find somewhere quiet and picnic. Settle down with my book.'

She's reading a book about a Suffolk village. It's a painstaking piece of social history, lovingly worked up by the author from hundreds of stilted interviews with senescent peasants. She likes to think of herself as in some way partaking of this panoply of rootedness, this weighty garb of staying put, but knows it isn't so. She shops in the Co-op, wondering if she'd be more at home hobbling after a chicken in a shtetl; and wonders as well about her girls – the younger is on a trendy kids' camping holiday, the elder off skiing. She tests how tight are the ties that bind her to them. They're slack. They're nearly grown. Her job is over. She could in all reasonableness make good now all those screeched threats to 'hand in my motherhood badge'.

Neither of them was anywhere near the Flixborough explosion, or the Red Lion Square riot either – another of Lily's concert venues. There are so many ways to die – burnt to a sludge by overreacting chemicals or bludgeoned by a law-ordering stick – can it matter which one will claim you?

143

Raisins – with the bountiful Mediterranean lovely on the box – 5p. An orange – 3p. Crispbread – 23p. Six segments of cream cheese – 18p. A tin of Top Deck lager and lime – 10p. Total = 59p. Good going. There might be enough cash left for a minicab on from Snape to Saxmundham, forestalling the late-afternoon effort to insert underwear where it shouldn't be. Shove it up Lily, as she pushes herself in the direction of the train station. Heading home to Crooked Usage. Total = 59p.

'Was there anything else?' It's a near-eyebrowless girl at the cash register. Can it be a locally inbred characteristic? Plucking hell. Gross, of course, both the register and her.

'I'm sorry?'

'Was there anything else, or is that all you'll be having?' She realises that the girl wouldn't have spoken at such length were it not for Lily's American accent.

She must assume I'm a tourist. Christ! That chocolate looks good. One a day. One chunk of nougat and toffee and chocolate. Mmm. I mustn't. This trip means slender, means healthy, means sexy. Means a prelude to all the alfresco lovemaking I haven't done since a class ring gashed my ass and blood flowed under the bleachers. 'And a Mars bar.' Ferchrissakes – I've already eaten it with my eyes.

Outside she finds her cycle and stashes the picnic in the panniers, carefully tucking each item in amongst her squished socks and nightie and cagoule. It's still cloudy, but there's no sign of rain. She looks to see if the eyebrowless man is still there, if he's now observing her, and noting her sportily efficient packing. But he's gone and in his place is a pear-shaped woman in her sixties with her ivory hair in a chemical fix. 'Chuck a match at her,' Lily sardonically, internally observes, 'and *she'd* be a mini-Flixborough.'

Yup, not a lot to Aldeburgh, save for a few substantial houses on a low eminence. Yet even this rise is enough to wind

Lily as she pedals her way up. Foot 1: corn-awareness first, then bunion-awareness, then a third, sharper wave of blistering unease – it can only get worse, because here comes Foot 2: and the same again. In between each downward spiral of effort there are other, inveterate sensations – rasp of lungs, pain in rib cage, stricture of underwear, stab in belly. Such is the go-round of discomfort as her fat legs revolve that Lily is entirely absorbed in it, adding her own mantra of self-hatred to each stab in the direction of self-improvement. 'Uneasy and faulty, ignorant and bumbling, neither generous nor giving . . .' Absorbed to a point where she cannot notice giant hands peeling away the greyness overhead. Absorbed to a point where she cannot hear the voices of the future sonic-booming over the flatlands. It's been quite a morning.

— Mrs Elvers?

— Yes.

— We're going to move your mother to a small room at the far end of the ward. There'll be more privacy there.

— Thank you. Sister?

— Yes?

— I know . . . I know you can't – don't – like to say, but –

— It's not long now.

— Not long now.

To lunch. Lily stops to consult her map. Not that she knows how to read it that well – all she wants to do is confirm the distance as superable. Map-reading was a Yaws thing. He used to read maps while crapping in the lavatory at Crooked Usage. A lavatory that was never locked – because it never had a lock. Not that this was evidence of progressiveness on either of their parts – simply more don't-do-it-yourself inertia. Never locked – so that from time to time the women of the house would walk in on the old bull and find him, peering at tiny countryside, while sitting over his own dung.

The lane is a tedious straight line, mercifully flat, which runs alongside a coniferous plantation. Should she crawl in there and try and cuddle down among the spiky trees? It hardly appeals. To the left of the road there is at first a golf course – which reminds her of Yaws's recent demise – and then fields full of either flowering potatoes or crapping cattle. Nowhere in this worked-over landscape to rest and read about the dignity of labour. How ironic. The Mars bar gibes at her hip as she pedals. The little log of chocolate feels absurdly bulky. 'Must be my conscience.' Lily has promised herself not to eat chocolate until the evening – and then only one item. She has five days away on this cycling trip and she wants to get home, climb on the scales and see firm evidence of the ounces and pounds jettisoned along the Suffolk lanes.

dreedle-thwock-dreedle-thwock-dreedle-thwock

Oh the fucking effort of it all – why can't effort be effortless? The effort of it, and the still worse effort of not thinking about chocolate. Lovely runny, brown, amorous chocolate. Chocolate penetrating your belly with its warm, tingling sweetness. 'I can smell it,' she thinks, her nostrils flaring for air, 'I can smell the Mars bar.' At the very least she should wait until she's smeared cream cheese on Ryvita, picked the peel off her orange, slurped her shandy, but Lily isn't sure she's able. How can such pathetic little instances of self-control ever amount to anything? Would it even make it into the local paper? MIDDLE-AGED WOMAN ON CYCLING TOUR DENIES HERSELF MARS BAR FOR FOUR HOURS. No. Not even in East Anglia, in the bulbous seventies, is there such little news.

She finds the traffic scary as it ploughs a windy tunnel past her labouring flanks. With a little extra energy this ride would go that much faster. It's nearly one already. She left Dunwich at eight-thirty; surely the intervening hours must have chomped away some of her hips? She wishes. She yearns. Most middle-aged women, it occurs to her, must consider taking up cycling once they've reached the menopause – for obvious reasons. Why are there *always* dead leaves in the roadway regardless of the season? When things die they should rot. Can I make it to Snape at all? Why bother? To see some pansy sing Nazi love songs? I think not. Still the forestry plantation to one side, the fields full of cow poo to the other. Oh fuck it! I *must* stop! I *must* have chocolate!

And so she does – the nudnik. Belly-kvetched into being stationary. As she brakes, slows, and her Daks-sneakered undercarriage comes down to absorb the impact, another motorised peasant-wagon peals past. Shaken, she miscalculates, barks shin on pedal and doesn't so much collapse as retract into herself – an uncomfortable huddle of steel, rubber, nylon, wool and fat. Tears before snack time. Lily hauls the bike with its stupidly bulky panniers off the road and into a gateway leading to the coniferous wood. She claws her comestibles out and, cradling them like nutritious babies in her woolly arms, she clumsily negotiates the five-barred gate. She can feel a trickle of blood lazily snaking beneath her slacks, down her shin, into her sock. Something to pick at later.

By a tree upon which a sibilantly bloodthirsty notice – 'TRESSPASSERS WILL BE SHOT' – has been nailed, she makes camp, dumping her mishmash, claiming her steak. And when she eases herself down to the damp ground of twig and leaf mould, she smells the moribundity of the wood rather than its life force. And she cries, 'Do I belong here?' Questioning the pine-stale air. And the answer comes back not in an echo – but in a sodden silence: no, not here. Not anywhere.

She fumbles the Mars bar out from her pocket and tears the wrapping off within the compass of the same movement, so that she can bring it directly to her misshapen mouth. Mmm . . . salty. Her upper plate sucks apart from her gum as she works the chewy goo around, feeling the loving trickle down her loveless and unloved throat. 'I might as well die here,' she ruminates, vilely aware of the fact that nothing can ever change, 'and now.'

Her wish is granted. A curtain of black rain is drawn through the darkling wood. The stuttering burr of a tractor in a far-off field is suddenly stilled, as are all the lowings, tweetings and bucolic burblings. Chill invests everything from within. It's a total eclipse of reality itself, because a well-formed arm a hundred feet long tears through the curtain of rain and shucks it to one side. Four giants loom there, three hundred feet high. A giant in blue, a giant in white, a giant in red. And a scrawny giant in black.

'Push!' That's how they adjured you. 'Push!' And they're doing it now. Doing it again. Pushing me up the corridor. Pushing me in here. Pushing in syringes. Being generally pushy. I wonder if this time I'll shit and give birth simultaneously? With Natasha it was a welter of shit and blood and fluid. Then they stitched me up like a fucking turkey. So embarrassing – they made me feel so embarrassed. Actually, both times I gave birth here, there was this oh-so-English attitude of prurience combined with prudery, then horribly diluted until it was a thin gruel of disapproval. It was as bad in the States in the late forties when I had Dave Junior. I can only hope it's finally changed now; that if fucking feminism has won us anything at all, it's a right to our dignity in labour and our joy in birth. No matter how difficult it is. How shitty.

'After yer dead, Lil', there'll be time, yeh-hey?' It's the aboriginal man again. He props his flat-iron butt on the bed and chats away unconcernedly. Not for him the overworked anxiety of the doctors, midwives and relatives. I'm not dying, though – I'm giving birth. 'Whatever. Hey – y'know I'll tek y'over, girl, yeh-hey?' Over where? 'The Styx, yeh? The river. See, yer karkin' it, Lily – b'lieve me, girl. Goin' to godzone. Like I say – but you gotta chance to get in the ungud, hey-yeh? T'git away from the go-round, y'know?' I haven't the faintest idea what you're talking about, but that being said, you're an enjoyable companion. 'Yuwai – we gonna be mates allrighty, Lily. Big-time, yeh-hey.' The contractions are getting closer together . . . will you hold my hand? What should I call you? 'Phar Lap Jones – you call me Phar Lap.' It's an unusual name. 'Racehorse. Big winner for me when I was a lad, y'know. It's a nickname – not my real one.'

He takes my leathery talon in his matt hand. He's smoking a hand-rolled cigarette. Astonishing, on a hospital ward in this day and age. The smoke flows up over his more than full lips and gathers in his mirror-backed sockets, boiling like mist in a mountain defile, or the marcelled hair of my senior class, Long Island, 1939. I concede – it's a late arrival, this child called Death. Who would've thought – given the long months of painful flushes, sweats and bellyaches – that I still had it in me? 'Y'don't, girl. Lily, listen . . . Y'dyin'. Me – this,' he waves the cigarette, 'not here. None of it. Not the ward. Not the hospital. Not cancer. Not death. Not here . . .'

Push! Push! Push! The high, distempered walls of the hospital room belly out then squeeze in, as if they were the womb and I the baby. Push. The stupid fucking baby. First one tiny foot emerges – all yellow with corns, bruised with bunions – then a second. A breech birth – no wonder it's so fucking painful, it's pedalling its way into the world. Then a thick hairball at the join of the yellow thighs, then a belly slack with births of its own. Then hacked-about dugs, then puny wattled arms – and finally, a brave little keel to keep it stable in the watery world. A brave keel and a full head of blonde hair. There it is, toothless, wizened on the bed, not arriving gently with that 30% cotton nightie all rucked up about its neck. How can a corpse sweat so?

'Yer not a corpse.'

'I'm sorry?' So fucking English, that – I don't like the person I've become.

'Yer not a corpse – yer dyin'.' I feel a sarcastic rejoinder swell in my mouth, but bite it back down – with my own teeth. Phar Lap is sitting at the end of the bed, still smoking, but I'm upright and I have my own teeth. My own teeth and my own fat, back again. Just as the crab has finally snipped it all away, so some other beast has pitched up and slapped it on to me again – like clay. I can also smell Phar Lap's cigarette – and Phar Lap himself. The aboriginal man is feral and meaty, sanguinely scented. The whole confused rondo of death – the blue rhapsody, the gurgled fight, the crashing breakers of pain and nausea and fear – has abated. The others have gone and there's only us, a woman in late middle age, not that well preserved, but still with her own teeth; and a middle-aged aboriginal man wearing black Levis, a plaid shirt and a white Stetson.

There's an Anglepoise, the white, conical shade bent back to the wall, so that it spews out yellow light in a large circle. Through the open door I can see the ward is bathed with the dim, jaundiced light of nighttime institutions. Through the window I can see the orange-haloed streetlights. In the near distance I can hear the giant cutlery-drawer crash of lorries slamming down Gower Street. On the high locker by the bed is a digital clock. One of my daughters must have dutifully brought it from Bartholomew Road, so that its red eyes might blink the hour of my death: 3.27 a.m. I can smell Dettol.

'We've a few minutes, yeh-hey?'

'What's that?'

'We have a few minutes – see?'

'For what?'

'Like I was sayin' – for you to see the Clear Light.'

'The clear light?'

'That's right – the Clear Light. Wasn't it you who once wrote, "The attachment to reality is horrible and possible"?'

'That's bizarre – I must've written that in a letter years ago. How d'jew know?'

'1961. Listen,' and he hunkers forward, 'everything adds up here, you don't have teeth any more, you don't have fat, and aboriginal men don't hang out in London hospital wards, in the middle of the night, smoking – geddit?'

While Phar Lap has done me the great service of making this speech in as near to Standard English as he can achieve – he's still not getting through to me. 'What're you saying?'

'None of this is real, Lily. None of Lily is real. None of it ever has been. Dump your Lilyness now, girl. It doesn't suit you. Dump it or go round in it again like a set of old clothes. Sell it on again. Sell it out again. You geddit?'

'So you – you're not real?'

'Yer fuckin' teeth woman, think about it – yer fuckin' teeth!' Back comes the aggressive Strine. He grinds his roll-up out on the lino, stands. He's wearing elastic-sided boots. Riding boots. They're all dusty. I'm doing my best to think about nothing – but I'm thinking about my teeth. I'm thinking of all the uses I could put them to, how they can chomp and grind and chew and crunch lovely food. And I'm thinking about my flesh – how it can be held and stroked and palped and needed. And Phar Lap says, quite out of the blue, 'Fuck it, girl – too late.'

Dead

'I plan to retire around five years after I die.'
Warren Buffet

Chapter Seven

The corpse on the bed is childishly small. On that point, at least, it transpires everyone was right. The sight of my body after death moves me to self-pity. Poor little me. Poor little old me. Poor little old dead me. There was a final 'Hereugher – '. A breath left unfinished – like a drink too many. Then the last quiver of the pallid, caved-in cheeks. Then nothing. The digital clock blinks 3.28 a.m. and it's over. My life is over. This has to be the major breakthrough in cancer treatment we've all been waiting for, for so very long. Now they're no longer needed they come, if not exactly running, at any rate briskly to the scene. The junky daughter itching and scratching in her dirty daywear, the straight daughter businesslike in showy pyjamas and a presentation dressing gown. She didn't fucking bother to bring one in for me, now did she?

It was the efficient sister, the brunette, who alerted them. She has the air of a major-domo – she's officiating at this burlesque death scene. I'm surprised to see her lean down and put her ear to the slack pocket that was once my mouth. Is she checking for breath, or words? She straightens up. 'Yes, your mother appears to have passed on.'

'Oh,' Charlotte replies. She's shocked certainly – for this is an indifferent 'oh', an 'oh' someone might come up with in response to the news that a cup of tea had been made for them. Shock is the body's way of rendering profound experiences temporarily prosaic. Shock is a badly constructed narrative. News of tea that's been made is followed, in a contrived fashion, by the pretext for drinking it.

'I've paged Dr Bowen – she's on call.'

'Oh – right.' And they wait, visibly swaying – all three of them – from heels to balls and back again. There's no small talk to be made about this admittedly large situation. I suppose I could've hoped for some hysteria – if not from sensible daughter, at least from over-emotional junky daughter. But clearly – she's fixed. She always scratches when she's fixed – and then everything is just peachy. Serrated nails paring peachy skin.

Bowen, a sad-faced lesbian in her early forties, comes up sneakily in flats. The lapels of her white coat are heavy with madly protesting buttons – SANE, MIND, MENCAP – any old acronymic crap she can lay her quick-bitten fingers on. She's a pitiable thing. I recall her telling me that oncology wasn't her 'thing'. I should say so, she's too sluttish to make a good cancer doctor. For cancer you need the offices of a dashing blade – like Steel. Anyway, dear old Bowen – or Jane, as she would prefer to be called – has her way with me. She rummages around in my sad sack nightie, partially exposing my hacked-about dugs, then applies her stethoscope. Ho-hum, while you're dying they'll expend resources on the fanciest of technologies, but once you're dead all they do is put a rubber tube in their ear and listen – for nothing.

Bowen and the sister run through a checklist of vitally absent functions and the sister ticks them off – each with a flourish of brushed-steel Parker on clipboard. She then hands the list to Bowen, who signs it without any emphasis, muttering me 'dead at 3.47 a.m.'. Time flies when you're disembodied. 'What happens now?' Natty asks. She's still in the prosaic phase of shock, the enquiry seemingly about plans for a group outing – although this is belied by the goo that spews from her nose. She may be stoned on heroin, but she's withdrawing from her Mumu.

'Your mother's body will remain here for tonight, but

obviously you'll need to engage an undertaker as soon as possible. Did your mother have any strong opinions about what she wanted?'

Both of my girls laugh at this, but it isn't a nervous titter of English embarrassment, it's a dirty chuckle of Jewish cynicism, one that should rightfully be accompanied by a derisive reiteration: 'Did my mother have any strong opinions?' Like, is Paris a city, you shmuck? But they don't follow through – neither of them has the necessary gall. 'No, no,' Charlie answers, 'she was very much an atheist, and didn't want any fuss – '

'Yeah,' Natasha butts in, 'she said we should just burn her and dump her in a skip . . ,'

Strange to relate, while my daughters are actually talking, giving the first speeches of any kind to be uttered on my behalf since my demise, I find myself moving, drifting away, strolling off. I can still hear the conversation under way behind me, but it's quite irrelevant. It's like snatches of surrealism – '-ime for', '-eared we would', '-entional mistake' – overheard as you wend your way through a crowded airport departure lounge. I've strolled outside the death chamber and see that it's no more than a glassed-in cubicle, partitioned off from the rest of the ward. Death on national insurance, well, it had to be better than death on the instalment plan. American death.

I'm gliding along the cool, stone floor of the ward, peering at the faces smeared on the pillows, when the hem of my nightie billows, and there's the clattering of stone hitting stone. I squint down and there, pirouetting between my knees, is a tiny grey manikin. It's no more than a couple of inches high and has the aspect of a foetus, but a foetus of around twenty years of age. Curious, I bend down to examine the creature. Its tiny mouth opens and closes, and hunkering right down I can hear that it's singing: ' 'Cos I lu-urve yoo! / I just like the things yoo-doo / Wo-on't yooo-doo-the-things-yoo-doo / Nya-nya-nya-nya-nya-nya-nyaaa! / Nya-nya-nya-nya-nya-nya-nyaaa!' I'm not exactly shocked – that would be prosaic – more amazed. This amazement must be a dam in the present, because banking up behind it I sense an inundation of awe about what's transpired. I'm thinking. I'm me. I'm dead.

The grey manikin has twinkly black eyes. It's a good dancer. It keeps right on with the nonsensical ditty, shimmying between my ankles. What the hell can it be? 'See you here, girl. This is a lithopedion, little dead fossil baby of yours, yeh-hey!?' It's Phar Lap, the aboriginal man who hung out with me while I died. I must say that during the endgame there he began to irritate me considerably. I couldn't altogether get where he was coming from – but needless to say it sounded religiose.

'How would I know,' I snap.

But Phar Lap pays this no mind, he simply squats down himself and gives the manikin a pat on its wrinkled brow with the very tip of his little finger. 'Could be much worse y'know, girl,' says Phar Lap Jones. 'Much worse than the little feller. You never have no abortions, no?'

'No.'

'Stillbirths?'

'No.'

' 'Cos they snag round yer head some – to begin with, hey-yeh?'

'What d'jew mean?'

'Dead foetuses, newborn babies, whatever. With mothers who have kids, y'know, and they're young then – little, right. Well, when that woman dies they come back – see? But see, hey, if they're real small they're still attached to the woman, danglin' off her, yeh-hey? Older kiddies – they don't stick with you as much, grown-up kids not at all.'

'Like life?'

'No, not like life . . .' He pauses, allowing some nurses to pass by. 'In life, death drive you 'part, yeh-hey? Now it drag you all t'gether. I wonder which you'll like more. Anyway, you had a dead child, right?'

How typical of life – you have to fucking *die* in order for anyone to discuss what's really bothering you. He's like a reversed mushroom – this Phar Lap Jones character – with his white hat and black stem. Still, his quiet insistence is beguiling. We link arms without touching and, guiding me as if I were a horse, with dips of his Stetson's brim and cheek-sucking clicks, he leads me towards the stairs. Down we glide, following the dirty whorl of the rotten old Royal Ear, talking the while of David Junior.

The lack of touch I understand – no pain, no touch. The obliviousness of the staff we pass I get too – no touch, no pain, no pain-murderers, stalking in the night. This consciousness after death – well, clearly I made a colossal booboo. That painful, embarrassing world through which I dragged myself, smiling thickly, throwing the occasional tantrum, beset by irrational fears – that was purgatory. And this? This must be heaven.

Down past the posters advertising upcoming events in the worlds of pregnancy, lunacy, dental caries and drug addiction. Across empty seating areas where water-coolers gurgle indulgently. Then down past the painful paintings executed by the maimed, and the insipid, pastel watercolours of the whole. Finally, past the somnolent security guard, nodded out over his newspaper, and into the street. I look down to see what's become of the lithopedion, but it keeps up well enough, grabbing the hem of my nightie and swinging itself from step to step. Tiny Tarzan.

Until we hit the street when, mysteriously, I find that the

nightie has gone with the night, and I'm standing in the roadway naked and wattled, with the dawn seeping in. 'Oi!' I hail Phar Lap who's rolling a cigarette one-handed. 'What's all this, then?' All this is all this wobbling cellulite, all these spongy pounds the crab had snipped away. All this *fat*. I didn't figure on being pudgy after death. Plump in the nether world. Rotund among the shades.

'You can't take it with you, girl.'

'Not the nightie – this.' I make fat shapes with my hands to cup what's implied.

'Oh, yeh-hey! That you get to keep. Heh! Not so subtle a subtle body, yeh-hey?'

This I don't get – but I keep on at him. 'I can't go anywhere looking like this' – absurd, I have done for years, we're all naked underneath our clothes. 'Anyway – where *are* we going?'

'Dulston.' It sounds like.

'Dalston?'

'No, *Dul*ston.'

Dulston, eh, and I thought I knew most of London's suburbs by name – even the utterly samey inconsequential ones. 'What're we going there for?'

'Thass where yer gonna stay, Lily girl. Thass where yer new unit is. No more gabbin' now – here's the cab.' A minicab pulls up to the kerb. It's a sloppy, medium-old, four-door saloon. A Ford Granada or something like that. When I was a young woman I took an interest in cars. Cars like the eight-cylinder Buick I had in the late forties, which would pull up a one-in-eight hill at sixty in third. Big cars like spunky men lying underneath me – controlled by my feet, my calves, my thighs, my hands. The men grew older and less powerful. The cars smaller. I gave up on both kinds of transport.

The driver of this jalopy is a Greek Cypriot. This I can tell from the iconostasis that is the dashboard. Tiny, gilt-framed pictures of a variety of saints, Madonnas and patriarchs, all looped together in a tangle of Christmas-tree lights and rosaries. On the back shelf of the car lies one of those nodding dogs, a black one with three yea-saying heads. The Cypriot has a greasy tonsure, a brown label of skin stuck down in thinning hair. He's grinning, and rinky-dink bouzouki music is plinking away. All the seats in the car have those knobbly mats strapped on to them, as if this were orthopaedic transport for back-achers; the kind of people who say 'My back's killing me' as if it were fucking cancer.

Phar Lap folds his length into the passenger seat and I take the rear, together with the lithopedion, which executes a neat forward flip from the sidewalk into the seat-well. Not I, though, I have to climb up into the car the way that fat people do, sideways, one leg provisionally advanced. For us fat, each footstep is an act of testing the world's surface, trying to find out who'll give way first.

No destination is requested, yet the Cypriot flicks into drive and we pull away smoothly up Huntley Street. But it's not until we're turning out of Grafton Way into Tottenham Court Road that I begin to appreciate how comfy this car is, how it glides along – more like some flying machine than an urban potholer.

But then it comes to me, I've forgotten that . . . 'I can't feel anything,' I exclaim to Phar Lap, whose face cannot be seen in the rear-view mirror. The cabbie snaps off the tape machine.

'Yer not gonna,' growls my mentor.

'I mean . . . it's strange . . . but I can feel the insides of me . . . the disposition of my parts . . . And I can *see* the way my body fits into this seat, but it's as if I'm *resting* on the surface, not pressing into it.'

'Yairs.'

'What?'

'Yeh, thass right, Lily-girl. You ain't got no physical body no more now, kiddo, jus' this like *subtle* one, yeh-hey? This subtle one. It can't reflect light. It can't feel pain or pleasure. It don't sleep or smell. It don't need tucker. It don't need grog. It don't need this one.' He makes a schoolboy's obscene gesture with an eye and a hook of fingers. 'It don't need no-thing.'

I think for a moment before coming back at him. 'But no pain, right?'

'Thass it, girl – no pain. Not for now, leastways.'

So, all have won – and all shall have prizes. My prize being the smashed crab, its pincers dislocated and laid alongside the white and brown mush of its flesh. No pain. It looks like an excellent deal to me. It *feels* like a great deal of numbness, like a whole body-shot of super-Novocaine, and an epidural for all eternity. I love it.

The cab pivots through ninety degrees under the bland graticule of the Euston Tower and glides on to the Euston Road, where we're confronted by the unwelcoming Wellcome Institute. How many fucking times have I laboured along here on the way to work. A fat, old, bourgeois bag lady, weighted down by a Barnes & Noble book bag full of second-hand culture and wicked, carbohydrate snacks. The gritty city air gusting up my dress, blowing shrapnel in my eyes. My dentures clenched with the artificiality of my own efforts.

Dentures? Dreaming of teeth. Dreaming of teeth again. I have my own teeth back – that much I *can* feel. My own filled, bridged and promiscuously uneven choppers. Dunce-prize cuspids – hardly worth dying for. They should never have taken them out in the first place, but hell, they used to do that before they put fluoride in the water. They'd rip your fangs out without so much as a by-your-leave. Parents used to give their halitosis-haloed kids fucking *dentures* for their twenty-first birthday. The keys to the door leading away from pyorrhea. Jews especially – as if we were anticipating an evil demand for rotten enamel to build another foul shower-surround. So, then I had no teeth and a big appetite. Now I have teeth and no requirement for them. *Quelle blague.*

'What y'thinkin' 'bout, girl?' Phar Lap swivels to show me his yellow eyeballs, his yellow teeth. Aboriginals – unlike African blacks – are entirely matt, there's nothing oleaginous about their skin at all. No sallowness either. Just matt black. They're definitely the ethnic minority the eighties have been crying out for.

'You.'

'What 'bout me, hey?'

'What're you *for*?'

'Like I say, Lily. Like I tell you back in that place – I'm yer death guide, girl.'

'So – guide me. Where the hell are we going?'

'Do you know where you're going to?/ Do you like the things that life is show-ing yoooooo? / Do you know!' This is from the lithopedion, who perches on the very edge of the back seat, actually managing to *swing* its calcified little legs. I shall have to have a serious word with it about this behaviour when we arrive.

'Like I say, girl – we're goin' to Dulston; it's a 'burb like any other, yeh-hey?'

'And where is Dulston?' The minicab has nosed on to Pentonville Road. 'I mean, we appear to be heading in the direction of Dalston.'

'Yairs, well. It's right alongside of it, y'know. It's like a skinny district, yeh? One minute yer on the Kingsland Road, the next yer turnin' into Dalston Lane. If yer not quick you can miss Dulston.'

'So, it's between Islington to the west and Dalston to the east?'

'Thass right.'

'And what's to the south?'

'Dalston again.'

'And the north?'

'Stoke Newington.'

'That doesn't make any sense. There isn't anything *between* these parts of London. Not unless Dulston is a made-up estate agents' kind of place.'

'Could be that. Could be y'don't know London quite as well as you think.'

'I'm sorry – and how fucking well d'jew know it, then?'

Phar Lap waits a while before answering. Long enough for us to turn into Barnsbury Road and pass the Metropolitan Cab Office. Long enough for me to conclude that this isn't the way I'd go to Dalston if I were driving. I'd head north and go over the Archway – detouring via Jack Harmsworth's comfy, musty flat, at the top of the priests' house off Hornsey Lane. He'd still be sleeping off last night's gin when I tiptoed in. I'd have to prise the bottle from his blue hands. Still, I know he'd be glad to see me and we could have a cup of coffee together. Or I'd head south from here, cut through Covent Garden and pass by Emma's chichi flat off Bow Street. I've never been by her place this early – I bet she sleeps clutching one of those teddies she collects, like a diminutive furry lover.

What am I thinking of? Neither of these routes to Dalston – or Dulston – is anything like direct. Anyway, I haven't even driven the last couple of years. I gave the old runabout to Natasha, who, predictably, ran it into the ground. Also, I never call unexpectedly on these people. Not at this hour – not ever. It isn't, as the prissy English would say, the *done thing*.

'I know London well enough. Y'know, Lily, I'm a traditional feller, yeh-hey? I still sing the songs. So, when I came here for the bicentennial, yeh?'

'The Australian bicentennial?'

'Yairs. Mebbe. Anyway, when I came here for the bicentennial – on account of someone needing to point out what
wholesale fuckin' gammin it was – I planted my kayan right
down on the carpet, in the terminal building at Heathrow,
gave me bullroarer a swing, an' dropped dead, hey? Dropped
fuckin' dead. Heart attack.'

'So that was when?'

'January, thereabouts.'

'January? You've only been in London since January?'

'Thass right.'

'And you presume to tell me the way around town?'

'Like I say, Lily, I'm a bit of a traditional feller. So I had to
find out what the city songs were, y'know – '

'So how can you tell me you're lo-one-ly, and say for you
that the sun don't shine? / Let me take you by the hand and
lead you through the streets of London . . .' the lithopedion
croons, but we pay it no mind.

'Had to go walkabout the place. Find out what makes it
tick, yeh-hey?'

'Are you dead?' I lean forward and ask the Cypriot cabbie. I
was going to tell him where to turn off the Liverpool Road,
but I suspect my directions are of little use to him either.

'Me – four years,' the man replies, smiting his breast with a
closed fist, as if proud of an achievement. 'And the name's
Costas – if youse don't mind.'

'You must . . . You must . . .' – I can't believe I'm saying
anything quite this trite, but still it trickles out – '. . . miss
them a lot?' In among the empty-eyed halo-heads on the dash
are snapshots of curly-haired kiddies smiling out of lace,
taffeta and other ruffs.

'Not rrrreally,' he rolls out a devilish *r*, 'I see more of them
now I'm dead than I did when I was alive.'

'And . . . and they can see you?'

'No-no – I'm not about to do this to them – they're little childrens. I wouldn't want to scare them none. Now – theirs mothers, that's not same thing.'

I want to pursue this subject a little more but Costas has to execute a tricky manoeuvre which I myself know only too well: the slide down the side of the station, the whip round Highbury Corner and on to St Paul's Road. By the time we're halted again at the junction of Essex Road I haven't exactly lost interest, but I've collapsed into a state which – *faute de mieux* – I can only call a colourless stupidity of indifference. I've always thought London was this, anyway – a colourless stupidity of indifference. Even in this lemon dawn of late spring, with the sunlight turning everything Janus-faced with darkness and light, there's still no relief. The city is an encrustation upon a scab, cigarette ash flicked on to cigar ash. Terrace upon terrace of knock-kneed, terminally warped Victorian townhouses, with shitty council blocks sticking them apart. The shopping parades aren't festive enough to warrant the moniker, they're parodies of commerce, every third window boarded up and plastered with flyposters for pop and politics. Very occasionally a triangle, or a quadrangle, or a trapezoid of closed-off space insinuates itself between the brick bluffs, the dirty turf marked out for the lost game of life, with no-goal posts in its pissy corners.

Five a.m., and the city is rolling over in its clay riverbed and feeling the gravel of sweaty repose. Five a.m., and the human collectivity is rubbing the gunge of urbanity from its filmy eyes, farting the gas of lack-of-utility, and yawning asthmatically as it struggles to inhale another day. Planeloads of sleepy dust are touching down at Heathrow. Terminal morning. Is it my imagination, or is this road even more saggy and daggy than usual? True, it's a journey I've only ever done for workaday purposes, or to undertake merciless errands. Going to squats to pick up my junky daughter, prise her loose from the carpets of 'friends'. Or to discharge her from dying in hospitals, when she's anaesthetised herself against the intolerable pain of her bourgeois affluence.

Even so, I know the Balls Pond Road – who doesn't? And this isn't it. This is some further division of the polarised city – with its poor to the east, its rich to the west. The terraces are more warped – totally cockeyed, with their front steps collapsing, their roof tiles flaking like hard scalp. The little council estates seem even littler, their red-bricked walkways but pill-box slits from which the inhabitants might indifferently regard – should they even be able to – the colourless stupidity of the city all around. And the shops – is it my imagination, or are they more run-down than ever, offering fewer goods, with hardly any cards taped in their filmy windows, offering utterly useless services?

Phar Lap Jones sits with sharp knees against the dashboard, sharp shoulders against the seat, the crown of his white Stetson floating along the black crown of the road. He turns from time to time, adjusts his sunglasses, peers at me with world-weary amity. Costas drives with surprising verve for a man who's been dead since the early eighties, swerving the car this way and that, grabbing at the shift and banging his corpulence forward on to the pedals, then back on to the knobbly seat. The bundle of votive knick-knacks dangling from the rear-view mirror jangles. 'How can he drive,' I interrogate Phar Lap, 'when he's immaterial – or isn't his body as subtle as mine?'

'Yeh-hey. Well, yer gettin' curious, girl – an' y'know, more'll be revealed. You didn't learn life in one day – death won't be any different.'

Not only is Costas driving with considerable ferocity, but there are other vehicles doing just the same – making a getaway into the Islington panhandle. Apart from the occasional doodling milk-float, or heavy lorry stomping through, these dawn racers have the roads to themselves. From what I can see they're all driven by Costas's brethren, and they all have nodding Cerberuses on their back shelves, and they all carry recently expired passengers. Fords full of infarctions, Toyota-loads of tachycardia, Vauxhalls freighted with valvulitis. I guess they aren't playing chicken with one another – because they've nothing to be afraid of. A Datsun of such raddled antiquity that its bodywork is entirely oxidised orange cuts in front of us by inches as we slow for a light. But Costas, instead of beeping or berating, merely laughs, 'There's Spiro – he's frisky this morning!' Then pulls alongside. The Datsun also has bead covers on its seats and another Greek at the wheel. In the back sits a whey-faced man who clutches the driver's headrest. He's agonised, on shpilkes.

'You see that, girl?' says Phar Lap. 'Another one of the newly dead.'

'I gathered that, but where're they going?'

'Hey-yeh, girl – y'know there's only one destination in the final taxi – '

'Dulston?'

'Right.'

'And . . . and this is it?'

We've zoomed off the Balls Pond Road, zoomed down a one-way street, turned in front of an old Victorian pub – which looks like a waterworks and is called The Waterworks – and are now standing at a junction by a gas station. Its oil-stained forecourt is like a dirty diagram of the world. And my death guide replies, 'This is it.' He lifts one of a pair of big, black boomerangs, which he has tucked between his seat and the door, and deftly slices the air. 'There's the cafe. All the drivers gonna stop, yeh-heh? Gotta get some tucker in – s'been a long long night for us, hey-yeh?'

The cafe is underneath one of the arches of a suburban branch line. It's a Nissen-hut-shaped enclosure full – I assume – of steam and smell. But all I can see from the outside are whited-out windows, with star shapes of card taped on to them – menu items, presumably. Costas slews the car to a halt on an apron of tarmac, alongside twenty or so similar vehicles – rusting Fords, Vauxhalls, Toyotas and Mitsubishis. All of them have wonky aerials stuck on their trunks, earthed by scraps of old plastic bag. Across the bellying brickwork, which weeps mortar and bird shit, snakes the graffito 'GEORGE DAVIS WAS GUILTY – AND NOW HE'S DEAD'. We clamber out and my calcified foetus comes with, hanging on to my foot. I'm not sure which aggravates me more – the lithopedion or my own bare-assed nudity. 'Jesus, Phar Lap,' I say, 'I can't go in there like this!'

Costas waddles round to where we stand. He's even fatter than I am – and no one's ever counselled him against the optical effects of horizontal-striped shirts. He's so hairy he has noselocks. He's one of those ugly people who used to make me feel happy to be alive. He unpops the trunk and there amidst oily clutter is a sad piece of individual Samsonite, identical to the case Charlie must've packed for me to go to the Royal Ear – but this one is brand-new. I open it. Inside are big, soft, old woman's panties, ditto vest, ditto tented dress ('Not the wigwam, Mumu!' Natty silkily whines in my inner ear), ditto pasty shoes for minced feet swollen by half a century of standing still. All of the pathetic kit for this – my biggest adventure – is brand-new. All of it – and that makes it all still sadder. I pull the dress off its midget hanger, decant the shoes from their box, rip underwear and tights from cellophane. I dress without chagrin under the dark eyes of the dead men.

Costas leads the way into the Turkish baths of a cafe. Gushes of steam from an urn toiling on the Formica counter are doing mighty but insubstantial battle with the kraken tentacles of smoke from the fifty-odd fuming fags stuck in fifty-odd fuming faces. The tables are packed tight, twenty playing-card shapes laid out for a game of impatience. At each sits a trio as mismatched as Phar Lap, Costas and I. The newly dead are easy to spot – we all look simultaneously bemused and relieved. Relieved from the pain – whether it's the hammer blow of violent extinction, or the quick-quick-slow scuttling crab, or the lightning lobe strike – and bemused by the outrageous dullness of the afterlife itself. The Charon-substitutes are Greek Cypriots to a man. They're all paunch and trouser wrinkle, they make burning points with their cigarettes and chatter loudly. They sit back in their chairs, or forward, or ride them back to front, the way car jockeys habitually do when out of the saddle.

I whisper to Phar Lap, 'Why're all the final taxi drivers Greek Cypriots?'

'Yeh-hey. Well – s'matter of opportunity, y'know. Big community of these fellers all round Dulston – in Dalston, Homerton, Hoxton, Clapton, Hackney, too – they know the territory, see? So they get the pick-ups. Still, it changes – used t'be all the drivers were proper Cockney cabbies, but last ten years gone death's bin kinda deregulated. Yeh-hey?'

I trail after him to where there's a vacant table. Our trio – black face, brown face, sallow face – sit down with the red, brown and yellow sauce bottles. Yup, I can cope with the hacks, but the assembled death guides are much harder to come to terms with. These guys are all fucking weirdos. There are Amerindians with lip plugs the size of their own breakfast plates; saffron-robed Buddhist monks; Samoyed shamans in trimmed, reindeer-hide robes; Korean Taoists in shiny, black origami hats; Wolof witch doctors wearing ebony masks; Dayak cargo cultists sporting wickerwork beanies; and several ringers for Baron Samedi, all togged up in voodoo suits. 'What community do *they* belong to?' I say. 'What unites these guys? Nothing save for worshipping the fucking fairies in lieu of the mighty dollar.'

'Yeh-hey,' Phar Lap predictably tics. 'Fair dinkum, Lily m'girl. All us mob here – we're mostly what're called traditional peoples, yeh-hey? Seems like you Westerners can't get no grasp on the death stuff, on the ungud, on no-thing.'Less you have one of us to guide you. See – seems like when you b'lieve in nothing you gotta have guides who b'lieve in the never-never, see?'

'Erm . . . I suppose so.'

'No you don't. Yer jus' sayin' it, Lily-girl. But anyway this ain't no settin' face to face with the Clear Light. Plenny of time for that. Now – let's eat. What'll y'have?' He points a big black boomerang at the star-shaped bits of cardboard Sellotaped to the window. These announce the awful permutations of egg (poached, fried, scrambled to fuck), sausage, bacon, beans, black pudding, white pudding, fruit pudding, slice, two slices, beans and tomatoes. One is headed 'Full English', another 'Full Irish' and a third 'Full Dead'.

When I first came to London in the late fifties the very words 'full English' gave me heartburn. Just saying them left a sticky film on the roof of my mouth. Mindjew, in those days – with rationing still within gut feeling – the cafe breakfast was more commonly 'tea and two slices'. Two slices of thin white bread, lifeless flour slunks smeared with marge. Slices of no kind of life at all. Truth to tell, the English *really* loved rationing. It was the only thing that prevented them from swelling up and fucking exploding – given the lashings of carbohydrate they were wont to eat. Unnaturally, in time I too became inured – even accustomed – to the messy business of coating the walls of my stomach with a thick layer of grease.

Like a cross-Channel swimmer I'd dive into the choppy, inland sea of my neuroses, fully, greedily, daubed.

Still, the past is another pantry. 'Would you like breakfast in America?!' the lithopedion warbles. I'd forgotten it – but here it is, squatting on the table, in between the sauce bottles.

Phar Lap ignores it. 'Jeezus, Lily – what'll y'have, girl?'

'What d'jew recommend?'

'I'd go for the full dead – '

'Youse *are* going for the full dead,' Costas interjects, 'youse always do.' And the cabbie lights a Benson & Hedges, blows blue smoke in my face.

'Full dead it is, then,' I murmur, and Phar Lap sticks up three fingers, a signal acknowledged by the barrel-chested character tending the urn, who shouts back, 'Three full dead – being exhumed!' But I ignore this, because I'm on the verge of castigating Costas for his insensitive puffing, into the face of a woman who's died of cancer only a few hours ago, when it hits me that the smoke doesn't sting or irritate – it doesn't even *smell* at all.

Nothing smells any more. I sniff the polluted air of the cafe with flared nostrils – but there's no odour. None. No grease, no egg, no condemned meat – no whiff, no pong, no no-thing.

'Phar Lap,' I say, 'I can't smell.'

'Whozzat, Lily-girl – yeh-hey?'

'I can't smell.'

'No, you can't – nor will you. Yer dead, girl. Like I say – you've a subtle body now. It don't make no reflection. It don't get tired. It don't need sustenance of any kind, no tucker, no rooting, no nothing – see. So, no smell – whyd'you need to smell, girl, see? Yeh-hey?'

'But the breakfast – why do I need a full dead breakfast? And anyway – what do I do with the thing?'

'You'll see.'

'Yeah – youse'll see,' Costas puts in, jabbing the air with his pill, 'thass all youse'll do now lady – see. Being dead is all about seeing and *listening*.'

And I do see – *really* I do. I see the full dead breakfasts approaching, rolled out by the barrel-chested Cockney man, one plate in each hand, the third balanced on his right wrist and a plastic bucket dangling from the left one. I see that all the other tables have a bucket beneath them, and that all the death guides are chomping up their full dead breakfasts; giving them a thorough mashing, then regurgitating the mush into the buckets – not always with the greatest accuracy. The newly dead all look pretty green contemplating this gross-out – and I guess I must too. 'Ferchrissakes, Phar Lap, is this what you guys do instead of eating?'

'Yesh,' he says, spearing a sausage, shoving it in.

'But why – why bother?'

'Ritual, Lily-girl. Me – I only have breakfast when I bring someone in, but the others, hell, they've eternity to spend here in Dulston, so why not bloody eat – even if they can't swallow?'

'And smoking,' I turn to Costas, 'why d'jew bother with smoking?'

'Youse smoke one time, lady?'

'Smoke? Of course I fucking smoked – that's why I'm dead!'

'OK, OK – well, youse ever smoke in the dark?'

'Occasionally.'

'But not much – right?'

'No, I guess not.'

'Thass right – 'cos youse have to see it, right? See the smoke. Smoking's as much seeing as feeling, so why not smoke – youse want one?'

I want a B&H more than the full dead – which anyway is exactly the same as a full English – so I take one and Costas gives me a light. The smokes plays painless chords in the accordion of my diseased lungs. 'What's this place called, anyway?' I ask through my own ectoplasm.

'No p'ticular name,' Phar Lap replies, 'we just call it the cafe.' He wipes a glossy rime of egg from his matt top lip.

'Is that because it's the only one in Dulston?'

'No – it's just the one that's bin 'ere the longest, yeh-hey? Dulston is what you'd call a cystrict.'

'I'm sorry?'

'A cystrict – it swells up, then it leaks, then it swells up agin. It's a cystrict.'

'I don't follow.'

'Aw – y'll see – finished?'

'I never began,' I say, and stub my cig out in the egg's yellow bull's-eye. Full dead indeed.

'Fine – we're elsewhere, then.' Our trio rises, weaves between the tables to the counter where, to my surprise, Phar Lap pays.

'Why d'jew pay?' I ask him as we stroll back to the car. 'Surely you don't need money in this place?' He rounds on me. 'Why not! Place has gotta run like any other. Streets gotta be cleaned, teachers paid, sewers sluiced out – it's no bloody hotel, I'm tellin' ya, Lily, dead people are jus' like the livin'.'

'Except we can't feel, or smell, or love – '

'Or hurt! Or smell ourselves, or sweat, or any of that. There's an upside to this, y'know,' says Costas, who seems buoyed up by his gruelly repast, swinging himself into the front seat of the car with deathly vigour.

As we reverse into the roadway I press Phar Lap more. 'So, if that's where the newly dead and their guides eat breakfast, why are they serving ordinary meals?'

'Yeh-hey. Well, the other mob come in, y'know.'

'You mean the living?'

'Who else.'

'Oh, right – and you mean to say they aren't terrified by the sight of a load of weirdos spitting pap?'

Phar Lap cants round to deliver his next line. 'Lily – this is London, the whole bloody city is full of weirdos.'

'So, there are living people in Dulston as well?'

'No, I'm not sayin' that, it's just the place accommodates them if they turn up – like I say, it's a cystrict.'

A cystrict. I think I'm getting the point, for, as the minicab slops along the road I begin to appreciate the character of Dulston. Sure, the clumps of houses, flats, commercial premises, warehouses, used-car lots and light-industrial units are the same as in any of the adjoining districts, but Dulston is even more characterless than other inner North East London suburbs I've known. The overwhelming impression the place gives is of colourlessness, an indifference towards municipal airs and graces.

Dulston is one of those districts you're always finding yourself lost in, rather than arriving at. It's the place you wind up in when you overshoot your destination or take the wrong turn. It's the 'burb as displacement activity. Without even needing to question Phar Lap I realise that Dulston must be as big or as small as its beholders. It's a hidden pleat in the city's rolled-up sleeve; an invisible flare flapping in its trouser leg; a vent in the back of its jacket. Presumably, if the living stray into Dulston they see nothing of its true nature. For them it's merely a drive-by span of inattention, a glimpse of their own speeding car warped in a showroom window – before they find themselves traversing Hackney Marsh, or gawping at the Stamford Hill frummers, or heading into town. Dulston: you wouldn't know you were there at all – unless you were dead.

It's no revelation to me either when Costas angles the minicab into a road lined with late Victorian houses not dissimilar to the one I lived in in Kentish Town. No bolt from the blue when we halt outside one midway along. Costas and Phar Lap are out on the sidewalk by the time I've disencumbered myself. Peculiar, to move with the gait I used to have yet feel none of the discomfort of swollen feet, or riding underwear, or fatty ballast. The lithopedion comes too, chanting, 'This is the sound of the suburbs!' as I start for the stairs up to the front door. I'm gonna have to address this problem – but for now there's the new apartment to consider. 'Am I on the first floor?'

Phar Lap is encumbered with his wooden paraphernalia; bits of wood clack against the railings he's walking beside. What a kid. He calls me back. 'No, Lily-girl, you gotta go down, y'know. Basement, for now – mebbe go up a floor in time.'

So, down we go into the tawdry little area with its bins that look like rubbish. Phar Lap has a bunch of keys chained to the hip of his skinny jeans. He deals one out and unlocks the heavy door, with its architrave of London grunk, its lint-trailing draft-includer, its four whirl-of-distortion glass panes. He shoves it open into a vestibule which is dank to the point of musty saturation. I follow his flat ass; Costas comes behind with the sad Samsonite. The lithopedion warbles, 'Another suitcase in another hall / Where are you going to?' And we tour my new quarters.

The deformed corridor staggers along the left-hand side of the basement, and the first door off to the right limps into a mouldering bedroom. The bed's a shapeless pagoda of three double mattresses. There's a naked dressing table with a tip-tilting oval mirror; a freestanding thirties wardrobe, like a mahogany plinth; and three sash windows which aren't admitting much at all. There'd be dust motes in here if it wasn't so damp. The poor mites in the soggy old mattresses must be swimming for their fucking lives.

176

The next watery closet along is a sitting room. This comes complete with a Danish ancient armchair (x 2), some crappy lamps set on insignificant occasional tables, and a period gas fire piled with a miniature, flame-snagging ossuary. Somewhere Sweep could commit fucking suttee. Oh, and a bad-news bookcase with a *Good News Bible* in it, together with eight mildewed copies of the *Reader's Digest*. Perched on top of this is a tiny, old, black-and-white telly – like a bird box. But there's more – less more. With the lithopedion batting past my ankles, the party gains the end of the corridor and the fetid horrors of the kitchenette and bathroom. Shitty units clutter both pigeonholes. In New York – given the overall decrepitude of the basement – these would be rustling with roaches. But I know what'll be in these without needing to look: six laid-off wads which were once copies of the *Daily Worker*, seven mismatched Tupperware cups and saucers, five belly-up wood-lice. That's it.

The kitchenette has a gas stove and a fucking *meat safe*. Still, I shan't be cooking in it – so what the hell does that matter. No cooking – no reheating a saucepan of coffee even. And no ablutions in the bathroom, where a pre-shrunk shrink – Shtikelberg perhaps? – might sit alongside the dugout enamel couch on a cork-topped *stool* of unspeakable shoddiness. The very heads of the rivets that pinion the mirror to the seeping wall are rimmed with *shit*. The splashback is grouted with *effluent*. And throughout the entire apartment the walls are covered with bilious lozenges, or garish parallelograms, or clashing cones. Wallpapers of sixties vintage, which were designed by English hicks imagining a psychedelic experience, when succumbing to the effects upon their inner vision of two pints of fucking *Strongbow*. There's unfit carpeting too, the kind that looks like underlay. If I could squidge it with each footstep – I would.

It's unspeakably awful. I slump down on one of the chairs in the sitting room and my gaze wavers from Phar Lap to Costas to the lithopedion. This is the spring season in hell. Sitting room is right, I guess. Yaws used to call the ratty reclining space of the house on Crooked Usage the 'drawing room'. The pretentious shmuck. Still, 'living room' is *so* non-U, and totally out of the question now. 'Ferchrissakes Phar Lap this joint is *terrible*. If I weren't dead already this'd *kill me off* once and for all – you can't expect me to stay here!'

'Everyone's gotta start somewhere, Lily-girl, yeh-hey.' He's unfazed. 'An' anyways – what choice you got? You don't know bugger-all about Dulston. You need this unit – which is mine t'give, yeh-hey? You need me big-time. You need the meetings as well.'

'Meetings?'

'Yairs – meetings. Induction kinduva thing. They're held all the time, all over Dulston. You gotta go, Lily – else you won't know nothing about death, won't get to yabber with the rest, won't be able to function, yeh-hey?'

'Mores than thats,' Costas puts in, lowering his broad bottom into the other Danish ancient chair and sparking up another B&H, 'iss frightening, y'see. There's scary stuff you need to prepare y'self for.'

'Scary stuff?'

'Sure.'

'Scary stuff in a suburb called Dulston? A suburb full of dull cafes, tedious streets, boring buildings, and this – this *crappy* flat?'

'Yeah, even *in* this crappy flat.'

On cue, there's the most peculiar sound of murmuring and cackling from the bedroom. It's faint but clearly audible. Colourless voices intoning, 'Fat and old, fat and old, fat and old, fat and old . . .'

'What the hell's that?' I snap.

'Fat and old, fat and old, fat and old, fat and old,' the murmuring continues. Phar Lap and Costas have sly little smiles perched on their foreign faces.

'Well – aren't you gonna tell me?'

'Fat and old, fat and old, fat and old, fat and old – '

'Looks like you got the Fats, girl,' my death guide finally answers. 'Lotta people – specially women – do. Better go see 'em – they're like the lithopedion here.' He gestures at the lithopedion, who sits on the gas fire's brick surround, swinging its grey legs, singing, 'I'm just a poor boy / I get no sympathy / Caught in a landslide / No escape from reality . . .' in bizarre counterpoint to the 'Fat and old, fat and old, fat and old, fat and old' coming from next door.

I rise up and strike out for the door; Phar Lap and Costas follow me. In the bedroom there's a terrible sight. It's not scary – it's terrifying, yet oddly pathetic as well. There's a doppelgänger of myself, naked and shining, beneath the window. Another is trying to wedge itself under the bed, a third sits on the plush-covered mini-banquette in front of the dressing table. They're disgustingly obese versions of me, all wobble and jounce, huge dewlaps of belly dangling to their knees. They've no eyes, hair or nipples, and they've the slack mouths I saw last on my own corpse. They're the Pillsbury Dough girls of total dissolution. The one under the window has a hank of intestines wound round her forearms; which the one on the banquette is paying out, pulling off loop after loop of goo and feeding it through to the one under the bed. I can't see what this one's doing, but I can distinctly hear the 'shuk-shuk' of garden shears. They've got a beat going – these obese versions of me; and the 'Fat and old, fat and old, fat and old, fat and old' is a work song of sorts.

But when the gut gang see me they break off, huddle together, fall silent. Phar Lap and Costas nod their heads significantly. 'Fair dinkum,' says my death guide, 'they're Fats all right.'

The Fats whisper sour nothings to each other which sound like tummy rumbles: 'What'd he say? Who's he? There she is – '

'And what, exactly,' I assume a sang-froid worthy of the Aboriginal himself, '*are* the Fats?'

'Yairs . . . well . . . Y'did a fair bit of dieting while you were alive – yeh-hey?'

'Um . . . yes . . . I did.' Did I hell – I dieted for suety Olde Englande. I obsessed about my weight so much that I probably *put more on*, simply by thinking it into existence. Kerrist! Those endless doodled figures on the wallpaper, those thick supplements and insipid juices, those minutely calibrated snacks – trimming the edge of a lettuce leaf in an attempt to negate another calorie. Those fucking Weight Watchers meetings. Did I diet? My whole existence during the seventies and eighties was defined by the continual struggle not to eat, not to stuff the hated world in my face.

'See these Fats here, Lily, yeh-hey, they're your fat. The fat you shed during all that dieting' – a black mattock digs in the direction of the skein-holder – 'and the fat you put back on again.' And he gestures at the one who's taking up the slack.

'What about the one under the bed?'

'She's the fat you lost for ever – the stuff you dag-tailed.'

'Oh, so I did actually manage to lose some . . . overall.' Why should this give me any satisfaction now? Yet it does.

Phar Lap doesn't answer. He's extracting bits of paper, booklets and envelopes from a small straw bag he has slung over his shoulder. 'Listen, Lily, I got you a few bucks here

in me dillybag, sit-down money, see? And I've got you a
map of Dulston and a list of meetings. Come in the other
room.'

'But what about these . . .' I can't address them so casually,
the fat fiends with their Edgar Allan Poe faces.

'The Fats? They won't trouble you any more than the
lithopedion here. They're part of you, Lily-girl, see? No more
terrifying than yer own mind, yeh-hey?'

So I follow him into the other room, and the Fats carry on
muttering and unravelling the loops of gut. Phar Lap counts
out exactly seventeen pounds and thirty-six pence. Both the
notes and the coins are old, distressed.

Then Costas weighs in, 'Youse gotta pay me now, Lily –
gimme youse plates.'

'Plates?'

'Yeah – youse falsies.'

'But – but I don't have them any more.'

'Look in the case,' Phar Lap advises – and I do. There they
are, wrapped up like they used to be on the rare occasions
when I took them out. Wrapped up in new fat old lady's
pants, looking more fleshly now than prosthetic. I feel an
affection for them – these prised-apart jaws – they were more
a part of me than what I've become. Still – Charon is Charon, I
guess, even if he only drives you across London, so I go next
door and hand them over.

'There's a store up at the corner there, Lily, yeh-hey?' says
Phar Lap. 'You can get cleanin' stuff, give the place a goin'-
over, hey-yeh?'

'And what're you going to do now?'

'Work – I got work t'do jus' like Costas. We *all* gotta
work, Lily. Maybe I'll see you at the meeting tonight? Maybe
not.'

'And if I don't go to the meeting?'

'You stay at home with the Fats, then, and – '

'Me and you and a dog named Boo, loving and a-living off the land!'

' – the lithopedion here.'

He was right – I'd rather go to any kind of a meeting than sit around with the tiny calcified cadaver, the reanimated reminder of my sexual fecklessness. Let alone those Fats.

Chapter Eight

Well, what can I say, that's how it was for me. Not so different to anyone else's death, I guess. We've all got our own fucking sob stories in here – that's for sure. Still, you might've thought that with the Fats kind of gibbering in the next room, and the lithopedion belting out its seventies ditties as it dragged at my feet, I wouldn't have had any difficulty at all appreciating I was extinct. Not so. I can remember that first afternoon in the basement flat at 27 Argos Road as clearly as I can recall anything that happened to me before – or has transpired since.

Sure, I didn't know it was Argos Road at that point – any more than I knew that the house number was 27. It was just a damp basement, in a dull suburb, of an immense city which I'd learnt to tolerate – but never love. And being dead? That no more registered with me – metaphysically speaking – than the ineffability of God's name, or the Marian cult, or the Red Sea parting, or any other bit of religious mummery. An afterlife was as vastly improbable as Atlantis, a sunken continent of silly supposition, believed in only by credulous fools.

I suppose you'd expect my subtle body, the resurrection of my teeth, Phar Lap's and Costas's eccentricities to've made a big impression on me too, but this wasn't so either. You've gotta believe me when I say that the hereafter, as it revealed itself to me on that spring day in 1988, seemed no stranger than my arrival in England for the first time in the winter of '58, when my pregnant belly – stuffed full of Charlotte – pressed against the railings of the *Queen Mary*, as it honked its way towards the dockside; while down below spread the waiting crowd, a field of cloth of gabardine, scattered with pink-featured flowers. One of which – and I searched it out at the time, believing, or willing myself to believe, that this meant love – was Yaws's. So much for belief.

England, a country of profound, antediluvian backwardness, where the hearty homes wore their circulatory systems on the outside; a savage reminder of the fact that come winter, your own pipes would freeze quite as surely. England – quaint it ain't. Not now, not then, not ever. I never loved the place, or the culture – or the people for that matter. I always kept my US passport in my handbag, ready to jump ship if the need arose. As for the Yaws family, with their nursery nicknames, their gentle bigotry (never hating anyone because they were black, or a Jew, or a woman, but simply disliking them for themselves alone – *and incidentally* their blackness, their Jewishness, their femaleness), their casual drunkenness (were they drunk, or slow-witted, or both?), and their determination to mortify themselves internally with vast carbohydrate repasts – set beside *them*, my death guide and the minicabbing Charon weren't all that peculiar.

No, I figured this was only another scene change, a further forced march in Lily's war. In the same way I'd jumped from Kaplan's bed to Yaws's, from the US of A to shitty little England, so I'd relocated – via the Royal Ear Hospital – from Kentish Town to Dulston. Now I'd have to go through the whole tedious business of acclimatising myself again. Getting the utilities sorted out, finding out where the local Sainsbury's was, applying for a library card – all that crap. With the deficit of hindsight – and since when, for the neurotic at least, has it ever conferred any benefit? – I suppose it should've occurred to me that my indifference to the more cohesive aspects of life – such as mail redirection and healthcare – implied a rather more significant change of address than earlier moves. But take it from me – it didn't.

Yeah, like I say, I recall the first day of the rest of my death perfectly; and see it as the other bookend to my arrival in literary ol' England. Southampton, winter of '58, where ice streaked the cranes' davits, and the land, the sea and the sky vied to out-murk each other. When it came time for me to quit the ship I cowered in my cabin, like a pale cow in an iron barn, until the lowing Yaws – 'Lily? What's the matter? I've been waiting on the quay for simply ages' – came to herd me down the gangway. Simply ages – *so* Yaws; everything with him was *so* simple. How true to say that simplicity is all too often the last refuge of the complex. Yes, *simply ages* – that's how long an eternity would be in Yaws's company. Actually, that's how long *five fucking minutes* was in Yaws's company, once the thrill of leaving Kaplan, escaping the Eight Couples Who Mattered and avoiding the banshees of guilt surrounding Dave Junior's death had worn off. Oh – and fleeing Jewmerica – that was a great escape as well.

Who was he, this big, pink, wet-mouthed guy, who'd roughly taken me a couple of times in the back of his rental Chrysler? He bit my tits. I think with Yaws I mistook shock for orgasm, and inevitably orgasm for love. But the weird way of it was that as with any other lover, Yaws became a physical archetype to me. All men in one – and all therefore hateful.

Yaws took me back to the first of a succession of uncomfortable flats; where drying racks hung with diapers and underwear were forever collapsing in tangles of cloth and strut, like the wrecks of early aircraft. Miss Wrong-Brothers couldn't fucking keep them clean – let alone aloft. Then, when I was pregnant with the second Miss Yaws, we ended up at Crooked Usage, where everything settled into a routine of neglect. Jesus-fucking-Christ, if *you*'d lived in Hendon in the sixties you'd know what living death was like. Dulston, by comparison, was a gas – albeit an odourless one. After all, I'd been living in purgatory the last fifteen years of my life. Extinction was all I'd expected – so is it any wonder that the very shoddy solidity of the basement was enough to stifle my normally raging curiosity?

I ignored the Fats and suffered the lithopedion. I went out to the shops to get cleaning materials. Surely, I reasoned, I'd still be able to smell ammonia? To tell shit from Shinola?

In the street it was sunny. Phar Lap was right – the subtlety of a subtle body was lost on a clumsy simp like me. It *felt* drier, crisper, warmer than the dank basement. Free of pain and the galumphing towards death, I felt as if *I* were drier, crisper and warmer too. Besides, so much of life consists in such distancing, such purely conjectural sensual delights – could death be any different? There was even fucking *cherry* blossom, pink and white frou-frous of unseemly frivolity, frothing from under the solid skirts of the late Victorian houses. Houses which, with their four storeys of frigid urbanity on top and their dank basements submerged, were like inverted icebergs. As I trolled towards the corner shop, with my death grant jingling in my dress pocket, I was buoyed up, almost girlish.

I passed a few people on my way, but they looked no more nor less zombie-like than any you veer past in any city street. A too tall girl with ends split from crown to collar, dabbing leaky lids with a slunk of tissue; a decayed stump of an old man in a tent of mac, testing each paving stone with a rubber stopper; an off-colour Asian gent with a meticulous fringe of grey moustache. Their eyes took me in, blinked me out.

The corner shop was set *into* the corner – like a corny postmodern piece of detailing. Inside it was a turmeric-scented grotto festooned with merchandise of all kinds – from cardboard bandoleers loaded with penknives, to plaits of onions, to hanks of liquorice strings. In the darker recesses of this trading lair lurked freestanding postcards racks, plastic baskets full of vegetables, shuddering freezer cabinets, and forgotten shelves clustered with the souls of soup cans.

The counter was almost submerged by a wave of cheap stuff, but through a gap between the till, a stack of the *Dulston Advertiser* and the albino dreadlocks of some mop-heads, I received instruction from a tiny, Indian woman in an immaculate sari. She sent me hither and thither, paying me out on a threnody of directions, to save from her labyrinth this lovely canister of bleach, that beautiful bottle of all-purpose floor cleaner, and those alluring scourers. Sitting behind her on a high stool, a small boy in pressed grey shorts played with a toy metal car, a toy plastic cow and a toy plastic harmonica. As I went back and forth I observed him carefully balance these atop his thighs. He tried car on top of cow on top of harmonica, then harmonica on top of cow on top of car, as if he were investigating the possibility of new Hindu cosmologies.

When I'd liberated the cleaning materials, I paid the tiny lady.

'You must be the new lady,' she said – clearly she was a ladies' lady. 'The one who's moved in at number 27.'

'That's right,' I replied, pleased to've been acknowledged. Perhaps this move to Dulston, this further assimilation, would be easier than I'd feared. 'The flat's a terrible mess,' I told her, 'it looks as if it hasn't had a decent spring-clean in twenty years.'

She gave a subcontinental snort, 'Er-hoo' – impacted with layers of meaning – 'yes, that is rightly true. Rightly true. Mr Buzzard was never one for cleaning – an unquiet spirit, you understand? He has moved now. Moved on to Bicester outside Oxford. Honestly, Mrs . . .?'

'Bloom.'

'Mrs Bloom. There are a lot of unquiet spirits at 27, don't let them annoy you. Don't let them get the upper hand. Is this your lithopedion?'

She leaned through the gap and peered at the lithopedion, who was sitting on the very edge of a banana box, swinging its stubby grey legs and fluting another of its tacky ditties: 'Streets are all empty / No one around / Everyone's gone – to the mo-on!'

'And what is your name then, Sunny Jim?' she asked. I was dumbfounded – it hadn't occurred to me to address it directly.

'Lithy,' the lithopedion squeaked.

'Do be quiet now, Lithy – there's a good child,' she told it – and it was. 'You have to be firm with a lithopedion, Mrs Bloom. They know no better than to be blurting out any old nonsense that comes into their heads. It's usually pop music because it penetrates through to where they've been caught up in your . . . folds.' She bunched up her sari to illustrate her point.

I was impressed by this useful dope – so much better than Phar Lap's pidgin mysticism. 'Um . . . You don't mind me asking, Mrs . . .?'

'Seth.'

'Mrs Seth. I've got some . . . Fats, is it . . . Fats in my flat – are they dangerous?'

'No, not exactly, Mrs Bloom. Most people's Fats are rather adolescent, if you see what I mean.'

'Adolescent?'

'Yes, you see they're totally made up from gained and lost fat. Fat that is usually the result of those childishly indulgent binges on chocolate, sweets and what have you. So the Fats have that character. They'll sulk, answer back at you, mutter unpleasantly, and play loud music, but you can get them in line – if you are persistent.'

A bell tinkled and another customer descended into the

shop. It was a shocking-looking man of indeterminate middle age, his hair a fright wig, his chin a frightful beard. A toilet brush of a man. What skin I could see – his hands, his cheeks, his forehead – was covered with burns and abrasions. He wore flared jeans so small they rose up like culottes on his scrawny shanks, and a cheap nylon anorak zipped up to his throat. His eyes were small-calibre bullet holes, shot through to the wreckage of his mind. Near the door he bent down in slow stages to seize a metre-long box of tin foil from a bottom shelf. Junky, I concluded, and gave Mrs Seth the conspiratorial look of the socially acceptable.

To my surprise she didn't return it; instead she returned my change and whispered, 'I know what you're thinking, Mrs Bloom, but he's a good customer. You'll be wanting to go to the meeting later on – I'll call by for you at seven o'clock.' Then she turned to the junky, who was staggering towards us, and beamed at him. 'Hello, Mr Bernard, how are you today then?'

I gathered up my shopping and left.

All that afternoon I did my best to put the basement in some kind of order. In the cupboard under the stairs I found one of those ridiculous old carpet-sweepers, the kind that ploughs the dirt and fluff into two parallel lines. I dragged the damn thing back and forth, back and forth, over the dank carpets. I shooed the Fats away from the sludge pile of mattresses in the bedroom and hauled them out into the front area, where they dried in the fresh air. 'What's she doing?' they chided me. 'Cleaning – ha! Silly old cow – why bother?'

Every wipeable surface I wiped, then scoured with Flash. In the kitchenette I attacked the greasy lino with a clean mop-head and didn't leave off 'til it resembled the pomaded conk of a fifties zootsuiter. In the lavatory I turned five J-cloths the same colour as the urine-stained fitments. Then I had to chase the Fats off again, flicking globs of crap at them with the daggy rags. 'What's she doing! Ooh! Stop that – ooh! Leave us alone!' Mrs Seth was certainly right about the Fats; despite their bizarre appearance there was nothing intrinsically frightening about them at all. Their blindness was for real, and it took them ages to grope their way into a room, or turn the telly on, or even creep up behind me so they could stand wobbling like three hideous turkeys, gobbling, 'Fat and old, fat and old, fat and old.' I soon grew used to herding them ahead of me, just as I became accustomed to telling Lithy to 'pipe down!' – one of Yaws's Victorian catch-phrases.

I hadn't planned on resuming domesticity quite so soon – in fact, within hours of my death. But what the hell, when I considered the torments I'd left behind it didn't look too raw a deal. Anyway, cleaning wasn't so bad when you couldn't *feel* the filth beneath your fingernails, or the dust as it shot up your nose. Sure, if I homed in on the task at hand, the sight of what I was doing and the disposition of my limbs as I did it were enough to remind me of a lifetime's faithless prostration before the household gods. Of the repetitive taking of the Pledge, the endless staring through Windolene darkly, the eternal coming of the bleached Lord in a burst of Vim.

By seven that evening I was fed up to the back of my resurrected teeth with the whole sordid business. The very *lack* of fatigue – of knee-ache and house-crone's elbow – that these labours should've made me feel was exhausting. My vigorous cleaning wasn't doing much for the place anyway, only provoking the patterns that screamed from the walls, harping on the ancient distress of the abused furniture, goading the sick fixtures and the ill fittings. When the bell rang I put on my coat – which I found in the bedroom folded over my suitcase – told the Fats to 'be good' while I was gone, tucked Lithy in a pocket and met Mrs Seth at the door.

'Is it far to this . . . this meeting?' I asked as we set off along Argos Road, the diminutive Mrs Seth taking five skinny steps to each of my thick strides.

'Oh no, not at all,' she replied, 'it is a few streets, turns this way, turns that way. No more.'

I wanted to chat volubly with the kind Mrs Seth as we paced through the Dulston gloaming, but now that she'd been prised out of her shop setting it was hard to get going with the bejewelled woman. What kind of sally did I dare to hazard? How long have you been dead, Mrs Seth? Have you got a lithopedion of your own? How about Fats? Are there other dead Seths in Dulston? Or perhaps a less personal approach would be better, like – tell me, if you will, Mrs Seth, how exactly *do* the dead live?

It didn't matter, for she was right, we were soon there. This, the first of many such meetings, is still the one that stays with me most clearly. It was held in the South Dulston Community Centre, a dead modernist building – flat-roofed, grey-concreted, blank-windowed – which was neither central nor communal. The Centre had a piece of waste ground on one side, where hulks of adventure-playground equipment were bound in vetch and nettles. On the other stood a derelict warehouse, whose ill-starred panes suggested perverse attempts to break out – into Dulston.

It's my considered opinion that while the history of the twentieth century may've been typified by design innovations, the community centre remains, resolutely, a World War One creation. A Methodist church hall marooned in no man's land, withstanding the bombardment of history's howitzers. We entered via a concrete trench. It was the vacuous barn I expected – scuffed lino floors, whitewashed cinder-block walls, doors leading to equipment stores, cubbyhole offices, and toilets. In the Men's, three full-size urinals would undoubtedly be set beside one tiny dauphin's ear. Through a serving hatch I could see an institutional kitchen where an urn steamed, while a couple of individuals primed plastic beakers with tea and Tupperware plates with Nice biscuits, before handing them out. Overhead, five big bars of light were chained to the fire-resistant tiles. The oblong suns beat down on the assembled company, thirty-odd men and women, who stood about in uneasy groups, all of them shifting from one leg to the other, as if they were the possessors of a single, very full, bladder.

At the time I thought it was an optical effect – caused by the striplights flickering against the night which loomed behind the blank windows. For I saw beams of even yellower light emerging from the people's heads, from the very apex of their skulls, and bouncing off the ceiling to create strange nimbi about their ordinary heads.

I expect you've been to a few Personally Dead meetings yourself; still, what can I tell you about these people, these attendees? Only this, that they were the sort who show up for such meetings – ambiguous events organised in anonymous premises by shadowy parties. Pro-tem seekers after provisional truths. Sure, there was a sprinkling of lip-pluggers and neck-banglers – like the ones I'd seen at the cafe that morning – but they only leavened the general London brown bread. The middle-aged women, the old women, the very old women, and the withered crones, who, with their lumpy heads slack-wrapped in plastic headscarves, their shapeless coats and their swollen hands, were Cockney peasants. Chaucerian phenotypes. The men outnumbered the women, but they were greyer still. They carried batons they'd forgotten to relay, tightly furled newspapers or umbrellas. They were younger – on the whole – than the women, but so fucking colourless! They weren't men – they were cut-outs of men, snipped from old knitting patterns in *Woman's Realm*. They were men from the middle rows of group photographs. Men pictured in advertisements seen from the indifferent vantage of moving escalators. Men whose cocks were merely details noted on forgotten index cards in the dusty filing cabinets of the Kinsey Institute. Statistical men. They reminded me of every shnorrer I'd ever botched a transaction with – 'Missus – this is a fiver not a twenny' – or crossed the street to avoid. They were the sort of nebbishes who skulked for no reason. Always disappearing around a corner ahead of you, inducing mild paranoia.

As this gauzy crew pulled stacks of plastic chairs away from the walls and arranged them in a loose oval, I noticed other features of the meeting. Cards were taped on the walls with peculiar exhortations written on them: 'LIVE AND LET DIE'; 'DON'T THINK, DON'T THINK, DON'T THINK'; 'IT'S HARD GOING'; 'FOR ALL ETERNITY'. The lettering was as inelegant as the sentiments – someone had misused a Magic Marker with a shaky hand. The cards were bad enough, but by the serving hatch leaned two placards which were far worse. These read as follows:

The Twelve Steps of Personally Dead

1. We realised we were dead and that our lives were over.
2. We came to disbelieve everything.
3. We made a decision to painstakingly remember our former lives.
4. We made a searching and fearful inventory of our nervous tics and mannerisms.
5. We shared this inventory with our death guides, and subjected ourselves to their ridicule.

6. We became entirely ready to abandon ourselves.

7. We waited for nothingness.

8. We made a list of all those we hated.

9. We remembered them.

10. We continued to make a daily inventory and when we noticed disturbing personality traits we embraced them.

11. We sought through meditation to improve our unconsciousness and isolation.

12. Having spiritually annulled ourselves as a result of working these steps, we carried this message to the newly dead.

and:

The Twelve Traditions of Personally Dead

1. Our common annihilation comes first – individual dissolution depends on dead unity.

2. For our group purpose there is no ultimate authority; our leaders are usually petty bureaucrats.

3. The only requirement for membership is death.

4. Each group is autonomous – after all, frankly, who gives a damn?

5. Each group has but one primary purpose – to carry the message to the newly dead.

6. A PD group ought never endorse, or lend the PD name to, any living facility or enterprise, lest we scare them to death.

7. Every PD group is fully self-supporting, incapable of receiving outside contributions.

8. Personally Dead is non-professional, although our death guides – who belong mostly to traditional peoples – may be appeased with cowrie shells, bullroarers, penis sheaths and whatever other tat appeals to them.

9. PD is over-organised, consisting largely of a purposeless and inefficient bureaucracy.

10. PD has so many opinions, that they should – all things being equal – cancel one another out.

11. Our public-relations policy is based on deception. We must always maintain the illusion of being alive at the level of press, radio and films.

12. Individuality is the basis of all our traditions, ever reminding us to place personalities before principles.

Now, at this stage in death, thinking of my former life had become a delicious irrelevance. Why worry about my junky baby when I couldn't change her shitty diaper? Why fulminate against Mr and Mrs Elvers when it wouldn't make them even remotely uncomfortable? And so I slackened all the daily ranklings with which I'd strung my catty cradle. The two Daves I'd been indentured to – well, fuck 'em. Could I make them better and more considerate lovers, fathers, friends? I think not. My shyster father – my sadistic mother? All the slaps in the face and kicks in the shins that had been dealt me over sixty-five years? Gone – or at least *not relevant*. It seemed that even my leading persecutors had had only cameo roles; and now they had no more significance than the protesting brooches on Jane Bowen's lapels.

It should've dawned on me how awful it was that in my life gall had been all – but it didn't. I suppose it should've sunk in how unbelievable my new-found coolness was – but I simply took it on trust; death, I figured, must've mellowed me.

As for the trappings of the Personally Dead meeting – the bowdlerised twelve steps and twelve traditions, the pie-chart slices of humanity wedged alongside me – why didn't they jerk me into comprehension? Why didn't it even occur to me that there was only one person who could've arranged these particular elements of *my own experience*, and cobbled them together into this dreary scene? I dunno. But at the time I'd forgotten all the weary weepfests of Families Anonymous I'd attended – along with other fucked-up mums and fucked-over spouses – to try and get a handle on Natasha's limitless capacity for destroying herself and others.

Jesus Christ, I sit here with you, leafing through yet another fucking *Woman's Realm* and I still don't know. And even now I've had more than enough time to give the question *all due consideration*, I don't think I'll ever know. Not on this go-round.

So the zombies took their places in the oval of chairs. Deadening silence was achieved. Thirty-odd cigarettes and cheap panatellas were sparked. The smoke-streams flowed through their searching headlights. It was a community Nuremberg. A fishy little fellow in a blue shirt and a grey V-neck flipped the proceedings off. He called upon three members to read the screeds printed on some laminated cards. The first of these – entitled 'Why Are We Dead? – spoke of how dying was an uncomfortable and fearful experience for us all; how disturbing it was to realise that style *was* personality, and that our sense of self was nothing but mannerisms and negative emotions. The second reading explained how the members of PD thronged together on a regular basis to remind each other that they were dead, and to inculcate the newly dead into the ways of the afterlife. The third reading proposed a solution to this malady, but by then I wasn't concentrating. The readings went on and on. If I'd been in the least bit tired I could've fallen asleep, but no dice. God knows my interest in life had flagged all too frequently, but clearly, being bored was now going to be even duller.

My gaze, like a fat fly, droned about the large room, alighting on a flyer for intermediate aerobics classes, a fire extinguisher, some stacked gym mats. As the other dead smoked and I fidgeted with nothing, it did occur to me that this queer Kaddish had some justice. That it was suitably hellish for me – who had always prided myself on not being a joiner – to end up like this, in a terminally banal club, whiling away the aeons under strip lighting.

I was winched back up to earth by the personally dead, who all thanked the last trumpeter in unison. The human tiddler – who was, I gathered, dubbed 'the Secretary' – then introduced Robin Cook, who, he informed us, had come along this evening to share his experience of death with us. Cook, a smouldering twig of a man, as spindly as the cigarette he kept permanently tucked between his thin lips, rasped his words. His eyes were hidden by the yanked-down peak of his tweed cap. He was all sharp knees, sharp elbows and sharper Fitzrovian tones. Cook had, he told us, been agreeably surprised, given that he had no religious belief whatsoever, to discover that there was an afterlife. Of sorts. He'd been a thriller-writer while alive, and as he'd always published pseudonymously, there was no problem with his continuing his career after death. Indeed, the books he'd written since moving to Dulston sold marginally better than the ones he'd published before. Even if they weren't too well received by the critics.

Yes, it was difficult to get used to not feeling, touching, eating or sleeping, but the relief from the pain and the indignity of terminal illness had always stayed with him. Cook was grateful for death – considering what a crock of shit his life had become. True, there were awful psychic manifestations caused by the dissolution of his mind – but hell, he'd always had a dark imagination anyway. There was nothing more horrible than he could've conceived himself. He found the cynicism of the PD programme a balm for disincorporation. 'What do the steps mean?' he croaked. 'I've no fucking idea. Do I work them in any sense? I haven't a fucking clue. It seems to me – and I've only my own experience to go on – that this whole set-up is a bit of joke. Who's the joke on? I don't know – and what's more, my loves, I don't think I ever will.' He spoke – as you can see – to my condition.

After Cook had finished, the Secretary announced that he was 'throwing the meeting open for general sharing'. They called it 'sharing' – how ridiculous, how risible an expression. Only corpses could've failed to corpse when uttering such jargon. Anyway, what this meant in practice was a lot of halting, garbled complaint. One after another, introducing themselves 'I'm so-and-so and I'm personally dead', the members of PD gave vent to their smoke and their complaints. The bizarre thing was that while what they described was pantomimically over-the-top, the manner in which they expressed it was leaden. It was like the visitation of the Fats; the terrors faded out suddenly, like piano notes stifled by a foot-pedal. I guess it should've hit me then that I really was dead, and more so, that all life's piquancy had been solely a function of the fear of death. But it bloody well didn't.

The PD members spoke of the gods of the Hindu pantheon – elephant-headed Ganesh, monkey-bodied Hanuman, skull-garlanded Kali, quadri-armed Vishnu – smashing through the thin walls of their Dulston bedsits, rehearsing their ancient grievances, then re-enacting their epochal battles. A whirl of avatars in the toilet bowl. They moaned about Christ emerging from the Golgotha of their fan-assisted oven, to deliver a quavering sermon from the mount on their secular kitchen floor. In the Babylonian suburb they inhabited, the Four Horsemen of the Apocalypse exercised their mounts by cantering across the municipal park. Death, War and Hunger hitched them to the swings in the kids' playground; while Civil Strife shared out ham sandwiches and tea by the boating lake.

In the confused realm of the personally dead, houris bathed in the small sinks left behind in the corners of spare bedrooms where dead builders had undertaken spurious conversion work. These eternally pure courtesans, capable of conceiving at the will of the faithful, drank sherbert, and laughed lustily long into the night. Even the gods of the pre-Buddhist religion of Tibet could get flat-shares in Dulston. So, psycho-physical chromatism came to Corinth Way, Sparta Terrace, Syracuse Park and Athens Road. Blue gods the size of car dealerships loomed over the car dealerships; red gods the size of buses dodged among the buses; and green gods – temporarily entombed in the raised, grass-covered embankments of the Dulston Reservoir – surged forth when the personally dead approached. The florists sold demoniacal flesh-eating plants at a pound a stem. Very dear.

Some were visited by deities appropriate to their denominations. A Wicklow man gossiped in thick brogue about Mary-next-door's open-heart surgery. A quavering member of the Brethren bore witness that, before the deluge, he was required nightly to cut Methuselah's prodigiously large corns. The dead horny skin of nine centuries. But others were pretty confused. Why was this intense old Portuguese man tormented by Osiris? Why was that foolish frummer shaking his locks over the manifestation of the Rainbow Serpent? And what did any of it have to do with me? The Secretary had impressed upon us the importance of 'listening for the similarities rather than the differences', and there were those who spoke of more physical apparitions – personifications of hiccuping, blinking, burping, farting and yawning – which sounded suspiciously like the Fats. Still, my attention wandered. Lithy had found a couple of its own, and the three grey foetuses ran in and out of the shadowy corners of the room, chanting in their reedy voices, 'We are fa-mi-ly / I got all my sisters an' me!' until the Secretary told them to shut up and behave.

Behave like what, exactly? I mocked to myself. How *should* a reanimated, minuscule, petrified cadaver behave? How should any of us behave? I mean to say – 'can't do' could no longer be made to do. And what if you *simply don't like* kreplach?

After an hour or so, the Secretary shushed up a slight, nervy woman who was complaining about Mithras – he lived in her icebox, conducting improbable, pyromantic rituals – and informed us that the last ten minutes would now be available for 'the newly dead' to share. 'This is to embarrass you flatliners into admitting your own extinction,' he crowed. 'After all, if you aren't defunct – what're you doing here? Even if you can't face saying anything, you can grunt or rattle, or do whatever it is you did when you gasped your last.' As he pronounced these cruel words, a rictus tore in his papery face. All the dead eyes swivelled to fix me, all the bony fingers wiggled as if to clutch me.

Seeing Phar Lap Jones and Costas come in by the swing doors opposite – the very ordinary swing doors – and feeling a sense of relief, I decided to brazen it out. 'I'm Lily,' I said, 'and personally, I think I'm dead.' That was it. That was all I said. It seemed that was all that was required – some admission that I was dead. Cut off from everything. A tumour of a woman excised from the world. Phar Lap's Stetson brim dipped with the weight of his cool approval. His mirrored shades tilted and the two tiny sections of floor reflected in them sank down. Costas filled his ample chest with unnecessary air and the hairs flared in the V of his shirt. My fellow members mumbled their approval.

Then it was over, we all stood, held the shape of each other's hands and muttered the prayer: 'Gog grant me the stupidity to deny there's anything I cannot change, the temerity to neglect the things I can, and the ignorance to be incapable of distinguishing between the two.' Phar Lap and Costas moved forward to join in this balderdash.

As soon as it was over I went up to them. 'What the hell was that about?' I asked Phar Lap. 'It made no sense at all. It certainly didn't teach me anything about Dulston, or death, or how to cope with it.'

'Yeh-hey, well, I s'pose it might seem total fuckin' gammin – but thass the way of it girl, yeh-hey? Thass the way of it – '

'Yes, Lily-lady, that *is* the way of it,' Costas added. 'Youse should listen to my friend here, he's youse death guide. Youse can't get back in my cab and leave Dulston – this lot here know the only routes out. Listen to him! Now, I have peoples here I must talk with.' He sidled off, and Phar Lap indicated with twitches of his snaky hips that I should follow him into one of the cubbyhole offices.

Here, he got behind a desk, squatted on a swivel chair, pressed the back of his Stetson against a cork board – so that the front poked up, releasing a puff of black curls – and regarded me with wry detachment. 'Yairs, nothing here fer you, Lily-girl. Thass true enough. All this gammin, see – it's 'cos yer dead but won't accept it, yeh-hey? It's gonna get worse – b'lieve me. It'll get worse than the lithopedion, yeh-hey? Worse than the Fats – and it's all in yer head, girl. None of it's real. None of it at all – you, this, me, whatever. You get me, girl? Don't you remember how you felt back there in the hospital, when we walked out of the ward, quit the place? It was like a mirage, hey-yeh? Like hot wind movin' across bush, all shimmery, yeh-hey? That was *you*, girl – b'lieve me. It's you who're no-thing. Recognise it an' all this . . . this guna will evaporate, y'see that? Doncha Lily? Doncha?'

But I didn't see it at all. I saw Phar Lap's amazing apple

cheeks, his ebony eyelids, all the Epstein planes of his handsome head. And behind him I saw the cork board, with its thumb-tacked schedules, notes and newspaper clippings. I saw rain spatter against the black window pane, and tiny dusty dervishes whirl across the floor. I saw piles of undone folders on the dun desk, I saw the personally dead all smoking away in the hall, and I saw Phar Lap prise open a can of Log Cabin, his fingers forklift a pinch of tobacco and grind it into rollability. I saw the pennant of paper appear on his lower lip. I saw him contrive another cigarette and light it with a Redhead match. I saw it, and while it may have been wacky, disconcerting, troubling – I didn't disbelieve it for a second.

Christmas 2001

I didn't give it any less credence than the colossal rampart of MDF that rears up above me now, tier upon tier of crappy possessions, like the steps of a Toltec pyramid. All the valueless things the Ice Princess and the Estate Agent stole, then couldn't fence or pawn. Grown-ups forget quite how huge their material transgressions are – so preoccupied are they by tiny, psychic misdemeanours. I simply couldn't understand what Phar Lap Jones was driving at – I couldn't hear him. No more than I can reach the mobile phone that I know is up there, way beyond my reach. And anyway, even if I could, it's a dead chunk of circuitry now – an immobile, an uncommunicator. It's as incapable of receiving anything as I was of understanding Phar Lap's clicking and palate-slapping. At the time I thought he was trying to drive me crazy – but hell, I managed that all by myself.

Chapter Nine

I settled into Dulston well enough. I hummed, 'Little boxes, little boxes, and they all look just the same / And they're all made out of ticky-tacky, and they all look just the same / There's a red one, and a blue one, and a green one, and a yel-low one / And they're all made out of ticky-tacky, and they all look just the same,' as I sluiced the depression out of my basement. I got a job. Not in Dulston, but down the road in Hackney. Phar Lap had explained it made no odds if I worked for a living company or a dead one. And believe me – it certainly didn't *seem* any different. I'd only six weeks earlier left off working at the public-relations business where I'd toiled when alive, yet here I was at another PR company, on the other side of town, typing up still more releases on fresh kitchenware, country club launches, innovatory thermal socks – whatever new effluvia were next to join the ever widening torrent of increasingly trivial innovation. Or so *it seemed to me*.

Just as when I was alive hardly anyone at Chandler Communications had bothered to ask me who, what, where, or why I was – so nobody at Baskin's Public Relations gave a rat's ass either. Each day I stomped to work down Argos Road, turning into Corinth Way with its coursing traffic, taking the short cut along the gentrified Sparta Terrace – who says the dead can't be upwardly mobile? – and traversing Syracuse Park, before catching the bus that ran down Athens Road. Usually in the fusty warmth of the upper deck, where pensioners and kids squeezed together, cutting out the middle-aged, I forgot about my own death, neglected Death in

general, ignored metaphysics, and instead read crappy women's magazines. Eventually, after much diesel grunting, I'd
look up from my *Woman's Realm* to find that the bus was
trundling down Dalston Lane, or Queensbridge Road, or
already turning into Mare Street. Back – laughable as it
may seem – in what's called the land of the living.

Every interface between the worlds of the living and the
dead was just this prosaic. Utilities – well! They were as hard
to organise now as ever, despite there always being a dead
person working in the relevant office. Getting everyday stuff
together was a real hassle now I was so very subtle. The
boundaries between life and death were as provisional, confused and indeterminate as those of Dulston itself. The living,
foolishly, comfort themselves with the notion that in death at
least things become *clear-cut*, as if death were a definable
barrier, a wall or a line. But I was finding out that death was
far trickier, and as hard to locate as the exact edge of your
own visual field. I now understood why spiritualists' communications with the hereafter are invariably so ludicrously
trite. If anyone had been bothered to tap my table, without
hesitating I'd have asked for a nice cup of tea.

Baskin, a bearded-Lothario emeritus, hired me because I
boldly announced that I'd take twenty per cent less than any
flibbertigibbet who was prepared to flirt with him. In truth it
was Mrs Baskin – a marcelled monstrosity who came in to do
the accounts from time to time – who took me on. Wasn't it
always the way. So, not much in the way of shekels from
Baskin PR.

It took me ages to get the basement tricked out to my
satisfaction. There was no sense in getting workmen to do the
painting and decorating. At the Personally Dead meetings
they were good enough to tell me that dead artisans were
incredibly unreliable. Anyway, I was free from arthritis, from

bronchitis and from gingivitis – free from anything that could have stopped me doing the work myself. I bought black slacks and a man's white shirt from the flea market at the end of Sparta Terrace. I tied the shirt-tails under my jugs and crawled on top of the furniture to slop and roll the paint about. The Fats crowded round me and giggled at my efforts. 'Look at her great white belly! He-he, it sags like a sack when she stretches . . . He-he, she's a fat old thing. Fat and old, fat and old . . .'

So it went on. It should've driven me right round the bend in a few long days – but it didn't. Now I had no need for sleep, I really missed repose. Shit, if I'd known the afterlife was going to be a relentless 24 x 7, I'd've had thousands more lie-ins, heaps more hot-water bottles, gallons more fucking *hot chocolate*. All that fucking dieting – yet here I was, pear-shaped for eternity and beset by the blind bogeywomen of my own vanity. Sure, I did have Lithy. I'd stuck with the name Lithy for my lithopedion, because I couldn't figure out any alternative. Gus Junior didn't seem – how can I say – wise. Besides, the past was the last thing on my mind, there was so much to do, so many bloody errands. Lithy was a trouble-some, precocious little thing, but despite its nimble pins and familiarity with seventies pop songs, it really didn't have much idea of the world; so, I took it upon myself to educate my never-born cadaver of a child.

I dressed Lithy in Barbie and Ken's little hand-me-downs and took it to work with me at Baskin PR. It knew enough to slump and be silent when told. 'What an unusual dolly,' said Mrs Baskin, while Gloria, the blowsy secretary, admitted she found it 'creepy'. Nevertheless, from the vantage point of my desk, propped up against the old plastic Cheops of a com-puter, Lithy was able to get an angle on the origami paper economy of the late eighties.

I confess, I used the same baby talk with Lithy that Natasha and I had shared, peppering every proposition with 'noo-noo's, 'goo-goo's and other gummy nonce words. Lithy became my itty-bitty plaything and in time I even began to enjoy its performances, as it danced through the basement singing, 'We had joy, we had fun, we had seasons in the sun.' I couldn't see any resemblance to me or Gus in its crinkly nearly-face, or its beady jet eyes. I don't think there's anything much in the world of the living that *does* resemble a litho-pedion, saving perhaps that horse's ass Spielberg's alien. And that – natch – has big, blue eyes. The big, blue, bootiful eyes that can only be worked up from the dreams of yet another Jew boy who yearns to date blonde shiksas. 'The Extrater-restrial as Shiksa – Discuss' would be a likely subject for the kind of term paper I'd set for the lithopedion itself.

Take it from me, Dulston was as good an arena within which to exercise the greyhounds of my contempt as any living suburb of London. Who'd've imagined it – but the late English middle class were exactly the same pompous pricks they'd been when alive. Still piling up infinitesimal gradations of accent, demeanour and education into staggeringly bar-oque edifices of class. There were U and non-U dead to the nth degree. The old dead and the newly dead, the dead who were the salt of the earth and the dead who were the corrupted soil. With grim inevitability it turned out that you *could* take it with you – your death grant was index-fucking-linked. Not only that, but despite their much-vaunted disregard for vulgar notoriety, the English dead doted on their famously deceased, being at great pains to report that they had met so-and-so, preferably while both parties were still alive.

Most of the famously dead people had long since moved on from Dulston – another thing that made me think it was merely a quarantine, a clearing house for the newly dead to reside in until our dispersal to more comfortable berths. In the meantime, all and sundry made it their business to tell me that *of course* they had known Countess Teresa Lubinska. How she'd always been *very free* with her stab wounds, and how she'd come directly to Dulston *on the tube* after the stabbing – only realising she was *dead* when the officious ticket-collector at King's Cross troubled her for her ticket and it struck her that she was changing trains *for no apparent reason.* What horse shit. Typical of the English dead that the only Holocaust martyrs they'd recognise were fucking Polish aristocrats, killed in fucking London. Just typical.

And they socialised – boy, did they socialise. They held parties where the liquor was sluiced round their mouths and puked in the geraniums, and the canapés parted from their wooden prongs only to be spat into buckets. Yup – drinks parties, the English dead were so fucking *happening.* They chewed quiche a lot – because it was easy to do so.

It was a long, hot summer for those of us who had to work, and frankly it wasn't my idea of fun to spend evenings standing about on terraces, chewing quiche, munching salad and then regurgitating into plastic buckets. True, not all the buckets were plastic, there was a vogue among the trendier dead for galvanised steel. These looked better, were easier to hit, but rang pretty loudly. Mrs Seth was always quick to defend the buckets, the chewing and the spitting. 'You have to let people do what they want, Mrs Bloom,' she told me, 'and what these dead people want to do is behave like the living – you can appreciate that.'

What I did appreciate was that Seth's Grocery and General Provisions did damn well out of the bucket business, the wine sales, and the bloody cheese trade too. They did almost as well out of flogging aluminium foil to Bernie, the unquiet spirit of a junky who lived in the attic of number 27. I never got used to the way these dead stupenagels got tipsy at their terminally dull drinks parties. I guess it followed from *acting* as if they were drinking – such is the power of ritual; but still it was foul to witness a lot of dead middle-aged people talking crap, singing old show tunes, and even making *passes* at each other.

So far as I could see, the only thing that distinguished these gatherings from those of the living – besides the sick buckets – was the fantastic number of smokers. In my experience *all* the dead smoke. Even those who hadn't smoked when alive took it up once they moved to Dulston. There was a real payback for smoking when you were dead. With a lung full of acridity there were a few, brief instants when you almost felt embodied. Then you'd exhale and revert to being no more substantial than the individual portions of cloud floating in front of your death mask. But these moments were worth paying for, worth *working* for.

Mostly prices in Dulston were low – after all, who'd *want* to live there? But cigs were as dear as anywhere else – and I got through pack after pack. I don't know what it's been like for you, but I found that the whole process of smoking acquired a certain dash once I was dead. The crinkle-slip-crunch of the cellophane as it came away from the cardboard, the very boxiness of the pack itself, its hard edges *defining* my hand. Then the rough silkiness of the inner foiled lining, and finally the cancer sticks themselves, so *deliciously harmless*. To smoke when one was so clearly fat and old – what high bravado blown in the face of the living, as they waited to exhale their last!

And it kept off the Fats. They couldn't stand cigarette smoke. It must've been something to do with their eyelessness. Whereas I could only see, they could only smell and complain, like the health-consciously correct, overweight adolescents they were. 'Ooh!' they'd chorus, as I greeted another dawn with my hundredth-odd smoke of the twenty-four. 'Ooh –

must she? Should she? Why does she? Can't she stop? Doesn't she know it's bad for her?' And I'd shoo them off with another blast of menacing wraiths. The sight of their wobbling butts disappearing out of the bedroom, fast, would've got me giggling; but now I realised – occupying as I did a wholly absurd world – that I hadn't been giggling at the absurdity of the world before I died, only wearily sniggering at my own.

At the PD meetings the 'old-timers', those who'd been dead for upwards of five years, counselled against getting involved in relationships during your first year of death. This was absurd, for if there was one thing the dead did even more than the living it was form relationships. Or rather – they moved in. A couple of dead oldsters would shack up with a dead middle-aged person in order to save on rent and keep up appearances. The dead middle-aged would take in the young dead for the same reason. It wasn't uncommon to see two middle-aged dead people walking along swinging a dead nonagenarian between them. In Dulston a second childhood really meant something. You might've thought the family units formed by these convenient liaisons would reek of oddity – not so. These shared households only brought home to me that blood had always been the most arbitrary basis upon which to order your emotional life.

What the dead discussed most was the past and the future. This explained their defiant lack of interest in Dulston, its environs and organisation. Dulston – which Phar Lap called a 'cystrict' – was as uncommonly like the adjacent districts as its residents were like theirs. Despite being deceptively thin – no more than a sliver of brick, masonry, concrete and tar – Dulston never felt the bustle of the living city that surrounded it. At night, after we dead were all safely tucked up inside, watching our own horror shows, we'd hear the living zipping through on the stunted stretches of arterial road that traversed our neighbourhood. If they did chance to stop, what did they find? Nothing much. A gas-station forecourt drugged with its own fumes, an all-night zoo store where the keeper cowered behind bars, a hooker selling her sad snatch on the corner of a council estate.

Drivers did pull over occasionally, by night and in the day. They bought petrol, groceries and forlorn fucks, for the most part never knowing what macabre exchanges they'd transacted. The live johns were numb to the dead hookers' insubstantiality. But the dead also refused to lie down under it. We rebelled and manifested ourselves as we actually were. The poor, sluttish women, dead from poverty and drugs, too many pregnancies and too much Valium, would appear in broad daylight at Dulston Junction, with their aborted foetuses floating around their lowering brows, bloody umbilici festooning their nylon housecoats. The suicides would gape their double mouths in the faces of lost travelling salesmen, or flash their crimson bracelets, or display the impacted sludge of their lower bodies, as snail-like they dragged themselves around the block. The murdered would exhibit their sliced-up, shot-through and bludgeoned bodies. The diseased would parade their chancres. The heart-attack victims would convulse and fall, convulse and fall, convulse and fall – an endless ring-a-ring-a-corpses. We all fall down.

How did the living react to this drop-in centre of annihilation? Why – they went crazy, natch. They were institutionalised, got religion, or left the country. They took the antics of the beyond for what they were, an eruption from a fifth, hideous dimension always suspected by them, but never witnessed. They were haunted. I very quickly saw, as I wandered the streets of Dulston, that everything I'd ever heard while living and disbelieved – about headless riders, or women in white, or screaming banshees – had been only the slightest of references to this disgusting limbo. As for the mentally ill, with their tales of alien invasion, conspiratorial control, and diabolic discorporation – *they'd been telling the absolute fucking truth*.

When alive I'd fought hard to ward off the darkness at the edges of my sight; the fear of my own mind's lintel collapsing, as I hovered on the doorstep between home and the world, claustro and agro. There'd been times when the phobias were so intense I could hardly withstand the sensation of being claustrophobic within the confines of *my own fucking head*. A little dolly-woman staring out through eyeholes cut by sadistic brain surgeons. Then I'd flee to the musty sheds of Christ, the cricket pavilions of the Lord. And how suitable it was that the English should find themselves sucking on such a meagre, rational, half-boiled sweetie of solace. My excuse was that I enjoyed the choir, or the admired the artwork, or found the atmosphere calming. But most English churches have none of these, and the raw fact of the matter is that I was *fucking afraid of the shit inside my head*. Desperately afraid it would get loose and overwhelm me. It was small satisfaction to discover I'd been right all the time. Right all along.

I didn't see a great deal of Phar Lap after the first PD meeting. He told me, 'I got work t'do, same as you, Lily-girl. I don't pick up no sit-down money. I go walkabout for new pro-spects, y'see, yeh-hey?' What these prospects were I didn't discover for a long time. Phar Lap commended me to the good offices of the personally dead. 'These babas'll teach you all y'need t'know, girl. Keep goin' t' the meetings. Speak up about yer own guna – they'll understand. There's nothing more I can tell you fer now, hey-yeh? No-thing.'

At the meetings I blurted out that I had an insuperable urge to attend my own cremation – to watch myself burn. 'Go,' said the personally dead, 'go, but don't expect it to do anything for you in particular. Neither to resolve the past, nor to make this purgatory any more pleasant.' Death was unable to effect any closure.

I took the tube from Highbury and Islington, and changed to the Northern Line at King's Cross, where, if I chose to see them, astonishing ghosts of human toast haunted the escalators. I sat on an Edgware Branch train to Golders Green, watching the reflections of the wan metropolitan faces, elongated into absurdity in the window opposite. On the dark walls of the tunnel, high-voltage tendons of cable flexed below the city. As it burrowed north from the West End I could feel the building-up above my head until, at Hampstead, its great clay weight oppressed me. Still – *en route* to my own funeral and I was experiencing only *mild* claustrophobia. Fantastic – when alive I wouldn't't've *dreamed* of travelling on the tube at all unless I were *drunk*, or sedated, or both.

Then the longest stop of all, from Hampstead to Golders Green; from the old and intelligent to the new and smart; from the villas on the hill to the chalets in the valley. Golders Green, where short-ass *nouveau riche* women of unspeakable vulgarity, their shnozzles just visible above the dash, piloted their husbands' Mercedes with absurd legerdemain along the Golders Green Road. Treating the huge Kraut saloons as if they were ten grand's worth of bumper car. Then oblique-parking them and pedicuring into Lindys patisserie, or Grodzinski's bakery, or some other calorie shack, to stuff themselves plumper. And it was like this in the sixties! Only twenty years after their fucking mothers and fathers had been *slimmed down* for the ovens.

I always hated Golders Green. I'd take the kids there to see a movie at the Ionic cinema, but only if it wasn't on anywhere else. Because I hated to be in that press of Jewry, all munching and gabbing and shmoozing their way through the ads, the support – and then the fucking feature. Ferchrissakes! It was as if they were in fucking shul! I couldn't help myself. I couldn't hide my racial self-disgust from my mongrel kids. So, once we'd got out of the joint, I'd *swear* we'd never go there again. That if they wanted to see another movie there they'd have to get their fucking *father* to take them.

I'd hold out for a month or two, or even three. Then on a dull winter evening we'd be driving back from shopping in town, grinding up the Finchley Road in whichever clunker it was the Yaws family had that year, when the thought of getting home to Daddy with his goyish air of pernicious, pipe-and-slipper anaemia would become *too much* for me. I'd find myself stopping outside Bloom's, ushering the girls in, waiting in the homey-smelling takeout area, while the old shlepper in the stained white coat made up our order of salt-beef sand-wiches and latkes. Even the food at Bloom's – where, let's face it, the bland were feeding the bland – tasted exotic in this city of carbohydrate. Then we'd go sit in the jalopy and gobble it up. I'd tell Natty and Charlie how fucking brilliant our people were. How we'd produced all the great thinkers of this century *and* the last. How even Bloom's was full of wayward Ein-steins, Freuds and Marxs, waiting table for food money while they finished their PhDs. And how when our dander was up we could hold off an entire army of Yaws and his Latin-conjugating ilk for months at a time, until we committed fucking *suicide* rather than surrender.

It was utterly unchanged – Golders Green. The same Becks stood becking in the station forecourt, about whatever non-sense was in their heads. I turned away from them, and under a London sky with superb vertical hold – a static greyish band below a whitish static band – walked north along the Finchley Road past the uncomfortable semis, squatting behind their prickly, privet barriers, to Hoop Lane.

It was the third day after my death and there I was, resurrected outside the Express Dairy. I didn't know how I knew it was the right time, but I knew. I hadn't wanted to go to my wake, organised by Mrs Elvers, natch, with Esther in self-pitying attendance, together with a slew of the English indifferent. Why would I wish to be present at the start of my own forgetting? No, it was the cremation I cared about. I had to make sure the coffin was of the cheapest possible manufacture, the undertakers of the sloppiest deportment, the hearse a Yawsmobile. I wanted to creep round the back, into the room where the conveyor belt disappeared the coffin. I needed to see the crematorium thieves rip my corpse out of its two-hundred-quid box. I needed to see them rip off my estate at the same time as I quit it. I'd spent years being appalled at the industry of death – I didn't want to miss out on these gonifs doing their very worst.

It wasn't like that at all, though. Eleven in the morning on a gloomy Tuesday, and the gentle swoop of dull, moist tarmac empty save for the intermittent swishes of Volvos, Volkswagens and Mercedes, carrying monied matrons the long mile from the Hampstead Garden Jewburb to Golders Green for a wallet workout. Sodden leaves underfoot, and up above the square chimney of the crematorium supporting the sky with a swelling column of fleshy smoke, while sucking the greyness into its red-brick Lutyens heart. A paradoxical brightness illuminated the Jewish cemetery behind me. I laughed mirthlessly to think of all the fools who'd paid top dollar, imagining they'd end up safely ensconced here, when the prevailing wind meant they were destined for a reverse diaspora after death, back to the East End.

Strange to relate, Natasha Yaws came alone, from the opposite direction to me. From the Hampstead Garden Sub-urb. Why, I couldn't imagine. It didn't seem a likely place for her to have scored. Scored she must have, because it was early for her, and if she didn't exactly look perky, she was at any rate composed. I followed her on in, keeping a good fifty paces behind. I had already been well enough schooled by Phar Lap in the arts of exiguousness to know that she wouldn't see me if I didn't want her to. How like childhood death seemed, involving as it did such games of grandmother's footsteps.

Natasha hadn't had to consider whether it was appropriate to wear black for this human barbecue – because she always did. Even so, I was faintly pleased to see that she had her best black on today. A three-quarter-length black silk skirt, flared from the knee; a black silk blouse with an exaggeratedly long, pointed collar; her good, black chenille woolly; a long black scarf; and a high-waisted, full-length black overcoat – this latter essential on an almost balmy morning in early May, to keep her junky chill wrapped up tight. It was an outfit I'd bought for her, which explained its smart co-ordination. Natasha added the mores of a beautiful woman to the messy lessons of her father. And anyway, for years now she'd been in the habit of shooting up *everything* she got from Marks & Spencer. She'd go in with her pal Russell, boost a load of stuff, then take it back for a fifty per cent refund. M&S had the best returns policy of any of the high-street chains. Those Jews! They understood that it was far better to roll with a problem like this. So, fifty per cent Jew, fifty per cent refunded – that was my Natty.

As she clacked by on the worn heels of her cheap, plastic ankle-boots I saw that she had reasonably presentable black tights – or at least not running at the knee. She asked a lingering, baggy-suited man which chapel. The sepulchral underling looked at her with sarcophagus eyes. She tripped on. I followed.

A hearse stood by the doors to the chapel. It looked bog-ordinary to me. Goody. The coffin was a plain enough deal as well. There was no toilet-seat wreath, or trumped-up tribute.

Not even a loose bunch of my namesake. As we stared, four hirelings dragged the thing out and oomphed it up on to their unsteady shelves of shoulder. Who'd've thought the old bag had such weight in her? They shuffled a little in their square-toed, Freeman Hardy & Willis, orthopaedic-lookalike shoes. They adjusted the coffin with their ugly hands, bracing each other with thick arms held across heavy-set backs. Then plodded forward. Ah, the leaden death march!

'Goin' to the chapel and we're gonna get mar-ried!' the lithopedion went off in my coat pocket. I damped it down, padded forward, slid into one of the pews at the back. Natty stood two pews from the front, wavering in the narrow aisle as the undertakers undertook to dump my coffin ceremoniously on the plinth at the front, which I knew from previous visits concealed the conveyor belt.

Then nothing. Or, as Phar Lap would phrase it, 'no-thing'. Meaning a great desert of negativity, an ultimate tundra, a vanishing-point veldt. No readings, no music, no flowers, no weeping, no no-thing. The undertakers stood, ranged across the front of the chapel, displaying to the ungregation their four elephant asses. After a while one of them came back to where Natty stood and said something in her ear; she murmured in return. The lift attendant of death strode forward across the lobby and without bothering to conceal his action hit the concealed button. The conveyor belt jolted, took up the sad slack, and propelled it offstage left. *Exeunt*.

Natasha came past me fast. All I saw were her pin-prick pupils, her paper-pale skin, her ineffable cheekbones, and she was gone. What did she see? No-thing. I waited 'til the undertakers had passed, rubbing their hands, getting out their packs of Benson & Hedges, then walked forward, up the aisle and round the back of the belt, to where I found the expected door.

They say it helps people to see the bodies of those they've loved one final time before disposal. Helps to confirm beyond any doubt that the dead are dead. Deanimated. Gone. Perhaps it would've helped if I'd seen the rip-off I'd anticipated. My corpse helped out of its pine jacket and speedily dispatched; the cheapo coffin shoved straight back in the hearse and returned to the showroom, like a used car with a number of careless owners. As we all know, there's nothing more comforting than being confirmed in one's long-held prejudices. I was out of luck. Backstage two men in the khaki overalls affected by Englishmen on the calmer shores of manual labour checked the seals, the paperwork, the dials on the big chundering oven; then, without even adjusting its position on the conveyor belt, opened the doors, hit another button, and off it went. It, you note. Not I – it.

Had I expected anyone else to be at the bonfire? To wave sparklers of feeling about, let off fireworks of emotion? No, not particularly. Although I was surprised at Mr and Mrs Elvers's non-attendance. I supposed they must have had an important meeting – they were that kind of people. Meetings for them were sumptuary affairs. Such that, were either of them to be asked at around teatime if they wanted a slice of cake, they'd reply, 'No thanks, I had an important meeting at lunchtime.' Both of them were growing fat on important meetings; and as time went by, and the Waste of Paper chain grew and grew, a crumpled streamer of premises wreathing the office world, they grew fatter still.

No, it was left to Natty to mourn in the now sunny morning. Under the plane trees with their dancing leaves, amid the cherry and apple blossom, looking imposingly beautiful, ridiculously Russian. She dallied outside a small exterior office, which, like everything else there, was solidly built with dark Dachau brick. As the undertakers were stubbing out their cigarettes and swinging into their hearse, one of them paused, a crease neatly slicing his ham's brow. Was he thinking of consoling Natty, or hitting on her? Or both – she was that kind of a girl. He thought better of it and shuddered.

And Natty, did she cry? Cry she didn't – and this did rile me. She'd cried at fucking Yaws's funeral. Admittedly she was only ten then – but still, her own fucking mother. Her Mumu. The fount of her own incomparable narcissism, her wayward charm, her rampant needs. How come she didn't shed at least one, meagre, drip of grief? Couldn't she wring out her emotional wet blanket of a character just that little bit more? I mean, I *know* she was sad all right, sad for her own fucking self. Miserable as hell. Desolate beyond belief. Or was she too like Yaws? Another fucking Yaws, with a fresco of his face painted on the wet plaster *inside* of her own. So it seemed.

After half an hour they brought her an urn. Well, not exactly an urn, more of a giant, bronze-coloured, plastic Nescafé jar, complete with screw top. She cradled this bulky thing in her skinny, shot-to-shit arms, her shabby gloves grasping the lid of her dead mummy of a baby. Then she turned and walked away, back up Hoop Lane, still dry-eyed.

Now I concede, the smack must've stunned her along with the shock of it all. And having to do it on her own little lonesome had to've put a spanner in her Fabergé works. But even so – not to cry *at all*. Well, this did cut through my colourless, odourless, insensate stupidity of indifference. I tried rage on for size, like a hat, and it nearly fitted. I pronounced an anathema on my junky daughter. I lit a ciggie and, inhaling, remembered the words of a more famous puffer than I. Camus, dead at forty-seven in an auto wreck. 'If a man does not cry at his mother's funeral, the world will chop his head off.' Quite so, Bert, quite so. And as for a daughter – well, I shuddered to think. I shuddered to think.

Christmas 2001

I shudder now. It's cold in here. For some reason the Estate Agent opened the window in the kitchenette before it all happened. Before he lay down in slow stages. I stand in here hungry, cold, and not a little weepy, looking up at the underside of the leaves of the hideous spider plant. How can you tell that a property's empty? Because the spider plants have taken it over, colonised it with their sharp fronds. A very domesticated day of the triffid. Perhaps the spider plant will take over this property, now vacant save for little me? Proving that this was no symbiosis on their part – squatting in the corner looking fucking ugly, in return for three drops of Baby Bio and a few shaky dribbles of tepid tap water – but a rampant, parasitic war. Spider plants against all the rest.

Naturally it was the Ice Princess who did the watering, tending this appropriately ugly garnish with one of her characteristically absurd attempts at housewifery. In a while I'll crawl up and take a look at her – but not now. Now it's sufficient for me to stand here, under the spider plant, in the corner. If I turn round I can observe the ganglia of cabling sprouting from the back of the television, which once yoked it to the amplifier, the CD player, the tape deck, the record deck and the speakers. All the technically musical appurtenances of this most unmusical of households. This gravely quiet household. It's amazing they managed to hang on to these black-box recorders for as long as they did, but they're gone now – and so are their sounds. The least the Ice Princess and her swain could've done would've been to put the television on.

But then I was forgetting – there's no electricity.

Chapter Ten

I 've always managed to have a certain cold objectivity about my daughters, perhaps because of losing the loved son so early. And in the years following my own death I excelled myself. But then the perspectives afforded by my pulverised condition – the view from the Nescafé jar – supplemented my own Dulston prospect. Everyone who touched, or even beheld, that plastic pot of me, took a little bit away with them – a sarcastic smear of ash.

Natasha Yaws strode with purpose up Hoop Lane on that balmy morning in early May 1988. She'd descended a scant hour before from a house on Central Square. An oblong-fronted, mock-Regency affair of fake solidity but credible rectitude, where she'd spend the latter hours of darkness sitting, half-naked, on the edge of a man's marital bed. She'd fallen in with the man at Russell's in Kentish Town, where he'd been scoring cocaine. His wife and kids were away, and the nameless, never-to-be-named man had taken Natasha home with him in the first, cocaine flush of certainty that he'd be able to fuck her. Natasha had been confident he wouldn't be able to – and she'd been right. She needed to be north in the morning – so why not grab two kinds of lift?

He'd lain in the marital bed casually rubbing the mush at his central juncture, while Phil Collins cried melodramatically from concealed speakers, feeling him coming in the air at night . . . O Lord!

Natasha had sat on the edge of the big Slumberdown, half-naked to give the married man the necessary visual fodder, while she snarfed up the remains of his cocaine. She interspersed dirigible lines with chases of smack off of a generous foil hanky torn from a family-size roll, which she'd found in the immaculately white, family-size kitchen below. She'd only needed to strip off her funereal woolly and funereal blouse and funereal M&S black bra to give the man what he wanted. Ach! Such loveliness. Such high breasts, such long pink nipples, such a smooth back. Such a *pity* he was too far gone to see the raw pink pits in the crooks of her arms. Such a *shame* he wasn't able to insist – once Rémy Martin and cocaine had done their work – on her removing the black skirt and the black tights, so that he might see the truly awesome mess she'd made of her nether regions with her sharp nails. Picking and slashing at her own long thighs, as she vented her hatred on half of herself. But he didn't.

Now, Nescafé urn in her arms, Natasha banged the brass knocker on the big white door and waited for the married man to come running. Which he did, jerked awake from spunk-sodden sopor with a sudden awareness of *all* that had transpired. Could it be wife and kids prematurely returned? He pulled on trousers, shirt, kicked drug trash under the bed, limp-staggered down to the front door. But no – it was the tart without a heart. 'G'gaa wh' what?' he gagged on the fresh, spring air. He was confused; the last time he'd seen her she'd been half-dressed, now she was over – and holding a bizarre jar. 'What's that?'

'My mother,' she tartly replied. 'I need a cab for her – and me. I'm going to Regent's Park. Give me the money, call the cab. Don't worry – I'll wait on the bench over there.' She pointed with a black-sheathed finger.

Worry he might, at home in the mid-morning, his motherly neighbours perambulating around the square, greedy for indiscretion. 'B-b-but . . . I thought . . . What?'

'Don't think – act,' said Natasha. 'Give me the money.' He groped in his pocket and found a tenner. She swivelled on her synthetic heel, clacked across the road to the bench and sat down on it. He called the cab and as he dialled reflected, quite rightly, on his lucky escape.

At the sumptuous Cumberland Terrace apartment an odd trio awaited Natasha: the two mortally tubby Elverses, and the eelishly thin, immortal Esther. They talked small while anticipating large events. They sat at a big, round, pine table, with big, round, china teacups in their hands. This was domesticity with a generous shot of growth hormone. They weren't to be disappointed.

The day before there had been a characteristic Natasha-Charlotte row, about the cremation. Esther had wanted to attend and Charlie didn't see why she shouldn't. Should-shouldn't, shouldn't-should had, in due course, given way to did-didn't and the whole dull grind of inter-sibling abrasion. 'If she goes, I don't!' Natasha plainted. 'Mumu couldn't stand her – and nor can I. Mumu would've hated her being there – and so would I. If she goes, I don't – and you *know* what Mumu would think of that!'

Charlie had sobbed on her husband's upholstered shoulder, beat her plump fists on the arm of a candy-striped divan, reversed the procedure. She decided she couldn't go without Esther. That she'd better sit it out and endure developments.

Now, the entryphone burped and Charlotte went to spy on her sister courtesy of the CCTV system. How bad might she be looking? But of course, she was beautiful in her black pillbox hat – toque of the devil. The trio braced themselves as Natasha made her way up the wide, carpeted treads of the staircase. Richard Elvers said to his wife and her aunt, 'Let's humour her on this occasion, she's been through a lot – we've all been

through a lot as well.' But there was nothing funny about
Natasha and no point in humouring her.

'Where the fuck were you – you bitch!' Natasha spat at her
sister from the door, ignoring her brother-in-law, blanking her
aunt, and putting her jarred mother down on the thickly
carpeted floor.

'B-but you . . . You – ' such stuttering is all Natasha can
elicit today.

'I what? *What*?!'

'You, you said you'd go alone. That you'd only go alone. I
was only doing wh – '

'What! What were you doing – sitting here! With that . . .
that . . . *bitch*!'

And you might've thought that Natasha had *really* gone
too far now, if it wasn't that this elegant, Nash apartment had
– for the purposes of this shtick – become another waiting
room on a timeless Ellis Island of crowded, over-emotional
Jewry. Esther – far from swooning, or screaming, or otherwise
manifesting Anglo-Saxon attitudes – sank quite disgracefully
to the boards of her niece's histrionic play. She trilled, 'Oy!
My faygeleh! My little Natty! Oy – come here darling,
darling! Don't cry so. Your mother dead – and you so sad,
so sad.' She sprightly rose, advanced towards Natasha and
the two skinny Jews embraced, while the two tubby Gentiles
looked on. What's bred in the bony – and all that jazz. As if all
this wasn't bad enough – they smoked, Natty and Esther.
They smoked big-time. Charlotte and Richard had given up.
They were the kind of people who'd given up everything at
least twice. Although when they'd taken it up again – in order
to give it up once more – was difficult to ascertain. They'd
given up smoking, drinking, eating and – the unkind might say
– thinking. But they had to tolerate the junky and the aunty
smoking two packs of Kools and drinking their tea, while

goading each other into more emotionality than could rightly be contained even in this vast apartment, with its aircraft-hangar ceilings, its cliff-top cornicing, its massy mouldings, and its outsize eighties furniture arrayed in pastel riot. Esther and Natasha smoked and sobbed while the long, lipstick-stained butts piled up in the ashtray, building a burnt pagoda. Mumu's cremains were tidied away.

It's not easy being good, so the goodies eventually retreated to the kitchen, where they propped their comfortable rumps against the range and the worktop, while they deliberated on what to *do* about Natty – who so clearly was *out of control*. (Although, in truth, she had always been; it was just that now, given Mumu's demise, they'd decided to take responsibility for it. Big booboo.)

'I've already taken two days off from the office,' said Richard, his face pinker than ever, his sandy hair ruffled with emotion. 'I mean,' he hurried on, 'not that that means any-thing.'

But he needn't have worried about upsetting his wife; Charlotte had had quite enough of her mother's implosive death, and didn't like the fall-in either. 'Darling, I know what you're thinking, but Esther won't stay for long, she'll want to get back to New York as soon as possible – but Natasha we'll have to deal with. I think we should ask her to stay here, she's got to kick the drugs. I spoke to Dr Steel about her and he had a word with a colleague. They'll have a bed for her on the psychiatric ward at the Royal Free if we can hold on to her for a day or so.'

'D'you think that's wise? D'you think she'll do it?'

'It's worth a try – we have to try. I've called Miles as well and he's coming over – perhaps he can persuade her?'

Two hours went by, and forty-odd butts accumulated before Esther and Natasha went to lie down in adjoining bedrooms. The heroin had leached through Natasha's system – and the cocaine was long gone. But it didn't matter any more which end of the narcotic seesaw she was perched upon – she still lurched in short arcs of hysteria. Natasha was broke, of course, or she wouldn't have dreamed of staying in this centrally-located country house hotel, with its plump, square flunkeys. True, Russell might well have scored for her, or given her tick if he was holding, but lately he'd been making odder demands upon her. Demands so peculiar that Natasha couldn't get stoned enough to fulfil them without feeling *very bad*. She knew that she ought to get away from her sister's, that soon she'd be immobilised, that the seesaw was rocking to rest.

She lay down on the Elverses' brass one-and-a-half-size bed. She squirmed under the quilt and immediately was concussed by unconsciousness. Smack – such a good word that; such an apt example of psychic onomatopoeia. Natasha Yaws, smack-head. So true, so *just*.

When Natasha awoke, seven hours later, in the early evening, Esther had already gone. Esther, a fleet old bird, winging her way back to the US of A. Ageless Esther Bloom, her stem of a body propped up in a padded first-class vase, on a British Airways flight out of Heathrow ('the best bit of Britain so far as I'm concerned – yooknowhatImean?'). Esther, watered by passing hostesses and leafing through the current number of *Fortune*, was already putting the last few days behind her. She'd take time out to process her little sister's death when she'd dealt with her broker, her accountant, her tenants, her friends, the committee at the Met, her pet dogs, her tame faggots, and all the rest of the Manhattan menagerie which kept her from brooding. Kept her alive, in the present, not sunk in the hopeless past like her sad Lil, not endlessly reliving it and chewing it over, as if there were any way to change it. What could that provoke? Only a trip and a tumble, down the basement steps and into the jumble of memory. Their parents – their fucking parents. Ach! Such pretentiousness! Such stupid foolery! Denying their race, their religion, their debts, their lies – and for what? Doodly-squat. And Lily, sprinting through life bearing the eternal flame of internalised race hatred. Carrying it all the way to this grey, wet little island, where she ended up the widow of some dumb Englishman. Now she was dead herself, poisoned by her own incompatibilities.

Lily had always joined in with this idiocy – but not Esther. Esther went to shul, gave money to B'nai B'rith, visited Israel, wailed at the wall, screamed at Yad Veshem. Esther didn't simply resign herself to being Jewish – she accepted it. Lily had nearly always tried to hide it from the world. 'If no one knows,' she told Esther one time when they were still young enough to speak seriously with each other, 'I won't have to react when some swine makes an anti-Semitic remark.' Esther had roared with laughter. 'If anyone makes an anti-Semitic remark around me I'll smack him – or her – in the keister!' And now Lily was dead of all that ulcerating self-hatred, those phobias, those useless husbands, these nudnik kids – and Esther? Esther was going to live for ever – so she lit another Kool and stayed that way.

Miles and Natasha sat and wept apart in the second spare bedroom of the Elverses' apartment. Despite the late hour, Molly, the Filipino peon, was vacuuming up after Esther, trying to eradicate her smoke-cured, ageless air. JAP jerky. Through the wall came the distinctive noises of someone throttling a robot.

The two cried apart – because they couldn't do anything much together any more. Not with Natty like this, skinny, scabby, sweaty; her black hair stuck down on one side of her pillow-creased face and flying away from the other; her nails bitten to the quick – the only thing that prevented her from picking at the sores on her legs. What a turn-off! Or so Miles, hypocritically, thought. For, in truth, he'd made love to her for the first time when she was precisely like this – and done it many times since. He'd pressed his soap-smelling, nicely compact, firmly muscled body against this scabrous streak, and hoped that at each contact point his own vitality would flow into her. He pushed himself up and moved over her with his electric mouth, pulsing between the abrasions, jolting to the side of wounds, conducting into her cunt.

Natasha would lie almost inert during these Frankensteinian sessions, only shocked a little by her own tardy orgasm. For what was Miles *for*, anyway – save this: to make love to her, to admire her, to bail her out of jail, or the clutches of other men, or the sludge of gutters. It was his *métier*, his expertise. He'd been trained up to it from birth. No, with Miles Natasha would allow herself to be made love to, like the exquisite mechanism she might've been, had it not been for this dynamo of self-indulgence which was her animating principle. And for a big-cocked, hard-assed, cranked-up, solid fuck? For that she went to Russell. Russell who, with his pimp-size prick and his own implausible good looks – hawk-ish face, olive skin, chestnut locks – was in every way a match for Natty. Russell with his endless patter, his casual anarchism, his plangently sexy amorality, his violence, his madness, his not-being-nice-Milesness.

So, Miles cried for himself and Natasha cried for herself, and eventually Miles broached the subject of his quest into the bedroom. 'Natty, Charlie and Richard and I – '

'What?' Quick off the mark there – such consensus was, in and of itself, deeply suspicious.

'We wondered if you might consider going in for a detox now . . . now Mumu's gone?' Good way of putting it, that, for Natasha is far too selfish to think of doing anything for herself. She's entirely centred in what others might do for her. But Miles is too thick to leave it there – he pressed on regardless of her dangerous glare. 'Charlie's spoken to the Royal Free, they'll give you a bed – your own room, even. It'll be a good detox – not too fast. Nothing heavy . . .'

He tailed off because she'd uncoiled her feline length from the bed, avoided his entreating arm and was bending down, groping for her black plastic ankle-boots, her little black bag full of crumpled foil and wads of tissue paper.

'Natty – what're you doing?' Dolt – wasn't it obvious?

'Getting the fuck out of here . . . this-this *clinic*.'

'Natty . . . Natty . . .' Natty what? Dread? He was such a twerp. 'You're in no fit – ' He didn't have to go on, for she was performing the end of his sentence by doubling up and retching. Her forehead was braced against the carpet, her fingers scrabbling and clutching at the pile, as if she'd been taken with the plague in the very act of fitting the fucking thing. 'Oh Natty – Natty my love.'

She allowed him to help her back into the soft, soiled bed. Allowed him to smooth the henna-tipped bangs away from her knotted forehead and wipe the sticky slick from her sharp chin. She moaned, 'I can't, Miles, I can't . . . I jus' can't . . . specially without Mumu . . . ach-oh- eurgh . . . I can't. I've got to have something – anything – *I've gottoo*, *dammit*, *gottoo!*' Natasha Yaws yowled and yelled.

Miles proved himself at the *very moment* when he was physically resisting her to be entirely conducive, completely deserving of what Fate would deal him out. 'Natty, if you'll stay here at Charlie and Richard's you can have this – and these.' Yup, he had some drugs. One hand came up out of the pocket of his uniform black jacket, in it a little brown jug of methadone. Crazy drug – crazy boy. A heroin-substitute, named Dolophine for the Führer when it was synthesised by the Germans during the war. So, Miles medicated the emaciated Jewish junky with special Nazi drugs. Swiss ones too, for in his other hand appeared a littler vessel of Valium. Resourceful Miles had bought one from his mother, Isis, and the other from the junky who lived upstairs from him. He hated doing it. Not.

Natasha snatched them both, hunched to protect *her* supply, unscrewed caps, washed down pill with potion, dropped the bottles clinking back over the side of the bed, then subsided on to the pillows.

Miles looked on, pretending to be aghast. He muttered while he stroked her hair. 'That's twenty mils.' He knew the jargon – well he would, wouldn't he? Nice boy, in his last year of law studies, although he'd be righteously fucked if the powers that be were to find out about *this*. 'It should hold you for twenty-four hours – and now you'll sleep. I'll get you more, Natty, but only if you'll stay here, see the people at the Royal Free on Friday. Please?' He didn't have to go on with this ordinary pleading, because Natasha was sleeping, or pretending to sleep, or ignoring him, or all three.

Near to sleep, Natasha Yaws was delivered from the awful death of her beloved Mumu. She escaped the Furies of her own addiction, avenging, implacable, disputatious. She lay quiet, as the drugs percolated her raddled young body, turning filthy blood to distilled water, distressed flesh to waxy purity. She waited for the tearful irritation – which made her feel like smacking nice Miles in his pretty face – to turn to the tearful impersonation of love. And in these moments of half-sleep, with the narcotic undertow pulling her out, Natasha became the person she would've liked to be, her beauty as yet unmarred, thin and young. Sexy, yes, but not the Charybdis of venality she'd fast become, sucking men down into her, wrapping her long legs around their waists as many times as there are carnal sins to commit. Simply sexy. And free – not free like a loosed horse, or a runaway train, but capable of sustained and voluntary action.

Capable of the concentration, application and creativity required to paint the vast and splendidly-achieved frescos that processed behind her eyelids as she sank into sleep. Frescos on the ceiling – it was always these that Natasha dreamed of painting, because all her ambitions were approached from a recumbent posture. Yet, what frescos! What a teeming new mythology! What boldness of composition! Sureness of line! Brightness of colour! Such a shame they always faded as she metabolised, until, on cracking her crusty eyes, Natasha was confronted yet again with the painfully uncertain, cramped line drawings of her very real life. The old realism.

Dusk fell and Natasha wheezed on the pillow. Miles moved a high-backed armchair to the window. As the sun set over the arboreal park, and the gibbons in the zoo – now denied human subjects – impersonated each other, he took from his case a book which nearly filled it. He resumed reading where he'd left off early that morning, about the law of tort.

The cremains of Lily Bloom sat in a bronze plastic, outsize Nescafé jar, in a fitted cupboard, in an alcove, in the Elverses' front room. Lily had always wanted to live between here and Oxford Street. It's the only part of London that has anything approaching a grid system, a tiny gauze patch of American antisepsis set in the infective core of the Great Wen. Mindjew, the ironic recursion of the past few days wouldn't have been lost on her. Her cadaver carted north to Kentish Town, filed in a giant desk drawer at the undertakers' for two days, then carted further north, then burnt, and now the residuum carried unsteadily back here, to within carping distance of the Royal Ear. Yes, Lily Bloom appreciated an irony – arguably she moved to England mainly in order to experience its green, unpleasant irony at first hand. To play out her overdramatised internal conflicts in a theatre where she could be assured that the audience were laughing at her heartily. Behind their hands.

Given that the Elverses' Cumberland Terrace apartment is on a twenty-five-year, Crown lease, it's not quite as dear as you might expect. But still, this is 1988, and London's funicular property prices are at the peak of one of their ten-year wind-ups. A hundred per cent has been put on the value of every bothy in the burg. So, given the settlement of that troublesome tax bill which – along with Minxie – gnawed her in her last days; and given the settlement of death duties; and given her mortgage on the flat in Bartholomew Road; and given the fact that she could never, ever save, Lily could just about afford the cupboard her cremains are to tenant for the next five years. In death there are smaller premises, littler ironies.

Through in the master bedroom the Elverses were having sex. This was no joyful affirmation that they were alive while the greyish Nescafé next door was dead, nor was it a defiant assertion of marital fidelity in the faithless faces of the pair in the second spare bedroom. No, this was *having* sex, owning sex in the same way that the Elverses possessed two hundred Waste of Paper outlets, three homes (London, Norfolk and the Algarve), four cars (his Mercedes, her Volvo, their Range Rover and the little Seat down south), fifteen notable canvases (Jasper Johns, Lichtensteins, even a Warhol – their fresh-bought modernism was conservatively American), twenty-odd minor prints, and lots and lots and lots of chattels. The Elverses had more than one mug tree – that said it all.

So, the Elverses, as plumped-up as their 100% pure

eiderdown, forty-tog, emperor-size duvet, disported themselves on their daddy-and-mummy-bear bed, desperate to become a daddy and a mummy. They possessed the sexual act in the way that they might wish to have a baby bear – securely, cherishing it, nurturing it, raising it up, giving it everything it might conceivably need in the way of porridgy caresses. Charlotte – as, I daresay, has been remarked – was a fine figure of a woman, broad-beamed, pink from nape to base, big-breasted, saucer-nippled, blonde-maned and square-shouldered. And Richard was big enough to fold all this motherly potential in his own heavily-freckled bulk, his own white and ginger enormity.

Richard Elvers, curiously enough, even had the same Yaws mouth as Charlotte, the same red turbine of a kisser. Observing them sucking saliva in and out of each other made it difficult not to fear for any progeny, who might well have this characteristic reinforced by heredity. It was only early evening and here they were possessing sex. But then Charlotte had researched thoroughly and discovered that there could never be *enough* sex when it came to manufacturing more Elverses. That Richard's vas deferens – like a wrinkled, brown udder – would fill up with more little Elverses the more it was milked.

Moreover, that morning Charlotte had gone for her weekly reflexology session. Her feet were palped by an old Kiwi hippy in Harley Street, so that her endocrine system was, it was to be hoped, in as much harmony as the flower pensioner's stock portfolio. Not to mention the herbs Charlotte regularly grazed on, and the flower decoctions she regularly slurped up, and the essential oils she regularly sniffed, and the needles that regularly riddled her – all in the service of regular ovulation. No wonder they went about the business of this regular sex meeting with a specific agenda. Specific because it fell within the three days that Charlotte knew – by dint of keeping a very regular cycling diary, taking her temperature frequently, and watching her cervical mucus like a peculiar hawk – were most likely for ovulation. And specific because their movements were co-ordinated so as to discharge the maximum number of elvers, from his Sargasso into her internal waterways.

It didn't matter if Charlotte went on top – which she mostly did – it was still essential that she stay still once they had come. And come they must. Orgasms had to be achieved like the sales targets throughout the two hundred card houses of their paper imperium. Orgasms must also be as simultaneous as possible, and consummated not with a second try – fatal that, over-stirring the generative broth – or a clammy cuddle, but with Charlotte pancake-flat on the mattress, with her feet higher than her head. Every possible natural force was brought to bear on this natural process – even gravity itself.

Richard did his best too. Not that there was much he *could* do. His was not a frame that took tight, hip-hugging briefs anyway. He was to boxer shorts and pleated cords as to a baggy manor born. He cut his commitments back to the bare minimum, slackening his grip on the business so there was plenty of time in hand for regular sex. Regular sex and, unfortunately, regular snacks. Not that either Elvers thought of their biscuit-barrel blow-outs as regular. No – they were highly *irregular*, unscheduled, unpremeditated – but they happened often. Even if only a fraction of the space in the fridges, cupboards and freezers in their three homes was filled, there was still enough delicatessen pigswill to fatten several porkers. The Elverses, for such plump presences, had an immaterial way of absorbing nutriment. Their big hands blurred from plate to mouth. They didn't know what they were doing themselves. Often, they only realised they'd had yet another cookie-monstering when they rolled over in the fluffy bed and felt the shingle of crumbs grate beneath their stranded bodies. You could only feel sorry for them – or not sorry at all.

Natasha was kept in a chemical straitjacket for the next few days. It was murder on the Elverses' furnishings and on their nerves, already frayed by death. Natasha couldn't figure out why it was she felt so crappy, despite the little brown jugs that Miles brought by. But then she didn't know that the cunning, legalistic fellow was watering each draught down more and more. Natasha dragged one of the portable Trinitrons into the spare room and got it into bed with her. She yanked a phone in as well, and ran up the bill calling her one remaining friend, who lived in Australia – natch. She burnt holes in the carpet, the duvet and the sheets with her ceaseless smoking. She raided Richard's drinks cabinet and downed cherry brandy, advocaat, and Chartreuse – then puked on the pricey Persian kilims. She wouldn't bathe. She prevented Molly from cleaning the apartment by engaging her in endless disquisitions on domestic exploitation. She'd tolerate Miles's presence at night, but only if he sat in the chair by the window. She would've had him pacing up and down the Outer Circle if she could've.

It wasn't necessary to tell Natasha what the family's plans for her were – that much they knew. Natasha and Lily had been like the two weighted balls on a gaucho's bolas, hurtling through space, revolving around themselves, tangling savagely in the running legs of the world. With Lily gone, Natasha was simply thrown.

Dr Steel had Natasha's number all along; his very steeliness was itself a psychic scalpel with which to excise tumours of false, junky emotion. 'She can take up a bed at the Royal Free and get a detox,' he told the Elverses; 'there's one available at the weekend. But she'll be discharged within a fortnight and go straight back to using – that I can, unfortunately, guarantee. Or else you could consider putting her in a treatment centre.'

'Would that work?' Charlotte asked, as if contemplating a new accounting system for the business.

'It might – it might not. Your mother's death should've broken through some of her denial, put her in a more receptive state.'

'How long would she need to be there for?'

'Well, as far as I know the primary-care programme lasts around eight weeks, then they might let her out if she had a stable environment to go to, but she doesn't, does she?'

Charlotte pictured her sister's environment. It wasn't so much not stable as fragmented like a refugee camp bombed by the Israeli air force. Five bin-bags full of dirty laundry at Miles's, three at Russell's, two at Lily's flat, one at Cumberland Terrace. Natasha had no money, no abode, no prospects. Her job at Hackney Dogs had indeed gone there. Her habit had become a skilful practitioner of negative arbitrage, talking her out of everything she – and significant others – had. 'Erm . . . no, not exactly.'

'Well, they'd probably want her to stay in for a secondary-care programme as well. All in all you could expect her to be away for six months.'

Charlotte heard this as 'you could expect to be *rid of her* for six months', and resisted the impulse to whoop and holler, because: 'She'll never agree, Dr Steel. Never.'

'She might if you shock her into acceptance, confront her forcibly with the reality of what she's done – of how her behaviour is affecting you all. What's her boyfriend's name?'

'Miles.'

'Is he an addict?'

'No – but he's pretty spineless.'

'What I mean is – will he back you up on this?'

'Yes, he'll do that . . . But there's another boy – man – she's involved with. He's dangerous – a drug dealer, a criminal.'

'Is she in contact with him?'

'I think so.'

'Well, I don't know what you can do about that, but what I can organise is an interview with the admissions people from the centre – '

'We'll never get her there.'

'That's all right – they'll come to you. To be blunt, Mrs Elvers, they need the sale.'

Sale – a word Charlotte understood. 'How much is this likely to cost?'

'That's something you'll need to discuss with their people, but from what I understand . . . if she completes a full programme . . . not far shy of six thousand.'

'Six grand!'

'I know, it's a lot, but the DHSS will pay a proportion. Mrs Elvers . . . it may not be too tactful, but your mother – Lily – did she leave anything for Natasha?'

Charlotte pressed the plastic squares of inner calculation, a thing she was good at. 'Um . . . yes, well, she could afford it, not that I'll let her know she's paying. I'll get a power of attorney if necessary. Fortunately I alone am my mother's executor – she wasn't altogether a fool in such matters.'

'So it seems.'

The people from Pullet Green, the treatment centre, arrived with sinisterly avaricious promptitude the very next day. But they had the disconcerting honesty to explain themselves to Charlotte Elvers at once. In the hall. 'We have a waiting list who want to come in on state-assisted beds, but we can't afford to take them unless they're subsidised by full-payers.

And those are in short supply,' said Irene Theakston, a dumpy presence with frilly blonde curls, a neat blue suit, and brown moles on her face and neck, so heavy they hung down, like tiny dewlaps.

Her companion was a vigorous young man in his early thirties with beaky features, who wore a most unfashionable, green nylon jacket, even duller brown trousers, and never-been-on-deck shoes. He introduced himself as 'Peter Landon, I'll be doing the admissions interview with . . .' – he cumbrously consulted a file he withdrew from a briefcase of achingly sensible utility – '. . . Natasha?'

'That's right.' Charlotte was taken aback. Natasha would eat this one alive and spit his bones out all over the carpet. More mess. She hadn't known what to expect of the Pullet Green people, but surely not these two, who looked recently cashiered from the Jesus Army. Strangely, Landon intuited Charlotte's scepticism. 'I do admissions because I look soft but can act tough. Two cops in one if you like. Not, ha-ha!' – he laughed abruptly – 'that I've ever had much to do with law enforcement – except on the receiving end.'

Charlotte arched her brows in query.

'I was a major cocaine-trafficker for ten years – I found recovery in jail. All of our counselling staff are recovering addicts and alcoholics, so, I hope we know whereof we speak.'

'I see,' said Charlotte, now entirely flummoxed. 'Would you . . . like some tea?'

'Coffee, if you have it,' said Irene Theakston. 'I'll handle the boring, administrative stuff with you, while Peter takes his gloves off.'

Landon meanwhile had withdrawn a two-inch-square yellow paper sachet from his briefcase. 'Just some hot water for me, please – I've brought my own tisane. No caffeine, you see – I find it too speedy.'

The preceding night Dr Steel's suggested intervention had taken place. The Elverses and Miles stood round the beddy mess where Natasha lay, and hit her first with their anger – why did she behave like this, the lying, the stealing, the cheating, the abuse? – and then with their love. Didn't she understand how much they cared? How much they wanted to help her get better? That there was some hope. But only if . . . only if . . . only if . . .

They succeeded in wearing her down, but all sensed it would be temporary. They got her agreement at least to speak to the Pullet Green people. Miles's sole contribution was to withhold her evening potions for a few minutes – he had no stomach for intervention. He'd never intervened in anything in his life; if a self-sealing envelope wouldn't seal – he'd cry. Richard didn't do too much of the intervening either. He did dislike Natasha and wish her ill, but only on principle. Only because she so distressed the sister he loved. And anyway, Richard had another kind of intervention ahead of him that evening, one he suspected he'd enjoy rather more.

Richard put on his old jean jacket from his Kenny Market days. He drove north with casual finesse. He parked the big, blue Mercedes in the alleyway behind Kentish Town Road and got a stainless-steel Big Chief baseball bat out of the trunk. There were hidden sides to Richard Elvers, sides that included intimidating rival card-shop proprietors in the provinces. He mounted the steps to the rear entrance above the bookie's, and leant the bat between two bins. He knocked with all due respect, in the way he imagined an addict might knock – 'tap-t'-tap-tap'.

With disconcerting abruptness a tough, full-bodied, Cockney voice enquired from within, 'Oozethere?'

'I'm a friend of Natty's,' Richard replied in a wheezy voice. 'Wotchew after?'

'This and that,' said Richard, hoping this was sufficiently vague.

It was. The door swung open. 'Wot this? Wot that?' The speaker had to be Russell. He was both better- and tougher-looking than Richard had suspected. Around six foot, with black shoulder-length hair, and more black hair lying flat on his hard head. His nose was hooked, his eyes heavy-lidded, his complexion olive. He wore a loose black sweat suit, with Olympic rings embroidered over the left breast and upper thigh. What, Richard wondered, could Russell possibly be working out for? The two-metre sprint to the ashtray? Miniature-javelin throwing – into the vein? Or perhaps the one-gram smacklifting contest?

Over Russell's shoulder Richard could make out, moving in the dark interior, another large shape which emanated dangerous energy. 'Who is it, Russ?' the shape challenged from the shadows.

Richard edited the Big Chief baseball bat from the frame – this would require a more flexible incentive. 'I've got a message from Natty' – he addressed the shadowy shape as well as the war bonnet in the doorway – 'and some money for you, a debt?'

'Oh really – Natty's gonna pay 'er wedge, is she, wonders'll never cease. You'd better come in.'

Russell stood back a half-pace, allowing Richard space only to insinuate himself in the manner of a table being manoeuvred around a corner. His belt buckle snagged against the door; he felt his vulnerability as intensely as a chilly plunge. The contrast with the smoky airlessness of the flat completed the reverse sauna. The flat was also the size of a sauna. A corridor long enough for a five-year-old to turn a somersault in led to a narrow room with shelving units on all four walls – the kind featuring half-size supermarket baskets suspended

240

from vertical tracks. These had been screwed in from floor to ceiling. Each of the baskets – there must've been near to seventy – was prominently labelled with Dymotape: 'SOCKS', 'PANTS', 'CASSETTES', 'DHSS' and so forth. This smudging of exteriority and interiority was as deranging for Richard as the fussy orderliness, the heat and the claustrophobia.

The only other door in the room – which must lead to still tinier apartments – was blocked by the bulky presence of a portly middle-aged man. He was bald save for a horseshoe of brownish furze, wore a white T-shirt, the trousers from a long-since dismembered suit, and a scowling mien on his crushed, Gladstone face. He would almost have looked comical were it not for the fact that in his pudgy hand he held a long-barrelled revolver. Next to the man was a crappy little kitchen table, and on top of this were a set of electronic scales and two square pieces of plastic, one featuring a miniature beige slag heap, the other a milky-white one.

'Is that real?' Richard asked, nodding at the gun barrel which wavered over the rucked surface of thin, stained carpet. He had no idea why he'd had the temerity to come out with this – it hardly seemed diplomatic.

The pigskin-faced man, however, took it in excellent part. 'Heurgh-herg,' he gurgled, 'nah – not exackery – s'won of them replicas. But you can file out the guard they weld across the front, an' put in a real firing pin – then they work, sort of.'

'Oh,' Richard replied.

'I know a bloke who's dead handy with his file,' the man warmed to his theme, 'so I've got meself quite a number of these . . .' – the barrel described a gestural figure of eight, like a steely index finger – '. . . replicas.'

Russell came into the room, and then there were three big bears in the little house of knick-knacks. Russell sat down on one of the plastic office chairs by the crap kitchen table. His body was a jerky toy which contained an eccentric inner movement. He pushed up the cuff of his track-suit trousers, disclosing the top of a high-performance track shoe and a white padded sock. He withdrew from his pocket a flat plastic case, and from that a one-millilitre diabetic's syringe, already primed. He administered the fix with Dr Steel-y efficiency, the bunched cloth and the angle of his crossed-over leg serving as a tourniquet. He flushed the works in a mug of water on the table, replaced them in the case, and replaced that in his pocket. He began to wrap the wraps of cocaine and heroin, while speaking. 'So, Tiny Tony . . . this is . . .?'

'Richard,' said Richard, oddly fortified by Russell's grotesque performance.

'Charmed,' said Tiny Tony, offering Richard his left hand. They clasped.

'Richard's come to pay back that dozy cow's debt – issatso, Richard?'

'Erm . . . yes, yeah – that's right.'

'So you're givin' her one, are you?' Russell looked up from his task at Richard and gave him a glance of malevolence mixed with sympathy. Tiny Tony gurgled with evil merriment.

'Err . . . no-no, not at all – I'm her brother-in-law.'

'Okeydokey, brother-in-*law*, are you. Hard to imagine Natty having anything so legit, the moody bitch. Well, whaddya gonna give me then, brother-in-*law*?'

Miles had managed to screw out of Natty the approximate figure. Richard drew out a wallet from the inside pocket of his jean jacket; an incongruously large wallet, with double rows of plastic credit-card holders, set like teeth in its leather mandibles. From this he began neatly peeling pale-purple twenties, dealing them out on to the tabletop, next to Russell's fussing hands. Richard did this rather well, in keeping with prevailing gangster chic. There were hidden depths to Richard Elvers all right.

Tiny Tony kept count in a whistling undertone: 'Twenny, for'y, sixty, eigh'y, ton, ton-twenny, ton-for'y, ton-sixty, ton-eigh'y, two tons – '

'Oi – hold up!' Russell had finished bandaging the bindles of smack and coke with clingfilm, and they lay like small packages of meat between his lean hands. 'Thass double what she owes – what gives brother-in-*law*.'

Richard sighed, aware suddenly of the unpleasantness of the atmosphere in the room – a stench of hostility as rank and as palpable as shit. On the floor beneath the table a radio receiver hissed, then squawked, 'A37, TDA in progress . . . Royal College Street . . . Request backup.' 'Roger Control . . . received . . . on our way.' And then went silent. The two drug dealers didn't appear to notice it. 'Yes,' said Richard, 'it is. But I'd like you to do something for me . . .' He went on adding more notes to the stack on the table, and as he did so continued, '. . . or rather, *not* do something. You see, we're putting Natasha into treatment, or rehab, or whatever it's called, and I know that you're the only person who'll carry on giving her drugs – who could stop her going. I want you to keep away from her until she's out of town – '

'Wot!' Russell expostulated. 'You want me to go away – I can't do that! I've got the business – '

'No-no, I'm not expecting you to go anywhere. All it is is – don't answer the phone or the door to her. Don't let her have any drugs – she can't pay for them anyway. Don't see her . . .' Catching Russell looking at him with dangerously beaten, narrowed eyes, Richard pressed on, 'Look, her mother died a few days ago, and . . . well, I think it's the right time for her . . . psychologically . . . I think she might actually give up . . . with treatment . . . you wouldn't begrudge her that – would you?'

A siren whooped down Kentish Town Road, towards the room full of insincere men, and Richard's eyes slid involuntarily to the window, framed by Russell's basket-case belongings. Through a vertical sliver betwixt blind and frame, Richard could just make out the roof of the speeding police car, with 'A37' blazoned on it, as if for his eyes only. 'Fucking good, these scanners,' said Tiny Tony, who was positioned in such a way as to have a better view of the roadway and the rushing vehicle, 'you set 'em off an' they run right frew the filth's frequencies – over an' over – only stop when they pick up a ca – '

'I don' – I-I don' . . .' Russell broke in on Tiny Tony's hissed patter with his own request for backup, his own emergency squawk, 'I don' be*grudge* her – who fucking would . . . Richard . . . who wouldn't want out of . . . of *this*.' One of his lean hands flipped over, and fell open on the table to grasp the pathetic tininess of the situation – the drugs, the thugs, the paranoia-receiver underneath it.

Richard took the profound risk of looking Russell full in the eyes and saw there things he undoubtedly shouldn't have. Self-pity, certainly, but also shame. Monstrous self-obsession – without doubt – but also a kind of loving. Russell's eyes had large hazel irises, with browner lines spearing them – pretty eye tie-dyes. His pupils were inexistent. Russell's eyes burned with anger and welled with tears, as if an internal, emotional sprinkler system had been activated. Richard hurriedly broke contact, allowed his own gaze to waver away over the Dymotaped labels: 'SHIRTS', 'BOOKS', 'NAT'S STUFF'. Nat's stuff? Was it the case that this pair were that well integrated? That much of a storage unit?

'Yeah well, hreugh, yeah,' Russell snuffled, 'I won't speak to her, then – but you – *you*' – he leant forward and caught Richard's forearm, held it with pincer fingers, and in that moment the dim light in the flat seemed to intensify, the swirling smoke to eddy and clear, the hissing scanner to fall silent – 'make sure you tell me where she is once she's gone, right? You'll do that, right? I'll want to . . . I'll want to write to her, call her . . . and stuff.' Richard saw that the fingernails that clamped him were bitten into recession, and that the lean hands were really swollen sausage meat. He saw the track marks that wormed over the backs of those hands. And Russell saw that he saw. Then he turned back to the table, began unwrapping one of the packets he'd only just bound into its clear winding sheet.

A voice which was self-preservation spoke in Richard's head: 'You'd better leave.' He turned away abruptly, walked the few paces necessary to take him to the front door. Neither of the men in the room made any motion as he undid the chain, undid the two mortise locks, flipped the catch on the Yale. As he was closing the door, Richard saw that Tiny Tony was lifting the purple fan of notes from the table. The fat thug looked at Richard and nodded curtly, as if to say, 'Cut out the middle man, yeah.' Then the door was closed. Richard retrieved his baseball bat from between the bins, not altogether certain who'd been struck out by whom.

Christmas 2001

Even when adults make the greatest possible effort they can't imitate the handwriting of small children – or our drawings either. They can't fake the wonky strokes, botched loops and exaggerated serifs, nor the curiously prosaic orthography. It would be neat if adults, when imitating children's handwriting, ended up with something that looked like children's imitation of adult handwriting – but they don't. There is no mirroring here – only a vast strangeness.

When I was last a little girl, sitting in a hot cotton dress, under the hot, cotton-boll sun, I'd imitate adult handwriting with a bridge pencil in a green, narrow feint book. That's what I remember – the stationery, the writing implements. The feelings are all gone. I'd loop the narrow loop clear along one line, then smear to the line below and loop all the way back again. My idea of adulthood was one of such loopy continuity. A crazy kabbala of curlicues. On that last go-round I had all kinds of ideas about young children. When my own were small I thought them all little Wittgensteins, biding their quiet times scrawling in blue and brown notebooks, until they were ready to publish their philosophical investigations; garbling gobbledegook until they felt the need to translate it. This was, of course, entirely down to the influence of mother-hood and that overwhelming sense we all have of giving birth to a unique personality, a timeless individual. Adults who're children giving birth to children who're adults. Then, as they grew, and the hated lineaments of their forebears began to test the limits of my own forbearance, I concluded that I'd been wrong all along, and that babies were merely stupidity in waiting. Doubly dumb.

Now I'm a child who'd like to imitate an adult's writing. I'd like to be a little Scott marooned in this walk-up antarctic apartment. But these chilly mummies, lying at the bottom of their terminal moraines – they never had much time for writing. They were too busy failing life's examination. I stalk the main room, wending my way from the horrible spider plant, around the entertainment stack, around the coffee table, past the stairs, into the defile between the shelving unit and the door to the kitchenette, but nowhere can I see so much as a half-chalk, or crushed crayon. And believe me, I'm well adapted for searching – ground-hugging as I am; I'm perfectly contrived for looking under furniture, or squeezing behind it.

I once put considerable effort into designing ideal writing implements – now I can't even find a real one.

In the course of the first few stunned hours I spent alone here, I espied the handle-less mug on top of the shelf, inside the serving hatch, which makes this lower floor one not-so-roomy tomb. A present from Bangor – banged up here. Had it been an ironic gesture to buy this incurious curio, this souvenir of nothing? I couldn't give a flying fuck – but what I could see, from down here below (and now I see everything from below, everything soaring up and away from me; that's what you get for a lifetime of looking down on people – another, shorter lifetime of looking up at things), was that it held a stook of pens and pencils. It took me quite a while to get up on the divan, longer still to achieve, precariously, the back of it. I fell a number of times, bounced, rolled to rest among the highly flammable cushions. When at last I managed to knock the mug from the shelf, the implements nearly impaled me as they rained down, although none of them had a point – so the exercise was pointless.

There was one, blue, Berol Rollerball, but it lacked its pillbox cap. The ink had long since evaporated, leaving only a trace in the ball itself. This I discovered when I began pretending to be an adult and tested it on the corner of last week's Cable Guide. *This pretence was, of course, too good for a child. Kids don't test pens – not little kids. They just pitch on in and draw a wonky house or a turd-bodied man. But I tested it – and the pen donated a few, short blueish grooves in the shiny paper, then gave out for ever.*

Anyway – what would I have written? This adult imitating a child imitating an adult. There's nothing much to say except that I'm cold and I'm hungry and I'm lonely and I'm frightened. And what's so fucking novel about that?

Chapter Eleven

Phar Lap introduced me to HeLa, which was really the only wall-covering adequate for a Dulston basement like mine. HeLa wasn't a paint, or a wallpaper, or plaster, or even anything in the synthetic line, oh no. HeLa was the product of abnormal karyology. A vigorous cell line which had originated from the cervical tumour of one Henrietta Lacks, who died in Baltimore in 1951. That was a good year for innovations of a polymorphous nature – what with Disney releasing *Alice in Wonderland*. HeLa was immortal and grown in suspension cultures. The living used it for virus research – and it almost always produced tumours when injected into animals.

We, the dead, had nothing to fear from this material, and it made a fine wall-covering: flexible, durable, and softly murmuring the words of the dying woman herself – 'I'm cold, so cold . . . so very cold' when it was hot, and 'I'm burning up . . . I'm bur-ning . . . Oh, I'm so hot!' when it was cold. I suppose the living would find this grotesque in the extreme, but then they can walk away from such horrors; until, that is, they tread on the rake of their own short-term view, and it smacks them in the face.

There was a factory behind Dulston Junction which churned this stuff out, and Seth's sold it in four-litre cans. Very popular it was too.

In August, Dan Quayle was adopted as Bush's vice-presidential running mate. This made me think of the little birds served up by Bunny Yaws, and all the weird dinner parties of the living, with their smells, burps, grunts and slurps. In November they decided the Turin shroud was a hoax, and at least five Dulston trainspotter types – personally known to me – claimed responsibility. They wished. Fuck it – these characters also said they were behind the Stealth Bomber, the mobile phone, satellite television and several other technical innovations – none of them beneficial.

In December there was an earthquake in Armenia. Many thousands dead – many more thousands mangled and starving. But this meant little to us; after all, they were unlikely to pitch up in Dulston, unless they had family here. The same month saw the Clapham rail crash and the Lockerbie bomb. A few of these people did come to us – burnt, crushed, bemused, and bearing a certain enviable cachet for having been so randomly and rapidly annihilated.

In March of 1989, middle-class liberals in the cystrict were transfixed by news of the Tibetan riots. *Tout le monde* had street plans of Lhasa pinned to their cork boards so they could discuss the finer points of the action, while serving up rösti, masticating it forty times, spitting it out. The Hillsborough disaster claimed little attention in Dulston – after all it was an away match in every sense. Indeed, I'm ashamed to say that many dead I knew laughed uproariously when Kenny Dalglish, the manager of Liverpool Football Club, made his famously understated appeal: 'I think everyone knows there have been a few problems. Please try to stay calm. We are trying to help you.' But then even the most crushing events can acquire an unwarranted irony – when you're dead.

Ah me! Dulston days. The Tiananmen Square disturbances in June of '89 affected us not at all – but the same month, Freddy Ayer moved to Dulston. He pitched up in an elegant, ground-floor apartment, two blocks away from me, on Athens Square. Fucking academics, they always wind up with cushy berths. Ayer I'd met a couple of times when living –

Yaws and he had been distant colleagues. I went to a kvass and goat-cheese party given for him by his death guide – an impressively furry shaman. I was always trying to wring some truths out of these reindeer-piss drinkers and shrunken-head merchants, but no dice. Everyone else's death guides were just as uselessly enigmatic as my own. They all muttered about 'go-rounds', the 'Clear Light' and the 'hooks and eyes of grace', as if this jargon was self-evident.

Of course, Freddy always thought all metaphysics was mumbo-jumbo, and death hadn't thawed his notoriously glacial logic. He even suggested to me that it might be the case that all of my sense data since expiring – Lithy, Dulston, Phar Lap, the Fats – were no more than fragments of my disintegrating consciousness. To give him his due, Freddy included his own manifestation, along with the collapse of the Berlin Wall, within the elastic confines of this set.

When I pointed out that this left *him* with little more than a phantom existence of his own, Freddy giggled indulgently. He liked death because he could smoke again, and put his hands up young women's skirts with total impunity. I figured that only such a relentless rationalist could gain any succour from these, the nervous tics of the afterlife. Still, it was fun to run into him from time to time, dapper, distinguished, wholly disengaged.

Not so Ronnie Laing, who died in August of that year. His was a *most* unquiet spirit. Clad in tennis togs, swishing his racket, he wandered the streets of Dulston looking to kindle fights with everyone, but the dead – as we know – aren't combustible. So he exercised his volleys of rage on the living, smashing into schizophrenia mere drivers-through, who'd never had a moment's mental ill health in their lives. In death, I suppose, he did at least have the satisfaction of confirming his own prejudices. Or theories.

We only had Larry Olivier for a few matinées before he transferred to the provinces. But you can bet every star-fucker in the whole miserable joint did their splendid best to try and rub up against his commanding nothingness. I stayed out of the crush bar. I'd other things to worry about. Work every fucking day – only the subtlety of my body made the slog tolerable. Two disruptive kids now, one a petrified club singer, the other an all too bumptious delinquent. Yup – that Rude Boy. He pitched up and acted out. He arrived barefoot and buck-naked from Heathrow, hula-hooped down the steps and came screeching into the basement, coonskin cap wagging, ass wiggling, all blacked up for the nigger game. Sure, I tried to placate him with glasses of milk, peanut-butter and jelly sandwiches, *Captain America* comics and Hostess Twinkies, but he wouldn't wear them any more than he would clothes, or manners. Rude Boy put the mockers on any kind of social life I might've got going in my freshly HeLa-decorated apartment. He was totally unmanageable.

When the *Marchioness* sank in September of '89, Rude Boy had been around for nearly a year. Mostly I could get him to stay home with the Fats, who could cow him a little, with his own mother's future bulk. But when the poor drenched kids were driven into Dulston by their death guides, there was Rude Boy to make their extinction thoroughly miserable, screaming, 'Got a little muddy, did you – you fucking disco dancers! Not making so many waves now, are you!' And – natch – Lithy had to chime in with 'All I need is the air that I breathe, and to love you!' Not that Lithy was a sick or resentful creature itself, you understand; it was just that sibling thing, that badly mixed blood cocktail.

I wanted the hell out of Dulston, where the new arrivals were mostly damp *and* déclassé. In August I wanted to be in NY, where Irving Berlin died, or in Paris where Simenon died, hobbling to Ennuyeuseville with his tailored trousers down round his ankles. He claimed to have had sex with ten thousand women, and I'd've liked to see him confronted by the stadiumful of drabs. Shit, I could've even handled Hollywood, where Bette Davis was headed when she died that fall. I'd always admired her – or rather her screen persona. But then if death taught you anything, it was that a screen persona was as good as any other. A cigarette held just so, a devilish smile, an inscrutable gaze. We lived through our mannerisms – and died through a lack of them.

At a PD meeting I struck up an acquaintance with Clive, a man of my own agelessness. Clive was an investment banker, who hadn't taken retirement until five years after he died. Like most of his ilk he remained stuffed with down payments. Through the winter of '89-'90 Clive and I began to go about together, taking long zigzagging walks which allowed us to escape the confused borders of the cystrict. Clive had a wry sense of humour and tolerated the Fats, Lithy, Rude Boy and all the rest of my death baggage, which tagged remorselessly along. 'Ah!' he'd exclaim as Rude Boy launched another assault. 'The young Rosicrucian.'

Clive's own baggage was exactly that – baggage. For reasons I never discovered, he inhabited an austere, one-bedroom apartment in a five-storey block on the Thebes Estate that was full of luggage – suitcases, holdalls, tool bags, attaché cases and steamer trunks. This luggage moved around morning, noon and night, like the plastic counters of a 3-D puzzle. We'd be sitting, chatting, in one of the irregular spaces left between mounds of Gladstones and piles of kitbags, when one of the valises would ease out of its confinement, as if propelled from behind. Clive would grunt, 'I think . . . ahem . . . Lily, we'd better vacate this area.' So we would. He never explained what was doing it – and I never asked. Clive's sparse hair and lustrous, gold-rimmed bifocals were in keeping with this rectitude. These qualities, which in a living Englishman would've been bloody irritating, I found curiously seductive in dear, dead Clive.

During those days I often awoke in the small hours of the morning, having been visited by incubi as I slept. Comforting phantoms of unspeakably sweet, erotic loveliness, who hugged me to their ecstatic nothingness, clasped me to my own subtle bosom, breathing into my toothy mouth their gummy nullity. In the corner of the bedroom the Fats murmured, 'Plump and ageing, plump and ageing, plump and ageing . . .' while beneath the bed Lithy boogied and belted out, 'I feel lo-o-ove / I feel love!' and in the corridor Rude Boy romped, rending the air with his ranting.

But I hadn't slept, I was wide awake in the colourless indifference of death. Comfy Clive and I were having shady sex. Strange, isn't it, how among the dead all sex is intercrural – a matter of penises placed in the crevices of the body, but never the vagina. Clive would put his stubby dick beneath my armpit, in the join of my thighs, between my breasts, or even lever apart two dewlaps of belly to interpose what might be him. It was as if, in attempting these contortions – which enabled us to see the afflicted portions – we believed we might achieve the least little bit of friction, of *touch*. But there was nothing, nothing nuzzling nothing.

Clive squired me to dinner parties where the most elaborate meals were prepared by hosts and hostesses anxious for our approval. Such casseroles, brown, vinous and creamy. Such cuts of meat – pink and juicy! Oh, the colourful collations of the freshest vegetables, dew-selected from the finest greengrocers in the capital. And for what? For no-thing. They didn't even smell. We guests played with our portions – for this was all we could do. One mounding his mashed potato into a semblance of a Rodin; another arranging her glazed carrots and broccoli florets so as to imply the garden at Giverny; and a third experimenting with lumps of meat, transplanting them into chewy torsos with gristly limbs and bitten-off heads. Grimly anticipating the coming decade's conceptual excesses.

That was Dulston dinner parties for you – wasteful, costly patty cake. If we were deluded enough, gripped by whatever tittle-tattle was doing the rounds, like the San Francisco earthquake – nothing that exciting could ever happen in London – or the death of Samuel Beckett – oh happy day – or the last exit of Greta Garbo – alone at last, she wishes! – then perhaps we'd make the effort to bite it to bits, chew it to shreds, ruminate it to slop, then shpritz it into an ever so echt pail. In March of 1990, Clive and I attended a dinner party for the late Jane Grigson where all her finest recipes were served up, barely played with and then speedily discarded. How we all tried to laugh, but that evening sick humour was lost on us, who were forever bulimic.

Clive – God knows how – even knew racier characters. Dead yuppies who dwelled in the fashionably minimalist, rubber-floored, down-lit warehouse conversions in back of Sparta Road. These types served up newly dead cuisine. Tiny cuts of meat – the flensings of fidgeters; itty-bitty parings of root vegetables – thrown carelessly on to huge white plates, like the haymaking of elves. And over everything they drizzled *jus*, as if these stripes of edible semen could compensate for their own infertility, their own inability to eat; while at the same time proving that this – and they – were absolutely, totally, *really*, the *dernier cri*.

We sat by abstract picture windows, on poufs among gays, while dead people dressed entirely in black – it really doesn't suit us, does it? – chattered on remorselessly about the invasion of Kuwait, or the extinction of Leonard Bernstein, or the cultural relevance of Teenage Mutant Ninja Turtles. After dinner, mirrors would be produced, coffee tables cleared, and fish-shaped lines of cocaine laid out on the slick surfaces. Meticulous exercises in the preparation of anti-nutrition. Astonishing – for even the dead have to pay for their drugs. And they weren't cheap. Astonishing, because after the assembled company had stared at these tiny drifts of numbing snow for five, ten, or twenty minutes, whoever was the provider fetched the vacuum cleaner and hoovered them up with the big, plastic, mechanical nostril. Gone – just like that! Gone, in a dinky expensive vortex. Look what God just did to us! No-thing – as Phar Lap would've said.

So, Clive and I didn't rub along. We went to PD meetings together, where, one evening, we listened inattentively – chins rammed against hands tilting faces; have you ever noticed quite how many ruined Rodins there are in London? – while a young woman, with eyes sunken for her age, recounted her day. 'Well, there was a knock on the flat door and I answered it. I mean to say, what's the point in not answering, d'you know what I mean – they'll only get in anyway. So, I answered it and this bloke says he's one of the executive Furies of the Lord of Death. They always talk like that, don't they, all pompous like. Then, without so much as a by-your-leave he chops off my head, removes my heart, extracts my intestines, licks up my brain, cuts my flesh and gnaws my bones. 'Course, I'm incapable of dying, and even though my body's all hacked to pieces, it revives – then the fucking bastard does it all over again. Every time as painful as the last. Every time. Well, at the end of the day, I suppose that's the executive of the Lord of Death for you. Well, I just wanted to open my mouth . . .' And the other members rustled, examined their nails, each other's nails, the floor.

I should've given her sharing some credence, but I assumed

she was making it up. The dead don't feel. The dead have subtle bodies. This kind of torment isn't visited on us – or so I thought. I didn't pay attention and instead I looked at her face, not so much freckled as an amalgam of freckles. Ach! Let's hear it again from the Katzenjammer Kids – and *don't listen*, never *listen*.

Mostly Clive and I went to the meeting at the Community Centre, but from time to time we'd vary it and promenade to St John's, at the top of Argos Grove. It was an undistinguished, gloomy church. The Almighty was not accustomed to visiting it. Here, pinioned below the neo-Gothic needle, we'd sit in the asbestos vestry on wooden chairs in wooden rows. The Secretary there liked to officiate as if he were a priest. He set himself up behind a row of school desks so old they had built-in inkwells. I recalled the steel-nibbed dippers of my childhood; how the good kids always had dirty hands, because they got to fill the wells from the big, ribbed bottle. But the deceased members of this infantile class had fingers smudged with cigarette ash, and sat retelling the kind of tales that would've got you larruped senseless when I was a girl. Larruped until your union bodice was *inside* your tiny chest and your bob blown all to shit. Larruped by Mummy, when all you'd wanted, at the end of the day, was to open your mouth.

All this through a long hot summer. All this while the live culture was set in its soccer ways. The global tournament now had its own signature tune. At Baskin's, where I laboured over press releases for water-coolers – even though the boss wouldn't shell out for one for his own downtrodden – they played it all the time. *Nessun dorma*. Sleep-no-fucking-more. Abso-fucking-lutely. I lit another ciggie, Lithy vibrated in my dress pocket, a joyless buzzer. Baskin stared at me through an arch of ruptured ring binders. I mused, some men have hats of hair, others hair like hats, but how does a man get the urge to make himself *appear* as if he's bewigged?

Natasha and Charlotte were both pregnant that summer. What peculiar duetting for these mismatched progeny of mine. I learned about it through Bernie, the unquiet spirit on the top floor. For two years now I'd been privy to his awful existence. The scrape-thump, scrape-thump of another home-coming from Seth's, with yet another tin-foil crutch. The leaden tread on the creaking stair that meant he was off for his weekly trip to the heroin cash and carry; then the more sprightly thumping that betokened his return. These occurred with metrical regularity, you could've calibrated a nuclear clock by the ebb and flow of the man's junk tide. Late at night, early in the morning and all through the day I was bothered by his customers' peculiar cries. They stood by the front door, their feet level with the top of my bedroom windows, pressing their needy mouths against the brickwork and calling up to him. A vertical whispering gallery. 'Ber-nie. Bern. Ber-nie. It's me.' So many mes – so much human mess.

It occurred to me, being the old sourpuss that I am, that I should challenge Bernie over this relentless traffic. It wasn't altogether credible that anyone could go on shovelling this much heroin into themselves, and putting this much out, for bubkes. Mrs Seth was good enough to set me straight on the matter. 'You have to understand, Mrs Bloom, that Mr Bernard was not having the intoxication from all the heroin he was taking when he was alive. That is the way with the junkies, you know. When they are addicted they take it solely to be normal.'

'Yes, yes, I do know that – my daughter – '

'Of course. I am sorry to be telling you what you know already.'

'But what about once he'd died? Surely he noticed the difference?'

'Well, absolutely not. No – not at all. You are knowing your neighbour Mr Cox, up in the second-floor flat. Well, one day he heard an almighty crash from Mr Bernard's attic.'

'Not so remarkable, that,' I interposed, 'it happens when – '

'Yes, yes, it happens when he lifts up one leg to put on his underpants – '

'And forgets that he's already lifted the other.'

'Absolutely so. Anyway – that is precisely what happened on this occasion. But furthermore, the unfortunate man fell right across his bar heater, which was on at the time, and, having mildly concussed himself on the bare boards, he remained lying there for a sufficient period.'

'A sufficient period?'

'Long enough for it to burn Mr Bernard to death. However,' she lifted a jewelled finger, 'not long enough for all the rubbish in the flat to catch fire. The first thing that he knew about it was when he came in to buy some foil and the boy here noticed that his belly area was all burnt away.'

'And didjew tell him – inform him that he was all burnt up?'

'Well, yes. We did. But it didn't register with the man. Intoxicated in life, I suppose – now intoxicated in death. He merely zipped up his anorak. That is why he keeps it zipped up all the way like that. All the time. Besides that, he has kept on very much the way he did when he was alive. His room, you know, you should go up and see it, Mrs Bloom, it is an absolute messy place, all burnt and littered besides.'

I didn't want to see Bernie's room – I didn't want to see Bernie. I had my own kids to think of, calcified Lithy, mud-spattered Rude Boy. In death it was the lack of feeling that counted. And the live girls? Well, I'd visit them from time to time, braving the tube down to Regent's Park, stomping to Cumberland Terrace where I'd catch Charlie and Richard trying to make a baby for their very ownsome. I even tracked out to the sticks and dropped in on Pullet Green, where Natasha was taking her medicine. Pullet Green turned out to be a Lutyens mansion, set among parched beds of tea roses – the soil so friable it looked like kitty litter – and balding lawns fringed by dusty rhododendrons. Here, in circles of dry yet weeping alcoholics, and clean but filthy-minded junkies, my younger bitch crouched and snarled, while being expensively coaxed out of her heroin kennel.

She bloomed – the roses didn't. In four short months she went from dropping dead to drop-dead gorgeous. Ah Natasha! In this, the short, incandescent summer of her womanhood, she was the most beautiful she'd ever be. That springy structure was upholstered with genuine *curves* of olive flesh. Her breasts, when she exposed them – which she did with charming, apparently inadvertent frequency – were of a prominence and succulence to stare down any man of average height and commonplace tastes. Eyeball him into puling submission. I know so. I stood at her shoulder and looked into the mirror while she disrobed. My subtle body unseen behind her not so subtle one.

Yes, I sat in, not integrating with the group, while Peter Landon squeaked about the scuffed herringbone parquet in his rubber-soled deck shoes, fuelled by camomile and attempting to implant a particle of common sense in Natty's fickle frontlet. No dice. Natasha never saw herself as on a par with her pickled peers, and in fairness to her – nor did they. She was so fucking lovely they all wanted her. Even Landon – and believe me he tried – found it so hard to be insensible to her charms that after one-to-one counselling sessions he had to go and jack off in the john.

No, you could take the drugs and booze out of Natty, but the addiction to the power of her own private place remained as deep and smooth and moist as the orifice itself. Nope, all they did at Pullet Green – all they *could* do – was to dry her out, set her up, and send her out again. Worse than that, all the group therapy, the individual therapy, the browbeating, the ego-cracking amounted to, in the end, was a peculiar kind of pruning. The tea roses withered in their cat trays, but the hungry bloom inside of Natasha simply put down deeper roots, put out more shoots, grew stronger, more convoluted. Then stronger still.

At the Elverses' place I crouched in vestibules, hid myself behind sideboards, squeezed alongside overstuffed armchairs. I sought out places in the capacious apartment where I could witness the earthshaking rutting of these giant beasts. It occurred to me that this was the explanation for the extinction of the dinosaurs, all this monstrous coupling to so little effect. But let me get it straight, there wasn't a scintilla of voyeurism on my part, that wasn't what kept me coming back. I had enough fat action on show back home in Dulston. And enough in and out, claustro and agro.

No, I watched my daughter and her husband fuck because that was the best way to catch up on the world of the living. While they bucked and plunged, they tittled and tattled. Ripley, can you believe it – or not? But if I could've been jealous – I would've. All of my latter years, lovelorn, imprisoned by flab, ignored by men, I'd obsessed that everyone else was screwing on this industrial scale, making such masses of love.

If I phoned the spinster at Kentish Town Library to see if she had a book I'd ordered, I'd picture her, her cardigan sleeves stuffed with tumours of congealed paper hanky, face puckered up as she enunciated the dry words of our factual discussion. But below the desk I'd imagine a crouching satyriasis-sufferer, licking her out as if she were a huge ice-cream cone. His hindquarters crammed into the kneehole, his head rammed between her knees. Cowled by her tweed skirt and nylon slip, his jaws worrying at her like a terrier with some scraggy end.

But then that was my ill fortune – to reach obsolescence when around me the entire world was stripping off and flinging itself into paroxysms of limbs. By the early eighties I wouldn't've been *that* surprised if an Iranian ayatollah had pulled off his black robes and streaked through the precincts of Qom. Or Margaret Thatcher had gone down on one of her ministers in the House of Commons, the rest of them forming a clapping, chanting circle – 'Maggie! Maggie! Maggie! Out! Out! Out!' Yup – everyone was fucking save for fat old me. And it wasn't fair – I hadn't *had enough*.

Richard had just about had enough, when finally, with one last slap and shudder, he unleashed a single spermatozoa feistier than all the rest. One little elver strong enough to swim through the seas of hostile mucous. One shred of DNA, which, if it could only burrow into the ball, set off the chain of replication, would, after many moons, be in a strong position to inherit an extensive chain of Waste of Paper outlets. Branches now such a part of the economic tree that to visit a shopping precinct was to be visited by one of the Elverses' stores. In between Woolworth's and M&S, or in between McDonald's and Barclays, or in between the NCP and the war memorial. Leaves within branches.

Natasha, on the face of it, kept to all the suggestions made to her by the counsellors at Pullet Green. But then when did Natasha's face mean anything but betrayal? They told her to go from primary to secondary treatment – so she did. She stayed in a bungalow at the bottom of the grounds. She attended many, many more group-therapy sessions. She began going to Alcoholics Anonymous and Narcotics Anonymous meetings in the vicinity, where she made a highly personal impression on all who saw her, and heard her speak.

She did voluntary work at the local old people's home, where she listened to the whisperings of the temporary residents. Although not too closely. Had Natasha been truly attentive, leant into the toothless mouths, placed her tidbit of an ear within a tongue's length of these old slobberers, she might've interpreted their whispers for the imprecations they truly were. 'Go away! Piss off! Fuck off!' That's what they were saying, irked by her beauty, peeved by her youth, and annoyed by her useless concern.

At the bungalow she mended the leaking shower-surround with a giant syringe-like device, which extruded pink mastic. It made her think of shooting up. It made her think of penetration by Russell. The two were scrambled in her addled mind. The counsellors suggested she not make any major decisions for the first year of her recovery – so she put a brave face on it. She'd stay with Miles, who, although branded an 'enabler' and a 'codependent' by the counsellors, was also held to be a steadying influence. Yup, she'd stay with poor Miles because he was Natasha's ticket out of the institution. Charlotte waived her share of Mumu's flat – what need had she of this leftover space anyway? The plan was that Natty and Miles would move in there together. Their world would be steady.

Miles came to Pullet Green and booked a room at a bed and breakfast in nearby Reigate. He attended a family meeting with Peter Landon, who couldn't believe this pretty boy's good bad luck in catching the tumultuous termagant who was Natasha Yaws. The next day Natasha went out on an afternoon pass and met Miles in the town. They had a strange burger. They looked in shop windows. With much sarcasm they bought postcards at a branch of Waste of Paper. If the pus fairy had sprinkled their cheeks they might've been teenagers. Eventually they snuck into the B&B and Natasha milked Miles dry. Under the cold scratchiness of the quilt, he asked her if she loved him. Natasha shuddered, despite the black sweater she'd declined to remove – she had the goose bumps of the rejector. 'Of course, silly,' she said. But really it was he who was silly, of course.

In his trademark Adidas black, silk-effect track suit, and with his innately black, silkily violent, depraved heart, Russell entrained for Reigate from Victoria. Having engaged the jolting toilet, he smoked crack in a stem of Pyrex piping. He vigorously exhaled the toxic spume through a ventilator grille. When he was vacant, he vacated the toilet and went to stand, jolted up and decoupled on the jolting coupling between two carriages.

At Reigate station Russell encabbed, instructing the bemused Sikh driver to take him to a grid reference he'd marked on a 1:50,000-scale map of the locale. Having successfully negotiated two parallel barbed-wire fences, Russell angled across a wheatfield towards a ship-shaped copse. Chest-deep in the golden waves, Russell checked his diver's watch and noted – militaristic, efficient bastard he was – that all was in synchrony.

Natasha waited for him, crouching in a small hollow of last year's dry leaf mould. When her commanding officer arrived she wasn't required to rise, merely to salute his thick stripe with her lovely lips. She was completely naked – he fully clothed. But she hadn't felt so hot in weeks. When he was spent, he ordered her about face and fired a salvo inside her – he had so much ammunition to give. There were no words wasted between them. There were no words at all. What a relief for Natasha, who was saturated with talk. What a balm to have at least twenty minutes of non-communication; sandwiched as they were between a group-therapy session and a counselling session with Peter Landon. The previous day she'd used Miles, then she was used by Russell. That afternoon Natasha sat with twigs, frass, seed cases and pupae in her hair and euphemised to Landon. The sick Ceres. The blighted Aphrodite.

So, who fathered Natasha's child? Perhaps nobody – since neither Miles nor Russell could exactly be pegged as remotely paternal. Was it, then, a destructive feat of parthenogenesis on the part of my daughter Kali, frigging herself with one hand, tossing off the donor with a second, readying the instrumentation of insertion with a third, leaving one free for petty gestures of supplication? No matter – she was knocked up. Miles tended to her as she puked and moaned and kvetched in all her specialness. And while he was out dogging at the lawyers' offices in High Holborn where he now worked, Natasha, the bitch, headed off to Dulston – which to her was simply another nondescript part of a city she was incapable of describing – and spent his gelt on Bernie's gear. She'd been introduced to Bernie by another girly flake who'd failed to take recovery seriously; a young woman who, like my Natasha, attended the meetings of recovering addicts in a spirit of social enquiry, taking notes on the counterfoils of stolen chequebooks.

What a perfect cover for using heroin this pregnancy was – or so Natasha thought, caught up in her own cunning awfulness. You can fool some of yourself all of the time.

I'd watch her from my front window. Or rather, watch her ankles, trim – for such a tall, disorderly woman – in her trademark ankle-boots. I'd watch her bump ballooning above me. Then I'd hear her throw her voice up to Bernie, and see the Yale thrown down. The Fats saw her as well, and burbled to themselves, 'So lovely, so lovely. Young and blooming, young and blooming,' while Lithy dug into its trove of popular song for a serenade – 'It's all too beautiful! It's all too beautiful!' I'm not saying she did it all the time, but once every fortnight I'd see

Natasha on the front steps, waiting to cop from the other side. And once a fortnight I'd troll over to Cumberland Terrace to see how Mrs Elvers was getting on with her swelling.

Saddam invaded Kuwait and my girls indulged their own cravings. In their second trimester, the towelled heads unravelled on Temple Mount. On the cusp of their third, Maggie-Maggie-Maggie – that cross-dresser – was finally out; and a film opened at the Dulston Odeon, in which a woman is pleasantly haunted by her dead lover. It played to packed houses for months. How we laughed at this light comedy of extinction. Then, at the close of the year, as big, steel, Arab phalli flopped on Tel Aviv and the shmendricks all scattered for cover – they lost them. Both of them, Natasha *and* Charlotte, lost their babies – within a week of each other.

Peculiar, this, given that they had so little to do with one another, bar the occasional anti-social call, when Charlie decided there was an item of pregnancy prêt-à-porter she could do without, and gift her skittish sister. Peculiar that their bell-shaped bodies should resonate like this, especially considering that their pregnancies had been ministered to so differently: Charlotte regularly sitting, leafing through glossies at the London Clinic, propped up by a duchess to one side and an arms dealer's paramour to the other; while Natty occasionally crawled into the Elizabeth Garrett Anderson, to rub the midwives up the wrong way with her invincible hauteur.

Strange that both foetuses died the same way – poisoned by their own backed-up piss, their puny bladders blocked by congenital knots. Not that Natasha didn't blame herself, didn't fear she was sunk because of the tin-foil flag of inconvenience she'd been cruising under. For if one thing's for sure, in the realm of the emotions all contingent events are causally felt. I smoke heroin, then my baby dies, therefore my addiction killed my baby. Too true, missy. Too bloody true.

They both found out the same way as well. Lying on the padded couch with the ultrasound technicians making with plastic pucks, ironing their big bellies with little echoes. There was a cheerful, running commentary to begin with, and then . . . silence . . . looks of anguished confusion rippled both operatives' brows. Both pregnant women had been having a hard time with nausea and then, magically, ceased feeling sick a couple of days before. Both mothers had been getting an internal kicking – and this too had stopped. 'Um . . . err . . . there's a problem here . . .' The operatives both struggled for the words with which to describe this intractable situation. *In utero* death can do this to the most consummate rhetorician – it's so *previous*.

On the padded couches both ex-mothers, weighed down by the awful dead things inside of them, stretched out anguished hands to clutch at their menfolk. Hysteria welled up in all four of them. Richard vented his bad feelings on the doctor, when he eventually arrived to tell the Elverses their baby was dead. Miles didn't intervene. Both women were prescribed *plenty* of Valium. Charlotte stayed in the London Clinic and that very night they dripped the drugs into her that contracted the womb, which squeezed the corpse, and evacuated it into a cardboard kidney dish. Natasha went home to Kentish Town wearing a self-pitying sackcloth woven entirely from blue, ten-milligram sedative pills. Two days later she presented herself, back at the Garrett, smacked out to the gills, and they sucked the dead fish out of her too.

Both slunks came to join me at the flat in Dulston. Natch. They lay alongside the nodding Cerberus on the back shelf of Costas's cab, like bloody, discarded rear-view-mirror dingle-dangles. He scooped them into a Sainsbury's bag – It's Clean, It's Fresh – and dumped them at my door. All through that winter, while young Iraqi conscripts were being entombed by

British and American aerial gravediggers, and into the spring, when once again, Famine drew the Sudanese as stick-figure parodies of human figuration, Charlotte and Natasha's start-wrong kids haunted the basement flat at number 27.

I couldn't get them to stay inside. Once admitted they slimed right through and out the cat-flap in the back door. They flotched around the tiny concrete area out back, beneath the miniature clothes-line pylon. They sat, side by side, on the three dank steps that led up to the sunless strip of garden. Two little red cousins with unformed faces hugging each other. Dead babes in the concrete jungle. We all did our best – Lithy, the Fats, Rude Boy and I – to coax them in. It was to no avail. Only in the middle of the night, when the Fats gyred in the front bedroom, and Rude Boy roamed the corridor spitting imprecations, and Lithy sang, 'I'm gonna wait 'til the midnight hour . . .' did the poor mites climb up on to the sill and slither against the window, their tiny maws opening and closing. If I opened the bottom sash and bent down close, I could just about make out what it was they wanted. 'We need to go wee-wee,' they said. 'We need to go wee-wee.' And of course they did. For eternity.

Clive departed. The dead never broke off relationships, as such – we simply drifted away from one another, each suspended in our own wispy cloak of cigarette smoke. You're never alone with a Strand. There was no rancour, no weeping, no sense of loss. He couldn't really take the horror show in the basement – and who could blame him? He'd rather squat in his apartment full of baggage, while the lost principles of his office lifetime pushed the valises, rucksacks and steamer trunks this way and that.

Anyway, the Balkans were revolting, while in Milwaukee they'd discovered an apartment not unlike Clive's, but stacked with dismembered corpses. How much more disgusting were the flights of fancy of the living than those of us mere shades. Miles Davis was dead. Miles with his impeccable sartorial taste, his sweet shofar, his infinite cool. Miles whose jizzy horn had limned in the fins of the fifties. Miles, who did battle with Dizzy on the hot afternoon at the party, when the poet said, 'September, when we loved as in a burning house.' So sexy, that – quoting poetry. It'd never failed to turn me on. Not that I'd ever needed much turning on, my heels were ready-rounded. Miles was dead. I should've suspected that something was afoot.

I'd been dead for three years. In the sixties we'd all been shocked by the Living Theatre, but I'd grown accustomed to a dying one. I was barely fazed any more by the antics of the Dulston shades, the way my nostalgia for the beautiful babies I'd once had had been transfigured into a menagerie of ugly abortions. The PD meetings, the lazy manifestations of Phar Lap Jones – how could I've been expected to realise that this was the peaceful side of the afterlife? Because while the dead hoovered up useless cocaine and tried to rub up against one another, the living were going on and on. Life bobbed like a cork caught in an ever widening torrent of trivial innovation. The century gurgled towards the artificial plughole. And if in those three years I began to accept that I was dead, in the ones that followed, it was made transparently clear to me that I was even . . . deader.

Christmas 2001

Soon I'm going to have to attempt some serious climbing. I can't expect to hug the ground indefinitely, a deserted rug rat. I try to comfort myself by imagining this is a test, a probationary period; and that if I do well the delegation will eventually arrive to announce that I am, indeed, the living goddess. This shoebox maisonette occupies the corner of the building, two flights up. There's another, empty box, between the front door and the piss chute which serves all the apartments as an external staircase. Even now, in the dead interstice between the years, I can hear children running up and down the stairs, along the landings, the soles of their trainers slapping the concrete. But they seldom venture along here to the corner. Even if they do get as far as the neighbouring flat it's only to rattle the letterbox with a stick, or bang it on the steel shutters the Council have bolted across the windows. Anyway – kids never listen. We never really listen.

What're they in training for anyway? Every one of them shod in complex vehicles of rubber, leatherette, suede, Gore-Tex, and even, I daresay, Sympatex. I wonder if anyone else has noticed the sinister convergence of training shoes and cars? Both cars and shoes are now designed so as to appear as if they're plunging down and forward. They're ass-up, their squared-off butts anticipating the tragic congress of a rear-end shunt. And the cars are getting smaller, more garishly painted, their plastic bumpers, wing mirrors and functionless spoilers just like the useless ridges and corrugations of training shoes. Training shoes which are, natch, getting larger. Soon people will find themselves inadvertently parking their shoes and putting on their cars. I wish. Even police cars are fashion statements. Calling all queers – there's an all points style bulletin. Graphic law and garish order.

Sympatex – rich, isn't it. But it exists, I know it does. I saw it advertised on the tube, in the days before the Ice Princess had degenerated so much she could no longer head up west to Marks & Spencer, and make use of their generous returns policy. I guess Sympatex must be an artificial material that adapts itself to the shape of the wearer's body. If only it could adapt itself to the wearer's intentions, but then they'd have to call it Unsympatex, certainly so far as my fellow residents here in Coborn House are concerned.

What're they in training for, a lifetime of being unfit? I used to think it absurd enough to share a country with people who wore baseball caps – back to front, natch – when they'd never played the game in their lives; but during the few, short months of this latest go-round it's struck me that I've been living with millions of worshippers of the wind goddess. Everywhere you look, NIKE is emblazoned on sweat pants and tops, jackets and hats, shoes and even socks. Often there's only the ubiquitous tick that's the shmutter vendor's logo. So droll, that; when to me, who's lived through times when people didn't feel the need to put on sports gear before lighting a cigarette, the tick looks like nothing so much as the symbol on an old packet of Newport – but turned upside down. The logo – the logos. The world's been turned upside down. The daughters are the mothers – their former nurturers are now their neglected babies. Mummy, why's your skin so rough and hard? Because I'm a fucking corpse.

Yes, they walk the shitty streets of this fucking hole, Mile End, East London. They walk these shitty streets, sucking on their cigarettes, marked off with the ubiquitous tick, and exhibiting all the florid symptoms of schizophrenia. I used to see them, hanging about the precincts of Coborn House, right up until the last few days, when the Ice Princess couldn't even get it together to get up at all. She used to think I was complaining because she was removing me from the rusty swings, the groaning seesaw, the wonky roundabout – when really I was protesting that she'd taken me there at all. Close by us the wind-worshippers stared into the air, while addressing the voices piped into their inner ears. Like modular, electronic talismans, their mobile phones performed the magical feat of convincing them that they had a relationship with these disembodied individuals.

Why do I sneer? I could use a phone myself right now, but the land-line is cut off and the chunks of plastic the Ice Princess and the Estate Agent used to wield are simply that now: chunks of plastic. If a delegation did arrive it wouldn't be to find the living goddess, it would be to dun the Ice Princess, or drub her consort. I suppose the GP or the social worker might've been anticipated, if this wasn't the dead interstice between the years. Instead they're tucked up in their own warm homes, gobbling fat fowls, advocating another thimble of advocaat, doing their level best to forget the human wreckage they sort through during their working lives. 'Did you have a good Christmas and New Year?' their colleagues will enquire of them when they get back to the surgery in the early part of January. 'Oh yes,' they'll reply, 'I remembered I was middle-class. And you?'

Even at 32 Coborn House the season of joy has been, if not exactly celebrated, at least alluded to. The hideous spider plant down here has been indecorously draped with a twist of tinsel. I know she dangled some shiny balls from the fronds of the yucky yucca upstairs. On top of the TV there are at least three cards, only one of which is from the world's most unsuccessful lawyer. Who're the other two from? Fuck knows. I wouldn't be at all surprised if both are from members of the 'crew' the Ice Princess and her consort associated with. 'Crew', marvellous euphemism this, as if that raggedy gang were in fact a bronzed cockpit full of Ivy Leaguers, plunging through the surf off of Cape Cod. But the only America's Cup this 'crew' have ever been associated with is a crushed Coke can, punctured with a bent pin, and fumigated with crack smoke.

There's the tinsel, the cards, and in one of the kitchenette

272

cupboards there's a hunk of Christmas cake on a Tupperware saucer. It isn't even wrapped in tin foil, because they used that up a few days ago during one of their experiments in domestic nescience. Still, I know it's there – I saw it when I was last fed a little pot of heated purée, sitting up on the out-of-worktop, while the Ice Princess negligently poked a hard plastic spoon at my soft little mouth. But that's all there is in there, save for a couple of crumpled, cellophane, sad pasta packets and three mouldy jars of unpreserved preserves. There was a shrunken-head apple on the edge of the serving hatch – but I ate that yesterday.

So, I'll have to do some serious climbing. It's fucking cold in here – as I think I've had cause to remark – and if I want to make it through another night I'll have to eat something. I'll have to pick my way over the lianas of cabling, circumvent the coffee table, climb up on to the divan mountain, climb up on to the arm of the divan, crawl along the high back of the divan, gain the serving hatch. Then, leaning out on the slick melamine of the surface, while teetering over the void, some-how contrive to get the door of the cupboard open. Why is it that in this fucking hovel, where everything that ever had any utility has long since broken, there are still functioning cup-board doors?

Even if I manage this exhausting expedition there's no guarantee I'll be able to reach the cake. Even if I reach the cake there's no knowing whether I'll be able to get it down without falling. Still, if I do, at least there's someone there to break my fall; I won't smash my little head in on the hard floor. No, because that's where he lay down in slow stages, the Ice Princess's handsome consort. I watched him go – so I know how decorously he managed it. And it had to be, for there's only just enough room for him to stretch out there, full length, in his own training shoes, his own sweat pants and top, *all of them marked with the ubiquitous tick. He had delusions about dealing in property – but this is his real estate.*

I suppose I should be grateful they saw fit to put me in my own little pair of Nikes, so that I could train to walk. But you know what – I'm not. The only thing I'm grateful for is that they left a packet of ten Benson & Hedges filter cigarettes on the coffee table. Without these I'd really be in shtook. Now, wouldn't it be amusing if the delegation did turn up to find me alone here, preternaturally mature, not simply playing with a box of matches, but using them to light a cigarette as well? Har-de-fucking-har. Still, it's good to smoke properly again, to feel the stuff ooze into my living tissues, to sense the nicotine hone my mind, to watch my puny exhalations. To smell again.

They used to say it stunted your growth – and I thought they meant smoking. But it wasn't the smoking – they meant death.

Deader

'I'm still here – where are you?'

*Field Marshal von Paulus's last telegram to Hitler
before surrendering at Stalingrad*

Chapter Twelve

I 'd made a death for myself and was pleased to tell Phar Lap so when I ran into him in the street outside Seth's. He was his normal self, denim-clad, boomerang-toting, roll-up-smoking, looking as if he'd blown into Dulston in a dust devil. 'Yeh-hey, Lily-girl, whaddya 'bout?' he clicked.

'Oh, this and that, this and that,' I snapped back.

Rude Boy came running between us and tried to kick Phar Lap in the ass, screeching, 'Nig-nog, nig-dog, walk your dog, nig-nog!'

Phar Lap made as if to grab at the tail of Rude Boy's coonskin cap and chuckled indulgently. 'He never gives up, that Rude Boy, hey-yeh? Ne-ver.'

'Will he ever?' I asked, knowing full well that Phar Lap wouldn't give me any kind of answer at all.

'Mebbe not, but you gotta split the swag sometime, Lily-girl.'

'Meaning?'

'Meanin' maybe iss time you moved on, hey? It's always thirsty Thursday roun' here, ain't it?'

I passed him the lighter I was using that week, which was clear, blue, plastic and eminently disposable. Lighters filled and emptied, came and went. I remained the same. They were alive – I was not. He lit his dag-tail, I my B&H. We both stood puffing, our smoke simulating the misty exhalations we should've had on this, a chilly December morning. Moved on? What could Phar Lap mean? Not, I hoped, a tedious intra-city trek down to Dulburb, Dulston's corresponding cystrict in South London. I'd been to Dulburb a few times – and it was exactly that. It was where the more comfortable dead liked to rest, in substantial semis, behind shaven privet hedges, in back of broad sidewalks, beside quiet roads, the tarmac surfaces of which were so bluey-brown they seemed like infinitely slow-moving, turbid waters.

No, not Dulburb, at once illimitable and confined, like all the parts of London the dead inhabited. Not Dulburb, where every mile or so the houses pared away from a brief stretch of dual carriageway and you found the same mouldering parade of identical shops – the butcher, the baker, the greengrocer, the ironmonger – as you'd encountered a mile back. Not Dulburb, where the roundel of the tube station at Dulburb North was followed by the roundel at Dulburb Common and then, eventually, the roundel at Dulburb South. Dulburb – which its gentrifying incomers jokingly referred to as 'Dahlb' – sounded a little too much like 'dull burg' for my taste. Anyway, I'd had enough of the Dulburbs of this world when alive – ferchrissakes I'd raised two kids in Hendon!

But if not Dulburb there could be worse destinations. The deatheaucracy – which I knew was as powerful as it was nebulous – might have in mind a move to the provinces. And what would lie in store for me there? No jobs available in the vicinity for a fat old woman, and no bus service to take me anywhere else. My life would become a series of Women's Institute cake-bakes, neighbourly cups of tea-spit, walks through fields of crops committing pesticide. It hardly bore thinking about.

'Don' see you at the meetings much, Lily,' Phar Lap said after some smoking, changing his tack. 'Wossamatter, doncha think they've anything to teach you?'

'Since you ask – no. As far as I can see it's simply an excuse for a lot of saddies to get together and moan about being dead. If the intention is to make the condition any more bearable it's a waste of time. If the aim is to alleviate it – then it's about as effective as getting tuberculosis-sufferers together in a room and having them cough over each other. I've got a death – thank you very much. I've got my job, I don't need much money to die on. I've only the rent on that grotty little flat to pay, my ciggies, and a few cents for lighting – why should I spend my time listening to a lot of mumbo-jumbo?'

'You remember what I said before, girl?'

'What, exactly – you've said so much and it's meant so little.'

'About it all being gammin, rubbish, lies.'

'What? What you say to me – that I don't doubt.'

'Yaka! No! Don't be a fool, girl – yer no buju. Act yer age – think!' I hadn't seen the man so exercised before; his mirrored sunglasses shimmered as he jerked his head about, his angular arms sliced the chilly air. He even snatched up one of his precious fucking boomerangs and waved it in my face, as if this could possibly intimidate me. 'The meetings, girl, this place, the Fats, Lithy, Rude Boy – all of it. *Don't you geddit?*'

I stared at him, and pictured two little mes staring back out of his lenses. I wondered if I was still keel-nosed and log-faced, and my complexion remained sallow. Or were the lines on my face incised a little less deeply? The grooves not so groovy? The bags under my eyes not quite as capacious? Had death, perhaps, mellowed me?

Anyway, what the hell kind of a psychologist could possibly be observing me from behind these two-way looking-glasses? I tried to think about what he was saying, but it didn't mean nix to me. On the other hand, everything I'd experienced of the afterlife these last few years made perfect sense. Especially the way I was able to go on working for year after year at Baskin's, Lithy propped on my desk, with no one making more than a perfunctory connection with me – this was so true to life.

When alive I'd always been stunned at how, if you were raddled, ringed and accented, once you got into an English office environment you became an ageless, stateless single. You might be asked about your holiday, or your new shoes, or even – on certain, vital occasions like the outbreak of war – what your 'views' were, but anything that defined you as more than another plastic-piano player was irrelevant. Husbands, kids, homes, beliefs – these were beyond the ken of anyone at the office. I came, I wrote press releases on integrated shelving systems, I went again. I remembered thinking when I had to hobble from Kentish Town to Chandler PR, bunion-shod, arthritis-gloved and latterly cancer-clad, that this kind of life was a living death. Now it was a deathly life. The awful symmetry was appealing – and entirely believable.

'I *am* thinking, Phar Lap – truly I am. But I don't "geddit", as you so succinctly put it.'

'Yeh-hey, Lily-girl, no way t' 'tach you to the hooks and eyes of grace if you don't.'

'I guess not.'

'Still, if you change yer mind you'll know where t'find me.'

'Where's that, then?' I never had any idea how to locate the man; he'd told me he was going walkabout for ever – and I took him at his word.

'No-where.' Phar Lap said and snickered, palate-slapped, cheek-sucked – did all the things that reminded me what an alien he was.

'Don't be funny, or I'll begin thinking I had your fucking number from the get-go.'

'Hey-yeh – I'm serious, girl. Doncha pay no attention to what goes on in this city?'

'Meaning?'

'Meanin' iss nearly 1992, girl – the recession's over, yeh-hey?'

'So – how does that effect you?'

'When the London mob gotta little more dough in their pockets they wanna spend it – thass how the whole fuckin' show gets back on track.'

'So?' Christ, I hated joining in debate with Phar Lap. The marriage of aboriginal enunciation to the quintessentially Australian, meaningless interrogative made for the most irritating exchanges.

'So, they want their kuyu y'see – their meat. An' I'm the feller to give it them, yeh-hey? Smokes?' He poked the little round tin of Log Cabin in my direction and for a change I accepted it. I'd seen Phar Lap grate the coarse tobacco in his coarser hand, then deftly marry it to the tiny ensign of paper that flew from his bottom lip, enough times to do it by rote. In death I was becoming unusually deft. He matched me with a Redhead. We puffed. If I could've tasted it I bet the smoke would've been woody.

'How, exactly,' I asked, spitting out the shreds of tobacco that caught on my lip with little 'paf's, 'are you going to give the Londoners their kuyu?'

'Nowhere,' he snickered again. 'Iss a restaurant, see – like a roadhouse, yeh-hey?'

'*You* are opening a restaurant?' I thought of eating at Overtons in the sixties with Yaws; the bill – as I recall it – was six pounds for two. Well wined, natch, but being Yaws, near tipless. When I moved to London in 1958 there were two kinds of restaurant in the whole city, bad and worse. Now a dead Australian Aboriginal was about to open one.

'Yeah – Nowhere. Thass what it's called, yeh-hey? Kinduva themed joint, y'see. Themed Centralian, yeh-hey? I've got some traditional fellers to cook bush tucker for me – damper, 'roo, goanna an' such. Customers'll come an' sit out on a sandy floor round a fire, yeh-hey? Keep it fuckin' hot in there.

Big video screen on the roof showin' pictures of the sky over my country, hey-yeh?'

'And you believe this will be successful?'

'Bound t'be. Can't fail – this kardibar mob'll eat any old guna, an' the stuff at Nowhere is gonna be good, yeh-hey?'

'And where, exactly, *is* Nowhere?' Why, why, why did I let him draw me into his absurdities? Phar Lap's conversation was like Yiddish, always querying to solicit another question.

'Oh – y'know,' he shouldered his boomerang, adjusted his shades, pulled down the brim of his Stetson, showed me his boot heels, 'it's around the place. Ask anyone – they'll tell you. B'lieve me, Lily-girl – yer gonna wanna know, yeh-hey? Come by for this one,' he tilted his thin hand to his plump lips, simulating taking a drink, 'it'll be my shout.'

With that he was gone, striding off down Argos Road, roll-up tilted up, hat brim bent down, his dusty figure blowing past the front of Seth's. Nowhere. Honestly, was there any limit to the man's impossibility? And to think I'd once imagined I could learn something from him, that he could guide me somewhere. Nowhere indeed.

But I ignored him on this occasion – and what kind of a klutz did that make me? Fumbling with metaphysics, cack-handedly assembling tiny cosmologies in the greyness of my short everyday. Mumu in a mumu. A sad sack in a sad sack. It should've begun to come together in my mind by then – surely? Or at least when I discovered that Natasha had split with Miles in the wake of losing the baby. Especially when I found out she'd contacted an old friend, and decided to head out to Australia for a year's travelling.

The old friend was teaching in Sydney – which was why she'd remained a friend of Natasha's at all. Natasha had a way with friends; far from cultivating them, she rubbed her salty tears into the wounds she'd inflicted, rendering them incapable of sympathy towards her for the next thirty years. But this one had been out of the loop since they were in art school together.

Polly Passmore was her name. I remember her as a plump, comely lass, with a healthy, sensual appetite for hairy thighs against her smooth ones. She laughed, drank too much white wine, cosseted the children in her care when she ended up teaching. Her life was like the brightly coloured collages she liked to make – full of disparate shapes and textures, harmonised by her own good nature. At school she'd been burdened by her own good looks, pushed into a popularity she found wearisome. But when she got to St Martin's she found Natasha. What a boon, for set beside Natasha's sinister beauty, Polly became a fat, plain young woman. She was able to take up the second fiddle she'd always longed to play.

Polly didn't get enough of Natasha. She presided in a tea-doling, tissue-passing capacity over Natasha's first few spirals down into dissolution. She provided a shoulder for the young men to cry on impotently, the young men whose imperfectly fired hearts Natasha had smashed on the kitchen floor of their shared flat. She scraped Natty off the same floor a couple of times, after early, poignant, never-do-it-again heroin overdoses. She attended court with Natty when her pal was had up for shoplifting. Again. She blocked in the blank areas of pictures Natty had hurriedly sketched out, so that they could be presented for tutorial assessments.

But Polly cleared out before things got truly heavy. Perhaps she'd had as much of Natasha as she needed. She knew now, at any rate, that she could never be as beautiful – nor as damned. Polly left London still thinking that one of her friend's wings was broken, not comprehending that it had been amputated. She went to Glasgow, she went to the Isle of Mull. She spent time in California and in Banff. She taught art quite artlessly and had many many unsuitable liaisons with men who treated her quite unforgivably. She grew into the fat, plain woman her friend had licensed her to be; and while swilling sweet wine became appropriately bitter. How else could Polly Passmore have been dumb enough to keep in touch? Stupid enough to offer Natasha a home once the life had been sucked out of her?

Natasha snorted the last of her heroin off a metal soap dish, in a toilet cubicle, in the transit lounge at Abu Dhabi. When the plane touched down in Sydney all the passengers applauded, while giving Ocker cheers and piercing squeals of glee. Our little sophisticate clutched her sweaty head between her scrawny upper arms and vomited into one of the bags provided. A classic antipodean already – chundering the dreamtime into a nightmare.

Charlotte had coped with so much for so long. With her father's face, with my death, with her sister's addiction, with fucking to order. But this . . . this . . . *global* injustice. With this she could not cope. A woman called her a month after the event and asked if she'd like to attend a group, where women whose babies had died *in utero* got together to show the Polaroids of their tiny lifeless progeny. The ones the medical staff had thoughtfully taken. It wasn't Charlie's style to snack on such meagre leavings, crumbs of maternity on the expensive empty plate of her life. So she shrugged it off, declined the invitation. She'd rather suffer the trauma. She saw her dead son in nightmares of savage reality. Each night he came slithering, the poor mite, up the façade of Cumberland Terrace. He tapped, the lost soul, against the pane of the large sash window. Charlotte rose from the marital slough, padded through the soft pile to confront the hard truth. 'What is it, my love? What do you want, you poor thing?' His tiny maw opened and closed in the orange light of the streetlamps. She heaved up the sash with a whoosh and leant in close. 'I need to go wee-wee,' he said. 'I need to go wee-wee.' For shame on the little bugger, shlepping all the way over from Dulston, simply to lay this heavy trip on his poor mother. Jesus – even I felt some sympathy for the woman, for a change.

In the daytime, every toy dog Charlotte passed trotting along the sidewalk was a furry foetus. The Elverses gave up on the spreadsheet analysis and abandoned systematic fornication. They now had nearing a thousand Waste of Paper outlets and there was no sign of the expansion slowing down. Sure, there'd been something of a glitch during the end of eighties, but now, like some rocket rounding the moon of recession and utilising the inertia, the Elverses' enterprise accelerated into the boom. In the nineties the economic cycle began freewheeling on what people wanted. It was no longer a question of establishing people's needs and providing for them, it was a matter of encouraging them to want any old tat – then supplying it. That's what the Elverses did so well – supply any old tat.

Never before in the history of the world had so many pictures been framed, presents wrapped, knick-knacks boxed, books covered, prints masked, stamps hinged, photos cornered and shelves lined. And with the daily grind of encrypting information now computerised, never had stationery been such a decorative, luxurious item. The populace no longer so much as sent each other a note – but by Christ they had notelets. Weren't they tortured, as I'd always been, by the tyranny of this much blank paper? Or was it, as I suspected, that the enormous Waste of Paper was itself the cosmic complement to their unformed, unbecome and untold stories?

Not that the Elverses didn't diversify – they were no fools. Like Esther Bloom they bought art galleries, properties and business publishing companies. They moved from being merely frivolously wealthy – to being seriously rich. Richard Elvers, who'd left school at sixteen to sell collarless white shirts on a stall at Camden Lock, and Charlotte, who'd bought one of them – neither of them even knew that the country's constitution was yet to be written; so they'd no shame when it came to entertaining legislators, lordlings, and stars of the musical theatre.

Yes, I felt some sympathy for Charlotte – and that alone should've alerted me. Where was my stupid colourlessness of indifference when I needed it most? *Les Miserables* had been running for nearly ten years – didn't I comprehend the true nature of my own? As I crouched by the poor, professionally dumb waiters, while they ministered to the ministerial chums, the millionaire thriller-writers and the televison executives who made up the Elverses' little coterie, I grew angry. Angry at the gaucheness of this, a newly-fabricated dining cubicle that made a crass mezzanine in the once airy apartment. Angry at the chatter that emanated from these privileged mouths. Had anyone heard that the FDA was warning women with breast implants against flying, lest they explode? Given half a chance I'd give them a fucking breast implant they wouldn't forget. I wished I was an unquiet spirit. A Bernie who didn't know I was dead.

And wasn't it the case that it was useless airlifting food to the former Soviet Union? (At this time none of them could yet contemplate the word 'Russia'.) And had anyone yet been to Nowhere, the new, Australian aboriginal, themed restaurant? It was *très très amusant*. For night after night I gnashed my own teeth in my daughter's Nash apartment. The Cold War was over and these jerks had won. Everyone was a liberal now. 'I'm basically a liberal,' they'd say to each other, as if this freed them up to affect the jacket of a fascist, or the trousers of an anarchist. Apparently the only people who didn't get it were satanic covens of fat, black, poor trade-unionists, riddled with Aids in the Gambia.

Yes, good, old-fashioned, righteous anger. Bottled bile. Canned gall. Draught choler – this being England. Richard and Charlotte were encouraged by their short, swarthy, successful, Semitic friends to contemplate a shopping trip to Phoenix, Arizona, where they might be able to purchase, from a stud of an orphanage, a tall, blond, Aryan child. A child who would come with a form book of its very ownsome, out of Mormon by Swede. Richard and Charlotte were advised by sterile friends who had a 'liberal' conscience to fly to Manila, or Managua, or Mauritius, where, for hardly any gelt at all, they'd be able to shop freely for a mulatto. Browse, as it were, in the birthing bazaar. Richard and Charlotte were adjured by charitable couples of unimpeachable rigour – the kind who fully appreciate that charity begins as far away from home as you can possibly get – to take a camper van of medical supplies to Romania, or Somalia, or Rangoon, where – with considerable effort and bribing of UN officials – they'd be able to secure a little leper, or a burgeoning haemophiliac, or a cute encephalitic. 'Isn't his swollen brow *so* cute.'

Ooh – it made me mad! Then I'd get home to Dulston, to find Rude Boy resplendent in his coonskin cap watching footage of the LA riots, his muddy feet up on the arm of the chair. 'Get those niggers!' he'd scream with approval. 'Ream those boogies!' Cowering at the back window were Charlie and Natty's slunks – 'We want to wee-wee' – and hoedowning on the kitchen lino was Lithy – 'Oh the concrete and the clay / Beneath my feet begin to crumble!' And in the bedroom the Fats, naked as the day they were shed, gained, or lost, spun their hanks of flab and muttered, 'Ooh she's mad, yes she is. Ooh she's in a rage. Fat and old, fat and old – and in a rage. Fat and old.' Then there was HeLa as well, whispering along the walls. Why the hell didn't these kids *listen* when I told them not to track dirt into the house? Here was I, suffering all the weight of these, the family's dead progeny, while junky dearest took another instalment of her gap life and Charlotte contemplated fucking *buying* out.

Rude Boy never spoke to me, he only shouted at me. But one evening he took my old hand in his young one, in such a way as to suggest that we might be holding on to each other, and he led me. Led me out of the flat. Led me up the steps to the front door. Rude Boy shouted up to Bernie's window, 'Chuck down the key, you miserable fucking smack-head!' And the Yale sailed down.

As we mounted the stairs, turning awkward corners by grimed-up windows, passing the shabby doors to the flats on the first and second floors, I saw a change in him. If you ignored your children's moods when they were alive, imagine how pervasive this becomes when they're dead. Rude Boy was simply that to me now – a rude boy, a troublesome presence to be blanked, especially when he frigged in the face of some stodgy Dulston lady, whose only terrors in the afterlife consisted in being unable to serve the vicar his tea. 'Less tea, Vicar?' But as I followed his ass up the stairs, his mud-spattered ass, his vulnerable ass, his nine-year-old ass, he ceased being Rude Boy and became Dave Junior once more.

At the top Bernie was waiting, anorak zipped up, grimacing teeth in beard. He made as if to ruffle David's blond hair. No, he did, he did ruffle it. He was, I remembered, alive after a fashion. Which is by way of noting that he thought he was. I followed David in. Bernie's attic was as Mrs Seth had said. Up here under the sloping eaves of the old house, Bernie had camped for decades, a filthy urban Bedouin who'd lost the urge to wander. Piled everywhere, like a never-to-be-begun game of pick-up sticks, were hundreds of cardboard tubes and boxes that had held the tin foil he'd bought at Seth's. Mixed up with them were frozen dollops of discarded clothing; milk bottles half-full of ancient, crusted, brown piss; heaps of mildewed magazines and newspapers. In the dead centre of the attic, under a spillage of light from a filthy skylight, sat a bare, single mattress, a vile stain in the middle of its ticking. Alongside it was the electric heater that had done for Bernie, both bars radiant in the gloom.

As if they were the remains of an offering that had been sacrificed at this domestic altar, dangling on the fireguard, plopped on the bare boards and splashed on the walls were melted and ashy bits of Bernie and his late anorak. From somewhere within one of the drifts of trash hiding the skirting boards came a choked, tearful voice singing, '. . . it's down at the end of lonely street – that's Heartbreak Hotel . . .' For a few seconds I thought Lithy must've climbed up here with us, but it wasn't the right decade. Then I realised it was Elvis, and that the sound came from the paltry speaker of a fifties transistor, muffled by an unspeakable item of Bernie's underwear.

Once I'd spotted this, other mementos popped out of the murk. The cover of a paperback lying open by the mattress, picturing a neat couple in an unruly embrace. The title was *Peyton Place*. Butting against a pile of cardboard tubes, trying to lift them with its bulbous forks of arm, was Robbie the Robot, whining with battery-powered frustration. David picked his way through the trash like he knew this room only too well – like it was *his* room; one narrow foot placed surely on a shiny, new copy of *The Cat in the Hat*, the second planted in the saucer of an upturned frisbee. Bernie stayed standing by the door, his bullet-wound eyes wavering from

David to me and back again, the grimace still splitting his toilet-brush beard. He'd had the junky daughter up here a fair few times – now he'd got her mother and elder brother. At the far side of the attic David reached a dwarfish door and pulled it open. This, I thought, must lead to some stinky kitchenette, or fouler bathroom. The boy beckoned to me to follow him – and I did.

Into 1957, into Vermont, where I'd caught him, playing in the back yard with two of his buddies.

What's more overpowering at first it's difficult to say – for all senses come rushing into me with a roar, all perspectives with a screech – and the memories, the memories *glissade*. First, it comes to me that around this time I smoked pot, three, maybe four, times with Bob Beltane, before we made love in his station wagon, parked up by Moses Lake. Second, that this was like being high – everything musically exaggerated, the sky such a deep and aching blue, the sap from the maples in the plantation behind the yard stickily smelly, the rasp of crickets and drone of hornets a veritable string section tuning up for *Fantasia*. Third, that this was Now, and I could *feel* the very spring of the porch boards beneath my feet, the beat of the summer heat on my smooth *young* face, every little waft of cooler air *play about* beneath my light, cotton dress.

Oh Jesus – what sweet *relief*! What *feelings*! What an inconceivably broad view, the creamy piles of cumuli dragging my eyes up, the green grass, brown earth and white clapboard houses dragging them all around. Whirling impressions of inconceivable richness and colour for someone come from mouldering Dulston, from the dead future. But then, within instants – and life is so very instantaneous, so very Now, don't you think? – come other, deeper, more pleasing sensations too. The warm bellyache of recently received and passionately enjoined caresses, the deep thrum of dick-beats inside, the salty gushes of orgasm, his and hers, sweet and sour, acid and alkaline. The scent of the other is upon me and I know – sure as the shit I am – that I've only just arrived from my lover's embrace. Waved him off from the front veranda, watched the fins of that shark-like cocksman's car pull around the corner.

I've only just now stridden through the house, revelling in the energetic languor of my long legs so recently clasped around his brown waist; the imprint of his ass cheeks is on my sweaty hands, the flavour of his poetic mouth is in mine. My vagina and pubic hair are still slick with him, for although he always has the Trojans, I insist he need not smuggle them inside this Helen. He can pull out in time, every time, so good at rhyme – without any reason – is my Bob. Yes, I've only just stridden through the house and my eyes are still blinded by the dark afterimage of the living room, with its scattering of David's toys – the new frisbee, the old Robbie the Robot, the tiny transistor – and my and his father's reading, open on opposing, uneasy chairs. *Peyton Place* versus *Delinquency: The Juvenile Offender in America Today*. Jesus H. Christ – how can I stomach such shlock? How can he digest such baloney?

I've left the three nine-year-olds, David, Gus and Gary from next door, for a long hour and they've got up to all kinds of mischief. Here they are naked save for their shorts, and smeared all over with black mud they've manufactured with the hosepipe. *Now a surfing of awareness and an undertow of consciousness, pulling back from the wave about to crash on to the beach. Stop this – stop this Now, stop this faithless, old geyser of rage, which is about to spew from my mouth.* 'What're you playing?' I call to David from the back porch. 'The nigger game!' he shouts back. I burst through the screen

291

door and am on him in two strides, I knock his coonskin cap off, I grasp his blond hair, I smack his head once, twice, three times. The way British actors playing Gestapo officers smack their interrogation victims.

He's only said it by mistake – this much I know. The red fog of anger is only the gas blowing off the forbidden planet where my own, selfishly sated lust resides. But it's too late, for the other little boys' faces are racist caricatures of minstrel shock, and my David is running out of the back yard, across the front yard, into the roadway. I reach the side of the house at the precise moment the fender hits him. The car can't be doing more than thirty – this is a sleepy, residential area, we all sleep with our fellow residents – but these gas-guzzlers are huge and the impact is enough to hurl him into space, my son the puppet. 'May all your children be acrobats.' Now I comprehend the Jewish curse. His astral body rotates a full one and a half times before crumpling to the asphalt, then I see that he isn't mine any more, he doesn't have a face – only a mush. I recall the line I always used when he rode me too hard – 'Go and play in the traffic' – and every instance whips me. Keening and tearing at your bosom turns out to be a reflex action. 'Jeeezus! Jeeezus! Jeeezus!' I run towards the scrap of dead boy in the roadway, and the driver is out of the car, keening too. 'Jeeezus! Jeeezus! Jeeezus!' Jew and Gentile stand over the dead child's broken body. Was there ever an era when so many faithless people cried out so loudly for the Messiah?

'. . . You'll feel so lonely you could die.' The tinny ululation loops me in, and in a single swivel I turn from young and thin and keening with grief to fat and old and boiling with anger. The blue sky falls away, the dirty walls rise up, and there at the door stands Bernie ushering me back into death, the permanent Then.

He grunted once as I squeezed past him to gain the stairway. Already, below me, I could hear Rude Boy's clattered descent, the rattling crash of the basement door to number 27.

'Aren't you ever going to clear this shit-hole up?' I enquired of mine host.

He didn't have an eyelid to bat. 'Yeah – well. Yeah. Busy at the moment, yeah?'

Oh yeah, busy all right, busy handing out paper packets of indulgence, busy listening for the wailing wall. Busy doing nothing, this Junky, the eighth fucking dwarf. If only I could've found a way to scare him off – but he'd already seen every horror show on offer. That much was clear.

Christmas 2001

High-heeled sneakers – verily, that's what they are. They're exactly like the basketball boots kids wore in the fifties – rubber-soled, black or white canvas uppers, thick white laces, cross-threaded all the way up to the ankle – but they've got high heels. Fancy that. Imagine such an asinine article of footwear being sung into being by a nigger minstrel. They didn't get to lie down by the waters of Babylon, nor did they rock in the bosom of Abraham, the chariot never swung low enough for them to catch a ride home, but they did get to wear high-heeled sneakers. If God exists, clearly he is a fashion-conscious queen, so much attention has he lavished on the accessories of this world, so little on its substance.

Not that I'm wearing high-heeled sneakers. The Ice Princess and her consort may have been ludicrous, but they never wasted hard currency on such soft tat. Not for me. Nope – I got a pair of fake Nikes, off a stall on the Mile End Road.

Gutter shmutter for a guttersnipe. 'Nah – they're not snide, mate!' exclaimed the shabby man groaning beside the board of shoes. 'Why're they only two fucking quid then?' replied the Estate Agent, cradling the little trainers in his swollen hands. 'Take it or leave it, mate,' said the shabby man – and the Estate Agent took it, because by then taking it was all he could do. Gone were his looks, gone was the fire in his belly, and his chutzpah was useless – there was no one left to charm save the Ice Princess, and she'd long since been inoculated. 'Ta-ra,' said the shabby man. 'Ta-ra,' said the Estate Agent. Tan-ta-fucking-ra, a futile fanfare for the common man.

Which English class do I truly prefer now I've had the opportunity to be the dunce in both of them? (I exclude the aristocracy on principle – and because they're all fucking Krauts anyway.) The middle, with their ludicrous sense of wounded responsibility for a phantom imperial limb? Have you ever noticed how it's they who apologise if you knock against them in the street or on public transport? 'Sorry!' they involuntarily bleat. 'Sorry!' Sorry for taking your land and the fruits of your labour, sorry for taking your men and killing them in our wars, and an especial apology for making you play fucking cricket. So very sorry for that, old black/brown/yellow chap (delete as required). At least they've ceased referring to themselves as 'one', that peculiarly arithmetical form of the royal 'we'. What can you make of people who talk about themselves so persistently in the third person? Only that they were doomed to be sucked into the estuary and have their vowels flattened by the tide of commonality.

And what of the lovelorn commonality I've spent the last year or two with? 'Orlright luv,' they say, or occasionally, 'Orlright luv?' they query. 'Ta-ra luv,' they say on parting, and, ''Allo luv,' on arrival. There's so much luv in their world – so little caring. Luv is to love as diesel is to petrol – a heavier, more viscous, less incendiary form of affection. Not that they're averse to petrol – these superannuated Cockneys, these fag-end easterners. They're pretty adept with the petrol-soaked rags. They're partial to posting them through the letterboxes of the black/brown/yellow (delete as applicable) who've cropped up on their estates. (And isn't that so fucking English – difficult to imagine an American blue-blood inviting you to his project in the Hamptons.) Oh yes, the middle class say 'Sorry!' and shoo them away, straight into the luving arms of these diamond geezers, these pearly queens.

I fell on him orlrighty. Fell on him as I lunged for the Christmas cake. The irony is that the Estate Agent could be well-spoken – when he chose to be. But somewhere along the hideous line he travelled, the wind changed and blew the glottals far back into his throat, where they stopped, for ever. I fell on him and he was cold and stiff and unyielding. So much better than when he was alive – for then he was hot and warped and endlessly pliable. I can tell you there was a curiously pink froth at his blue lips. I can tell you about his rictus and his rigor and the feel of his dead flesh beneath my windy feet, my chubby body – but I could never describe how fantastic that icing tasted. How scrumptious it was to devour gobs of suety cake, and how little I minded having to search for currants and raisins in his matted chest hair.

That was hours ago. Mid-afternoon I guess. Since then I've knocked about the apartment a little – but then nowadays I knock about everywhere. For the last two nights I slept downstairs on the divan with the cushions humped round me for warmth – but it was still cold. Tonight it's going to freeze, and little people like me feel the cold, don't we? And there's no one here to do hot potatoes on my chubby hands, or blow warm breath on my absence of a neck. The stairs here have treads but no backs, and as you ascend, the room below retreats in stripes of shoddiness, framed by worn carpet. Dead ahead, as I crawl up the second flight, there's a walk-in closet.

I've considered making every effort to get inside, by dragging stuff over so I can climb on top of it and reach the handles. But the only thing high enough is a table that the television up here occupies – and that television, portable though it is, is not portable by me. Even if I could contrive this platform, I know the closet doors open outwards. The jerk of the catch freeing would be enough to propel me backwards down the stairs. Even if I could get inside, there's little hanging there to cover myself with. How could a woman who made so many trips to Marks & Spencer come away with so little in the way of clothing? Oh, I know, I know orlrighty.

My bed is a barred cage-on-legs. It's squeezed in the corner at this end of the room, behind the television, between the two windows and the two cold radiators set below them. Even when the radiators were hot it was fucking draughty, and I usually ended up at the other end of the room, on their bed, in between the Ice Princess and the Estate Agent, balancing – in my own mind – the benefit of their two kilowatts apiece against the likelihood that one, or other, or both of them might roll over in their smack stupor and crush the tiny life out of me.

She's there, lying twisted at the hips, but her shoulders are flat against the single squashed pillow. She's there, wearing a Che Guevara T-shirt, one arm flung out across the pillow next to her, the other curled against her upper thigh, as if mortality has surprised her in the act of drumming her fingers with boredom, or irritation. She's there, the duvet – which is my only hope – mounded over her central parts. She's there, her dark hair lying in a fan around her face, and her dull eyes wide open in astonishment. Doubtless she's surprised at what's happened to her. But I know I wasn't.

Chapter Thirteen

For the next eighteen months I existed on that back porch, screened in by the red fog of anger. Sure, I did my go-round, 24 x 7, 7 x fucking 52, but I was a whiter shade of my former pale shadow. 'We skipped a light fandango!' sang Lithy, as it did just that. The little ones asked to wee-wee, the walls moaned, the Fats jiggled, and Rude Boy gave me a knowing eye. I went to Baskin's, I came back again. I went to Seth's, I returned. I watched TV, listened to my little radio and stayed angry. *Very* angry. For if ever I let the anger drop, let the geyser subside, Rude Boy would beckon to me, lead me outside, call up for the key and take me back up to that attic full of grief, guilt and loneliness. Heartbreak Hotel indeed.

I existed in anger – and rage awoke me. I'd always had a temper and usually temporised, so this was quite like life. The anger seeped into every part of my no longer subtle body, like Three-in-One lubricating a rusty engine. My fat, old belly gurgled with annoyance, my saggy limbs shook with irritation, my tired old sex grew gummy with pique, my internal organs played arpeggios of indignation. Even the parts of me that, when I was alive, were dead – my hair, my teeth, my toenails – *ached* with dissatisfaction. Have you ever seen a dissatisfied toenail? I think not.

I was disgusted by the escape of Pablo Escobar – I'd have liked to eviscerate him myself. The Serbian death camps revolted me – if I could've got to that fat fuck Milošević, I would've strung him up by his own quiff. In Nazi old Germany thugs burnt the hostels of the laughably-named *Gastarbeiter*; it would've pleased me mightily to stand these shaven-headed monstrosities to a drink of their own Molotov cocktails. That dimwit Polack in the Vatican had the temerity to admit that Galileo was right – as if the sun shone out of his own fucking heliocentric ass. The dishonourable, spunk-drunk governor from Arkansas planted his fickle shaft in the Oval Office before I could get to him – I thought I'd drown in my own gall. Those peaceful Hindus razed the Ayodha mosque until it was like unto a dungheap – what high, old Babylonian fun; eight hundred dispatched to the subcontinental twin town of Dultson – I wished I were Kali herself, so I might garrotte the lot of them. The Somalis shot each other's starveling bones to pieces with the West's charitable Death Aid – didn't anyone have the wherewithal to bang their woolly heads together? In Britain the bog-trotters went a-bombing again – I'd've delighted in stuffing their blarney-holes with Semtex. Bombs in Manhattan, bombs in Bombay, barking-mad cultists in Texas – they all had their moment in the megaton sun of my ire. And another clever, famous, Jewish wiseacre fought another million-dollar suit against the shiksa he'd discarded in favour of her adopted child. Oy-oy-oy gevalt!

In June of '93 twelve Bosnian boys were killed when the Serbian fascists shelled a football pitch in Sarajevo. Now this was excessive – *one* would've been enough; then at least they'd still've had a full team. It occurred to me that all violent deaths were like this – the elimination of substitutes. Mass warfare is the biggest confirmation that there's a mass at all. The twentieth century in a lethal nutcracker. Thousands march down Whitehall every day, yet no one thinks to throw a can of paint over the bombastic statue of Field Marshal Haig, a man who presided over the deaths of a third of a million men, during six, short months in the mud fields of Flanders. Europe's own Hiroshima.

When I came to Britain in the late fifties people still mused wonderingly over the way the First War had touched every-one. How there wasn't a town, a village, a hamlet, a school, a business or a club that hadn't lost its complement of men. On Remembrance Day, special reverence would be accorded to the sad old things who came tottering along Whitehall, beribboned with bravery, willing yet again to place themselves in the shadow of Haig's stone horse. Parliamentarians to this day rise up on their hind legs and bleat and baa about the way these khaki ants sacrificed their lives for the preservation of free speech, of liberty. Freedom to do what exactly? Freedom *in* what precisely? Freedom to be part of the nest? Freedom to die of cancer? We've been given the great and glorious choice to do multiple-choice questionnaires. Mr Khan's quality-of-life questionnaire for terminal patients.

Cancer and warfare. There are memorials in every town and village and hamlet to those who've shrivelled in the battle against the sarcoma; and of course, both forms of annihilation hammer home the same point – that those who survive do so arbitrarily. 'It could've been me!' scream the ones left behind – and only demented moralists dare to contemplate that it *should've* been them.

The anger subsided, leaving me deader than ever. Even if I could've been resurrected now, what place would there've been for me in the world? In the five short years since my demise, new models of car had come on the market, different makes of mobile phone; the people cut their hair in innovative styles. Beside these nineties folk – who were themselves unsurpassedly decadent – I would've appeared a walking continuity error. Lily Van-fucking-Winkle. I couldn't get myself connected. I lay in bed and I smoked. I smoked B&H. I smoked lots of them. I had twenty-four hours every day in which to smoke – and no lungs to damage. I was merely a subtle set of bellows, a temporary confinement for the genie that eddied about me in the cold, front room of the basement. Where the tissue culture on the wall muttered to itself, and the eyeless golems of my own indulgence squatted, and the calcified cadaver of my own lust did its shimmy, and the angry child I'd slaughtered raved. And, lest we forget, outside the back window my dead grandchildren shuffled from one vestigial foot to the other. They always say it's *so* much more satisfying being a grandparent – but compared to what, exactly?

I managed a cigarette every four minutes, fifteen an hour, three hundred and sixty each day. In two months of that summer I spent all of the money I'd saved working for Baskin. The front room became a worthless Fort Knox with its stacks of empty, gold, cardboard boxes. 'She's gone to seed, gone to seed,' muttered the Fats, 'she's awfully seedy – she's let herself go, let herself go.' I ignored them. I listened to my little radio. 'When a lovely thing dies, smoke gets – ' Lithy crooned and I tried to lash out. As required, I'd send Lithy or the Fats – they did everything together, entwined by flab – down to Seth's to get another carton, but I had no intention of sallying forth. To Baskin I explained that I had chronic bronchitis, a reasonable explanation for my absence, given my advanced years and my heavy, dutiful smoking.

In bed and without the need to plump my pillows – what could be finer? In bed, blowing blue ploots of smoke into the rank atmosphere (no lungs, so no moisture, no colour change). I considered smoking experiments. Might I be able to build a Rube Goldberg contraption with which to feed myself ciggies? A complicated and implausible arrangement of wheels, cogs, pulleys and conveyor belts, rigged up to the engine of a dismembered Hoover, all with the aim of supplying me with ready-lit, correctly aligned pills. I'd resemble an early animated short – *Steamboat Lily* – and add at least twenty minutes to my daily smoking time. I meditated on having my own teeth again, on how they did wonders for inhalation and exhalation. Smoking with falsies had always been absolutely that. The loss of the cigs and the loss of my teeth. Always together.

In late July they released Demjanjuk – the car worker who claimed he'd never been involved with the assembly line of death at Treblinka. I felt my old anger stir, but wouldn't let it get the better of me. My counterpane world was absolutely that; I lay, a shloomp in a humped muddle of duvet, gazing up at the letterbox view of the outside afforded me. The tops of the bedroom windows framed three portions of the sidewalk. This grey view of slabs was striped by the railings, so that as legs went by, they flickered like zoetropes, or stop-action photographs. Cars seldom parked up outside the house. The dead – for reasons never altogether understood by me – didn't bother too much with driving. Dulston was like the past in this regard; if you could get it together to drive, there was always somewhere to park. Like Crooked Usage in the sixties.

As I lay smoking, on the morning when the *Today* programme announced Ivan the Terrible's acquittal, two neat wheels squeaked, crunched and grounded against the kerb. I could see a foot or so of the immaculately dusted, half-timbered bodywork; then one trim, court-shod, tan-hosed foot; then its accomplice. They clicked past the railings, then out of sight. I heard them clicking down the steps. There was a pause, followed by – a sharp rap on the knocker. Most peculiar – the dead never knocked, the door was always open. There was no point in locking it; I'd long since learned that if the shades wanted to get in they'd simply manifest themselves in the dank corridor.

'Answer that, will you?' I snapped at the Fats, and the three of them blindly bumped out of the room, squashing together in the doorway.

'I've come to see Mrs Yaws.' The clipped syllables evaded big teeth. 'Is she at home?'

'She's let herself go,' gabbled the Fats, 'she's fat and old. Fat and old.'

'Could you tell her Dr Bridge is here?' The classy dullard was unfazed by watching my personified weight. 'No – don't worry, I'll tell her myself. In here, is it?' And in she came, *Virginia* Bridge no less, the whole dry, tweedy, twinsetted, headscarved, equine length of the woman. Her pale blue eyes blinked and watered in the pale blue clouds of smoke from my umpteenth B&H of the morning. '*Really*, Lily,' said Virginia, crossing to the bedside, setting down her Gladstone, removing her tan suede gloves, '*really*.'

And I was back there with her – really. Back at Crooked Usage. Back in that anachronistic period of the early sixties when there was nightly television news *and* coal was still delivered. Coal in dusty blue-black sacking; coal, as dense as the smog it generated. The sixties, a decade of thick, yellow smog and swinging sputum. On the crappy copy of a Hepplewhite bedside table sit several flat packs of du Maurier filters. Beside these is a Daphne du Maurier novel, its paper cover bent to buggery. There's a cut-glass ashtray full of butts – one of which is still smouldering – and I'm lighting up another with my smogodynamically-shaped Ronson.

The bedside table has three drawers. There's one for medicaments: sodium amytal capsules; a pot of attractive yellow-and-green Librium; the proprietaries – Venos useless cough syrup, dumb Disprin, asinine Anadin; and tampons – because, of course, I've got my period. Blood at one end – sputum at the other. It's enough to make you retch. Drawer number two has a bottle of Haig laid end-on in it, couched with Kleenex. Virginia has adjured me time and again not to drink liquor on top of the barbs, but what care I?

Drawer number three is full of snack food, purloined over the past few days from the cold kitchen. There's half a pack of fucking Huntley and Palmer's Toytime biscuits. They're square, slick things, with icing pictures of trains and teddies on them. When I crunch them with my rotting fangs, they turn my mouth painful and gritty. I do this frequently. I also munch on Crawford's Ginger Ruffles and squidge on Nestlé fruit drops, nor am I averse to the occasional excruciating worrying that's required to dispatch a tablet of Callard & Bowser's butterscotch. Yup – I sneak down to the cold kitchen and I steal the kiddies' cookies and sweeties. Then I come back up here and get snacked out.

Virginia's got me upright, the buttons of my nightie undone, and is sounding me with her smooth, Atrixo-creamed hands, while speaking to me with her dry English accent. 'Lily, really, I mean to say, you can't expect me to go on treating you for chronic bronchitis if you aren't prepared to give up smoking. I mean, it's not as if you don't know the facts . . .'

The facts are that every month or so Yaws goes away to play golf, with his peer group of permanently prepubescent, ex-minor-public-schoolboy pals. In provincial towns she liaises with him in prim guesthouses. They're so respectable that their adultery is never suspected. At night, on brushed-cotton sheets, they chafe together. He ejaculates dust into her sandy vagina. I tolerate this in the mad way you do when you're not sure you require the pipe that is his forever being knocked out on your mantel, the dottle gagging in your throttle. Not true. I was riven with jealousy, hacked out with the adze of it – a dugout canoe of yearning. *I* wanted to be the one who stood, with an ice lolly in each hand, not sure which one to lick. Not Yaws. Not Virginia, who, pausing from her soundless, insensate sounding, peers around the room at the blubbery golems, the lithopedion, Rude Boy, the sarcoma wall-covering . . . has she come to the basement flat in order to speculate as well as employ her speculum?

About what Yaws and I didn't do together? Or Kaplan? Or Bob Beltane? Or King Stuff? Is she imagining all this as a possible version of her own afterlife? I can believe that. She had a crippled husband. Paralysed from the waist down. Lucky for Virginia it wasn't from the waist up. Anyway, I lie here and black-and-white documentary clips of that era – showing baboons with masks lashed on to their muzzles, forcing them to smoke – spool behind my eyes. Give it up. I couldn't – I'd rather die again. Cigarettes are the best friends I've ever had. More reliable than liquor, comforting – but not fattening. I'd sooner die a thousand deaths. Roll me over in the clover. Roll me over and let me expire again.

The fucking cow – fucking with my bull. The whole fucking herd of them, being serviced by a husband with a dripping, yard-long pizzle. Jealousy courses through me – a green circulatory system. All the wives I ever betrayed, all the wives who ever betrayed me. I see them congregating in a field and cunting up to form a gay rondo of congress that excludes me utterly. I stand in a fucking cowpat, a sad little thing, while they whoop and low and grind and groan. Little boxes, little boxes . . . and they all look just the same / And they're all made out of ticky-tacky . . . and they all look –

Just the same. I close my eyes tighter still – '. . . it's an addiction like any other, Lily, it will take a few days . . .' – and will Virginia Bridge to die. O Great White Spirit, if I give up smoking will you take this woman in my stead? I *really* do this – I truly did this. I weighed up the Weights, the Passing Clouds, the Viscounts and the blessed du Mauriers. 4/- +

3/6 + 4/- + 3/6 – sums were so much kinder when they incorporated such tiny strokes. I piled them up into a huge bier of dry white twigs, threw Dr Bridge atop it – and she committed suttee in my stead. Poor Virginia. Poor, dry Virginia Bridge. Dead of cancer at forty-odd, when unlike me she hadn't been smoking forty-odd a day for twenty-five years. Poor Virginia – you could do the arithmetic yourself – she didn't deserve such malevolently willed extinction.

I reach for the bedside table. I'm gonna have a big slug of that Haig, before it gets too vague – but it's too late. Gone already. She's gone, it's gone. I'm still here.

I looked up through the nicotine-stained windows at the roadway above, and the trim wheels of her trim car had departed. 'She's gone to seed,' muttered the Fats, 'she's awfully seedy . . .' I lit another B&H and remembered all the peaceable hours I'd eradicated, all the joy I'd steered to avoid, as I whiled my bitter life away on a river of resentment, lustily sculling beneath the green envy trees with their parasitic wreaths of sexy jealousy. Under the grotty bed, Lithy gave reedy voice: 'Ah – ah – ah – ah – stay-ing al-ive!'

Who knows why Virginia Bridge found it necessary to climb in her ghostly Morris and make the long trip north from Dulburb to Dulston? (And I had no doubt that that was where she'd ended up – she was Dulburb to the very tips of her fingers. Dulburb through and through.) But she did. Again and again and again, for month after month after month – a twelvemonth in all. I bitterly regretted ever ever having called a doctor out on a house call, now that this shady practitioner kept descending on my basement. I got out of the fucking bed. I tucked Lithy in my pocket and went back to work.

That summer, Baskin had groped his penultimate fanny, shmoozed his final client, and rung down the curtain on thirty-two years of telling the world things it didn't need to know, or would've found out anyway. He and Mrs Baskin retired to Rainham to breed Bedlingtons. He sold what was left of the business to a thrusting conglomerate, whose PR arm had offices near Old Street. And what was left of the business? Only a client list that included such gems as the Queen Mother Leisure Centre in Stratford – 'You wet yourself – we'll clean it up!'; the Mile End Road One-Stop Fitting Shop – 'Tired of that Leaky Exhaust? So are we'; and the Leytonstone Laundromat chain – 'Stop Watching the World Go Round – and Let Us Watch Your Wash Go Round!' And me.

Yup – I went too. It was one of the conditions of Baskin's sell-out, the employee hand-me-down. You might've thought I'd look hopelessly out of place behind the mirrored windows of KBHL Corporate Communications – not so. I couldn't see myself in them anyway; nor could all the scented young pudendas, who tramped their knickerboxes in to play the plastic piano, see me either.

Mirrored fucking buildings – where did *they* come from? How could the modern city, with its vaunting ugliness, have the temerity to contemplate itself in these twenty-, thirty-, forty-storey pier-glasses? To ogle its own soullessness, while batting its vertical, textured louvres? I can recall the first time I saw such a thing – the John Hancock Center in Boston. Must've been the mid-seventies; the sleek rack of reflection was a pre-emptive strike by the future on that bulbous decade. But now London was stacking up with the things, as if the old hooker was intent on retouching her masonry maquillage in them. Every prospect became – on those infrequent sunny days – a postmodern Magritte, with fluffy white clouds oozing around giant external cornices. But inside the mirrored building was the perfect place for me to be. Me, with my tireless hatred of pretty young women and my newly recovered jealousy.

Christ I was jealous! I was jealous of the Filipino shoe fetishist when she went to jail for corruption – at least she'd stayed married. I was jealous of Hillary-fucking-Clinton – even when it looked as if she'd stay hitched too. I was jealous of the Israelis and the Palestinians, locked into the war congress with Slick Willie playing pander. Jealous of Arafat with his vaginal mouth, Rabin with his penile nose – jealous of what they did together. I was jealous of the kid in Pittsburgh who had seven major organs replaced during fifteen hours of surgery – she'd had more men inside her than I ever would. I was jealous of the Bobbitt woman who sliced off her husband's cock – to have *and* to hold. I was jealous when Fellini died – now there'd never be a bed for me in his dreamhouse of feminine archetypes. I was jealous of all the girls caught in the LA quake – they felt the earth fucking move all right. I was jealous of the Palestinian women when that crazed Yid shot their menfolk in the mosque – at least they could wail and rant and scream and *feel* their loss. I was jealous when Fred West, the home-improvement serial killer, was arraigned for his crimes. Imagine that – jealous of those poor young women, lured to their vile deaths. Could jealousy take me any lower? Yes. I was jealous when the massacres began in Kigali, simply because I hated to be excluded. But I *wasn't* jealous when Marcel Bich died; then I was merely beset by the old, stale envy. But I *was* jealous when the Channel Tunnel opened. Jealous of it as it was penetrated by train after train, each with its spermatozoa-load of men, eating *croques m'sieurs*, swigging beers, reading *Le Monde*. I was jealous of Winnie Mandela. I was jealous of OJ's wife. I was so jealous – I so wanted *not to be me*. I wanted to be loved. I wanted to be held. I wanted to slur sibilant Mama-loshen with someone to whom I'd always be – their baby.

'Be my, be my baby!' Lithy sang in the pocket of my sack

dress, as I wended my way between the girlish crowds streaming from the subways around Old Street. They'd've looked at me oddly – had they bothered to look at all. At work I considered offering the young men, with their brightly coloured braces and their dull imaginations, a crack at my withered sex. The subsonic hum of the air conditioning, the ultrasonic whine of the computers and the droning of the workaday chatter – all of it, amazingly, gingered them up. Most of them would, I knew, fuck *anything*. They'd insinuate their thin white joints into the photocopier or the fax machine if they thought it would feel good. But what'd be the point? I'd only feel the worst jealousy of all, the jealousy of my former, busty, lusty self.

In the late summer of '94 I was standing in the bloody basement of 27 Argos Road, by the open window of the bedroom, when I heard the familiar invocation of the Yale in an altogether too familiar voice. I craned up to see unfamiliar, expensive-looking, brown leather ankle-boots; unfamiliar, well-washed dungarees; and – thumb hooked in pocket, four fingers drumming on a flat thigh – a hand, the garden of which I once travelled round and round, like a teddy bear. Attached to it was an arm I used to take one step up, then a second, and an under-there which I'd tickle and tickle, until its owner's face scrunched up with giggles.

The key sailed down and she stooped to pick it up. Her hair was cut short – mannishly short. It didn't suit her. But her arms were tanned, almost muscled, with clean white sleeves rolled up on them – and that did suit her. 'She's fit and well, fit and well . . .' babbled the Fats, who'd joined me by the window and who huddled by my hips like loveless handles. 'But not for long!' I snapped back at them. Up above, Natasha turned and casually scanned the street, then her new clothes disappeared back into her old life.

Christmas 2001

I'm a chubby little thing – that I am. A regular piglet. The Ice Princess – to give her her due – was inclined to feed me on sterile pots of purée, gluten-free, protein-balanced, vitamin-enhanced. I suppose this careful feeding was by way of compensating for her own, increasingly erratic diet. Still, the Estate Agent made a mockery of this, because whenever the three of us were out together, and she'd disappeared behind one of those heavy, tomb-like doors, incised with the hieroglyphs of society's disadvantaged – the old, the wheelchaired, women with small kids – he'd buy me a bag of chips. Chips as thin as toothpicks, frazzled into spikiness in the grease bins of Burgerland, or McDonald's or KFC. Chips as sharply unpleasant in my tiny soft mouth as dental instruments – for, once again, I'm soft in the tooth department. Or alternatively, fat, blubbery, near-disintegrating chips, as white as Ouruobouros, questing towards my pink lips from within greasy flaps of grey paper.

Chips, chips and more chips. Chips clutched and chomped in shopping precincts, on street corners, or beside the twisted railings in shat-upon parks. Chips drenched in ascorbic acid, or bleeding Heinz. Chips hung on to by me for their warmth alone. My precious chips, always being solicited by kids with hooded sweatshirts – 'Gizzachip?' – their button noses silver-riveted to their gunmetal faces. In the bilious gloaming of the inner city they resemble a closed order of the shabby, the infantilised. Chips – always Prêt à Shit for me. Then the Estate Agent or the Ice Princess would lie me on a bench or a fold-down plastic scoop, or even on the cold earth itself, in order to wrestle with tights and trousers, to extract the wad of absorbency from between my rash thighs. Then the Wet Ones insinuated between my folds, then the slathered cream. All my life, underwear has tormented me – soon it'll be over.

But how soon? Two days now and all I've had to eat is the Christmas cake and all I've been able to get to drink is scoops of water from the toilet bowl in the bathroom. Several times I've inched along beside the banisters, avoiding looking at the Ice Princess, and gained the door to the bathroom. Here I've managed, only just, to climb up, scoop and drink, then sit down and pee, then flush. This death is child's play.

To think I was jealous of the Ice Princess and her consort – jealous of this pitiable pair, she up here, he down there. But they had their moments, cackling in minicabs as we slewed across town to score, steal or mooch, the African drivers navigating the ancient city by reference to their internal maps of Lagos, Dar es Salaam, or Addis Ababa. Cackling as the drivers slammed on their brakes and slide guitar slid from the speakers on the back shelf; cackling as they pictured tall, slim, tirelessly elegant Masai, puffing on filter-tips and staring out over the riven valleys of Marlboro Country.

But then I had every right to feel jealous of him – he wasn't anything to do with me. And her – well I knew her as intimately as anyone could know another. Knew her inside and out, claustro and agro. As begetter and begotten. Yes, I've edged past the Ice Princess's bier, this chilly slab of padding, disgorged from the fast-flowing glacier of her life into a terminal moraine of duvet and pillow. Edged past – now I must edge towards. Last night was cold – tonight will be colder. No one will come in this, the dead interstice between the years. Despite the muted bang and wail of the people who live in the flat above, cranking up for another evening session on the karaoke machine they got for Christmas. For they're as inaccessible to me as if this maisonette were an orbiting space station, with its communications failed, its computers down, its life-support systems a misnomer.

'Daisy, Daisy, give me your answer do / I'm half crazy, all

for the love of you . . .' She sang it to me – I sang it to her. Now, as I crawl over the carpet, struggle up on to the bed, pull a lappet of duvet from her, curl it around myself, I lisp the ditty in my own inimitable way: 'Daithee, Daithee, githee y'antha doo / N'yam na' athy, orcalovuv oo . . .' A shame to cry so – to void the toilet water. I could cry enough to flood this room, and send a wave crashing down the stairs, smashing into the door, busting the chains at top and bottom. Cry enough to flood the whole of Coborn House, so that its inhabitants have to assemble in the playground and run a caucus race so as to dry themselves off. Everybody has won and all must have prizes. Karaoke machines for the kiddy-winkies, karaoke machines for the leering adults. Then they can all sing something very very simple. I could never quite believe how popular popular music is.

From where I lie I can see very little and the Ice Princess is merely another bit of cheap furniture lying beside me. This place abounds with such meagre sticks. I can see orange beams from the streetlamps without, cut up by the louvres and ranged across the room. I can see a thin rime of ice forming on the windows. I want to sink into dreams of quiet, brown rooms, with slants of sunshine and poignant, boring atmospheres. Instead, I recall a trip the two of them took me on at the cold start of this year.

They were wrecked – natch. Stoned as crows. Flapping down through the Isle of Dogs, past the Celesteville of Canary Wharf to Victory Gardens. Then through the foot tunnel to Greenwich, then through the smoggy streets to the Millennium Dome. All the way they took turns to push my chair ahead of them. First one, then the other, giving it an almighty shove, then running a few paces to catch the handles of the caroming cart. Laughing like loons, imagining that this barely controlled sensation was fun for me. 'Oh my, my, my

De-li-lah!' he sang – she'd thought it amusing to incorporate her feared mother's name into her fearful daughter's. Why were we going there? Because they were high – yes. Because they thought the Dome would prove to be a hit, a trip for happy-go-lucky, hippy-dippy souls such as themselves. Oh – and the Estate Agent had pulled off some successful scam, or deal, so he had money for a change.

They did enjoy themselves – scampering from the Money Zone to the Play Zone to the Discovery Zone, all the time utterly zoned out. And what did I think of this huge, crushed boob, with its panoply of corporate playthings, its coursing multitudes of middle-class proles? Well, when they'd proposed the trip that morning, at our walk-up apartment in Coborn House, on the Coborn Street Estate, on Coborn Street, Mile End, I wanted to say to them, 'Let's not and say we did.' But that wasn't possible. My vocabulary has stretched a bit now – I could ask for the essentials if they were available – but then, all I could burble was 'Mumu' to her and 'Ruh' to him. Yes, Coborn House, with its three storeys of external walkways and staircases, so like a shoddy version of the Rhinelander Gardens on West 11th Street.

And the Dome with its cheesy evocations of a technologically advanced future that we know will never arrive, what did that remind me of, dear Mumu, dearest Ruh, as you shoved me hither and thither? Why, of another time and another place, where 6,700,000 cubic yards of contamination was removed so that the world of tomorrow could be built. It reminded me of a 700-foot-high tapered pillar, symbolising the finite, and a 200-foot steel globe, symbolising the infinite. It reminded me of the Helicline, the ramp that connected them, and of the giant NCR cash register that counted the visitors in. It reminded me of the giant powder box that served as a pavilion for ladies' cosmetics, and the humungous radio *tube that did the same for RCA. It reminded me that Lewis Mumford said in 1939 that the World's Fair represented 'a completely tedious and unconvincing belief in the triumph of modern industry'.*

Oh, the future – it's always so fucking dated. For you, for me, for all of us. If only there were some way out of it.

Chapter Fourteen

I went in search of Phar Lap to discuss this not so welcome homecoming. I didn't go into town that often – but I went. I'd been to the Courtauld fairly frequently since I'd died. The situation of the galleries – in those days tucked up several flights in back of Gower Street – was obscure enough to make me feel secure. The rooms were poorly lit considering the trove they contained, and visitors wafted over the sound floorboards. I favoured the Wigmore Hall for concerts, but mourned for the days when it smelt of Dettol. I avoided the grand galleries and booming venues, I skirted the wide esplanades. The London I traversed was a Dickensian city of snaking alleys and sunless courtyards, where the corroded bricks oozed pigeon droppings, and indecorous ledges were blanketed by sootfalls. What was the point of going to Selfridges, *they* didn't sell Benson & Hedges.

But even I, going on my wraith's progress, began to notice wedges of modernity, hammered into the creaking joints of the city, like plastic hips into arthritic old women. Flashy boutiques and garish eateries were opening up by the score. Down pissy passageways, brushed-aluminium frontages gleamed through the murk, where stray catwalk models picked their way between turds, *en route* to rest their heads on pillowy ciabatta and slurp frothy cappuccino. Of course, those of us who'd been here all along had seen it all before. The coffee bars and the themed restaurants, the drugs and the deshabille, the tourists and the travail, the pansies and the punters.

It transpired there were no fewer than thirteen branches of

Nowhere, the Centralian themed restaurant. Three in the Square Mile, five in the West End, five more in the 'burbs – but none of them in the phone book. It was easy to comprehend the success of Phar Lap's venture; the Nowhere concept evinced all of the foibles that passed for convictions among the city-dwellers: a willingness to embrace Ocker chauvinism, combined with a desire to lie down with the Aboriginal, and then complicated by the difficulty of actually finding the place. Nowheres weren't listed in the phone book, nor did Phar Lap and his partners permit entries in restaurant guides or listings magazines, or on tourist maps. To find Nowhere you either had to know someone who'd been, or had to go walkabout through the outback of London. This – in the jaded eyes of its beholders – made Nowhere an authentic transplant of traditional folkways into the urban context. You could only eat at Nowhere if you'd secret knowledge, or were prepared to seek it out.

There were also different kinds of Nowhere. The decor of the most basic outlets evoked the dried-out riverbed of the Todd, in Alice Springs, on a hot summer afternoon. Black shade edging pitiless glare. Vast mounds of empty cans and broken bottles. Extreme drunkenness. Very little to eat. As you ascended the hierarchy of Nowhere, so you moved – figuratively speaking – further out into the Centralian desert. The waiters discarded more and more K-Mart clothing and were to be encountered daubed with ochre, taking down orders on tjuringa-shaped pads, their hacked-about genitals concealed in leathery pouches. And these were the white staff – college kids from Perth, Melbourne and Brisbane – hired by Phar Lap because they were so much more reliable than the natives, and at least their accents were authentic.

In the most prestigious branches of Nowhere, which took up whole floors of mirrored office blocks in the City, there was nothing save for featureless expanses of cracked salt pan, ringed with spinifex. The walls were artfully painted with a continuous *trompe-l'oeil* mural depicting the hot air on the desert horizon; with perhaps the merest of dark smears to indicate, in the far far distance, a low escarpment, or was it the bar? Occasionally a goanna or a marsupial rat would be released from the far recesses of the establishment and would scamper through the dust, startling the clientele, who'd writhe in the dirt with delight.

Writhing in the dirt was a big part of the Nowhere shtick. Diners might arrive in a London midwinter, draped with cashmere, wrapped around with wool, suited and booted. But a few, short minutes in the dehumidified, forty-four-degree heat of Nowhere would see them stripping off their silk ties, letting them fall to the ground like limp snakes, unbuttoning their collars, unzipping their dresses, peeling off their tights, dropping their socks and feeling the grit between their soft toes.

The food was almost inedible: half-burnt chunks of kangaroo, witchetty grubs, damper – a kind of mushy campfire bread – and, if you were very lucky, a few handfuls of bitter herbs. But that wasn't the point. Overhead, the high-resolution screens drummed down on the dyspeptic diners a view of a sky so vast and encompassing that it entirely diminished the meagre earth. Cloud formations like continents wheeled by. The gibbous moon rose, its craters and mountains more sharply credible than Europe. The London without wasn't merely masked – it was annihilated by the experience of Nowhere. And there was the booze. Plenty of liquor. Phar Lap quipped to me, 'We put this stuff in the grog, yeh-hey? Kinduv makes this mob like blackfellers, hey-yeh? Takes out an enzyme – whatever. Makes it so they can't handle it.'

I didn't believe this for a second. What there was at

Nowhere was blistering dry heat and a pushy, personable kid by your side, for every second of your stay, mimicking the raising of a glass or a bottle, and interrogating you. 'This one?' he'd say. 'You want this one?' Then he'd bring cold bottles of good Australian white wine, or beers colder still, and slap the vessels, filmed with condensation, straight into your sweaty palm. No wonder people drank and drank, stripped off their clothes, and howled, and beat sticks together when – as was often the case at Nowhere – there was an inauthentic display of a bowdlerised initiation ceremony, put on by ex-anthropology students from the Australian National University. They drank, and during unhappy hour – when Phar Lap's staff released swarms of fresh flies into the joint – the drinks were half-price, so they drank twice as much. Yes, there was nothing in London quite like a trip to Nowhere. No-thing.

Not, you understand, that I ever saw the place in full swing. I arrived at the flagship branch of Nowhere, which was sited at the southern end of Blackfriars Bridge, in a prime piece of repulsive eighties rococo called Sea Containers House, during one of my lack of lunch hours. Nowhere never opened at lunch – although during the late nineties Phar Lap started up a hugely successful chain of themed Centralian sandwich shops, called Anywhere.

It was early August 1994. There'd been a car-bombing at the Israeli Embassy in London a week or so before, and the week before that a bomb in Buenos Aires had done for a hundred of my coreligionists. It was business as usual for us Jews, holocaust and diaspora, hand in oven glove. While in upstate New York they were limbering up to celebrate the twenty-fifth anniversary of fucking Woodstock. Ach! If the seventies were bulbous, and the eighties sharp, the nineties were nothing but bogus.

From the mock gilt and garbled marble of the lobby,

Schindler's lift took me up five storeys and disgorged me into a grim slot of space. The overhead video screens were showing naught but themselves. At the far side of a hundred feet of cracked white mud, a panel of desert horizon had been rolled back to reveal a patch of the Thames's north bank and a slice of Unilever House. A beefy blond boy in overalls was sweeping up a pile of dead flies and the occasional crushed lizard. Truly, I thought, we are as flies to wanton boys. A fat girl whistled as she vacuumed the spinifex, breaking off as I approached to gesture towards a pile of old clothes, which, as I tramped over to it, resolved itself first into a hat on top of a pile of old clothes, and latterly into Phar Lap Jones.

'Bin 'spectin' you, Lily-girl, yeh-hey.' He was toying with his big boomerangs and smoking his dag-tail cigarette. At his feet, on the floor of the mock desert, the ends of many many similar failed to reach any conclusion.

'Oh yes?'

'Yuwai – y'got wulu, girl?' He indicated that he needed a light – and I provided him with one. He took a long pull of the scrawny cigarette, the smoke leaked from his plump lips in thin pleats, staggered in a draught, then dispersed. 'Yairs – Natasha back, yeh-hey?'

'You know about that?'

'Know 'bout that. Know 'bout yer *feelings* – bin havin' them, yeh-hey?'

'I've been fucking angry – if that's what you mean – '

'And jealous. Deadly jealous, hey-yeh?'

'And jealous,' I acknowledged.

'The best is yet t'come, girl, yeh-heh? All yer feelings come down now, yeh-hey? Nearly yer last chance, hey-yeh? Make up yer mind, girl, get off yer go-round or shit yerself back into life, yeh – *your* decision.' Once again Phar Lap was putting the onus on to me, poor little fat old me; me, who'd endured so many twenty-four-hour Dulston days. My death, it occurred to me, was falling into the same pattern as my life, apathetic sojourns followed by spasms of inertia. He asked me if I wanted to get off this 'go-round', as he termed it. But as to what that was, or how to do it, he was as vague as ever.

Anyway, I couldn't bear too much of this twaddle, especially not there, not in a downtime themed restaurant, talking to a dead Aboriginal. I surprised myself by caring about Natasha. 'Natasha's back, Phar Lap, and she looks well.'

'She looks damn fine. Damn fine buju. But not for long, yeh-hey? Not for long. Y'see yer wonderin', Lily-girl, yeh-hey? Wonderin' how it all adds up, yeh-hey? How it kinduv fits together, hmm? Wonderin' why a traditional man like me has anything t'do with you girl, hey-yeh?'

'Yes. I think it has something to do with Natasha – to do with what happened to Natasha – '

'Down under?'

'Yes, down under.'

'Yuwai! Down fuckin' under, girl. Juda! What happened – you want me t'tell you what happened, yeh-hey?'

'You know, then?'

'Oh I know, Lily-girl. I know – I was fuckin' *there*.'

So he told me. It took the rest of the hour. I was late back to Old Street. Phar Lap told me in his own, inimitable way, but for your convenience I'll omit the cheek-clicks and palate-slaps, I'll translate the blackfeller terms and the Strine slang. After all – everything should be for your convenience in this, the most inconvenient of times. A waiting time in a waiting room.

But Phar Lap wasn't at Potts Point, where Natasha pitched up to stay with Polly Passmore. He wasn't present while she puked her way through hot days – so bizarre, the chill of withdrawal in this balmy clime; nor when at night the two young women would haul the mattress up on to the roof, and hunker down beside the swimming pool there, staring over at the entrance to the Sebold Townhouse Hotel. Watching the Caucasian big businessmen tramp inside with tiny Asian hookers dangling off their arms – like charmless bracelets.

Natasha stayed with Polly at Potts Point for six months, for her a triumph of mateship. She kept off the smack as well, more or less. She did score a couple more times at the Cross, and in so doing made less of herself. King's Cross, Sydney. How absurd – like Paris, Texas. Every facet of Natasha's London life was reflected back at her out of the hard diamond of the southern sky. She learned that you scored at Alice's Restaurant in King's Cross. Scored from surfer junkies. Ever seen a junky with a surfer's toned body, and who has no need to roll up a sleeve in order to find a vein, because he's wearing a fucking *singlet*? Totally bizarre. Natasha saw them and scored off of them, like I say, two, maybe three, times. But worse than that, one time she turned a trick to get the money. In London, Russell had taken to getting Natasha to do perverse things sexually. Fuck with him while men watched, so as to entertain dealers he wanted to get on the right wrong side of, or voyeurs he wished to be seen with. He'd also tied her up and slapped her around. All to get junk when they were coked up – or coke when they were junked up. Seesaw, Marjorie door, Natasha will have a sick master.

But this was different. Natasha strolled in among the milling tourist folk, beneath the low neon advertising strip shows, gripped by the need to get high. To let go of herself. To forget *all*. It wasn't the money *per se* – she had some. Miles sent her monthly chunks, the proceeds from selling the flat. But that was only enough to live healthily. That was her healthy stake. If she was going to get smack, she thought, she'd have to do something grubby for it, teach herself a lesson. What a mistake. Teach yourself a lesson and you become an autodidact. She thought it would be easy enough. She'd seen the street girls pick men up off the strip, walk round two corners with them, lie down in the bougainvillaea-planted border of a little park for all of two minutes of bumping. The men's white asses rising up from the hardy perennials like cloven moons. And everywhere she walked in the red-light district she was propositioned. 'G'day, g'day, g'day,' the men said to her. Which really meant – observing her long brown limbs, her blue-black hair, her still high-riding breasts – 'Good lay, good lay, good lay . . .' The Australian men, loudly dressed and clamorous, like gallah birds.

Natasha abandoned herself to this. She picked up the smallest, most timorous one she could find. A little clerk-type, barely up to her shoulder, come up from the financial district after work. He'd gotten a bit drunk and lost his mates. Remembered that he never got laid enough – if at all. Saw this beauty giving him the glad eye and whispered, 'G'day?' Natasha was drunk herself and willing to pimp her own irresponsible child. She took him to the park and got him into the bed full of shredded bark. All of her expertise came in handy here – all of those boys and men so expertly handled. She'd been so good at denying them what they wanted; how much easier it was to give it. To feed his soft kugel cock into a condom – no problem. To feed him into her – less of a problem still. Bit of spit on the dry bits. Mumu's spit heals every hurt. She turned her lovely face to contemplate the roots of the shrubs. She whispered, 'Ooh yes! That's good.' When oh no – it was *so* bad. Don't teach yourself lessons – don't abandon your own child. When real lust makes puppets of us all, how much worse to be the puppet mistress?

They got up and she took a hundred dollars from him. A hundred fucking dollars! Unbelievable. Within minutes she

322

was so fucking stoned she could've taken on entire football teams of beefcake. Natasha had learned a terrible lesson, an awful disappearing trick. She didn't know it, but she'd turned a definitive corner and henceforth things would never be the same again. But for now she basked in her warm opiate tank. See Natasha the clever pin-prick-pupil dolphin at Sea World.

People imagine that when junkies are loaded on smack, or alcoholics get drunk as lords, or coke-heads fly stratospherically high, they enter a fantastical realm of unlimited bounty, where they are possessed of great wealth, infinite allure and enormous talent. Not so. They may set out for an artificial paradise, but the real estate they all end up inhabiting is one and the same. In it they are *all right*. That's all. They're *all right*. Not alcoholics, not addicts – simply OK. Just like everyone else. Oh sure, they may have done dodgy things – lost a few jobs, broken a couple of marriages, had some kids taken into care, been deprived of the odd limb – but basically they're *all right*. And so this mighty traffic – bigger than the entire world's legitimate trade – goes, in large part, to service such a nugatory requirement. To supply deviants with the delusion of normalcy.

Natasha and Polly argued eventually. What was Natty *playing at*? Polly shrieked. Hanging out with deadbeats in Redfern and Paddington. Getting drunk. Going to bars. Pretending to assist a community project by doing yet another fucking mural. Another dumb daub which would dull out within a couple of years, as chaotic and unintegrated as the community it was intended to serve. What was the *point* in Natty's coming to Australia anyway? She was meant to be getting over losing the baby. She was *meant* to be getting herself together. She had – Polly knew for a fact – been smacked out last Wednesday. *And* come back to the flat without her fucking knickers on. What was all *that* about?

She lay on the sofa, smashed, and embarrassed Polly's friends. Nice people. Teachers. Lay on the sofa and babbled about gallah birds with soft cocks. When was she going to see something of the country? Why didn't she just get the *fuck out*. The entire continent had been giving Polly Passmore assertiveness training. Natasha got out.

For weeks, then months and eventually years, Natasha traversed Australia. This, a continental island so large that whole sectors of its drought-blighted territory received no radio signals – let alone the impress of a foot. A country like another planet, so distinct were its flora, fauna, and even landforms from those of the other, flatter sides of the earth. Over this immensity, a seeming culture was stretched, like a thin, tan drum skin across a cavernous gourd. A culture of knee-socked mock colonials whose overlords, the squatocracy, inhabited mansions built in the dunny vernacular. This, a vast slice of burnt toast, floating in the southern ocean, with only a few scrapes and smears of Vegemite on its chomped edges. This, a surrealistic nightmare, where men had laboured to construct rabbit fences visible from space, then unleashed an eye-exploding virus on Flopsy, Mopsy and – nominally – Cottontail. This, a noble democracy, ruled by a cerise goddess who lived in the day before. This vast unplace, where white men and women huddled together to play disco music, gamble, fornicate and watch soap operas, in a desperate attempt to keep out the cold heat. This oven, where a fall of half a degree in the temperature had its inhabitants scampering for fleece-lined nether garments. This parody of civilisation, where some seven million northern Europeans and some seven million southern Europeans camped in concrete tents along thousands of miles of littoral, wandering between each other's barbecues. While in the hinterland a handful of ancient, mystic wizards plugged the open veins in their scrotal sacs with beeswax, only uncorking them to mix their blood with the sacred earth itself.

Natasha felt right at home in this caricature of it. She took bar jobs in Brisbane and waitressed in Wagga-Wagga. She drove a sloppy Holden cab in Townsville. She ventured as far as the sauna-steamy shores of the Northern Territory and crossed the dry Nullarbor on the old Ghan. When she didn't want to work – she didn't. She sat and she thought. It would be nice and resounding to say of her that she thought often of her dead mother, summoned up Lily's loving sarcasm and her bitter wit – but this would be a lie. Occasionally Natasha would see a woman in late middle age, with thick, untidy, blonde hair, crossing a flat boulevard under a hot sky, whose lumpily angry emanations and canvas book bag recalled Mumu. Then Natasha would feel the gummy, toothless baby talk they used with each other rise in her dry throat, and wish she were the child she'd never been, impossibly again. The child she never could be, except in the unloving arms of Morpheus.

Hammer – as, in a doubly contrived version of rhyming slang, the Australian junkies termed heroin – Natasha avoided. There was so much of Australia, and Australia itself was such an avoidance, that this seemed easy. Anyway, this was a place where bulky youths already browned with incipient melanoma drank themselves into a whirl of projectile vomiting, in bars constructed like cages, or bars white-tiled, or bars with broad verandas – all so they'd be easier to hose down. Drinking in venues styled like toilets made its emetic aspect only too acceptable. Natasha drank, and in this dry climate it didn't seem to catch up with her too much; and if it did – who? what? with whom . . . last night? – she moved on again. There was always more nowhere to run to.

Australia, where affect itself was animated and you met

cartoons of the people you'd partied with in the city before, in the subsequent one – and the one after that. Hi Bob! Howzitdoin' Julie? Good t'seeya Steve, or Bruce, or Robyn, or Kerry, or who-fucking-ever. In a young country all relationships can seem, for a time, to be adolescent flirtations, cunts and cocks lightly entwined like sweaty fingers. No heroin – and very little sex. After the incident in King's Cross – the shredded ethics in the shredded bark – some part of Natasha did, at least partly, discern the danger of this.

On Magnetic Island, on the inner edge of the Barrier Reef, there was a brief liaison with a young woman from Melbourne – Cynthia, on the run from whoring and junk, not unlike Natasha herself. But Cynthia was artily unattractive. Legs, arms, chest, all flattened cylinders. A suit of a person, left out in the rain, on this, a monsoonal isle. They lay together, uncomfortably bunched in a hammock, for five days, and touched each other with hesitant hands not quite understanding why they – who'd never, either of them, done such things before – felt the need of this need. Cynthia collected crushed toads. Mashed roadkills scraped from the bitumen ribbons which ran for thousands of clicks between the chirruping cane fields. She kept them in an Ansett flight bag. The two young women sorted through the flat corpses, playing snap with them as they sat, cross-legged, on the veranda of the house where the hammock hung. An old house, for these parts, with a mansard roof of corrugated iron upon which the hard rain beat down. A house lent to Cynthia by a junky she'd known in Melbourne, a man very like her, on the run, escaping the spiritual auction, getting out from under the hammer. For those five days he was away prawn-fishing, out beyond the Reef.

So, like the lopsided cat's cradle of the Ansett Airlines route map itself, Natasha looped her way around the edges of the mighty ochre land. As she travelled she met more Cynthias, more internal exiles in a culture that was itself shut out from the rest of the world. Until, eventually, like so many others, she realised there wasn't anywhere much else to go – save for the interior. The Red Centre. In this upside-down realm the outback always felt – to Natasha – exactly like that. A chill behind her head, the sense of vacuity prickling hairs at her nape. It was a place that was no place. An open door in the back of the sub-urbanity of white Australia, which led elsewhere.

Not that Natasha was unaware of the traditional inhabitants. Who could be, when fragments of their metaphysical maps were reprinted all over T-shirts, tea towels and the menus of restaurants? And when their placenames now graced graceless suburb after slapdash subdivision? And when their sacred monody issued forth from hidden speakers on temperature-controlled shopping concourses? Another genocide that had ended in the textile department.

During Natasha's time in Australia the adolescent overlords had finally broken down in a wholesale attack of guilt, tasting at last the blood on their beefburgers. An entire hierarchy of weeping ministers and puling professors were intent on handing back, to the ancient wizards of the interior, something that had never really been theirs to give in the first place. The wizards – for whom all time is Now, and who understood their own thoughts to be merely the reveries of the earth itself – found it terribly difficult to explain what the fuck was going on. They were that fucked over. How to deal, in the vast land, with childish rulers who spoke in a gooey argot of babyish diminutives? Who called their own elders 'wrinklies', and their wounded 'sickies', and their campfires 'barbies'. How to share reality itself with tough, tough boys living in a Barbie world?

Natasha was staying with a kid in Canberra, the pseudo nation's bogus capital. The kid was a friend of a friend, of someone who wasn't really a friend of Natasha at all. Beyond an artificial lake, which did nothing to ornament the place, stood a parliament building with an enormous hypodermic finial poised above it. This was the theatre wherein barristers, bewigged like magpies, sought to divine how to do business with the wizards. Very occasionally a wizard could be seen, checking into the Holiday Inn on Manuka Circle, a gaggle of pink advisers fawning in his dark train.

The kid, who was the son of an anthropologist at the uni, was well-meaning and thought himself – like so many before, so many after, so many who saw her only for an instant, constructing imaginary lives of deep intimacy on the basis of a glimpse of her from a passing bus – in love with Natasha. They went out drinking in bars of exceptional ugliness. They returned to the kid's parental home in the pulsing night, to find curious, velvety cloaks all over the screen doors: an imbrication of bogong moths, who, tiny Australians themselves, had embarked on a long journey, orienting themselves by the moon, only to end up thus, glued to suburbia.

Down a musty corridor in the anthropologist's bungalow, Natasha lay in a creaky old foldaway bed. From the walls, bark paintings dangled on straps of kangaroo sinew. In the bookshelves, volumes of Pitt Rivers, Malinowski, Strehlow and Levi-Strauss jostled for elbow-room with contemporary periodicals. On the big kneehole desk, the anthropologist's carefully assembled collection of coproliths sat with utility bills and jars of Biros. These people will hunt and gather any old shit. Natasha lay naked, between linen sheets which had been carefully tucked in by her wannabe lover, and read *The Magician's Nephew* by C. S. Lewis, hearing her Mumu's voice in her inner ear. Mumu spoke to her of the Wood Between the

Worlds, where trees with tall, straight trunks were spaced with sinister regularity, between small pools of absolute circularity, beneath a canopy of utter impenetrability. And Mumu told her of how a child who dived into any one of these pools would find herself in another world altogether, whether it be Victorian London, or the dying empire of Charn, or Narnia itself, where God was cuddly and the creation myth easily anthropomorphised.

The next day the two of them left for Alice Springs. They had no exact plan, but in this casual realm of instant acquaintance, they presumed they'd find a berth with one of the anthropologist's postgraduate students, who was doing fieldwork in the Northern Territory. From the Alice, an airconditioned coach took them north, out of the pitiless, ferrous landscape of the Centre and into a no more hospitable environment of disorienting, endless verdancy. Stand after stand of thorny shrubbery spread out beneath the sun-full sky. On the coach, wrinklies sat in rows, wattled necks straining to see a video screen which entertained them with a film about a neo-Nazi conspiracy. Natasha and the kid watched the too much of nowhere roll past. It appeared innocuous enough – but it wasn't. To go out in it, without a compass, without litres of fresh water, would be to find yourself hopelessly lost in a savage parkland. Completely disoriented, succumbing to sunstroke within a few, short yards of the bandstand, or the icecream stall, or the duck pond. Instead of feeding the birds – being fed to them.

After six hundred clicks or so there was a waft of feral meatiness by Natasha's ear, and she turned to see an aboriginal man in a preposterous white Stetson hat, making his way to the front of the coach. When he reached the driver he said something to him, and turned back to face the wrinklies, none of whom wavered from their contemplation of the conspiracy.

He was middle-aged, thin to the point of wiry. He wore R. M. Williams jeans, R. M. Williams, elastic-sided bush boots and a plaid shirt. His face – fat-lipped, round-cheeked, leather-necked – was everything you would expect of a wizardly countenance. His eyes, shielded by mirrored sunglasses, reflected the wrinklies back at them. The coach slewed to a halt, outside wheels dropping off the metalled surface and sending up a clump of dust. The door whooshed on its pneumatic arm. The wizard stepped down, and without so much as a backward glance walked off into the scrubland.

'They have an innate sense of direction,' the kid told Natasha earnestly. 'My father's done research on it. Seems like they may have a kind of magnetic compass actually in their heads.'

Natasha told him to shut up.

At Stearns, a truck turn seven hundred clicks up the Stuart Highway, the postgraduate met them off the coach and took them to a dirty little guvvie house. It was empty save for a bundle of long hunting spears, with mulga-wood shafts, propped in a corner, and a slew of coverless paperbacks on the scuffed linoleum floor. Clamped to the windows of this un-breeze block were air-conditioning units like miniature versions of the house itself. These groaned and whistled with the effort of struggling against the big heat. Natasha, coursing with sweat, dribbled lukewarm water over her lankiness from a rusted spigot. She put on shorts and an old Che Guevara T-shirt. She donned an enquiring mien and went out to find the postgraduate, who was under the bonnet of his car, a big, yellow, rotting Ford saloon.

Natasha had no idea what she was looking for. She had the feeling that she had *incomplete information* about all of this. This journey, this hot coming to Stearns, with the ways dusty and the travel clerks refractory. But she also sensed that information was the least of it – and that it was the aboriginal man, who'd headed off into the bush, a hundred kilometres south of Stearns, who had the right approach. The correct methodology.

The kid and Natasha decided to hang out at Stearns for a few days. There was to be an initiation ceremony on the Thursday evening, held by the people who camped along the side of the track, the displaced people. The people who lived under corrugated-iron humpies, among twisted barbed wire and broken bottles. They were former ringers and gins, who'd walked here to be near their own country after they'd been thrown off the cattle stations to the east. They would be preparing their boys for the knife. The visitors couldn't see the ceremony itself – that would be taboo, not only for the kardibar, but for their own women and even for their dogs, who, after all, had their own complex lineages – but were welcome at a rehearsal for it. The postgrad had his own business in Stearns. In his mudicar he drove a quartet of the oldest men out to the country to the west, where they tried to remember their songs, in order to humour him.

The postgrad at least knew enough to know that he would never know enough, lying under the stars which hung from the inky sky like bunches of inconceivably heavy, lustrous grapes, dusted with the yeast of eternity. He lay in his swag, but – as he told Natasha and the kid – if one of the old wizards said 'Jump', he'd sit up and ask, straight-faced, 'How high?'

He took Natasha and the kid down to the people's camp to meet them. Natasha picked her way in slapping thongs through the broken glass, barbed wire and rusting Victoria Bitter cans, past the mean humpies where the liverish lay. The dogs spat hydrophobically, the children blew bubbles of lurid mucus from their wide nostrils, and the old people saw right through the luscious kardia, in her khaki Stubbies and her Che

Guevara T-shirt. Looked right through her with eyes whited out with glaucoma, scarred with trachoma, buzzing with flies. The people had bellies swollen with malnutrition, livers engorged with cirrhosis, legs warped with rickets, bellies studded with Natasha's namesake. Under the hard light they sat in the fourth world. From time to time first-world enforcers, fat in their short-sleeved grey shirts, came down the road in utes, with cages on their truck beds, the kind normally employed by dog-handlers. Then they'd fuck with the people.

An old woman – her face squaw-fat and dog-alien to Natasha, her breasts shrivelled – took the luscious kardia to one side, to her own private patch of dust, and showed her some undistinguished grey stones. 'These,' the old woman said, 'are solidified dingo-urine chunks, not only congruent, but concomitant, in their texture and colour, with the rain clouds, which at this very moment are rising up in the thermals to the east, over the Barkly Tableland, cooling and making rain. You might say – if you were mechanistically inclined, although I, of course, am not – that I was causing this rain to fall by shifting these stones in the palm of my hand.' But of course, to Natasha this merely sounded like a lot of cheek-sucking, palate-slapping and uvula-clicking, with the occasional 'ngapa' and 'yaka!' thrown in for added incomprehensibility.

Then there was a bustling among the people and they upped and went towards another old woman who came, distractedly wandering, across the road from the direction of the police post, her red skirt dragging in the orange dirt. Natasha and the kid hung back, but the postgrad went to the fringes of the group, then returned to where the duo stood, in the short spike of shade flung down by a dead tree. 'There's been an accident over at Hermansberg,' he told them. 'Some of this mob's relations have been killed. Ute rollover.'

'Did the police tell that woman?' Natasha asked.

'Nah – police don't know no-thing,' said the postgrad. 'Anyway, it only happened half an hour ago. Come on, we best go back to the house, this isn't our business.'

But in the car, the kid, evidently believing it to be his, said seductively to Natasha, 'It's telepathy. They know these things telepathically. Hermansberg is hundreds of clicks away – '

Natasha told him to shut up. The postgrad looked at her approvingly, his eyes narrowing in the rear-view mirror, as if noticing her for the first time.

The postgrad was friends with a mob of young men – black lads grown unbelievably fat on white bread. Most days he'd drive them all the way into Tennant Creek, where they'd spend their sit-down money on grog. They'd buy their grog, then return to the postgrad's guvvie house at Stearns where they'd smoke yarndi and play country and western on electric guitars. This was, after all, cattle country. While the band played on, the kid, Natasha and the postgrad did trivia quizzes in puzzle rags they found in Tennant. Did them addictively. They also played Trivial Pursuit, disdaining the use of the board, simply running through the cards, asking each other the questions. The postgrad had the Baby Boomer edition of the game.

During that week Natasha began to seduce the postgrad. The kid was desolate; he could see what was happening even if the older man couldn't, or wouldn't. Natasha impressed the postgrad with her unwillingness to be taken in by anything, the people's gammin, or the kid's, or anyone's. That and the fact that she never, ever, not even once, complained about the heat, or the flies. Natasha sensed that the postgrad had *incomplete information*, but he still had far more than she did. He knew something she wanted to know, although she had no idea what it was. The postgrad was tall and limber, with a triangular head and very green eyes. His cheeks were pitted with ancient acne scars; so deeply scored it looked as if some loony chef had once grabbed his face in lieu of Parmesan – and grated it. He wore sarongs in the house and filthy Stubbies when they visited the people. In the chirruping night, while the three of them did trivia, drank beer and smoked weed, sitting cross-legged on the concrete floor of the house, his bare knee touched hers.

On thirsty Thursday there was no point in going into Tennant – there'd be no grog for sale. Hence it was a good day for the initiation rehearsals. In the evening the rainbow serpent turned down its dimmer switch – from yellow, to orange, to violet, to grey. The trio spruced themselves up, then drove the kilometre to the people's camp. Here they found the dogs-who-were-almost dingos, shouting for their wargili – their cousins – out in the bush. They also found a rough oval of dust, defined by the people from the surrounding dirt. And they found the people themselves, chatting, chewing piltjuri, smoking, discussing prices at the store – for all the world like the congregation in an orthodox synagogue. Which is, of course, what they were.

The kid and the postgrad took their places in the oval. Natasha went with the women to the other side. From out of the grey dusk came pubescent boys and older youths, in pairs, their skinny legs scissoring together then apart, their feet kicking up the dust. They wore random bits of sports gear – one a singlet, the next some trainers, a third some shorts. They hoedowned to the sound of boomerangs clacking, one on another, big, black boomerangs carved from hard mulga wood. Scary, potent, ceremonial, each one a darkly affirmative tick. Pair after pair of initiates came scissoring into the oval, did their thing, broke the rhythm and, laughing, with their arms around each other's shoulders, like football players when the whistle has blown, made their way out of the oval.

Darkness fell. The fire was banked up. The dancing and clacking and chatting went on and on and on. Hours passed. Natasha saw the postgrad get up and disappear into the shadows – presumably to take a leak. She followed. She saw him standing over by a tree with his back to her; when he turned, straightening the leg of his Stubbies, she walked towards him. 'Take me for a ride?' she asked.

'A ride?' he snorted. 'But where?'

'Oh . . . anywhere,' she said, took his arm, and led him to where his mudicar hunched by the side of the track. Through the windscreen Natasha could see a few tired flies bedding down amid the unanswered mail he kept stashed on the dash. The postgrad had gone native – even though he didn't know where it was.

Beside the mudicar was a brand-new Toyota people-carrier, and leaning against it were a pair of fresh-faced Midwestern kids, with apple cheeks, blond DAs, white short-sleeved shirts with button-down collars, and grins so broad their teeth gleamed like burning grates in the night. 'Howdy Gary!'said one of the Mormons – for that's what they were – to the postgrad. 'Initiation rehearsal going well?'

'Oh, y'know, not so bad. Lotta the old fellers can't be here, though. Dunno why.'

'Gee – well, I guess they'll be going all night just the same,' said the other Mormon, who was taller, but otherwise – to eyes such as Natasha's, saturated in the strange individuality of the people – indistinguishable from his companion.

'S'pose so,' Gary replied, swinging himself into the car.

'Good evening,' said Natasha to the Mormons, as she got in on the other side.

'Good evening ma'am,' they chorused.

Gary started the mudicar and they drove off. 'Who the fuck?' laughed Natasha, but Gary was inured to all the lost tribes in this place, and merely observed, 'Mormons. They're not bad fellers. Gotta dispensary down the track. Helpful guys – not too pushy. Not like plenty of the fundamentalists. They can be fuckin' evil.' He pulled two tinnies from the Esky and cracking one passed it to her. 'So, where d'you wanna *go* for this ride, then?' No innuendo – the man was immunised against it. He could've been a Mormon himself, Natasha reflected.

'When we were on the bus up from Alice' – where were these words coming from? – 'I saw a man get off about a hundred kilometres south of here. In the middle of the bush. An aboriginal man – '

'It'd have t'be,' Gary cut in, wheeling the big car up on to the track, heading south. Natasha described the man she'd seen, his preposterous white Stetson, his shades, his air of possessing *complete information*.

'That'd be Phar Lap Jones,' said Gary.

'Take me to where he was going.'

Gary coughed, spurted beer, swerved the car so abruptly they rocked together, thigh on thigh, breast on chest. 'Jeezus, girl – you gotta be fuckin' joking!'

'Why?'

'He's only about the biggest fuckin' man in this whole slice of the Territory. No one – and I mean fuckin' no one, excepting his manager – would ever even *dream* of going near Phar Lap's country. Y'know those big fuckin' boomerangs I keep in the house – the black ones?'

'Uh-huh.'

'Walbiri punishment boomerangs. They're hard fuckers. The men'd hold me down and bash me with them here, here, here, here and here.' He pointed to his deep clavicle, the points of his high shoulders, his elbows, his prominent hips, his big bare knees, rammed against the sticky vinyl dash. 'Then the women would hitch up their fuckin' skirts and piss all over me. And besides,' he continued more comfortably, back on the logistical grounds, 'it's way out in the bush. There's dirt only two-thirds of the way – and that's bad dirt; after that, nothing. *And* this isn't even a 4WD. It's outta the question. Outta the fuckin' question.'

'But we could go some of the way, couldn't we? The moon's coming up and I'd love to see the bush under it. That wouldn't be such a shlep, would it?' Shlep – where did *that* come from?

'No – s'pose not.'

They drove out west on a clean dirt road which was like a river, running between the silver-nitrate trunks of eucalyptus, its sandy surface shining in the moonlight. How could anything so negative be so beautiful? At twenty clicks they stopped and fooled around a little in the front seat of the car, but as he reached for her red centre, Natasha stopped him, got him to drive on some more. At thirty-five clicks she helped him get his swag out of the trunk and spread it on the floor of the wadi. She found herself with no qualms at all. No qualms about crossing her arms and pulling the faded, flowery dress she wore over her head. No qualms about advancing, open to the man, open to the world. And he – he found himself ensorcelled entirely. Buggered and bewitched. Sure, she was beautiful, with her long, blue-black hair, and her all-over moth's-wing skin, and her silvered limbs and her hungry mouth and her fingers here, there, everywhere – but this was more. This was passion as art and magic. Passion forging a destiny under stars that hung from the inky sky like bunches of inconceivably heavy, lustrous grapes, dusted with the yeast of eternity. She lost herself entirely as he abandoned himself inside her. And in losing herself, she took him with her, crying, 'Me-shugg-en-eh!' Where could *that* have come from?

They drank more giggle juice, and in gassy spirits she

persuaded him to motor on along the wadi. At forty clicks the road ran out in a sandbank and they were almost bogged. Better for them both if they had been. But Natasha coaxed Gary, and Gary coaxed the mudicar, which growled across the flood-plain, betwixt the stands of savage thorn scrub, which loomed slowly by. They drove at walking pace by the light of the moon.

At fifty clicks she helped him get out the swag again and unroll it. Then she took his scraps of clothing off and lay him down. If anything this time their intercourse was even more strange, here in the deep country, while unicorns crashed through the brush by their thrashing legs. 'Oh you mensh!' she said, stroking his rough head. 'You mensh!' For he was a man of fine qualities, the postgrad. A good driver in the bush, with an excellent sense of direction.

When they were finished, and he slept on the ruckled slab of canvas and blankets, Natasha filled two empty beer cans from the canteen and left them by his triangular head. She walked on with the rest of the water through the moonlight, her rubber soles crunching on the tough grass, skating on the tiny ball-bearings of impacted earth, oblivious to the thorns slashing at her ankles. After an hour or so she reached a low escarpment, and threaded her way up it, through narrow defiles of rocks so cracked and spalled and smoothed they were like the backs of a school of porpoises. Gaining the summit she saw it, spread out below her, just as Mumu had described it to her. Phar Lap Jones's country.

Trees with tall straight trunks were spaced with sinister regularity, between small pools of absolute circularity, beneath a canopy of utter impenetrability. Natasha could see the first few curved lips, calling her in, but beyond it only the deepest darkness. Unafraid, she quickly descended and strode between the first few trees, marvelling at their natural artificiality. The water in the pools was oily black, but when she dabbled her naked toes in it she found it to be cool, not viscous at all. So cool, it could only be a relief to bathe in it, to plunge her hot, drunk head into it. To let this strange silent place, sober her up. Perhaps for ever?

The edge of the pool felt – to Natasha's bushed, deserted hands – marvellously machined. As if a curved mattock blade had sliced it. On the inky meniscus of the water the end of her dangling mane lay like the legs of an insect. Her black outline faced the darkness below, which but poorly reflected the darkness above. She leant down and down and, eyes wide open, plunged in through the ceiling of the room, noticing first the chain that fell away below her for three feet. An oily, black chain, liberally dusted and entwined with a flex like a caduceus, which led to a bell-shaped shade – saving that from this, precipitate perspective, the shade was round. Then Natasha peered past the shade and saw first a windowsill, and far below that a swatch of Manhattan street life, pedestrians milling like hatted bugs, cars soundlessly trundling, and the canopy of a building across the way. Only then did she take in what was in the room itself.

Directly below and slightly to the right of Natasha's vantage was the wide grey oblong of . . . a desk? Yes, a desk, with a grey steel surface. A desk, because at its edge was an onyx penholder, the old-fashioned kind with conical socket-housings set in ball joints. A desk, because of a fan of papers, some about to fall off. A desk, because of a black, buttoned box – an intercom? – to one side. A desk, because there was a man on it. A big man, naked save for an unbuttoned silk shirt. A naked man whose naked foot was pressed against the black box. A naked man, whose ass rested on the desk blotter.

Looking straight down, Natasha contemplated the flatly surreal juxtaposition of the flange of the man's ass and the cut-off leather corner of the blotter. His penis lay, purple and glistening, in a rick of ginger pubic hair. Spots and smears of semen dotted and dashed his broad belly. His face was averted to hold a conversation with someone obscured by the shade. Someone who said, 'And you wanna know why?' in her Mumu's tones, but half an octave higher, then moved out from below the lampshade. Blonde hair swept up and then rolled over bare shoulders in a wave which had recently witnessed a storm. Those shoulders were flushed pink. She bent, puckering deliciously at the hip, to pick up from the wooden floor a tangle of tan stockings and black suspenders, and Natasha could see, protruding from the deep ravine of her buttocks, the glistening spike of the woman's pubic hair.

'Why?' said the man on the desk.

'Because neither you,' the young woman down below came fully into view, turning, hopping up, so that her rump was supported by the edge of the desk where the man lay, 'nor your fucking pen,' she arched to reveal her opulent breasts, her round belly, lifted one, long leg up, and bending it loosely across the other thigh, began to thread the foot into a roll of stocking, 'has big enough balls.' In the middle of the woman's handsome face was a prominent keel of nose, to either side two steady, grey-blue eyes. In a big painted mouth a thin white cigarette burned, the smoke looping up lazily towards Natasha. Natasha couldn't help but admire the insouciance of this young woman, who, so clearly, had recently been fucked over. Natasha, who was perplexed by her sense of kinship to this vision. Natasha, who recoiled as a coil of smoke from the past curled into her open eyes.

And in a whirl of limbs on the forest's floor, Natasha had time to think of explanations – fatigue? the strangeness of the place? weak beer and strong weed? or had Gary perhaps spiked her with an antipodean psychotropic of rare exactitude? –

before her hands grasped the lip of another pool and the momentum flung her face-down into another world.

Natasha's lovely face projected from the unlovely grey surface of a dormant video screen. Below her on the stridently artificial desert floor, her Mumu – recognisable, instantly, by her thick wool tapestry-effect overcoat, her not inconsiderable bulk, her canvas Barnes & Noble book bag, her shoes like collapsed Cornish pasties, her prominent keel of nose – sat awkwardly askew, her legs curled to one side, one arm acting as stanchion, the other bringing a filter cigarette to her generously sour mouth. Mumu was in conversation with a white Stetson, the brim of which tipped up and down with wizardly emphasis, while from below came the clicking drone of blackfeller blarney. What could Mumu be doing here? Natasha might've asked herself. Why was she in conversation with the man who had got off the bus, the man Gary had called Phar Lap Jones?

Natasha might've asked these things – but she didn't. Visionaries, notoriously, are quite free from ratiocination and devoid of insight. Visionaries' prideful minds are, so often, like parted lips, ready to be filled by King Stuff. Natasha could've homed in on the Walbiri punishment boomerangs that lay on the false desert floor, and queried what exactly it was that they were affirming, these dark, sinister ticks. She didn't. She lost concentration and her eyes wavered to the far side of a hundred feet of cracked white mud, to where a panel of desert horizon had been rolled back, revealing a swatch of the Thames's north bank and a slice of Unilever House.

And all the rest of the night, Natasha Yaws pitched and yawed on the forest's floor, rolling in visionary ecstasy from pool to pool, lying in awe and shaking her face from world to world. In one she saw the blond head of the elder brother she'd never known smashed all over the asphalt, while within her breast swelled dark truffles of inherited racial prejudice. In a second she jealously witnessed Virginia Bridge, dimly remembered from her own childhood, sound her Yahoo Mumu with her smooth, Atrixo-creamed hands, while speaking through Houyhnhnm teeth, saying, 'Lily, *really*, I mean to say, you can't expect me to go on treating you for chronic bronchitis if you aren't prepared to give up smoking. I mean, it's not as if you don't know the facts . . .' In a third, Natasha saw the arms all out at angles like the limbs of trees. Winstons and Pall Malls and Camels and Luckys and Newports, all fuming away wherever these particular people congregate. And heard the lustful burr of her Mumu's voice: 'Is it going to take that long?'

'What?'

'For us to love? D'jew think I should set the house on fire now? We could let the calendar look after itself, huh?'

She peered between her Mumu's feet at the impacted leaves in Berkeley Square and felt the weight of inconceivable, middle-aged fatigue. She peered down the grooves of plebeian pine, as her poor old Mumu clawed the comestibles out and, cradling them like nutritious babies in her woolly arms, clumsily negotiated the five-barred gate. Natasha saw the trickle of blood lazily snake from beneath Mumu's slacks, down her shin, into her sock. Like something they might both pick over later. From realm to realm, from sloth, to lust, to pride, to anger, to greed – and back again. In this, a humble outer stand of Phar Lap's wood, a small plantation of the worlds available.

Dawn peeled back overhead and the gulf of the western sky drew a hard surface over the pools of the wood between the worlds. Natasha's face emerged like a Polaroid from the limpid water, at first blurred – then overly exact. Hyper-real. Within minutes the burners on rocket earth had been cranked up to full thrust. She rose to her coltish height and her scratched, bloodied calves bent this way and that as she took up the strain of planetary revolution. She stared about her at the shrubbery. It was like all the rest, a stand of eucalyptus and mulga on a rough underlay of grass. In the gums overhead, kookaburras laughed snidely. To the east was a low escarpment, the shadow already retreating in its lee. Around her in the ticking undergrowth the mounds of magnetic termites, like miniature Mies van der Rohes, or the tombstones of alien warlords, provided savage orientation.

Natasha found her way back. She was fortunate to have come to her senses when she did, when the sun was low enough, the shadows long enough, the water still plentiful enough. She made it to Gary's mudicar and woke him. The two of them drove back, east towards Stearns, all the baking day. It goes without saying that Gary was in it. Deep shit.

Natasha stopped long enough in Stearns to collect her little tote bag of pants and paints, her leather jacket and her R. M. Williams boots, her jeans and a trivia quiz book. She also took one of Gary's black boomerangs – as a sinister souvenir. Up on the track she flagged down a passing Mormon-carrier, and they drove her to Tennant Creek. From Tennant she took the bus to Alice. From Alice she flew to Sydney. At Sydney she didn't even quit the airport, but hung on in the terminal for thirty-six hours until a flight with a seat cheap and narrow enough became available. She boarded, and flew back around the world to the day before. From Heathrow she took the tube in to King's Cross, feeling utterly spaced out by the confinement of this ancient muddy city on the banks of its mini-Euphrates. This uh-Ur. This mistake.

In Stearns, Gary pined away. The kid split. Gary ignored the fat young black men who came to play electric guitars, and after a while they ignored him. He pined – and he drank. He staggered across the track to the stores and bought carton after carton of Emu Export and NT Draught and Victoria Bitter and even Castlemaine – which the locals referred to, contemptuously, as 'barbed wire'. Gary drank and the beer felt barbed in his rough throat. He switched to Bundaberg rum – but fared no better. He neglected everything. In front of the crappy little guvvie house, the once proud mudicar settled into the mud, which became dust, then became mud again. On the long-since rotted carpets lay greasy burger-wrappers and a mulch of mango pips, stalks and skin. In time a large mob of cockroaches moved in. Unlike Gary's mind, the mudicar had become a full, rich environment. The people understood.

The local quack understood as well. Gary would have to go south for treatment. He left the mudicar for the skinny old men, but the fat young ones took it, and ripped the shit out of the shocks in two days of 'roo-hunting. Gary went south and the treatment didn't work. The medics were at a loss to understand why a man as young as this had developed cirrhosis with such scary alacrity, his liver flayed with scars, engorged with sarcomas.

From King's Cross, Natasha took a cab up the Balls Pond Road, and at an indistinct point – not quite at Dalston Junction, nor exactly past it – she had the driver drop her off. From here on she'd only ever walked. There was a confusing character to this district, a delusive mounding and bunching of the streets, parklets and estates, that made it hard to direct a driver. Especially one who navigated the city using an internal map of Maputo, or Conakry.

In Adelaide, Gary's liver swelled and swelled – and then ruptured. By the time this news made it back to Stearns – and how soon is Now? – it was understood by all and sundry that his liver had 'just kinduv exploded – fuckin' blew up'.

It was summer in London, an intensely sticky summer, when the childish gods the citizenry worshipped seemed to have drenched the very fabric of the city in Coca-Cola, dripped it with melting ice lollies, gummed it up with old Wrigley's. With each long denim stride Natasha took, the city clamped its greedy, sweaty paw tighter round the seasoned stick of her, licking at her cool beauty with its tasteless, polluted tongue. She recognised the petrol station on the corner, turned down Corinth Way and continued until she recalled the phone box at the mouth of Sparta Terrace. She walked along the terrace, past the narrow house-fronts, where from the open sashes gauzy waves lapped at the paintwork. She crossed Syracuse Park, noting that while the one o' clock club had its share of plastic earthmovers and wooden trucks, the workmen and drivers were absent. She turned the corner of Athens Road and, hurrying now, failed to notice the one individual she'd encountered since turning off the Balls Pond Road. On a wall, outside the corner shop, sat a small, immaculately dressed Asian boy, playing with a toy metal car, a toy plastic cow and a toy plastic harmonica.

Natasha turned into Argos Road and strode along to number 27. She called up, 'Bernie, chuck down the key.' And after a junky's eternity – and how soon is Now? – it came sailing down, tied to some green sisal, like a tiny metal kite in the lifeless air. Was it Natty's imagination – which admittedly had been rather too fertile of late – or could she hear whispering from the basement flat?

Christmas 2001

I used to hate napping in the afternoon; I'd always awake feeling infinitely sad, or crankily wound up, or even just fucking miserable. It felt like the day had been broken in two – into two, short, unbearable days, instead of a single, long, barely tolerable one. 'Ooh,' they'd say, 'she's all cross because she's fallen asleep. Because she's napped.' Yeah, caught napping by the world, and whoever I thought I was turned inside out like a sock. So I'd wail and I'd thrash, and I'd arch my back like a seal – like a fucking seal – diving beneath the polar ice, until they'd say, 'All right, Miss Tantrum, we're gonna leave you until you recover yourself!' But I never did recover myself. I never fucking did.

The Ice Princess climbed under this cold giant nappy wearing her last trendy threads, her velveteen combat trousers. They have six empty pockets and are camouflage-patterned with malformed kidneys of black, yellow and khaki. I wish I could send every shmegegge I've seen in the last couple of years sashaying around wearing combat trousers straight into combat. I wonder how they'd react when tank-loads of huzzaing towel-heads appeared in the narrowed lenses of their fashion eyewear, and they had to put their militaristic gear to the test? The nineties ended with these pinheads observing a wide plain of destruction through such cramped apertures. Who the fuck did they think they were kidding? I've seen glasses come and go. In the seventies the dernier cri in frames were shaped like the rims of TV sets, or lavatory seats, and they goggled through these bulbous panes at the bulbous decade. Now everything's narrowed right down.

Yup, I wish I could send them into combat. And I wish I could send all the kids I see sporting full-length puffa coats – the kind that look like sleeping bags with arms attached – somewhere truly icy, to sleep off their identities. And I wish I could dispatch to a township all the creeps who flop along Greek Street in designer shoes modelled on third-world fucking sabots cut from car tyre. There they could drink puddles and get righteously screwed up the ass. Then they'd be copacetic. Truly, is there anything the world hath to show

346

more asinine than a footwear fetish? Shake-spear kick in the rear. The Ice Princess used to dress me up like a little accessory when she was in funds, natch. All that time I spent longing to be the kind of female who cared more about these things, who took the time to groom and dress and preen and prink. I got it – brother I got it. Then she'd say, to whichever shnook happened to be in train at the time, whichever ugly was burnishing her by association, 'Ooh, she hates getting dressed. Hates it. Come on, Delilah. Come on!' But I had – I have – a whim of iron.

Come on and let me buckle you into little combat trousers and track suits and even fucking dresses! All the while I'd buck and kick and yank at her hair, whirling my pudgy arms in wild haymakers, that would – har-de-har – every so often connect. Oh yes, I'm a past master of the voluntary involuntary action all right. Always have been. Yup, she'd dress me up in a velveteen dress, spangly tights, a miniature parka and tiny deck shoes. Then she'd let me clamp my plastic tiara on my head and she'd take this little JAP out with her when she went to make calls.

Her own wardrobe she was less fanciful about. This was dressing to undress, that much she understood. Gone were the days when she wore slinky fabrics for falling downstairs in. Oh no, her activities now demanded ligatures of slick material that cut to the quick of her, dividing her sex and ass like the core of a pear. Over this cord – pull it and she'd speak pre-taped phrases: 'My aren't you . . .'; 'Oooh, don't you . . .'; 'Mmm . . . can't you . . .' – went heavy, yet sheer, sixty-denier tights, which could be torn off easily without being laddered. She wore skirts like belts, and tops like sporting bras for this most unsporting activity. She put on zip-up knee-high boots and, to complete the dissemble, a heavy coat which could be wrapped round her then whipped open to reveal the goods.

Hey presto! And there was also the jewellery, the elongated rings – thumb, finger and pinkie – the angled bangles, the toe rings, all of them like the bits of a robotic exoskeleton. I suppose it pressed home the point that this was purely mechanical – what she was doing.

Yeah, she took me out with her, this mundane magician turning the oldest tricks in the world. She was that fucking mad and desperate. She'd leave me for ten, twenty, thirty minutes – however long it took – locked in some fucking vestibule at the Hilton, or the Royal Garden, or the Holiday-fucking-Inn. Playing with a dolly, while she was being one within feet. My presence kept them docile – the really mad ones – or so she liked to think. She'd even leave me outside in the minicab, brushing up on my Swahili. She had, like they all do, her cabbie accomplices.

Then we'd go and meet the Estate Agent in a restaurant or a bar in the West End, and he'd expatiate on his latest earth-shatteringly bad deal. Swapping this deed for that deed, indeed! The Estate Agent, with his mobile phone the size of a suppository and his handsome face all constipated with the rank, stinking jealousy which kept them both at it. Full-on.

They'd order up silly plates of food, expensive snacks for smack-heads – sun-dried this, wind-blown that, flambéed whatever – and cut off corners to poke in my little mouth. 'Try some of this,' they'd say, and, 'Ooh – doncha think she might like that,' my own burgeoning appetites putting to shame their diminishing ones – this fucking cuckoo in their nest.

Or nests, rather. We moved constantly, one step ahead of whichever Iranian, or Brazilian, or alumna of St Trinian's the Estate Agent had last done a number on. That's what they called it – 'doing a number'. 'Why don't we do a number on so-and-so,' they'd chortle indulgently to each other, and plan who next to fuck up or fuck over. Was there ever a duo for more indulgences than these two – they could've filled the medieval fucking Vatican's order book. They were mad and beautiful, for a while. You'll have seen their like, chucking chips on the wheel at Charlie Chester's, or stoking up with Bellinis at the American Bar, and wondered how the hell they have the gall to exercise their timeless gangster chutzpah. How they can get away with it, while outside whichever joint it is they're infesting crouch others of their ilk, the dirty panhandling ones, with stoles of giveaway blanket draped over their puny shoulders. The city's neglected children, trying to get home from the shoddy, alfresco sleep-overs that have become their entire life.

The Ice Princess and her consort only got away with it for a while. After all, neither of them was as young as they used to be. And there was the kiddy – such a drain. And the drugs. It's amazing they could take so many drugs, for so long, and still do any numbers greater than one. But then they'd both managed to get a few liver-enhancing years under their belt, and they both eschewed the needle, until this, their final tailspin down to the ground.

I suppose the question I ask myself now, as I hear the waking-up noises of newborn, Coborn House (trousers with writing on them being donned, dogs yanked, doors slammed, so that the scratch cards of no chance whatsoever can be bought from the meshed-in store below), the question now is – is this a good day to die?

It seems to me that it would be a sensible course if I decided this myself, rather than leaving it until, in a weakened condition, I fall down the fucking stairs and pulp my head on the fender of skirting board by the door. Or succumb to the wild, exquisite pain of being more hungry than even I can believe and, staggering, dazed, inject myself with tetanus from one of *the bent nails the Estate Agent left poking out of the window frames downstairs, when, in a crack-induced fit of late-adopted DIY enthusiasm (you couldn't call it paranoia – his fears were entirely justified), he attempted to board up this, his final, squatted castle, from within. What a mensh. Not.*

I could kill myself with their drug shit, but that is revolting. I could hang myself with any number of cords, ligatures and strings the terminally neglectful parents have left lying around. I could even – if the taps aren't frozen – drown myself in the fucking bath. All that guff about how ninety per cent of accidents happen in the fucking home, but hey, so do ninety per cent of fucking suicides. Statistically we're fools ever to curl up in bed with a good book, lest the madness seize us.

But I know I won't take any of these options. Won't take them as the cold day extends its fingers across the crappy carpet tiling, feeling up the exposed blue feet of the Ice Princess. Won't take them as it retreats again. What the fuck am I waiting for? And why do I find myself crying? Crying for Mummy.

Chapter Fifteen

Pride means never having to say you're sorry. I mean to say, if I'm so right about everything, then what the hell do I have to be sorry for, exactly? Pride is the necessary, deep mother lode, from which daily truckloads of self-righteousness can be mined and brought to the superficial surface. Pride can be husbanded, nurtured and laid up for an uncertain future. Think of all those aristocratic fools dusting their Meissen, while the Red Army rapes their womenfolk next door. Hey, *do* stand on ceremony, guys. And another thing – pride is heritable. Indeed, there's a prideful heritage industry. I mean to say, you don't want to spend all those years accumulating pride only to throw it away in some mad spree. No, pass it down, brother, pass that pride down. You can only hope that the next generation to the manner born understand what to do with the stuff and don't end up as deadbeat epigones, whiling their days away losing family pride at the humility racetrack.

Now, Richard Elvers had made a lot of pride of his own, and Charlotte Elvers had inherited a fair amount from her folks. And one final point needs to made about pride before I get on with the business of telling you how they spent theirs: there's no counterfeiting at the pride mint. Absolutely not. I can assure you of this; Mother knows best. I don't want to hear any of that crap about false pride, not now, not never. I don't care if you're Jonas Salk or a kid in a sulk – your pride is as good as any other cripple's.

So, Charlotte Elvers, proud of her attainments in the show business of big business. Proud of her womanly figure. Proud of her houses and cars and all her other chattels. Proud of her father, the late, eminent, ecclesiastical historian (and it's worth mentioning at this point that David Yaws came from a long line of Trollope readers), and proud of her mother. Not. No, not proud of me. So not proud of me that she'll avoid any mention of exactly who I was, who I am.

Charlotte, with her Yaws mask Scotch-taped to her broad brow, has no difficulty passing herself off as a goy, natch. No autobiography of a mongrel for her. Charlotte is subject to *not mentioning the fact* that she is – according to whomsoever you might fucking care to ask – a Jew. A *Jewess*, even. Mindjew, in our increasingly enlightened time there isn't much need for her to adopt – like the good, English chameleon she is – her protective colourlessness. Her studied indifference. Nowadays there are few of those awkward convocations where someone makes an anti-Semitic remark and everyone else gives silent assent.

Oh no, not nowadays. Not when the fucking Israelis are doing such a fantastic job of drawing fire by bombing refugee camps, cracking skulls, taking bribes, and generally behaving like an honest-to-God gang of .99-calibre fascist assholes. Nope, no need to be anti-Semitic with these shlemiels on the scene. Hell, even *Jewish* anti-Semitism doesn't seem that outrageous any more. To be a Jew-hating Jew used to mean something, you could take *pride* in it; it put you up there with some of the finest minds of the last two centuries – but nowadays any little cut-about prick with an attitude can get away with it.

So, let me set the scene for you, cue up the dénouement. It's the autumn of '94. Charlotte the shiksa, with her sad, comical, dead-man's face, stands in her squash-court-sized kitchen at Cumberland Terrace. Over the last couple of years the Elverses have bought the leases to several more of these apartments, and they're generous-sized to begin with. Knocked together they make a veritable fucking *mansion*, a country townhouse ready and waiting for the son and heir. Except that there isn't one. Charlotte isn't quite sick enough to trick out any of the bedrooms as a nursery for the Anointed One, the slow messianic train coming. But even if she was, where would she begin? There are far too many rumpus rooms where no one romps, studies where no one reads, bathrooms where not so much as a cuticle is trimmed, and conservatories full of freshly-cut fucking flowers – for her to get to grips with it. The Elverses' joint is so large now they have a fucking *switchboard*. And that's just the London branch of the chain.

Anyway, Charlotte, she activates a retro stainless-steel juicer and watches a column of bananas, prunes and what-not turn to healthy pulp, while ruefully contemplating her younger sister. Fresh back from the back of Bourke, and newly dubbed Natasha Bloom. Yup, that Yaws never suited her, too ugly a tubercule for such a flawlessly olive skin. And Natasha isn't simply olive now – she's positively *dark*. I mean to say, it's a wonder Immigration let her in at Heathrow, especially if they realised she was coming back to torture more victims with her sadistic pulchritude, her vicious beauty.

Yes, Natasha *Bloom*. Charlotte's gone one way – Natasha the other. And while Natasha wouldn't exactly say that she's Jewish, she is prepared to admit to Jewish blood. 'I have Jewish blood,' she'll say, as if – like the vampire she so clearly is – she keeps a vat of such in the fridge, to stop it congealing. Or, if pressed, 'I'm half-Jewish – I get all of the guilt, but none of the community.' Actually, Natty, there isn't a community that'd accept you as member, even if you did choose to join it. Shit, you wouldn't even be welcomed in at the Dulston Community Centre, and *that's* saying something.

The two sisters contemplate one another, two leonine halves of one prideful being. Antipathy crackles in the air between them as Charlotte strikes down the barb that's just been thrown. 'No,' she says, 'we haven't considered adopting.'

No indeed. *Absolument non!* I mean, what's the fucking point in acquiring quite this much pride if you're simply going to throw it away on the first fucking epsilon semi-moron the social services are prepared to chuck your way? I mean to say, it'd be like leaving your fucking property to the state, saying, 'Could we please pay more in the way of death duties? Pretty please?'

'Have *you?*' Oh, nice but futile try, Charlotte, for you know as well as I do that mother denatured here has no more need of adopting than a consumer has of trading a wide- for a flat-screen TV, a Ford for another Ford, or a Patek Philippe for a Longines. Yes, oh witty irony, how strange to relate that Natasha Bloom only has to *rub past* a man in the fucking *hall* to get knocked up. It's as if her entire, lusciously lucent, dewily downy skin were a fucking *flower*, tilted at exactly the right angle to collect whatever spore might be floating through the air.

Following a brace of scrape 'n' vacs in her teens, Natasha has always used a diaphragm *and* the pill, *and* insisted on condoms, *and* positively *slurped up* spermicidal lubricant, as if her vagina were possessed of capillary action. Excepting when she's zonked, of course – then, as we know, anything can happen.

There's nothing more seductive for the men who fall into Natasha Bloom's clutches than the way she puts a condom on them, muzzles their shlongs in latex. Curiously, it's the ultimate gateway to unfettered enjoyment for these saps. As she deliciously unrolls it with coolly deft fingers, they think to themselves 'Oooh!' and 'Aaah!' – she *really* doesn't want a kid, she loves me for my stiff little self. She – 'Aaah!' – wants the push and shove just as much as me, which is why she's fitting this one-fingered glove so expertly.

Ach! Such shtoopidity; they don't seem to realise that this proficiency is the very hallmark of cupidity. I was a pretty dab hand with the things myself. The point being that once those cocks are, as it were, shrink-wrapped, they're half-way to being harmless. Given the chance, Natasha would ply condoms with extra-thick, constrictor bands at their base. Bands that would tighten, so that, as with the devices farmers use to castrate sheep, eventually the portion would wither, blacken and then drop off altogether. Ah, Natasha, even the sight of a smoked eel makes her feel a little Bobbitty.

Still, her proficiency with condoms will stand her in good stead. She's gotta have it – she's gonna need it.

'Nope.' Natasha is munching on a peanut-encrusted chocolate bar which closely resembles a turd. She doesn't need to watch her weight, unlike Charlotte, and she has the flawless white teeth of Dorian Gray. Life can be so unfair. 'Although Russell and I are thinking of having a kid soon.' Yup, they're back together, and this time it's official. 'Now that he's cleaned up his act – well, I think he'd make an excellent father.'

'What! Russell!' And enter Richard Elvers on socking big feet. Richard Elvers, grown still more corpulent despite his personal trainer. Richard who, having spent the first part of the decade humping for English pride, will now spend its middle years under the auspices of the idiotically-named Lord Churchill. Poor Richard, it would be difficult not to feel sympathetic towards him, if I weren't so intrinsically unsympathetic, wrapped up in King Stuff as I am.

'Look, Richard,' she prettily mews, 'I know you and Russell don't exactly see eye to eye' – on the contrary, they have, that's the problem – 'but he's clean now and he's doing well with this property-development gig. In fact, he'd like to have a word with you about an old school he and his partner are buying down in Hackney.'

I bet he would. Probably wants some notionally clean capital for this, another of his filthy deals. Still, you have to hand it to Russell, he got out at the right time. Did his own cold turkey, his own six weeks at Pullet Green – Class of '92: 'A bad attitude can sometimes get you through – shit floats' – and has brought all of the twisted acumen he deployed engendering tiny dreams to this, the big nightmare of property development. Sure, Russell hasn't exactly stayed abstinent – he likes his puff and the odd glass of designer lager – but he's off the hard stuff. When Natasha turned up at his new place in Docklands, stoned again, ready to resume their old shenanigans, Russell, to his credit, slapped her about in a new way, cleaned her up again, moved her in, togged her out. Now they're very much the upcoming couple in town. Russell does up the apartments, Natasha furnishes their communal areas with corporate art.

'He's given me a budget of ten grand to sort out this other building, the one he's just finished in St Katharine's Dock,' Natasha boasts to her sister, 'and it's gonna look really good when I've bought the daubs. I'm going round some galleries this afternoon – you wanna come with?'

'You've got to be joking,' her sister shoots back. 'Anyway, Richard and I have an important appointment.'

There're other things I like about Russell as well. I admire his dark good looks – he and Natty go well together. I like his uncompromising, East End Jewishness too. Russell's family never moved beyond the pale, never went for the colourless indifference of the northern 'burbs. They stuck it out down the Mile End Road, shneidering out of premises in Whitechapel, attending services with the dwindling congregation at shul, going for the occasional shmeiss at the steam baths in Hackney. They kept faith with their Cockney patter – the word of God the costermonger – and have spawned another generation of chancers like Russell, living off his wits, winging it, like a dark angel passing over the feast of commerce.

They stand in direct contrast to the likes of Lord Churchill, the leading British authority on infertility, whose clinic is the venue that afternoon for the first of a series of appointments which, over the next five years, will steadily accrue phenomenal importance for Mr and Mrs Elvers.

Lord Churchill – paternal grandfather's moniker Jakob Rotblatt – has consulting rooms in South Kensington, within convenient hobbling distance of his own private clinic. It's there that the majority of his patients tend to put up, while visiting London for their treatment cycles. It's an irony which hasn't escaped Churchill himself that most of his success stories relate to the people of the Other Book. The women whose eggs he cossets and coddles, shakes and stirs, transports hither and thither, are black-bell-tent campers, with foil beaks, fresh in from the Gulf. He has to examine them in conditions of the most stringent purdah, the afflicted parts of their bodies portioned out for him, one at a time, like pieces of chicken-fed chicken. It's as if through such procedures he were undertaking to raise, through artificial conception, a West London army to further the jihad.

Not that Churchill's only patients are Arabs. Even to those very close to the good Lord, it's not entirely certain whether the 'Lord' part of his name is a title. It could be a first name, a student sobriquet, or only the first barrel of the shotgun combination 'Lord-Churchill'. Certainly, it's true that the good Lord has been instrumental in assisting friends – and even a few members – of the incumbent regime towards conception. But would this be sufficient grounds for ennoblement?

Richard and Charlotte think so, as they watch him make allusive shapes in the air with the index finger of either hand, delineating the possible diagnoses, treatments and prognoses. Lord Churchill conducts human destiny with superb artistry, knowing that the most sure-fire salesmanship a doctor can display is to *make* with the hands, *lay on* the hands. In some alternative lifetime Churchill would've been a spieler in Brick Lane, piling up dinner plates, side plates, saucers and cups into a great rosette of crockery, then pounding it down: 'Orlrighty, my loves – look at that! Never a breakage. Fine new china. Six of everything – t'you, ten quid. Only a tenner. Who's got the gumption? Who's got the cash!?' But instead it's petri dishes he's piling up, and injections of hormones, and incubators, and the knocked-up price is in the ten-grand region.

Still, the hands are superb. When Churchill rises from behind the desk and wiggles across the consulting room's thick, endometrial carpeting, his marvellously ugly face – like a clenched fist in a glove puppet – his barrel chest and skinny legs make him appear not unlike a highly motile sperm himself. Inspiring *enormous* confidence in the Elverses.

And me. Because I've accompanied them to South Ken. I've taken to hanging out with them again. I've begun to view spending time with the Elverses as being in the manner of an occupation. Accordingly, I've taken more – and increasingly protracted – leaves of absence from KBHL Corporate Communications. Until, at the point where it must've become clear to them that I wasn't really working there at all, they sacked me. The bumptious little prick who I reported to reported me to another bumptious little prick. Ah capitalism! It's gonna be a ten-thousand-year reich of a billion bumptious little pricks. Personnel had me into its drawer of the mirrored cabinet. 'You understand, Ms Bloom,' said Miss Ever-so-Modern, 'that given you haven't been with us for very long, we're in no position to offer you much in the way of a severance payment. I hope you don't mind me asking, but do you have a personal pension plan?' One more mirrored building I wouldn't have to look into, seeing nothing of myself, going nowhere.

I laughed like a loon all the way back to Dulston, Lithy gambolling beside me on the tube, singing in the street, 'It's good to touch the green, green grass of ho-ome!' Not that the dead chunk of calcification knew anything about grass, or home, or touching. Still, years now of shushing, tushing and generally admonishing my never-to-be-child had started to pay off. It was mentally growing up. It was now possible to hold a conversation verging on the adult with Lithy. Lithy who, it transpired, had the sassy irreverence and anarchic acumen I'd tried to inculcate in my daughters, but without Natasha's deep well of neediness, or Charlotte's constricting chain of snob shops.

With Rude Boy, on the other hand, there'd been no change. He was the same as ever, impersonating the wheelchair-bound by twirling his hands at his sides while screaming 'Um-diddy-um-diddy!', half-mooning the elderly with his muddy ass, freaking out small kiddies by manifesting himself in the margins of their vision. At least he wasn't so clingy. I'd leave him at Argos Road when I went to work, now I left him for whole nights as well. Shit – what could happen to him anyway?

'So, what do we do now?' Lithy said, back-flipping from gutter to sidewalk as we neared home.

'Well, I suppose we'll have to visit the deatheaucracy. See if there's an eternity benefit available, or anything of that ilk.'

The deatheaucracy were tenanting a busted car-hire operation in Acton that winter. One of those clock-card ladders was tacked up on the wall by the door of the place. When you arrived you were required to punch a card and put it in the appropriate slot. As you know, wherever the deatheaucracy pitch up there's a waiting system of a kind, whether deli-style tickets like these, or an electronic signboard like in a post office. Three or four of the dead – looking dead ordinary – sat on functional benches, leafing through a dismemberment of week-old newspapers.

Eventually my number was up, and leaving Lithy in the waiting area I trailed behind a clerk sporting a bumfreezer, through a claustrophobic succession of rooms, each one more crowded with life-size, cardboard cut-out, stand-alone figures than the one before. These rigid men leant about the place, their cardboard supports long since torn away. They were all the same guy, a young executive in a dark, double-breasted suit, waving a bunch of keys, with a speech bubble coming out of his mouth. This said, 'I'VE GOT HIRE POWER – HAVE YOU?' 'They put them in here when the business went under,' explained Hartly, the bumfreezer clerk. 'Frightful bore, but still, we won't be staying for long. Have you said hello to the *nyujo* yet?' I said hello to their precious fucking *nyujo*, which was being daubed with Copydex by one of the plain Janes.

A few of the suits were hanging around the place. Two sizes sat with their jackets off, trading baseball cards from their waistcoat pockets. Another, in a blue blazer, fired Buck Rogers's rocket pistol X2-31 at a hippy in a Mao jacket who sported a Zapata moustache. 'Zap-zap-zap,' the toy went. Other deatheaucrats were playing mah-jong or Diplomacy, Scrabble or Monopoly, or working their way through all 43,252,003,274,489,856,856,000 possible combinations of Rubik's cube. They ignored us as we passed. They concentrated on their dead crazes and their ceaseless smoking. Like Phar Lap, the deatheaucrats rolled their own. It gave them another excuse for a good fidget and pocketful of paraphernalia.

Hartly showed me into Canter's partitioned office.

'Ah, Ms Bloom.' Canter looked up from his paperwork, put down his Papermate, adjusted the collar of his Jaeger jacket. 'You may leave us, Hartly – do something useful, like taking Anubis for a walk on Turnham Green.'

'As you wish,' said Hartly, with ill grace. It was never possible for me to ascertain where authority lay with the deatheaucrats. While Canter nominally took control of my case, on occasions I'd heard him answer in the same surly fashion to Hartly, Glanville, or even Davis. The whole organisation has too many Indians and no discernible chiefs at all, wouldn'tjew say?

'Ms Bloom,' Canter pressed on, 'apparently you've given up your job?'

'News travels fast.'

'Oh, well-nigh instantaneously.'

'I'm getting too old for it.'

'You're no older than you were the day you died. Have you, perhaps, been having some . . . mmm, how can I put it?'

'Feelings?'

'Precisely so.' He shuffled a couple of file cards. 'Jealousy in the early sixties, anger in the late fifties, pride going back to the Second War and so forth?'

'Ye-es, those would be the ones.' The deatheaucrats always know everything, yet understand so little. 'But they don't altogether – '

'Impinge? Well they wouldn't, would they? Given your subtle body. It's more in the manner of seeing feelings, isn't it? Looking in on them from outside, revisiting the sights.'

Loathsome man. I was more than glad I hadn't got the job with them. A plain Jane came in with the obligatory Nice biscuits and the rancid tea. She looked at me with ill-concealed pique and eased herself out again.

'Going to the meetings, are you?' Canter pressed on, peering at me through a rimless pince-nez he'd poked up on to his shnozzle.

'Now and then.'

'Not according to our records. Listen, Ms Bloom, may I be candid?'

'What's the sense in being anything else?'

'You're still preoccupied with the affairs of the living. This observation of your daughters, this entering into their lives. Mr Jones should encourage you to desist. There's nothing to be gained now. You'd be far better off considering a move to Dulburb, or even further afield. I understand that your elder daughter, Mrs . . .?' Another search for facts – when were these assholes going to get computerised.

'Elvers.'

'Yes, Elvers. She's about to undertake fertility treatment, if I'm not mistaken.'

'Could be.'

'I wouldn't make the mistake of spending too much time with her during this, if I were you. There could be complications.'

'Oh.' I got up to leave; I'd had enough of the interview. I pulled my gloves on – it seemed the appropriate action. 'I'm not really interested in your advice on the matter, *Mister* Canter, I only came here to enquire whether there might be some cigarette money available now that I've quit my job?'

'Only the most nugatory amount. I think the current grant stands at around a hundred and fifty pounds per calendar month.'

'That will be sufficient. I won't bother you any further.'

'Good day, Ms Bloom, see the cashier on your way out. And do try and think about what I've been saying.'

But I didn't – why would I? I went back to Cumberland

Terrace, I took up my station at the Elverses'. I went with Charlotte and Richard to their consultations with Churchill.

My daughter had already been through a battery of tests and examinations with her own doctor, but the good Lord liked to do things properly. And although she'd been pregnant once before, it'd only been managed after the most strenuous sexual callisthenics. Churchill already had a picture of a complex of problems that were hampering the Elverses' ability to conceive. Charlotte had some endometriosis, although not enough to block her tubes. Richard's sperm were sluggish and some of them were abnormal, but they could still do the crawl. There was no doubt that Charlotte's tension and anxiety were affecting ovulation. Ha! Her inability to conceive had become a self-fulfilling prophecy. But there was also hostility between her refined cervical mucus and his coarse sperm.

Churchill did more tests. He probed her with his clever hands, both he and Charlotte revelling in mutual appreciation of each other's lack of embarrassment. This, Churchill reflected, is what gynaecology *should* be like – having a compliant patient, who had long since ceased to view her body as anything other than a vessel for procreation. He took blood, he took cervical mucus, he did a laparoscopy to check out her internal layout. He did a hysterosalpingography – purely because he liked impressing his patients by pronouncing the word. He did abdominal ultrasound scanning and an endrometrial biopsy. He pronounced himself satisfied and packed her off to lunch on the fifth floor of Harvey Nichols.

Richard came to see Churchill and the doctor talked to him, man to sperm. Churchill told him how lucky he was not to have idiopathic oligospermia – and Richard couldn't but agree. To have slow, fucked-up sperm was one thing, but to have *none at all*, that would look like carelessness. Churchill told Richard that even his normal, motile sperm might have undetectable chromosomal abnormalities. But he needn't feel singled out by this, it was quite possible that his wife's eggs were reaching their sell-by date as well. Some men, Churchill prated, are born without a vas deferens at all, or their urethra – foolish tube! – emerges on the underside of the penis. Others have retrograde ejaculation, which is pretty damn stupid; so they inseminate their own bladders, giving birth to their own pissy babies. 'But you've done that,' I mouthed at Elvers from the corner of the room, 'you've done that already – and it's I who must face the consequences. At the cat-flap, day after day, moaning for admission.'

Another possibility was – and Churchill was buoyed up by this one, for it was an area of doubly fruitful research – that Richard's immune system reacted to his own sperm as if it were a foreign body, as if he'd drunk some other guy's spunk. These weren't the good Lord's words – they're my own. Anyway, the important thing was to take the pith out of Richard and have plenty of the life force *on tap*. If he could've, Churchill would've demanded litres of the stuff from every man who walked into the room, the Lord's lust for sperm was so great.

Churchill told Richard to take his time; he'd go out and get a cappuccino while his patient frothed. There were any number of images on offer, carefully stored in a Chinese lacquer bookcase. Erotica of many stripes, woodblocks, etchings, dry points, even fucking *oil paintings*. Oh yes, Churchill certainly expected his patients to be of a refined character, the sort of men who whacked off to Degas and got a hard-on looking at a Gauguin. There were even – should Richard be of a coarser grain – actual *photographs* of naked women. Full frontal split-crotch shots, just in case he was forgetting what it was he was here for, and where it was all going to.

Richard thanked Churchill and took the plastic pot. He promised he'd do his best to come with the goods. Left alone, Richard eschewed the good Lord's cabinet of arty delights. He ignored the pornography and relied on his own procreative imagination. I watched him, a ponderous man, blurring into middle age, standing by the consulting-room window looking at the square outside. Staring at the posh, antiquated, knickerbocker-wearing kids, with their still posher, still more antiquated, Norton nannies. And visibly regretting – or so I imagined – every single lost ejaculation of his twenty-odd productive years. Every stiffened sheet and starched hand-kerchief, every wasted bit of tissue paper. All that wrist-ache – to no avail. He jacked himself off on lost time, did Richard, and I watched him. It's absurd, I know, but I thought I should *engage* with Richard a little more now, try and feel a little for him. He was, after all, still my son-in-law. Prince Stuff.

All this hanging around the doctor's office was hell on my smoking; I had to cut back to fewer than a hundred and thirty a day. I spent bizarre evenings watching Churchill and his lab technicians doing tests. They placed her mucus and his semen together on a slide and let the goo fight it out. They put bets on the results and drank beer out of Pyrex beakers. What a wag that Churchill was!

Come the winter, Churchill had us back in his consulting room and laid out the possibilities. He was no nearer to comprehending how the Elverses had managed to conceive once, but were now unable to, than when he'd started the hundred-guinea-per-hour meter. There were myriad possible factors, but none of them alone was sufficient. 'I don't recommend such a course lightly,' he said weightily, 'but if you're intent on trying, and you feel you have the *complete information* necessary to give informed consent, you might try *in vitro* fertilisation.'

Oh, they wanted to try – why wouldn't they? After all, they were now as rich as fucking Croesus, and given their grossly stultified imaginations, and their gross houses stuffed with chattels, they had little precious else to spend the money on.

Churchill described the treatment cycle. The drugs he'd use to suppress Charlotte's pituitary system and the temporary menopause they'd induce. The drugs he'd then employ to stimulate her ovaries and ruff up her follicles. The ultrasounds and blood tests they'd be doing all along to check everything was going OK. Then he got to the hard part. Even if she could cope with the mood swings, the abdominal bloating, the rashes and the muscle-aches, there was still no guarantee that any given treatment cycle would be worth completing. Did they *still* want to go through with it? You bet your ass they did.

Then came the hard-drug education. Churchill and his storky assistants showed Charlotte how to sniff Zoladex on the first day of her period. It made her feel high just knowing she was finally under way, even if in the wake of her sniffing sessions came these crippling mood swings, waves of hormonal *weltschmerz*. After day fourteen of Charlotte's cycle, when they'd checked to see that her ovaries were well and truly dormant, they taught Richard how to shoot his wife up with human menopausal gonadotrophin. He had to get a grip on a fucking big hypo for this job, and shoot the shit clear inside Charlotte's muscles. To begin with it made him feel quite nauseous – but not as sick as her.

All this time they had to visit Churchill's clinic for blood tests and scans. The treatment cycles played hell with their business cycle. Near the end of each one, Richard had to provide another semen sample, which was assessed, then washed – yup, that's what they called it – in preparation for fertilisation. Finally came the harvesting of Charlotte. The furrowed field of her laid out for Churchill's combined probes and needles. One last big hit of human chorionic gonadotrophin before bed. Goodnight Ovalteenies. At the crack of dawn, the eggs were sucked from the mature follicles in her uterus, and bunged into a nice fattening nutriment with Richard's squeaky-clean sperm. Then the whole primordial stock was chucked in an incubator to see if it would make soup.

Sometimes the embryologist found a normally developing embryo when she peered through her microscope twenty-four hours later – sometimes she found two. On other occasions there would be four – or none. There were decisions to be made – which to plant, which to discard, which to bung in the deep freeze to make Charlottes and Richards in the far distant future. The good Lord regarded this egg-selection business as his forte. Like a housewifely deity he would scrutinise the ontogeny through his microscope, then squeeze each egg with an eye-beam, deciding which of them were ripe, which ones made the cut.

Back in Cumberland Terrace, in the titanic flat, I watched Richard shoot up his wife with more human chorionic gonadotrophin, the two of them bent in grunting, painful, bloody consummation. Then the transfer. Back down to South Ken, up on the couch, in with yet another needle. There was an uncharitable première when she got to scrutinise Churchill's choice on a monitor – weren't they cute. Then, sedated, Charlotte was finally impregnated. What a fucking lottery! Only twenty per cent of the fertilised eggs had a chance of making it once they finally got back up Charlotte's cervix. One in five! Bad odds at the humility racetrack. Still, I've gotta hand it to her – to them – for persistence. For, as cycle succeeded cycle, and the seasons ran into one another like the watery colours on a child's painting, they kept right on.

More than this, I was actually proud of Charlotte and

Richard. They were fighters, they were sticking at it, they wouldn't give in. They were so charmless together; unlike Natasha they had no internal voices to wheedle them, saying, 'C'mon – give up. You know you'll never have a child. Give it up. Adopt while there's still the remotest possibility. Don't chuck away all your Waste of Paper . . .'

Yes, I felt proud of them, but then I daresay this pride had a good deal to do with the fact that during those years I was proud of *almost everything*. Proud of Russian plutonium-smugglers – hot dogs that they were. Proud of their president – sleeping through Ireland. Proud of the Jackal – finally brought to bay. Proud of the ridiculous Englishwoman who shlepped around the world in eleven years. They say that when she reached John O'Groats she was X-rayed and found to have the pelvis of a seventy-year-old woman. Tell me about it, sister – perhaps it was mine? Proud of the cultists suiciding in Switzerland. Proud of Dean Rusk – un-be-fucking-lievably. Proud of Rose Kennedy – welcome on board. Proud of those Russkis again – inefficiently demolishing Grozny with artillery rounds and small-arms fire. Proud of Fred Perry – thanks for the titty-patches, feller. Proud of the Taliban – crazy headgear guys. Proud of the Turks – once you've denied the reality of one holocaust it's *so much easier* to precipitate another. Proud of Michael Jackson, that whited-up shvartzer sticking it to the Yids. Proud of Timothy McVeigh – what a guy! Fascism American-style. Proud of the French – hey, they need all the pride they can get, to add to their European Economic Community pride mountain. Way to go, guys – starting up with those nuclear tests again, just what the world needs in 1995. And while you're at it – why the fuck didjew pardon Dreyfus? Surely some *humility gaffe* there. Proud of the British yomping into Sarajevo – you're only a couple of years late, fellers, with your army commanded by Yaws.

Proud of OJ – well, someone has to get away with it. Proud of Farakhan and his million men – give or take 600,000. Proud of Yigal Amir, who acted alone on God's orders and had no regrets. Yet. Proud of the dumb Princess Sloane, left home all alone, while her hubby the tiny horseman went a-rogering. Tally ho! Proud of the University of Texas researchers, who isolated the gene that causes breast cancer. Thanks guys. Proud of the Tamil Tigers – you're grrrreat! Proud of the First Lady with her legal bill *primus inter pares*. Proud of the Paddys bombing Docklands – a mere two dead and so much uggerly real estate demolished. Cool. Proud of the optical fibre that can transmit a trillion bits of information – twelve million phone calls at once, well just fancy that. Now we can all know what she said that he said that she said – to the power of fucking four hundred. Proud of the cloned sheep and George Burns – although it was hard to tell the difference. But mostly proud of the Unabomber arrested way out in Montana. Him I could've curled up with and done a little sly whittling. Doncha think?

Oh yes, with so much pride sloshing inside, I could afford to splash out a little. Hell, I even had some pride left over for Natty and Russ, that golden couple. Pride for them as they ducked and dived in the ponds of plutocracy, dipping their bills here, there and fucking everywhere. One month they'd be in an apartment in Mayfair – the next a penthouse in Paddington. They put on and removed their habitations the way other people did clothes. With their lunatic swaggering – driving down Aldgate in a Golf cabriolet, the City putting on a ticker-tape parade of unpaid bills – they parodied the comfortable wealth of the Elverses. While, with their latex-wrapped, spermicidal, easeful couplings, they mocked the Elverses' urge to conceive.

No, not strictly accurate, that, for, as I trailed across town –

sometimes on foot, often in buses, occasionally by tube –
reeling in the lifelines of my girls, I became aware that
Russell's occasional reefers were weaving themselves into a
full sisal jacket. That his odd half of lager was becoming an
odd bottle of Famous Grouse, or Stolychnaya. Then he did
odd things. They fought, the two of them, the two ruddy
ducks. They pecked at each other and complained, circling the
pond in the gathering twilight of narcosis, not noticing that all
the other birds had flown, that the hoary mantle was en-
croaching from the shoreline. That winter, with its chilly
austerity, was coming.

Yes, it was really the Elverses who parodied Russ and
Natty, what with their sniffing and shooting up drugs and
their washing of the milky-white lode. It wasn't to be long
before such playground mockery – and why, oh why, do one's
children *never* grow up? – got to Russ and Natty, and they
recommenced sniffing and shooting and washing up the
milky-white lode.

I could see the future – and it wasn't gonna work. The way
they watched so many soap operas lying on their sofa.
Listening to the synthesised arrhythmia of the signature tune,
as if it would introduce a little more drama into their operatic
lives. The way her voice impaled the octaves on its sharp
spike. And the distorted leviathan's moan of his lust – calling
out to her from the deep. When he took her by force – which
he did increasingly during the spring of '96 – it was distressing
to realise that it was *he* who imagined himself the vulnerable
one. The little girl.

After one purloined session, watching them tussle in a
rented house in Notting Hill, I walked back into town along
the side of Hyde Park. When alive I had, natch, belonephobia
– a morbid anxiety of being pierced by needles, or any sharp
thing. To walk like this, past a mile or more of iron railings,

would've been impossible. *Inconceivable.* Even if I could've, I'd've listed, an old ship overloaded with fat anxieties. Death, I supposed, had given me at least this queer stability.

The kids chased in and out of the beech avenues. Lithy and Rude Boy, death's kittens – ever sportive. We gained Park Lane and struggled across the three lanes heading north. We climbed the barriers on either side of the verge, then dodged the three lanes of traffic heading south. We tagged across Grosvenor Square and, as a small squall blew in, I looked back over my shoulder to see the tessellated greenery of Hyde Park, tossed with wind and drizzle, a verdant coping for the grey haunch of the American Embassy.

Even the noise of a city raving drunk on its own commerce fades if you tuck your head down and ignore it. While two-millimetre-thick hulls cut through the spray, I made my way to Berkeley Square and hunkered down on a bench. Here, then, there were never elms, simply great old plane trees, in a plain new place. I sat and lost myself in the damp leaves pressed into the pavement, a kiddy collage of anti-nature. Come in cigarette number 134, *your time is up.* I'd never felt, it occurred to me, more depleted by death. Or, to be correct, more indolent. The very effort needed to register my own fatigue was . . . too much. Seeing made me yawn.

Yawning summoned up Phar Lap, who came, picking his way between the sheltering tourists, from the Piccadilly side of the square. Phar Lap, looking unusually dapper in a brand-new Dryzabone, the waxed-cloth cape of the big coat giving him the gravitas of a black knight, or a city conquistador. 'Feelin' tired, are you, Lily-girl, yeh-hey?'

'Mmph – yup.'

'Feelin' all wrung out, yuwai?' He joined me on the bench, took the bullroarer and his boomerangs out from the coat folds, set them on the ground. We must've been visible because a passer-by looked at us with mild interest. The old woman, the Australian black – another pair of misfits in the ill-fitting city.

'My feet would be killing me if I weren't dead.'

'Ha! Issatso. Listen – you bin seein' Mr Canter, hey-yeh?'

'Oh, I went to see him a while back about a grant now I've stopped working.'

'And yer still hangin' roun' yer girls, yeh-hey?'

'If you can call it that – being unseen and not heard.'

'I can see I'm gonna have to remind you all the fuckin' time, girl. All the fuckin' time. Don't hang 'round the buju, Lily-girl, specially not yer daughters'.' He got the makings of his shrivelled cigarettes out and put one together. The rain didn't bother him. 'Wulu?' he clicked, and I gave him a light. 'Listen, go see Canter again. They're down off the Walworth Road this month, old office block called Providence House. Go talk to him – he wants to see you, yeh-hey?'

'What about?'

'Taxes – you owe taxes, hey-yeh?'

'Taxes? Whaddya mean? I'm not on any Revenue computer – I'm dead.'

'Yaka! Not now – before, taxes from before. You gotta settle up if you want to go back.'

'You're kidding, surely.'

'Listen, Lily-girl,' he stood to leave, 'there are some certainties, yeh-hey?' And was gone.

I went back to see Canter again. Admired their precious fucking *nyujo*, patted their bloody Anubis. I joshed the clerks playing with their clackers, or bouncing through the old offices on their orange Spacehoppers, rubber horns clenched between their decadently suited thighs. I listened to Canter, I watched him tot it up on an old Burroughs adding machine, crank the handle, pronounce the sum proffered to him on the paper tongue. 'Two thousand, three hundred and thirty-four pounds and twenty-three pence exactly. That's what's owing, Ms Bloom. You will have to settle via us before there can be any possibility of your regaining the before-death plane. You do appreciate this, I trust.'

'No, I don't fucking appreciate it – and I don't trust you.'

'One thing you may certainly trust is my advice in respect of the time you've been spending at the Churchill Clinic. You really should desist, Ms Bloom, now your, ahem, feelings are resuming – there are no simple mechanisms involved in this pro – '

'In reincarnation – that's what you're talking about, isn't it? Admit it.'

'Reincarnation is far too crude a concept for looking at these things. Why – the paperwork alone would preclude such an idea. There are numerous interview committees, each necessitating the most stringently-compiled presentations, and none of this cuts against the grain of pure chance. To adventitiously pursue the possibility of being – in some sense – *reborn* as your daughter's child. Well, surely you can appreciate that this is the flimsiest of fantasies, the vastest of improbabilities. You'd be far better advised,' he ran on in the face of my blank hostility, 'to consider the animating principle of an anencephalic stillborn infant, as I believe I've already mentioned.'

'You have – Jesus, you have. A more porous barrier – I know, I know.'

'Even a lithopedion, such as I believe you yourself conceived in . . .' – he swivelled his chair, banged open the cabinet, flicked through the cardboard squeezebox – '. . . 1967, would be, ahem, a better idea.'

'Why d'jew clear your throat?' I was on him in an instant.

'I'm sorry?'

'Why d'jew clear your throat? – You haven't got anything there to clear.'

'I hardly think – '

'No, you don't think. Listen, I'm not gonna sit around and sop up this mishegass for eternity, I've got kids to look after. And I don't trust you one little bit, Mister "ahem", not one little bit. I think you're holding out on me – I think I have *incomplete information.*'

'You can think what you like, Ms Bloom.' He was reinforced in his free-laced straight-thinking by the arrival of a departmental Jane, who picked up the Tupperware plate of Nice biscuits and looked down at him with an expression of protective admiration. 'You can think what you like, but until the monies owed to the Revenue are remitted, you won't be travelling anywhere much. Saving Dulston, that is. Now, unless you have any proposals concerning a payments schedule I bid you good day, Ms Bloom, I bid *you* good day.'

I swear he actually said this and, moreover (good Canter-esque word, that), took the lapels of his Shavian jacket in hand at the same time, like the skilled advocate of cycling and vegetarianism that he so clearly was, had been, and would remain evermore.

I went back to Dulston – grinding up to the Elephant and Castle in a shitty old bus, then tunnelling through the city to Bethnal Green in a fucking *new* tube train. Unbelievable, they'd finally got some new rolling stock on this line for the first time since I'd moved to London *forty fucking years ago!* I took another lumbering red dinosaur from the tube stop up Mare Street, then disappeared down Downs Park Road and into the hinterland of Dulston.

That afternoon in late spring of 1996, even the Fats were

pleased to see me. 'Ooh, she's tired and old, tired and old,' they said, 'she's overdone it, overdone it, she's tired and old.'

How right they were. I figured it out, though. I'd cut back to a hundred cigarettes a day. People say it's useless just cutting down, that you'll simply spend the time between cigarettes willing it to pass. That it's as bad as smoking all you can – if not worse. But then these live characters didn't have my subtle body, nor my unsubtle incentive.

Christmas 2001

Yeah, I don't have the fucking balls – that's what I'm blubbing about. An internalised British actor, playing a Gestapo officer, has slapped me three times across my face, and I've confessed. I don't have the fucking balls to do it. Although if I did, I wouldn't choose any of those easy options. Oh no. I'd go for the heavy, mulga-wood boomerang. I'd beat myself to death with it, administer the ultimate punishment. Then I'd derisively piss on myself, humiliating my own puny conception of what the world is.

The boomerang's there, downstairs in the MFI shelving unit. Authenticity stashed in fakery. It's propped up at the back of a shelf, a sinister tick this one – and not a bit ubiquitous. Hell, even the climb up there would be dangerous, given my weakness, my size, my clumsy misery. But I don't have the balls for it – the only balls I've got are super ones, hugely compressed spheres of oil, which when thrown bounce around this box, batting into walls, shooting through the leaves of the yucky yucca, fetching up in the blue hollow of the Ice Princess's throat. Super balls – the kind of pathetic little toy I was reduced to when the terrible twins ceased being able to do a number on anyone but themselves.

No, in the few hours of daylight I have available, I'll climb down from the chill mattress and get myself warm with a little super-ball action. It's a long way from pretending to be Joe DiMaggio in the sandlot to playing with my super ball here in a concrete shoebox, but I made it all the same. My toys are all in a crate under my cot, over in the far corner. This I can drag out easily enough, this I can tip over. But these plastic fragments of Chinese manufacture aren't as fatal to those under thirty-six months as their labels would have you believe. Not that the Ice Princess cared anyway, screwed up righteously as she was, tottering into the big M of merchandising, so she could buy me an unhappy meal with a free toy, and leave me, baby Nero, fiddling at a table, while she went down to the john to burn spoons. Here they are, my own little movie spin-offs, Simbas, Buzz Lightyears, Aladdins and Barbies, all ready to play. But oops! No – I need a pee. So it's back across the room, into the loo, drag over my old orange-box stool, and up on to the seat. Now I know why I took to toilet-training so well this time; it was because I'd be doing it unaided soon enough.

Ach! What a shloomph I am! Lumpy and ugly and stupid. I forgot to drink before I peed. Now I'm gonna have to wait ten minutes for the cistern to fill again, before I can dip one of my bath-toy scoops down into the bowl and get a dipper-full. The cistern – you guessed – is as kaput as every other fitment in this place. The Estate Agent – as I think I've had cause to remark – wasn't too hot on doing stuff around the house. No balls – fucked ballcock. Yeah, I'd like a drink – and I'd like to brush my teeth. There's no paste, natch, but I've a tiny brush with a glittery little handle. With this I can get some of yesterday's cake out of my milk teeth. I am, you will nowise be surprised to learn, inordinately proud of my teeth. When she tried to quieten me with sweets I'd scream and pummel her. 'Oh Delilah! Whassamatter? Mummy's bought you some sweeties – oh do calm down! Look, nice sweeties, you'll like them.'

Yeah, maybe, but they'll rot my teeth. I'm not about to make that mistake again, so I'll scream and kick and even bite you with the burgeoning incisors – until you back off, woman, back off and glare at me. A standoff badass mamas would be proud of down Mexico way.

Not a lot to look at here in the bathroom. I can stand on my stool and, if I stretch right up, peek out the small window. But there's not much out there either, only block after street after block, Plasticville E3. I had a toy like that in the 1920s, plastic buildings you arranged to build your own city. Now all that's done on computer screens. When the Ice Princess still had women she could offload me on, or freeload off herself, I'd see older kids playing at simulating cities, with pixel parks, trees, houses, stores, factories and city halls. Putting in infrastructure with a click of a button. In the country they probably have Ploughstation by now. Yeah, now they've got simulated cities, simulated relationships, and even simulated sex. All courtesy of their precious world-wide-fucking-web. The reticulation of early-warning systems which have demonstrably failed to warn them of anything. They'll never even walk to the fucking store again to buy a paper – not when they can click for it. Their legs will wither and drop off. They'll end up as two massive thumbs sticking out of a huge adrenalin gland. And no balls – certainly no balls.

If I could simulate London, I'd give it a better fucking climate. I'd give it a street life of sorts. Sure, I can hear the hysterical keening of emergency vehicles up here, but I can never see any of the emergencies they're heading for. The only toy humans I can make out are a few teenagers, their mental ages reduced by glue and truancy to the point where it's *perfectly reasonable for them to be stuck to the playground furniture all day. Every day. No, I want a street life, because my predicament would never be played out like this in Madrid, or Manila, or even – conceivably – Manhattan. I want a street life, because along with it comes a well-exercised tendency for people to stick their big fucking noses right inside your business and have a damn good honk. Shit, I wouldn't even mind being in Tel Aviv, or Jerusalem. Anywhere but London, where people are still so fucking reserved, so polite, so hidden behind gauzy indifference. Their politeness is killing me.*

Chapter Sixteen

Before I was sacked, I'd never really appreciated how much my work got me out of the house. Sure, I had my trips down to Regent's Park and South Ken to check up on the Elverses' expensive procreation-purchasing programme, but it was easy to skip a few now I had more information. I didn't kid myself that I had *complete* information, but c'mon – what could all of these warnings-off from Phar Lap and Canter mean? Canter clearing his throat like that and getting at me for back taxes. Well, he wasn't gonna fool *me*. I'm not saying that I began totting up exactly how many reams, quartos and grams per square metre there were in the family fortune, or how I was going to spend all that paper money. But it did seem fair enough that it should devolve on to me. Me, who was responsible for launching the pen cap that unleashed a million miles of memos, jottings and reports that girdled the earth. I'd done the pens – now I'd have the paper to go with them.

Still, I missed the daily grind, the vapid office chit-chat, the strap-hanging on the tube. Even the bumptious little pricks who were powering the economic cycle off on another steroid-fuelled mountain section of the Tour de Dollar. The whole go-round had kept me engaged with the world – after a fashion. As I lounged about the basement, chiding the Fats, singing along with Lithy, tolerating Rude Boy, giving HeLa the occasional cold wipe-down – 'Ooh! That's hot, so hot' – I began suspecting that I might come to regret my colossal lethargy. Because that's what it was – laziness. I'd always been a great, tall, heavy-minded, ageing girl, and now so more than ever.

At London Zoo, which I strolled through on trips to Cumberland Terrace, they had a sloth bear. It was a curious beast, definitely ursine, but with a pointed snout and hooky feet. They'd put it in an open enclosure, in front of the artificial rock formation. Way back in the sixties when I took the kids there, this was occupied by brown bears. Anyway, this sloth bear just couldn't get used to captivity. Couldn't get used to having that much pizza – it was within yards of the concession – dangled in its snout. It rocked like an autistic, or a Stoke Newington frummer davening on a mobile Jew phone. From side to side, from one pair of hooky feet to the other. Over and over. I felt a good deal of weary sympathy for the sloth bear; for two pins I'd've put it out of its fucking misery. But then, as Phar Lap would gnomically utter, voidness cannot injure voidness. What a jerk. Or, as Lithy would whine, 'Too much of nothing can make a man ill at ease.' The passage of the years was at least improving my calcified cadaver's lyrical taste.

But mostly I kept to the debatable 'burb of Dulston. 'And another child cries in the ghet-to / In the ghet-to!' Lithy covered the other King Stuff. Ghetto, natch, derives from the Italian for suburb – *borghetto*. Not a well-known fact, that, but one known to me. I'd like to be able to tell you that I found it out reading through the nights, laying up my store of useless erudition, but it'd be a lie. Truth to tell, an Italian guy at the Dulston cafe vouchsafed it to me one morning, when we were idly comparing pathographies over a full dead breakfast. Yup, it was that bad, I'd taken to chewing egg slop like all the rest. Perhaps this was the ultimate acceptance of death, the ability to pass the egg test of mortality itself? I dunno. But it wasn't so much a case of snatching an all-day breakfast – it was more a matter of all-breakfast days. I might not have been able to taste or feel, but I could at least hear the crunch of my prize cuspids on that mineralised scenery laughably known as fried bread. I ordered it up by the square metre. Like fucking carpet underlay – or a waste of paper.

I'd given up on the meetings altogether. It was blindingly clear that the personally dead had nothing to teach me. It was little more than an anti-social club, and I am – as I think I've had cause to remark – not a joiner. Also, I couldn't fail to notice, when I did from time to time drop in at the Community Centre, or St John's, that there were hardly any of the same people there, none of the members I remembered from my first few years in Dulston. What had happened to them? Gone to Dulburb? The provinces? Or had they taken up short-term contracts in the Gulf? Or maybe, like me, they'd simply dropped out of the loop altogether, decided they had better things to do with the unlimited time available.

It dawns on me at last, too late, that they weren't bullshitting after all. That they did have better leverage than I supposed. They were getting out big-time – getting out for good. Not simply dropping out to squat on the allotments behind Dulston Junction, like a few of the dead did. Growing vegetables they could never eat, while trying to 'connect' with the hop-head eco-warriors. This lot had taken up residence on platforms set among the branches of an ancient oak which leant over the railway tracks. They were gonna save it. What did they imagine would happen if it was hacked down? I mean, it's not as if it was the bloody Tree of Life. Amazing that these kids – allegedly so in tune with fucking nature – didn't even realise they were consorting with dead drabs. But then I suppose affecting a Palaeolithic line in clothing can scramble up anyone's feel for the stuff of life. Egg test indeed. Don't be vague – be vegan.

No, the personally dead weren't bullshitting. There was something – or no-thing – to their programme after all. There are no faces I recognise here in this ghastly waiting room, which Hartly has long since forgotten me in. We pitched up a while back (a long fucking while back), after Phar Lap, Rude Boy, Lithy and I took a black cab from Piccadilly. Suspicious, this, in itself – taking a black cab. The only cabs I'd ridden in for the past eleven years belonged to Costas and his pals who ran the Samsara Minicab Company. Sloppy old jalopies, driven with clutch-for-brake, by hairy dead men. But on this occasion Phar Lap gazumped the woman who had her arm up as if she were hailing Zeus himself. He wrenched the door open, and we all piled in. Not that the woman argued about it or anything – wouldjew? If you found yourself standing in Piccadilly, hailing a cab, and when it stopped a fat old blonde, a skinny Aboriginal and a naked nine-year-old boy beat you to the punch.

'Where to, guv?' said the self-employed Nazi in the front compartment, and Phar Lap replied, 'Palmers Green.'

Oh goody, thought I, Palmers Green, another jerking odyssey out to London's periphery. Another search for a run-down insurance office, or the colourless premises of a failed colour consultancy. Another visit to the deatheaucracy. Phar Lap and I settled down on the bench seat, Lithy and Rude Boy took the rumbles.

We U-turned away from the kerb. The Nazi shouted, as if throwing his grating voice at the back row of the Nuremberg stadium, 'Watch where yer fucking going, you wanker!' The intercom hissed at us, 'Traffic's diabolical up the other way – bin a bombing – orlright if I take the Embankment?'

'Yer the expert,' Phar Lap replied. How could he be so stupid? Even I, who hadn't ridden in a black cab since before they had intercoms, knew this was giving the shnorrer an open fucking season to rook us. Embankment indeed. Still, it wasn't me who was paying, so I sat back and tried to enjoy the ride.

Yup. Between May of '96 and Christmas '97, when I found

out that Mr and Mrs Elvers had well and truly done the dirty on me, I was Dulston's own sloth bear. I took languor to new troughs. Without straying too far from Argos Road, I entered an Olympic pentathlon in ennui and won every event. Running with boredom, hurdling over inertia, staying the put, throwing the indolence, shooting the tired breeze – I excelled in all fields of uncompetitive endeavour.

I was like the Inca sacrificial mummy they discovered that year, thrown up by a glacier in the Andes; perfect in every regard except for being frozen to death with my head bashed in. My little radio told me all the news that was fit for Estuarine accents to relate – and I'd thought the rotten plummy ones were bad! But I couldn't've cared less about peace in Chechnya – I'd outlast it. And even though I'd thought Timmy Leary a fraud when I'd met him in the late fifties (one of Kaplan's pals), I wouldn't've bothered to tick him off if I'd met him now, walking the beach at Santa Dullica. Land-mine bans were not my concern, bombs in Manchester and Atlanta left me cold. The tiny horseman coughed up fifteen fucking million for his coughing-up wifey. So what. Truth itself was relaunched as a downmarket tabloid – but hell, we'd seen *that* one coming. In Belgium they found a basement full of horrors. Tell me about it. Not. In Jerusalem they had an almighty brawl over the tunnel under Temple Rock. The Yids wanted it – the yocks wanted it. And all this for a tunnel? Try riding on the fucking *tube*, you shmucks. In the States a sixty-six-year-old had himself bumped off by a computer. Doh! Like – aren't we *all* being bored to death by the bloody things; no need to make a special *effort*. There was a fucking *auction* for Holocaust victims in Vienna. Kinduv like holding a sponsored pie-eating contest for Somalia – wouldn'tjew say? They re-elected the Prick in Chief from Arkansas – now that's boreocracy for you. OJ paid out.

Yawn. The dumpy Duchess won a million-dollar deal with Weight Watchers, and, I concede, I was mildly taken with the idea of what *her* Fats were gonna be like. The Human Fertilisation and Embryo Authority let a woman called Blood inseminate herself with her dead husband's jism. That's what I call tardigrade ejaculation. In LA some bozos tried to catch a comet tail and fell flat on their own overdoses. In France a poor everythingplegic wrote a novel with his *eyelid*. And they say the novel is *dead*. Another fucking Berg – this time the Gins – kicked the bongos and beat the retreat. Just down the road from Dulston, the off-the-peg mob cheered in a pop-eyed Bambi of a premier, as if it were some kinduva fucking *revolution*, when all it *really* meant was another excuse for a Waste of Paper. A computer beat the Jew Kasparov at his own game. *Au revoir*, clever clogs. The Swiss found four fucking *billion* of *our* money in their vaults. It was no good to me, but really, which *hole* did you lose that lot in, you Emmenthal-heads? The cancer-stick-makers had to cough up $370 million for Medicare. I wearily guffawed – too little, too late – and lit a B&H. Number seventy-six for the day. I was cutting down, remember. In Cambodia Pol finally got potted. In Florida a pansy nobody killed a pansy somebody 'cause he didn't like the cut of his pants. Or so I surmised. In Paris, the tiny horseman's clothes-horse bought the farm with weary predictability, galloping round the Périphérique late at night with her Arab rider. All London went meshugga. Even I hauled myself out of bed and shlepped down to Kensington Palace to get a look at this massacre of the blooms. Even I couldn't be altogether indifferent to this unbelievable waste of cut flowers. I mean to say, they might as well have passed the cheques *straight over* to New Covent Garden, and *cut out* the dead fucking middle woman. Who at that moment was probably having intercrural sex with Georges Simenon in fucking Ennuyeuseville. She should care.

After that I pretty much relapsed into total torpor until December, when my heart-throb the Unabomber was forced to plea-bargain with the Justice Department. He took life rather than death – the noodge. I'd hoped he'd plump for Dulston, and the two of us could idle a few years away whittling together. D'jewknowhatImean?

I must've missed out on the family-haunting for getting on for six months, but I was confident the Elverses were still hard at it. They had to be well on their way to completing twenty Churchillian treatment cycles by now. The good Lord had taken them for two hundred large and still – or so I suspected – Charlotte was no larger. When she did finally get pregnant, they were gonna be well and truly shtupped. I mean, what was Churchill gonna give them to go with their baby? A cuddly toy? A set of nursery furniture? What added value could his operation represent for people like the Elverses, people who had every material thing they already wanted, and plenty more besides?

It wasn't until I was out of the tube at Warren Street and stomping through the gritty winds that scoot down the Euston Tower that it dawned on me – it was Christmas Eve. We Dulstonians didn't set much store by religious festivals, and I think you can see our point of view.

There's no mileage in crying for the Christian saviour when you're dead already. I mean, the only thing that would happen on the Day of Judgement would be an influx of souls to our neck of the woods, pushing rents up to the fucking heavens. Not worth observing Ramadan either. So, food and water hasn't passed your lips, or transgressed your teeth? Well, if you're supping at the Dulston cafe, there's no way you're gonna *swallow* it. Honestly, I don't think even the maddest of dead mullahs could get up a doctrinal argument over what *we* put in our mouths. I did see the Seths make a bit of a show once or twice on Diwali, their little boy chucking colourless water over Mr Bernard. But that was the Seths for you – they took to Dulston far better than I did. Typical of British Asians, always prepared to up sticks, die, and move on to the next retail opportunity.

Yeah, Crudmass. Deck the halls with Boston Charlie, tra-la-la-la-la, la-la-la-la, Norah's bleeding on the trolley, tra-la-la-la-la, la-fuck-ing-la. Tin-foil trees in the shop windows, red nylon stocking hats on the boozed-up brows of commuters. Bad cheer everywhere. All along Cumberland Terrace the rich had seen fit to dress their windows with too dear retro baubles. The fashion this year was for painted wood decorations and candles in lieu of fairy lights. Anything that made turn-of-the-century London look like turn-of-the-last-fucking-century *Norway*. The Elverses had outdone themselves in this regard. Typical of a childless couple, without a scintilla of abandonment in their corpulent frames, to make so much of this infantile saturnalia. Typical of Charlie in particular – that egregious wannabe Anglican.

I plodded up the expensive stairs cursing heavily. I manifested myself in the big hall, with its Italian marble floor and redwood-sized coat tree. I could hear the clink of crystal from the drawing room and voices raised in happy chatter. Hmm, I didn't like that – what did they have to be so jolly about? Not only was the chatter happy, it sounded sinisterly familial, awfully child-oriented. I winnowed myself down to exiguousness, crept forward over the deep pile.

Jeezus-fucking-H.-Kerrist! There they were, Mummy Elvers putting pressies under a convivial pine, a maid standing by with a silver salver of mince pies, the sherry glasses sparkling, and, on the Mercedes-sized ottoman, Richard Elvers sitting with a cute little boy on his knees. The child was about three, grinning hugely, and as black as my cold dead heart. I had no doubt at all that he was their very ownsome. The way they looked at him, the way he looked at them, the Bob Marley playing over the Bang & Olufsen – doubtless part of their goody-two-shoes acknowledgement of his Afro-Caribbean heritage – all of it smacked of perfectly achieved domesticity. The Elverses were at home at last. But a shvarzer kid? I never would've believed it of them.

Sure, I was pissed, but for some hours I didn't believe the whole game was up for good. They may've capitulated and gone for adoption, but wasn't it often the case that once this happened the frenzied inconceivables relaxed enough to do it? It wasn't until I rifled Richard's desk, and found the letters from Churchill which finally – after, you note, he'd trousered the money – confirmed that my son-in-law's spunk was a tasteless condiment, irreversibly soured cream, that I accepted defeat. There was this – and there was worse. I hung around the New Elverses that yuletide, sopping up the atmos, and learned that they'd *sold* Waste of Paper, that they'd *given* a lot of the money away, and that they were *moving* to the boondocks, to concentrate on raising Junior. I was done for. I may've hated Dulston, but move to the English provinces? Fergeddit. I'd have to be doubly dead before I did *that*.

Twenty-seven quid on the meter and Phar Lap didn't quibble. Not only that, he even *tipped* Martin Bormann, despite his not letting us smoke in his precious fucking cab, *and* driving all the way out here to Palmers Green while gabbing to his friends on his mobile. What a shaven dickhead.

'So, what's it this time?' I asked Phar Lap, as we debouched on to yet another grotty shopping parade. 'A car-parts warehouse that's gone down the tubes? A Citizens' Advice Bureau that's run out of it? What *charming* premises has the deatheaucracy seen fit to infest this month?'

'Hey-yeh. Looks like it's an old tooth-puller's t'me, Lily-girl. We better head on in, yeh-hey?' And he shouldered his wooden clutter. There seemed to be more of it all the time.

'What's that one?' I asked him, indicating a painted stick a metre or so long as we trudged up the stairs.

'This feller? Iss a pukamani, girl – death pole.' He used it to push open the frosted glass door, and ushered me in for my long wait.

'Ah, Ms Bloom,' said Hartly, who we immediately encountered; he'd been trying to sucker a stuffed Garfield on to the door. 'I'm afraid Mr Canter is occupied pro tem, but we're pleased you're here. Good of Mr Jones to bring you over. I understand the monies owing to the Revenue have been paid in full now.'

'Is that so?'

'It is, it is.' Now he mentioned it I remembered that I'd paid it all off. I've alway been in such a muddle with money. 'There aren't, how shall I put it, any further lets or impediments, it's just a matter of form-filling, checking bona fides, sorting out the paperwork.'

'Oh, I couldn't have guessed,' I sneered.

Hartly smiled indulgently. 'I'm afraid our waiting room is none too salubrious – it's so hard to get the premises nowadays.'

'You're telling me.' I looked around me at this long, narrow room. The mismatched chairs along each wall: plastic stacking; kitchen, with basket-woven seats; and padded office, with castors. These racks fixed to the walls, still holding leaflets on fluoride, flossing, caries and other, vitally interesting tooth-rot subjects. I contemplated the usual highly-coloured posters of the human mouth, with personal ads stuck among them. 'Cat Seeks Good Home', 'Home Seeks Good Cat'. Somebody needs a cat exchange. Between the opposing rows of chairs there's this long, low table, stacked with many, many copies of *Woman's Realm, Reader's Digest* and *Tatler*. Presumably the only people who ever came here to get their teeth fixed were illiterate female snobs. Oh yes, there are the dead waiting, but then they're the usual gauzy crew, Cabbage Patch dolls without their identity papers, indistinct faces glanced at through the rain-spattered windows of public transport. Everynobodies.

'Nevertheless,' Hartly continued, 'the former tenants have left some reading matter behind, magazines and such, so please make yourself at home. You might like to pop in and see the *nyujo* in a little while – but only if you're feeling up to it.' And he disappeared through another door with a frosted-glass panel, briefly gifting me a view of the clerks, in their suits of all ages, drawing with spirographs, playing with Tamagochis, swapping Pokémon cards.

Phar Lap took a numbered slip from a dispenser and handed it to me. 'Here you go, Lily-girl, yer number 1,347 – so I s'pose it'll be a bit of a fuckin' wait for you.'

'Whaddya mean – for me? What about you?'

'Well, yeah . . . it's time I finally split the swag, girl, hey-yeh?'

'I'm sorry – are you *leaving me here*?'

'I'm a death guide, Lily-girl – thass my business with you. Yer not gonna be dead too much longer, so it's time I was Elsewhere.'

'Elsewhere?'

'It's a new night club I'm opening in Camden Town. Gonna be big, girl – no fuckin' gammin about it, yeh-hey?'

Make myself at home in this provisional place? The idea was preposterous. I felt a sudden nostalgia for the basement at 27 Argos Road, for Dulston, for my little routines. Even for the Fats. 'Oh well, I suppose I'll have the kiddies to keep me company, at least.'

Phar Lap sucked his cheek in the negative. 'Nah, the kiddies come with me, girl, yeh-hey? Iss not their go-round, girl, not theirs at all. This is all 'bout you, Lily-girl, all 'bout you.'

Lithy took it badly. 'With your long blonde hair and your eyes of blue / The only thing I ever got from you was sorrow! Sorrow!' I could almost see the tears glistening in its jet eyes. It staggered across the bumpy linoleum of the waiting-room floor, on the verge of being overcome, until Phar Lap scooped it up and popped it in his dillybag.

Rude Buy was equally moved. 'Fuck off, you fat old bitch. You fucking murderess. You Myra Hindley – fuck off!' He screamed his accusations one more time, before ramming his way back out the door. The last thing I – or should I say we? – saw of him was the tail of his coonskin cap. Why the fuck did I ever buy it for him? Oh, I remember – because he wanted to be the king of the wild frontier.

Phar Lap remained standing in front of me. 'So this is it, girl, hey-yeh? Gotta few things here in me dillybag for you – if yer goin', that is?'

'Whaddya mean *if*?' I was getting querulous – I've never liked goodbyes.

'Still one last chance to get off the go-round, girl.' His voice had that peculiar clarity it always achieved at homiletic moments. 'Still time to attach you to the hooks and eyes of grace. If you want it. If you can just – even for a few instants – achieve a one-pointedness of thought. B'lieve me, Lily Bloom, you won't regret it.' I stared into his mirrored sunglasses and saw there, peering back at me – and not looking nearly as bad as I'd thought I would after eleven years beyond the grave – myself. My own blue-grey eyes, my own prominent keel of a nose, my own high cheekbones – to *die* for. My own, thick, lustrous blonde hair. Nope – I didn't look too bad at all.

'So what've you got for me in your dillybag then?' I asked him.

He reached into the woven straw pouch and pulled them out one at a time: raisins, with the bountiful Mediterranean lovely on the box; an orange; crispbread; six segments of cream cheese; a tin of Top Deck lager and lime; and finally – a Mars bar. 'There you go, Lily-girl, bit of tucker t'keep you goin'. Yer hungry, yeh-hey?'

'Hungry? I'm fucking *starving*!' I took the snack food from his cupped hands and tucked the items in my coat pockets. The Mars bar was the last to go in; I knew it'd be the first to come out.

'Yer feelin' hungry then, girl, hey-yeh?'

I was. After all this time, it was back gnawing at me, that wild exquisite pain of being hungry. The need for food and the want of it doing chemical warfare in my retorting belly. 'Gonna put yer mind off rootin' for a change, yeh-hey?'

And it has – the hunger. It's got my mind off sex for the first time in months. The snacks were gone in seconds – you were here to see me gobble them up. And the Mars bar went first, as predicted. The little brown log of chocolate, turning to sludge in my mouth, trickling down my throat, penetrating me with its amorous sweetness. Gone in three bites. So good to eat with one's own teeth again – not a bonus I was expecting. Then the raisins went, and the orange, the crispbread and the cheese. I washed the lot down with the Top Deck and didn't even offer you any; but shit, you oughta assert yourself a bit more strenuously. When I looked up from my guilty repast, Phar Lap was gone. Very much his style, that – just fading out of the picture.

Since then the hunger's come galumphing back. Wild hunger come to drag me away. I dunno why Hartly said 'former tenants', because through the door at the far end of the waiting room I can hear, from time to time, the painful

391

whine of a water drill. If I'm not very much mistaken, somebody's doing dentistry in there. Still, no sex obsession, and that's a thing to be grateful for, because now I come to relate all this stuff to you, it occurs to me – perhaps just a tad belatedly – that it's sex that got me into this whole fucking thing in the first place. You wanna know about lust? I'll tell you about lust.

It was within a few short weeks of the revelations chez Elvers. I was lying on the bed at home, smoking and listening to my little radio. The announcer – now speaking in a broad, north-country dialect – told us that Benjamin Spock was dead. Fuck – Spock! Finally one of us. How many times had I leafed through his book looking for 'colic' while one or other of the kids writhed and moaned on the bed beside me. Spock, with his good, strict, common sense, which a nudnik like me found it impossible to apply for more than minutes at a time. If only I'd actually had kids *with* Spock, then there'd have been a chance of them turning out OK, not dead, or addicted, or mindless.

Thinking about Spock as a potential father led on, fairly logically, to thinking about *doing it* with Spock. Now what would that be like! I'd always fancied the idea of a doctor as a lover – they know where everything's kept and all that jazz. Suddenly I found myself not only giving the question due consideration – looking into his spectacles, helping him off with his white coat – but *getting aroused*. Getting horny. Obviously I couldn't feel my juices quicken, or my nipples erect – but my mind was in a fever of wanting it. And it stayed that way for the next year and a half.

I wouldn't have minded doing it with Pol Pot – sure, he was short, but in my experience the small, tough guys are often the best cocksmen. Such a pity he bought the killing fields in May of '98. And that guy Marcel Papon, I didn't doubt he sent Jews to the gas chambers, but you had to hand it to him, *so* dapper in court. He went down for ten years – I wouldn't have minded joining him in his cell for a little dual confinement, d'jewknowhatImean? And those crazy skinhead boys in Saxony-Anhalt. They scored eighteen per cent in the federal elections. I bet there was fine carousing in the bierkellers that night – and I could've handled a bit of rough myself. Yup, my lust was indiscriminate. I'd thought myself a puppet of it when alive, but this was *ridiculous*, if I could've I would've screwed *anything*. Bambi Blair and wet-lips Adams – I wanted to make a threesome with them during the Anglo-Irish talks. Hell, what about throwing in a brace of fat Unionists for good measure? Rioting towel-heads on the West Bank? Maybe they'd calm down if they had the opportunity to spend a few minutes apiece drying me off. You *know* what sexual repression can do to a man. I couldn't weep when the Ol' Blue Eyes dulled – but unlike the rest, I'd have done it with him on his fucking deathbed. I had no shame. Roy Rogers could sing in my country any time he pleased, I'd've known how to pull *his* Trigger.

All through the first nine months of '98 I lay in bed and psychically squirmed, while the Fats boggled outside, and Lithy faked orgasm humming 'Je t'aime'. Even HeLa got uncommonly hot, and as for Rude Boy – well, you can imagine. I had to get up in the end. I coped well enough with being dead, fat, and old – but filthy-minded? Well, I ask you.

With the Elverses gone and me jobless there weren't a lot of places to hang out. Anyway, I was worried that my new-found lasciviousness would make it hard for me to stay sufficiently exiguous. What if one of the myriad men I ogled in the street caught me at it? A fine old to-do there'd be then. Nope, I decided to go check up on my youngest and her swain. If ever there was anyone who could turn me off like a fucking light switch it was Natasha. Even before she'd become a thorough-going *whore*, she was nothing but a tart. It was bad attitude. The internal voices wheedling her: 'Why not let him screw you, Natty? You'll feel attractive – for a while.' That was her all right, bartering her diminishing stock of self-esteem for five-pound chips of men's lust. Attagirl.

Natasha and Russell were on the skids by then. They were still managing to keep up appearances, but then appearances were all they'd ever had. They were living in a ritzy apartment in Imperial Mansions, one of the modern blocks at the Lord's Cricket Ground end of Regent's Park Road. Russell had conned the place – fully furnished – out of some putz who thought he'd see a return for extending an arm of friendship to this duo. Idiot, they only extended their own arms nowadays in order to plunge needles into them. They kept up their belief that their lives were magical by performing elaborate tricks with smoke and mirrors. And when she was on crack, Natasha would crack herself open for anyone.

This particular afternoon Russell had gone out to score. Natty wasn't withdrawing – I could tell that. She was coked up and keen as mustard to get higher. She spent the downtime marching through the gauche rooms – white shag carps, glass-and-aluminium tables, leather-and-steel chairs – and back again, smoking all the while. She was collecting an impressive ash mound for the anticipated crack session. Even I, with my *tireless* smoking, was disgusted by the whole concept of a drug habit that actually *required* that you amass cigarette ash, set up a veritable fucking *store* of the flaky grey filth. Yuk.

She was wearing a slinky pair of black, sateen-finish trousers, my Natasha. And a slinky black lurex top. She still had the looks – if you fancy your meat on the lean, chemical-smoked side. Luckily, the one who came calling did. The buzzer went and down there in the lobby was . . . I went to the video entryphone with her to check out the visitor . . . Miles. How many had he dragged himself this time to visit his old paramour? He still didn't have the wherewithal for a cab, because when she'd buzzed him up, he explained that he didn't drive into London much, the parking was hell – and so expensive.

Yup, Miles, he'd moved to the sticks and married someone a little more suitable than Natty. But hell, Catherine the fucking Great would've been more suitable than Natty, even if you were her *horse*. They had two kids, non-identical twins. He showed her the smiley photos. Big mistake, Miles. Even going there was a mistake, but showing the black widow such an adorable reminder of her own maternal failures – that was deeply thick. But then you'd never exactly been on the fast track, had you, Miles? Stuck out in the boonies, labouring all day on legal-aid cases, barely making a crust. What a shmuck. And now you'd aroused her jealousy, her bad feelings, her huge dark whirlpool of self-disgust. *Really*, Miles, you ought to have known by now what went down when that happened. You did oughta, Miles, you did.

They were standing in the kitchen while Natasha made him a cup of tea. It was the only cup of tea she'd made in the place in the three months she'd been dying there. (Well, you could hardly call it living.) Miles never smoked anything, which gave him definition in this hazy joint. To add to his allure, for some curious reason he seized on this moment to quote verse to Natasha. 'September,' he said, 'when we loved as in a burning house . . .'

'Is it going to take that long?' she replied offhand.

'What?'

'For us to love? D'jew think I should set the house on fire now? We could let the calendar look after itself, huh?'

Suddenly she wasn't kidding – and I was appalled. She pulled a disposable lighter out of the pocket of her slinky trousers and applied an inch of blue flame to the corner of a cookbook, which was in a pile on the butcher's block. To do this she had to lean forward across Miles, so that her flat stomach momentarily nuzzled at his crotch. To give him credit, he recoiled – but not for long.

They did it in the master bedroom, without even bothering to pull the heavy, zebra-striped counterpane off the broad flat bed. Without him even getting his trousers off. Fuck it, she wouldn't have troubled either if it hadn't been she who was doing the thigh-parting. I stood in the doorway of the *en suite* bathroom, poised between the mirrors to watch yourself crap in and the crappy act going on on the bed. Claustro and agro. I was disgusted – true enough. But more than that, I was jealous. More jealous than I'd conceived of being ever before. He was *my* man, *my* Miles. It should've been *me* he was heaving into like this. I wanted to cover his pretty face with *my* kisses, hold hanks of his hair, shout into his mouth, grab his firm ass. I wanted him like I'd never wanted any man before.

And as for Natasha, the fucking slut. Always her father's Trollope – that's what she was. Another thick, feckless Yaws; just like a child, with an iced dick in each hand and not knowing which one to lick. If only voidness could injure such shallowness, I'd've scratched her fucking eyes out. To do it for kicks I could understand – but adultery out of spite, that was low. But like I say – it only took seconds. Poor old Miles, he probably wasn't getting too much action back in Stevenage, or whichever old new town it was he crouched in. He got her trousers off, got her pants down, got on top, lanced her a few times – and it was all over. He didn't stay for tea. He left to walk the long miles back to the station, leaving me with *her*.

But there I *stayed*. There I stayed until only weeks before my rendezvous with Phar Lap in Soho, the one I told you about at the beginning of this empty tale. Typical of the fucking deatheaucracy to keep us hanging about like this – but then it's lucky for me you've proved *such* a good listener.

Yup, I stayed. In fact – I had no choice. I was wedded to her by my lust, for whenever she turned a trick I had to be there. She turned a fair few in the months before she realised she was pregnant. I learned to experience the most exquisite torments of desire while she checked her watch over the juddering shoulder of unknown john number eighty-two. 'I've got to be there!' as Lithy so charmingly put it. I suffered the most intense agonies of insatiable sexual hunger, while she gagged on her seventieth cocktail sausage of the week.

How did she get into it, seriously tricking? Well, she wasn't one of those poor girls who have to get a card put up in a phone box, not our Natty. She didn't breach the sex descriptions act so blatantly. Those cards, with their pictures of pneumatic, unsullied, bounteous flesh, all strapped up in a waste of red elastic and white satin. Those cards, which read: 'Jasmine, 36-26-34. Eighteen-Year-Old. New on the Scene. Own Flat. No Hurry. Come and Relax. Stay for a While'; when what they should scream is: 'JANINE, TWENTY-FIVE-YEAR-OLD EMOTIONALLY SUBNORMAL CRACK ADDICT, GONORRHEA, BRUISES, NON-SPECIFIC URETHRITIS, HIV. I'LL JACK YOU OFF FAST FOR TWENTY QUID – I NEED A HIT SOMETHING FIERCE.' No, none of that for our Natty, she was a bit upmarket.

Russell knew *all* about it, natch, how couldn't he? It was he who introduced her to slimy Zimon in the first place. Yeah, Zimon, what a character; the type who thinks a *z* will turn him into Zorro, and his 'escort agency' into a convent in fucking Baja California. Zimon's big in the escort business, and his girls are the best when it comes to *escorting* drunken middle managers the seven feet from the doors of their hotel rooms to the middle of their beds. Yeah, Russell knew – not that they ever spoke of it. They were like every pimp-whore set-up the world over, his hook of inadequacy in her eye of disgrace, dragging each other down. Way on down.

They sank lower and lower. By the time the pregnancy was close to completion the Estate Agent had burnt down every business connection he'd ever had. There were men with writing on their trousers who wanted him dead. Literally. To give him some credit, credit where credit is jew. He did stop her putting out for money in the last trimester. I mean to say, how many perverts were out there who could fancy a methadone-swigging drab with a foetus visibly kicking in her stretched brown belly? Plenty. Yup, she was on the 'done. Twenty mils a day, picked up at the chemist and drunk there, standing beside shaven-headed kiddies, whose mums were shopping for nit combs. He nearly had to fucking wall her up in order to keep her off the other shit. But by then it was getting much easier to confine her – given that their residences had become so confined.

Down and down, from penthouse, to house, to apartment, to squat. They headed east, beating against the trade winds of affluence which blew in the opposite direction. Two skinny weather vanes, orienting themselves by an afflatus of extinction. They've come to rest now in Mile End, on a grotty little estate, along with all the other insecurity claimants. Still, what care I? There's a brave new world out there and I want to be part of it again. Hell, they've even managed to put an airstrip in the Gaza Strip – well ain't that something! They've finally impeached Slick Willie – although why they didn't get chopper Bobbitt in *ages* ago is beyond me. Bambi Blair has become Bomber Blair, doing his level best to convert his cub scout's woggle into a swinging, militaristic shlong, by wasting high explosive on the Balkans. At least Yehudi Menhuin didn't live for ever, and even if it wasn't a car that carried him off, there's still only one destination in the final taxi.

Which leaves us, here, with the *Woman's Realm*s, and all the other faceless waiters. I don't suppose you fancy popping in to see the departmental *nyujo* with me? You know about *nyujos*, do you? I guess it's the way the deatheaucracy get out of the go-round, as Phar Lap calls it. This department's *nyujo* is usually being encrusted, by some dusty clerk or fusty scrivener, with Copydex, Tipp-Ex, or any other gummy stuff they can lay their hands on. But this being a dentist's, they're probably turning it into Mr Potato-Head with fucking *amalgam*. No, not a trip to the *nyujo*? I can't say I blame you. It's been a bloody long sojourn here in this waiting room, hasn't it? We've seen a great mess of the dead come up the stairs, and go through that door to where the fucking drill keeps on whining. Whining like an infant machine; and as our Ford so perspicaciously said, 'Machinery is the modern Messiah.'

Thousands have priority over us. I guess they've got clout that you and I are lacking, an *angle* on the deatheaucracy. That, or – and it's a revolting thought – they know how to suck up to them. Sucking, that reminds me – did I ever tell you about the ballpoint pen I designed back in the forties? I did? Well, you know how it is, you tell a long story and you tend to forget the beginning. Bit like life, I suppose. I'm grateful to you, though, you're such a good listener, clearly the type who picks things up. But while I do think I may have recognised some of the others who've revolved through this room, *you* – sister? brother? – remain totally indistinct.

Who? Well, I think I maybe saw Yaws – or someone who looked like Yaws – come and sit for a time. He was carrying a bag of golf clubs, smoking a fucking pipe. If it wasn't Yaws it might as well have been. He was always a banality in an unwrapped commonplace so far as I was concerned. What do I wanna be? I'll tell you – anything that has the requirement to increase its body weight with extreme rapidity in the first few hours after entering the world. Anything at all. Personally, I don't care if I draw the fucking squid straw, as long as I'm a squid that gets to eat. I could kill for krill. Let's face it – not everything that has suckers sucks.

'Ms Bloom?' There's Canter . . . and yes . . . yes . . . it looks like it's gonna be me at last. 'Would you come through now please, he's ready to see you.'

Well, so long pal, I hope it isn't too much longer for you either. I don't know if there's anyone else here who's simpatico, but you could always work your way through a few more thousand *Woman's Realm*s. I find the banana-flapjack recipes a help. Sure, they don't deal with the wild exquisite pain, but they give it a point.

Well, whaddya know – it *is* a dentist's after all. And there's the dentist himself, another fucking ratty little Jew taking a part in my destiny. I wonder what this one's called? No, don't tell me.

'Blomberg, I'm Mr Blomberg – and you must be Ms Bloom. Please take a seat in the chair. Let me take a look in there. Mmm . . . my, you have been doing a little snacking, haven't you? Still, I suppose you had a long wait. Would you mind rinsing for me? Thank you *so* much. Now look, I'm not going to mislead you about this, Ms Bloom – may I call you Lily? Lily, then. Well, this is going to be painful – *very* painful. And I expect it'll be messy and embarrassing as well. I'd like to be able to offer you an anaesthetic, but you know how it is, our resources aren't what they used to be. All I can say is, I've done a lot of this before and I'm strong and quick. Is it absolutely necessary? Oh, absolutely – strictly, even. I mean there *is* the occasional sport or freak, but in the normal run of things it's unheard of for a human baby to be born with its own full set of teeth.'

Christmas 2001

I don't know if you've experienced being born – but I'll tell you what it was like for me anyway. It was fucking painful, disgustingly messy and truly embarrassing. Thoroughly unsavoury – not at all to my taste. Slobbering out of the Ice Princess's much-visited fanny, while she shitted and pissed and screamed and kvetched. Epidural be damned, they should've given her a fucking Caesarean and euthanasia at the same fucking time!

The clasp of firm professional hands, the enfoldment of a clean blanket, these were partial compensations. But then they had to go and clamp me on her fucking tit. Ach! The smell – you wouldn't believe it! But then smelling isn't your forte either, is it now. Still, in the days and weeks that followed, smell was an interesting rediscovery – if not an altogether welcome one. Far more to my liking were the colours. So bright! So varied. If I'd had the opportunity I never would've called anything 'grey' again on this go-round. Oh no, it would've been canescent, griseous, dove-grey, pearl-grey, cinereous, fuliginous, or écru. I revelled in those colours, and they were silent too. They didn't scream the way I did. Scream and whine, bellow and trumpet, whinny and gulp – do every fucking thing I could to persuade those bastards to give me drugs!

I almost wished the Ice Princess and the Estate Agent had been worse parents than they manifestly already were. That they would tip one of their little brown bottles into my plastic one. The doctors said they'd detoxed me before she took me home from the hospital – but what do those quacks fucking know. I was clucking, man. I needed a hit. I mean to say, if babyhood is all about rampant need to begin with, to be a baby junky is to experience overpowering fucking need. It's like being the whole world, waiting for something – anything – consumable, to keep you distracted from the silence of space.

There wasn't even a chance of getting it out of her, either. The Ice Princess didn't take to titty feeding. Well, she needed her metabolism for her ownsome – and her nipples for everyone else. Everyone who had a hundred quid that is. So, it was lumpy, barely dissolved formula for this kiddo. Usually it was the Estate Agent who got it together to feed me. But he'd give it to me boiling, tepid, or plain cold. It's a wonder I made it to toddlerhood at all. It's been a craven new world for me, that's for sure. I can't, in all honesty, recommend it. Sure, there are video screens by gas pumps now, so they can sell you something else while you're actually in the process of paying to denude the non-renewable resources, but what's so special about that?

I can't say I was surprised when it happened. I may not have been in a position to talk to them these last eighteen months, but I've listened. It was the same thing last Christmas – some asshole put a load of strong smack on the market and a fair few of their shooting buddies took a hot shot. They very nearly kissed off then, which, all things considered, would've been better for me. If only they'd kept on with the foil fucking hankies, kept on smoking the shit. Very hard to overdose that way. All in all, the demise of the Ice Princess and her consort rather tends to confirm me in my good opinion of smoking. Wouldjew like a B&H? No, I suppose you're a little young.

They were all cock-a-hoop when he brought the stuff back

this year. They hadn't had any money for days. The trousers were out for Russell, he couldn't have got tick from the fucking Rothschilds – even if they'd discovered he was a long-lost son. Then she managed to haul herself up and go blow someone. Well done, Natasha! That's my girl! What a snappy little sucker you were. So, she hobbles back with the gelt, and he goes off to score while she makes me the first pot of slop I've had in fucking days.

They both fixed up in the kitchenette while I was watching Teletubbies. No, I didn't disdain the entertainments available any more than you would. Then she managed to make it upstairs to their bed, as he lay down in slow stages. Kinduv touching, that, huh? Them heading off like that together, like Romeo and fucking Juliet, except older, more despairing, and devoid of any love for each other. Me, I barely stirred. Truly, I expected it to happen.

I also expected Miles to walk all those miles down to Mile End – it's so difficult to get a bus in this, the dead interstice between the years. Yeah, I knew he'd show. He kept in touch with her, always suspecting that I was his, despite the myriad other candidates in the frame. I mean, Russell wasn't ever a serious proposition for my paternity, I just don't look Jewish enough. Dear little snub nose and all. Retroussé – that's what I'd call it.

Yeah, that's why I've managed such bravado since you cropped up again. Well, now he's been and he's gone again, and I'm still fucking here. If only those swine upstairs weren't belting it out with the karaoke I might've heard him before it was too late. As it was, I was up in the bathroom drinking fucking toilet water when I heard the letterbox clack back. I got downstairs as fast as I could, but evidently he'd knocked many times, peered in, seen nothing, and decided to go. That's it – I'm done for. It's only – like everything else – a matter of time.

And to be frank, I haven't been enjoying your company too much either. I haven't a fucking clue who your father was, but when you came scampering off their bed three days ago I knew full well who your mother was. I guess you can't be entirely blamed; after all, her taste in music was never exactly developed. But even so, those ditties you warble, those snatches of idiotic pop songs, they set my teeth on edge. I wish you were the good listener I found when we waited together back at the Palmers Green dentist's office, in the waiting room between the lives. Still, what can you expect from a lithopedion – calcified little fossil baby that you are?

Nothing much. No-thing. Except this: forget me. Not.

A NOTE ON THE AUTHOR

Will Self is the author of *The Quantity Theory of Insanity*, winner of the 1992 Geoffrey Faber Memorial Prize, *Cock & Bull*, *My Idea of Fun*, *Grey Area*, *Junk Mail*, *The Sweet Smell of Psychosis*, *Great Apes*, *Tough, Tough Toys for Tough, Tough Boys* and *Sore Sites*. He lives in London.

A NOTE ON THE TYPE

The text of this book is set in Linotype Sabon, named after the type founder, Jacques Sabon. It was designed by Jan Tschichold and jointly developed by Linotype, Monotype and Stempel, in response to a need for a typeface to be available in identical form for mechanical hot metal composition and hand composition using foundry type.

Tschichold based his design for Sabon roman on a fount engraved by Garamond, and Sabon italic on a fount by Granjon. It was first used in 1966 and has proved an enduring modern classic.